Lost Track

XY Records Book #2

Heidi Hutchinson

www.smartypantsromance.com

Copyright

This book is a work of fiction. Names, characters, places, rants, facts, contrivances, and incidents are either the product of the author's questionable imagination or are used factitiously. Any resemblance to actual persons, living or dead or undead, events, locales is entirely coincidental if not somewhat disturbing/concerning.

Dedication

To Captain Awesome
Your heart is the wildest I've ever known
And the softest place I've ever landed

Prologue

D*RAMA CONTINUES IN LONE STAR STATE*

CelebX was first to report that Sunshine Capone's multi-million-dollar 19,000 square-foot mansion was on fire. Several hours ago, firefighters and emergency responders were called to the rapper's home as smoke filled the sky.

We can now confirm that multiple people were in the home when it caught fire and all were evacuated safely.

Police arrested Sunshine's girlfriend, Nora, on charges of arson.

Nora Cannon is a social media brand influencer with over four million followers. There have been no new posts on her accounts since the fire.

She was booked at the county jail earlier today but has already posted bond.

CelebX reached out to her sponsors for comment but have not heard back.

Nora and Sunshine have been dating for two months but insiders say rumors of Sunshine's numerous affairs made things at home volatile.

No one is talking when it comes to what's next for the couple who met at a party thrown by Sunshine's manager, where they were introduced by mutual friends.

This is the third time a woman who was dating Sunshine Capone has been arrested.

Click here to be taken to those articles.

Stay tuned to CelebX for updates on this developing story.

Chapter One
Sunshine

SABINE

In retrospect, she should not have taken her sweater off.

She should have suffered in silence until she was home.

She was an adult after all. Self-control was a cornerstone of her brand.

Wait.

Did tutors have a brand?

Probably not in the modern sense.

It didn't matter.

Because instead of waiting, she'd gone full toddler—tried to strip without a plan—and now she was in a pickle.

Hopefully Piper would be along shortly and she'd be rescued. Though being rescued by one of her students wasn't exactly the most professional thing she could have happen, it was better than having to wander out into the streets of Avondale to find a stranger to cut her out of her sweater.

She tried to calm her breathing, even as perspiration began to run down her cheeks.

She would not panic.

It was a sweater. She could breathe just fine. She would not die here—trapped with her arms over her head and the super soft sweater she just *had* to wear that day stuck to her earrings.

At least she had worn a camisole under the sweater. That made it a little less scandalous.

This was a perfect example of why she needed to practice dressing up more often. Except maybe at home. With supervision.

The sweater had been a hand-me-down from her roommate Kara who was a foot taller and two cup sizes smaller than Sabine. It was an orange, cowl neck, form fitting chiffon beauty that had very little stretch.

Which hadn't been a problem when she'd put it on that morning. In fact, she'd liked the way it hugged her body and showed off her curves. She'd been working out for more than a year and the sweater had fit *chef's kiss* perfectly.

Paired with the navy skirt, wool tights, and ballet flats, she had looked like she'd walked out of Teachers of Autumn Magazine.

If that were a thing.

But shortly after lunch, she'd become aware of a light scratching between her shoulder blades. It felt like something between an itch and a poke, and the longer it went on, the more bothersome it became. No matter how she'd twisted and contorted her body, she couldn't reach it.

By the time she made it to XY Studios for her last student of the day, she was heavily distracted by the bothersome sting. She'd been stopping in doorjambs and rubbing her back against corners all afternoon like a bear on a tree.

It had become the sole focus of her every thought.

Have you ever had something in a sock or your waistband that was relentless in its torture? Because that's what this was.

At lunch it had been a nuisance, by the afternoon she was convinced it was trying to kill her.

So, when she'd entered the upstairs lounge where she was to meet the eighth grader and it was empty, she dropped her bag, took off her coat and tugged the sweater over her head.

But she'd been so hasty in her desire to remove the offending garment, she'd made the mistake of pulling the sweater over her head with both arms instead of one arm at a time. It caught under her armpits and stopped moving.

Thus, she was standing somewhere in the lounge with her arms stretched above her and the sweater bunched around her head. She couldn't see. She couldn't breathe. And she couldn't move.

"Help," she whispered to no one.

Again, the panic threatened to take over.

She wasn't an overly anxious person. She liked to think of herself as fairly Zen.

But whatever piece of plastic or thread or glue that had tormented her all day long had driven away her sensibleness and she was now gulping for air, trapped in a jumper.

A prison of her own making.

New fear unlocked: small, confined spaces.

No.

Nope.

She would not die here.

Not like this and not this day.

The studio wasn't devoid of human life. She'd passed at least two sound engineers on her way to the lounge.

Sure, she didn't know their names, but she could ask them to help her. Maybe Nikki was working. Nikki seemed nice those two times they had almost interacted. Maybe she would rescue her.

She took a tentative step in the direction she hoped was the door. Another step.

Okay, so far, so good.

Another step and her hip bumped into the edge of the table.

Or was it the counter in the kitchenette?

She tried to rub her hip and butt along the edge to orient herself.

The sound of a door opening spun her around and she almost lost her balance.

"Hello?" she called, hearing the tremor in her voice.

"Hello?" a male voice replied and there was no mistaking the amusement in his tone.

She exhaled loudly and tried to walk toward his voice but collided with the table again.

"You are all turned around," he said, coming closer. "Just wait."

"Please help me," she said. "I'm stuck and I can't—" She wiggled her arms above her head uselessly. Her fingertips tingled. That couldn't be good.

"What can I do to help?" he asked, now standing in front of her.

She hinged forward at the hips. "Can you pull the sweater off?"

Silence for a beat and then a deep breath.

He smelled like coffee and fresh air. She wondered which engineer this was. His voice didn't sound like Johnny, the owner of the studio, and it definitely wasn't Johnny's younger brother Shawn because he would have just started laughing and wouldn't have stopped.

"Okay, I'm going to have to touch you. Is that okay?"

"Yeah," she replied, slightly confused by his statement. Because it was pretty obvious that if she'd asked him to help her, he was going to have to touch her.

But when cool fingers brushed against the exposed skin near her armpits, she flinched.

Oh, now that made sense.

He tugged on the fabric around her armpits and it didn't budge.

"Hm," he said to himself and she sensed him step back. "It's really stuck."

She bobbed her upper body in agreement.

Because, duh.

He stepped closer and tried again in a slightly different place.

Nothing changed.

"I don't want to ruin your sweater," he said, sounding distressed.

"And I don't want to die dressed like a traffic cone," she replied a little more hotly than she should have.

He chuckled and tugged at the sleeves over her head.

"Sorry," she mumbled.

"You do not have to apologize." His voice moved like he was walking a circle around her. "Though I don't think you look like a traffic cone. I actually saw you as one of those inflatable tube man things you see outside car dealerships."

She laughed despite herself. "That's not better."

"You think if I pull straight up, we'll end up with a finger trap situation? Because that's what I'm afraid of."

"I am very willing to risk it."

"Okay." He fiddled with the top of the sweater. "Stop me if it hurts."

She braced.

The fabric tugged, pulled and smashed her face as he worked it off of her. She held her breath, like that would somehow ease the progression. The hem pinched and rolled over her armpits and then…relief.

She sagged forward and then cried out.

"Earring! Earring!" She moved her head with the sweater. Her hands, newly free, gripped his wrists. "Stop!"

He already had stopped. The moment she had cried out he froze.

She let go of him and dove her fingers beneath the loosened fabric to detangle her earrings.

"Okay," she said, wincing in preparation for more pain.

But the pain was over.

The sweater came away and she took her first full breath in what felt like hours.

"Oh, thank you," she said, finally getting a look at her rescuer.

Sleepy indigo eyes met hers, and the smile on his face crinkled the stem of the rose tattooed near his right eye.

Here was the thing about working with famous people and their kids, they were too often hypersensitive to people's attention. She'd learned early on that most didn't like to be stared at. And because they were hyper-aware of being watched, any kind of eye contact could feel like it was staring.

Rational?

No.

But she understood it enough that looking *around* them instead of *at* them was a safe option. At least until new expectations had been established.

So, it was very off-brand (again) for her to have full eye contact with a rock star.

She immediately looked down, but not before she'd clocked the dove tattoo near his hairline and the words "As Yourself" above his left eyebrow. Her gaze dropped to his neckline where a large black and gray tattoo of the sun on his throat was just barely visible from the collar of his gray hoodie.

Sunshine Capone.

So… not really a rock star.

But kind of.

Pop star?

He was more hip-hop, right?

Why was she trying to specify what kind of star he was?

A star was a star.

"Thank you," she said again.

"Not a problem," he replied, and his tone caused her eyes to jump back to his, even though it went against all her instincts. He was still smiling. "Are you okay?"

She nodded and chuckled at her own circumstances. "I am now, thanks to you."

He handed her sweater back to her. She took it and rolled it into her hands, feeling like she should say something more.

He took a step back just as the door to the lounge opened again and Piper entered the room.

The raven haired thirteen-year-old tossed her bag on the table and removed her coat with a flourish. She scrunched her nose when her gaze landed on Sabine.

"What happened to you?" Her eyes flicked up to Sabine's head.

Sabine rolled her lips inward and lifted her eyebrows. Because where to start, right? She tossed her sweater on the table and smoothed her hair down as best she could. "My sweater tried to kill me a moment ago, but I survived. How are you today?"

Piper eyed her like she wasn't sure whether to believe her or not. Her brilliant blue eyes flicked to Sunshine Capone. "Shawn's downstairs."

"Sweet," Sunshine replied. He opened his mouth like he was going to say something to Sabine but then he just shook his head, his lips twitching, and left the room.

Piper grumbled and pulled the chair out where she flopped. "I was hoping you wouldn't be here."

"Thanks." Sabine hid her smile as she tucked her sweater into her bag, and took out her notebook and laptop. "I was looking forward to seeing you today as well."

Piper didn't just roll her eyes but her entire head. She straightened in the chair and wrestled her laptop out of the bag.

"We were assigned a stupid essay today." Piper jumped into all the reasons it was unfair to ask her to write a three-page essay on her favorite travel memory and what a waste of time it was.

Sabine listened and then helped her make an outline.

She easily and gratefully transitioned into teacher mode, allowing her uncomfortable afternoon incident to fade into the background of her thoughts.

Ninety minutes flew by, and Sabine was surprised when she glanced at the window that overlooked the alley and it was dark outside.

"Am I your favorite?"

"Favorite what?"

"Favorite student."

"You are definitely my favorite eighth grader."

"I'm your only eighth grader, aren't I?"

Sabine twisted her lips to keep from smiling. "You know I can't answer that question."

Piper rolled her eyes. "Where do I rank then? Like…among all your students. Where am I at?"

Sabine laughed because she really didn't know how else to respond.

"It's not a competition, Piper. I don't rank any of you. Geez."

Piper's expression turned flat. "Not like that. I mean, how do I compare to the others?"

Sabine scrubbed a hand over her face, not caring that it would cloud her already cloudy makeup. If she even had any left after the sweater incident.

It was fine. This was her last student of the day; after this she was headed home anyway.

"When I ask questions like this it drops me in rank, doesn't it?"

Sabine barked a laugh and slouched back in the chair.

If almost any other student asked these questions, she'd be worried about their self-esteem and other mental health concerns. But she'd been tutoring Piper for a few months now and she was familiar with the thirteen-year-old's competitive streak.

She liked to know she was always improving. A common metric for knowing that, was to compare yourself to peers. Sabine knew adults who did that all the time.

It wasn't an accurate measure of anything though.

"People learn at their own pace."

"No, I know that. But how is my pace? Am I keeping up? Pulling ahead? Falling behind?"

"Piper." Sabine patted the table between them. "I only compare your progress with you."

Piper blinked at her. Clearly, she thought her tutor was an idiot.

Not the first time Sabine had been misunderstood.

Which was why she sat up again and leveled a look at the girl.

"Every brain is different. Every single one. The best way to measure your progress is by comparing where you were before. Which I do. Your grades are coming up and your scores improve every week."

"But school measures everyone against each other," Piper argued.

"Yes and no." Sabine took a breath and forced the frown off her face.

Piper's observations were mostly correct. But it wasn't Sabine's job to cultivate rebellion against the system in her students. Her job was to help them be successful at the system so they could leave it behind them forever.

"Education is a complicated beast and we can get into all that some other time. But right now, you need to finish the essay. That's it. Just focus on this one goal."

Piper was poised to argue again when the door opened.

Both of them turned their heads at the interruption.

Sometimes, when Sabine was working, she'd forget where she was.

Her childhood had consisted of chaotic interruptions on a continual basis and she'd trained herself to focus on her tasks. It developed from a survival tactic into a useful skill that kicked in without her being aware.

Such as when she was working.

While she'd been tutoring Piper James in a recording studio, all she'd focused on was the student.

So, when Sunshine Capone walked back into the lounge, she was momentarily disoriented. They had eye contact and her mind was flooded with the events of earlier and she blushed.

Not because he was famous but because she still felt stupid about how he'd found her.

Feeling stupid in front of a stranger was right up there with not wanting to get eaten by sharks on vacation.

And he'd caught her at the dumbest she'd been in a long time.

Behind Sunshine Capone was a face that was familiar to her and she immediately smiled.

"'Sup, Sabine," Shawn Torres greeted. He approached them and rested his elbow on top of Piper's head.

"Ugh. This guy," Piper grumbled.

Which made Sabine snort because Piper adored Shawn, but always made a show of disliking him. Like she just couldn't help it.

"Pipsqueak." Shawn tussled her hair and Piper stiffened.

"Only Hannah gets to call me that."

Sabine pursed her lips at their interaction.

They may not be related by birth, but the sibling chemistry was real. It reminded her of her own relationship with her brother.

Shawn left them to join Sunshine who'd not even paused on his way past them. From what Sabine could hear they were making espresso at the coffee bar, but she didn't turn around to check. Instead, she watched Piper's expression as it turned introspective and stayed on the guys.

After a minute, Sabine nudged Piper's elbow with a pencil, getting her attention.

"What's going on?"

Piper shrugged. "I don't have any of what they have."

Sabine glanced over her shoulder at the guys who had moved to the window overlooking the alley and scrunched her nose.

"Face tattoos and matching vintage tees?" Sabine faced Piper again and cocked an eyebrow. "Because I know a guy who can hook you up with both."

Piper's dark laugh made Sabine smile.

"Can you imagine? Hannah would lose her absolute sh—crap. No." The thirteen-year-old sighed. "The music thing. I don't have that."

Sabine nodded. She understood that a little. It must be hard to be surrounded by music and a musician's life (they were in a recording studio for crying out loud), and not lean that direction.

"We all have gifts. None of them are more or less important than the others."

Piper forced a half smile. "You really think that?"

"I really do."

And she did. People were awesome in their uniqueness.

As long as they used their powers for good and not evil anyway.

"And what's my special gift?" Piper crossed her arms over her chest.

"Well, just going on the short time that I've known you, I'd guess that one of your gifts is athletics?"

Since that was the reason Sabine had been brought in to tutor Piper in the first place.

"Har har," Piper deadpanned. But she uncrossed her arms and refocused on her essay. A little less melancholy on her beautiful face.

Sabine watched her work for a moment. She could partially imagine what Piper's life was like as the younger sister of the world's most (in)famous pop star and having to live most of her current life in a protected bubble.

It couldn't be easy.

But when Sabine considered all the details surrounding Piper's circumstances, Piper was doing incredibly well.

Sabine flinched when the alarm on her watch buzzed.

Crap. Time to go.

She began to pack her things.

"I have to go. I want you to finish this essay the best you can—"

"Without you here?" Piper's voice was laced with annoyed panic.

"You'll do great," Sabine reassured her, holding her gaze as she spoke. "Send it to me and I'll go over it tonight before I go to bed. Then we can touch it up tomorrow."

Piper rolled her eyes but didn't produce any new grumblings.

Sabine zipped her backpack closed and shrugged on her coat.

"Where to now?" Shawn called across the lounge.

"That's classified," she replied, and Shawn grinned.

She accidentally (really!) looked directly at Sunshine and he happened to be looking at her. Their eyes connected. He smiled, making the rose tattoo near the corner of his eye crinkle.

Hm. Well, maybe he wasn't one of those who minded being acknowledged.

She sent a low wave across the room and hurried from the lounge.

It was Kara's birthday. And even though her best friend had said she didn't want to do anything for her birthday, Sabine had still ordered two Marilyn's—red velvet cupcakes with cream cheese frosting and edible glitter —from Kara's favorite gluten free bakery. They were gorgeous and so rich that they were very much a special occasion dessert.

But she had to pick them up before the bakery closed.

She was just about out the door when she was stopped by a voice calling her name.

Not just any voice, but one of the most famous voices in the world.

She turned to see Hannah Lee James aka Ashton James, world famous pop star, striding toward her in that badass, cool as hell way that seemed to come naturally to her. Two months into their arrangement and Sabine still wasn't used to it.

Which said more about Hannah than Sabine.

Lost Track

Sabine had been employed by a variety of rich and famous people over the years. She had a box of NDAs at home so full that she could use it as a stepstool.

She was (mostly) unfazed by celebrities.

But Hannah carried an energy with her that caught her breath and made her fingers tingle.

Sabine was pretty sure it was because of all the "celebrities" she'd met over the years, Hannah was exactly who she appeared to be. There was no pretense, no façade.

Which were equal parts enthralling and terrifying.

"How are things?" Hannah asked, crossing her arms over her chest. She jerked her chin back the way Sabine had come. "With Piper?"

"Good." Sabine tugged her earlobe, her earring hole still sore from earlier. "She knows the material. She just hates doing it. But I have some ideas to incentivize her."

Hannah's icy blue eyes studied her, and she finally heaved a sigh.

Sabine recognized that look and secretly she loved it. Sometimes parents or guardians were annoyed at the idea of needing a tutor. They thought their kid should just "know" how to do school successfully. Getting a tutor was used like a punishment meant to humiliate the student into "getting their shit together."

Hannah was different. It had been apparent in their first meeting. All she wanted to do was make sure Piper had what she needed to succeed. And she would go to the ends of the earth to find it.

Which made Sabine's job that much more delightful.

"What can I do?" Hannah asked.

Sabine's lips curved up and her heart warmed. "You're already doing it."

"Right."

"Right," Sabine replied. She held Hannah's eyes for a beat, and then left the warmth of the recording studio for the frosty air of a Chicago evening.

Well, of Avondale.

Which was basically Chicago but not really.

She jogged to her car and not for the first time lamented never installing a remote start. Three out of four seasons she'd convince herself she didn't need it, but then winter would arrive like a mugger in an alley.

She fired up the engine of the Toyota 4Runner and shivered her way out of Avondale down to West Loop.

"Whoever invented heated seats deserves a thank you note," she murmured. "And maybe a fruit basket."

She stopped at the bakery and picked up her order, and then hurried the last few blocks home.

Well, hurried as much as Chicago traffic on a Wednesday evening would allow.

By the time she pulled into the underground parking garage in her building, the heat was blazing and she forgot (again) that she wanted to get remote start installed.

The moment she stepped off the elevator onto her floor she heard it.

The oppressive and enthusiastic banjo playing from the loft across the hall.

"Not tonight, ya weirdos," she muttered, unlocking her door.

The loft she shared with her best friend Kara was everything they had imagined when they made all their big plans.

The top floor of a 1920s industrial building that had been restored and converted into condos and lofts. Complete with exposed brick walls, Bluetooth, granite counter tops, floor to ceiling windows, and hardwood floors.

Basically, it was Swanksville.

Did they need it?

No.

But it was the dream.

And both of them had learned a long time ago that dreams weren't handed to you. If you wanted them, you had to make them happen.

And so they had.

The only part that wasn't in the dream was the banjo playing vampires that had moved in at the first of the month.

And it wasn't even so much that they played banjo.

It was that they played it *so badly*.

And all. Night. Long.

Hence Sabine's belief they were actually vampires with a very specific torture fetish. One where they slowly drove their victims crazy with bad banjo. And then they swooped in for the kill.

"But today is not that day," she said. She set her bakery box on the butcher's block and pulled out her phone. She called up her Taylor Swift playlist and hit play.

The music pumped through the Bluetooth speakers throughout the loft and drowned out the undead Foggy Mountain Boys.

She took off her coat, stashed her purse, and set about making Kara's favorite dinner and poured herself a glass of wine. A half hour later Kara came through the door.

Sabine was in the middle of her "Fearless (Taylor's Version)" solo, using the ladle as her microphone when Kara joined her.

Kara used the wine bottle as her mic, and they danced around the kitchen singing to one another until the song was complete.

"Gimme that." Sabine took the bottle from Kara and poured a glass for her bestie.

Kara sighed and took the wine. "What's the occasion?"

Sabine eyed her, not even a little bit fooled. "Did you really think I'd forget your birthday?"

Kara's cheeks tinged pink and she shrugged, taking a sip of the wine.

"I just didn't want to… You know."

"I know, babe. And this is not me pressuring you to celebrate." Sabine touched her wine glass to Kara's. "I'm happy you were born, and I wanted you to know."

Kara's eyes glossed over and she hugged Sabine.

They held one another for a beat, just letting the moment be what it was. No need to explain or pretend anything away. Their decade long friendship had been filled with more than most people experience in a lifetime.

From the day they had laid eyes on each other in ninth grade, they'd been soulmates. Kara, the tall, blonde, perky cheerleader, had been the exact opposite of Sabine who was short, dark haired, and bossy.

It was a match made in a very weird part of heaven.

And it was the most important relationship of Sabine's life.

So of course, she wasn't going to let Kara's birthday just go by.

"It smells amazing in here," Kara remarked, stepping back and looking into the pot Sabine had boiling on the stovetop.

"Your favorite, sausage potato soup," Sabine replied. She went back to chopping her potatoes which was what she'd been doing before she got side-tracked by the music.

"You are my favorite person in the entire world." Kara kissed Sabine on the cheek and danced away.

"You only say that because I keep feeding you." Sabine smirked into the pot. "How was your day, dear?"

"Well, for starters, the five-year-old that reminds me daily of my place in the world told me he loved me. And then he asked if both of my hips were original or if I'd had them replaced yet. You know, like his grandmother."

Sabine chuckled, adding the bay leaf.

While Sabine tutored famous people's kids, Kara was their nanny.

That stepstool of NDAs Sabine had? Kara had one to match.

It was a good thing they could talk to each other, otherwise their social life would be way more difficult.

Kara sat down at the table and propped her chin on her fist. Her wide green eyes stared off into the distance and Sabine knew what was going to come out of her beautiful best friend's mouth.

"Maybe I should call John."

Sabine rolled her lips inward and focused on stirring the ingredients.

Kara exhaled a loud sigh and flopped her head onto the table.

"Or," Sabine suggested gently, "You could *not* call John." She waggled her eyebrows when Kara rolled her head to the side to look at her. She was rewarded with a smile.

"You make a great case."

Sabine shrugged because it was true. John wasn't that great. But he had proposed to Kara six months ago with an enormous diamond and so the struggle was real.

He just wasn't anything that Kara wanted in a life partner. It would have never worked.

"I just don't want to die alone."

"You are twenty-five, not ninety-five. And you won't be alone. Because you'll always have me." Sabine batted her eyelashes.

Kara laughed, sat up and pushed her hair back. "And what happens if I do meet the man of my dreams?"

"We've talked about this." Sabine closed her hands around the bowl of her wine glass. "You're going to make him build me a room above your garage so I have a place to grow old."

Kara's deep laugh made Sabine smile.

"This birthday is already ten times better than last year," Kara said. "Thank you."

That's because last year Kara's longtime boyfriend, Adler, had dumped her. On her birthday. To which Kara had responded by canceling all future birthdays.

It was also how she'd ended up with John for all of three months before the rebound proposed.

It hadn't been difficult to top last year.

The playlist switched to a lower volume song and the banjos could be heard through the door.

"Maybe I spoke too soon." Kara glared in the general direction of the noise.

And then the banjos were joined by the sound of vigorous foot stomping.

A growl rumbled out of the tall, lanky blonde, and Sabine reacted by dropping to the floor.

Kara cried out in surprise. She ran around the island to Sabine's side.

"Oh my God, are you okay? What happened?" Kara dropped to her knees, eyes wide and concerned.

Sabine blinked at her. "It's a hoedown, right? Am I doing it wrong? I'm doing it wrong, aren't I?"

Kara snorted and giggled and collapsed on top of Sabine, laughing into her shoulder.

"Okay, help me up. I have to check the potatoes."

They returned to standing and Kara refilled their wine glasses.

"How about your day? Anything cool happen to you?" Kara asked.

Sabine hummed as she thought about Sunshine Capone's dark blue eyes and the rose tattoo on his face that crinkled when he smiled.

"You know, the usual. Proteges, snarky teenagers, I was rescued from being strangled to death by my own sweater by a rock star."

Kara chuckled. "We have the weirdest life."

"But at least we have each other."

"Forever and ever, babe."

Chapter Two
Rolling Through

DAVE

It had been a little over a year since Dave "Sunshine Capone" Hansen had walked into Johnny Enamorado Torres' recording studio, XY Records, and had fallen absolutely, head over heels, in love.

With espresso.

Specifically, the espresso he could make in the upstairs lounge of the studio.

He'd always enjoyed coffee and caffeine and all the perks that came with it. But he'd never had espresso until the wildest week of his life.

It became a personal quest for him to recreate what he'd discovered. But after months of going into coffee houses, buying different brands of espresso machines, trying every grind and roast he could find, he hadn't been able to do so.

"You mind if I go mess with your espresso machine?" Dave asked.

"That's what it's there for," Johnny replied without looking up.

"I'll come with you." Shawn stood and followed him out of the control room. "So how did your first night go in your new place?"

Dave shrugged with a laugh. "I prioritize the wrong things. I got really into setting up my stereo and completely spaced on making sure I had somewhere to sleep. I woke up on the floor among a bunch of cords."

He followed Shawn through the door to the lounge and just like the day before, there was someone he didn't know.

The same unknown person as yesterday.

Except this time, she wasn't struggling in her own shirt and blindly bumping into furniture.

Which reminded him that he had never gotten her name. Which had been deliberate.

Because he was done with women for a while.

So even though after he'd freed her from the shirt and he immediately wanted to ask for her name and tell her he was famous and try to impress her in all the usual ways, he'd managed to avoid all of that.

Just barely.

He didn't think she'd be back the next day.

But then, just like yesterday, she glanced up, her hazel eyes caught his for the barest of seconds and then kept moving. Looking around him, but never *at* him again.

It was weird.

He didn't like it.

But he wasn't sure he'd be able to explain *why* he didn't like it.

"I can come over and help you get your stuff set up," Shawn offered, heading straight for the espresso maker. He raised a hand, palm out. "Sabine."

The unknown person smacked the offered hand in return. "Shawn."

She tugged her coat up around her neck, slung her laptop bag over her shoulder, and was gone.

Even quicker than the day before.

And again, it *bothered* him.

He had no business being bothered by a female brush off—as unusual as it was. He'd sworn off women, he reminded himself. A beautiful woman unimpressed by his credentials should not be driving him crazy.

Okay, that was an exaggeration.

But he couldn't stop the thoughts that bombarded him as she swept from the room.

Did she not like him? Had she read the articles about his exes? Is that why she wouldn't look him in the eye?

Why did he feel so judged by a veritable stranger?

But he did.

And unfortunately, he wanted to chase after her and *explain…*

No.

He didn't need to explain everything to everyone in the world. Even though he wanted to.

Maybe she was just embarrassed about what had happened the day before.

She didn't need to be. He had been happy to help. And he'd do it again if given the chance.

"Who was that?" Dave asked, jerking a thumb over his shoulder where she'd disappeared because he still couldn't help but ask.

"Who?" Shawn glanced around him, as if looking for who he was referring to.

"The woman who just left. Does she work here?" He was fairly certain he'd met the entire staff.

"Oh, Sabine?" Shawn asked, like Dave would know. "She's Piper's tutor. Hannah prefers her to meet Piper here. Just to discourage potential stalkers. You know."

Dave's lips twitched. He shot Piper a look who was already arching an eyebrow at Shawn's words.

"Correct me if I'm wrong but—"

"I was not stalking her!" Shawn protested. "I was just—"

"Learning her routine and following her around," Piper finished, dry as toast.

Dave snickered and Shawn scowled.

"Whatever." Shawn opened the cupboard and began to place all the different coffee roasts on the counter.

"Tutor for what?" Dave asked Piper.

Piper grunted and swiveled her laptop to face him for a second before spinning it back to her. "I'm failing English of all things. If I don't get my grade back up, they won't let me play basketball." She rolled her eyes.

"And Hannah found someone she trusted?" Dave asked, half-joking.

Hannah Lee James was notoriously paranoid. It took months before Dave was allowed to know her true identity. And it had felt like being read into an Eyes-Only file for a top-secret mission.

Which he was fine with. It made him feel like his occupation was more badass than it really was.

And finding out that the success of his sophomore album was due in large part to one of the greatest artists of their time had helped him to feel like it was a legitimate win, instead of…something else.

"Sabine tutors rich kids," Shawn continued. "She's used to being around celebrities and having to keep quiet." He motioned for Dave to come closer to the coffee bar. "All set up and ready for you."

The aroma of the coffee roasts assailed his nostrils and went right to his head.

He loved that smell.

It was like diving headfirst into happiness and brain cuddles.

He danced over to the counter and started mixing, measuring, and enjoying.

"What's that song you're singing"

"Hm?" He looked over his shoulder at Piper. "Was I singing?"

She laughed like he was being ridiculous, and he just shrugged.

"I've had that song…uh, by Zara Lorna?"

"'Good Intentions'?" Piper guessed.

"Yeah!" Dave pointed a finger at her. "It's everywhere."

She narrowed her eyes at him. "But you weren't singing that song."

He sucked in a thoughtful breath as he measured the grounds into the filter cup. "Nah, it was more of a remix of sorts."

"Dude, that would be so cool if you collaborated with her," Shawn spoke up.

Dave nodded and checked the water level.

"Unfortunately, I dated one of her besties a couple years ago and she has not forgiven me."

"Oh right. The Mandy Incident."

The Mandy Incident.

Dave grimaced.

"Mandy was a great girl. She didn't deserve to have her shit put out there."

"Is it true what they said?" Shawn asked.

"Probably not," Piper snorted without looking up from her laptop screen.

"About her stealing your car?"

Dave shook his head. "You know better than to believe what they say."

"They" being the entertainment media.

Shawn pursed his lips like he wasn't sure if he believed him or not.

Dave loved hanging out with these people. Not just Shawn and Piper, but the individuals in charge of raising them. It made for a nice break in his carefully constructed bubble of fame and notoriety.

Shawn and Piper spoke to him like he was just part of the family. So did Hannah and Johnny. And the entire XY crew.

It was nice.

He had that with his "entourage." Which was basically just his two childhood best friends—Max and Leslie. They had been by his side since the beginning and after he'd made his first million, they hadn't acted like anything was different.

Which wasn't something he could say about some of the other people in his life.

"So, she *didn't* steal your car?" Shawn asked.

Dave needed to introduce this kid to Max and Leslie because they'd get along.

"It was a misunderstanding." It was Dave's standard explanation for what had happened that night. It wasn't a lie.

Mandy had misunderstood why Dave hadn't called her back that day. He'd been sick in bed with the flu and she'd decided to take his car to get his attention.

Except it had been Max's car and she had driven into a neighbor's pool.

Max had called the police and she'd been arrested.

He went back to making his espresso.

"Isn't it kind of late to be having caffeine?" Hannah asked, joining them.

Dave clutched his chest. "Perish the thought."

Hannah bumped his shoulder with her own and he brought an arm out to hug her to his side.

Hannah was the reason he'd chosen Chicago.

After everything that had gone down in Texas a couple months ago, he'd needed to recalibrate. He'd realized he was swiftly painting himself into a corner he didn't want to be in.

His friends could only give him advice from a perspective of protection and loyalty. They would try to be objective, but it wasn't really possible.

His manager had one priority and that was to run the business of

Sunshine Capone as successfully as possible. That didn't always match with what Dave, the person, wanted to do.

But Hannah had been Ashton James.

She'd lived the roller coaster, had been at both the top and bottom of the industry and had somehow survived.

Plus, she was hella honest.

So, the day after Nora burned down his house, he'd called Hannah. Then he'd spent a couple months trying to make a decision as he went from Max's couch, to Leslie's, and back again.

Yesterday, he'd moved into the same building of condos where Hannah lived.

Decision made.

"Are you all moved in?" Hannah asked, bracing her back to the counter.

Dave snorted. "All my stuff is enclosed in the walls that I pay to occupy, if that's what you mean."

She nodded. "I've been there. Let me know if you want some company as you unpack."

"You're not going to offer to help me unpack?"

"Fuck no." A very unladylike snort accompanied the eye roll.

Dave smiled to himself as he watched the espresso machine finally dispense his cherished beverage. He brought it to his lips and the first sip greeted his senses like an old lover returning.

"It's the taste. There is literally nothing like it. Dark, light, in between…I love them all."

Silence followed his statement and he glanced at Hannah. One eyebrow was lifted in question.

"You wanna give me some context, bud?" she asked.

That was when Dave noticed Shawn trying to stifle his laughter across the room. Piper's eyes were glued to her laptop screen, but they were wider than they'd been.

"What did I say?" he asked.

"Well." Hannah spoke slowly. "Shawn asked since all your girlfriends keep getting arrested, why do you keep dating crazy women?"

Shawn couldn't hold his laughter in any longer and it tore through the room. Dave couldn't help but smile even though he felt heat spread up his neck to his face.

"And I said…"

"That it was the taste," Hannah finished seriously.

He cleared his throat and lifted the small espresso cup. "I was talking about the espresso."

He hadn't even heard Shawn's question. Not the first time. And it wouldn't be the last where he'd missed something and then said something that everyone laughed at.

When he was younger, it bothered him a lot more.

Now that he understood a little bit better how his brain worked and how those things happened?

It still bothered him.

Just not as much as it used to.

"Sorry," he muttered sheepishly.

Hannah just shook her head and let it be. She was one of those rare individuals who didn't try to change how he was wired. She just went with it.

"When do the boys get here?" she asked, changing the subject.

The boys she referred to were the forever homies. The OG crew. The goofballs who didn't make fun of him when he started making up rhymes in middle school and who had supported him through everything. Even the face tattoos.

Max and Leslie.

"Tomorrow night. They're just here for the weekend and then out again. But they'll be in and out as I settle. Just to make sure I don't do anything stupid."

"I'm glad you have them. They're really great guys."

"And I would tell them you said that, but I think I would have to tell Max outside of a hospital just in case he stroked out."

"That's ridiculous," she chastised, but she was smiling.

"He can be, yeah," Dave agreed. "He's just been in love with you since…"

"Sure." Hannah rolled her eyes.

"Right. I forget how annoying you find it."

"Find what?"

"Being adored."

"Hey, I'm trying to make a miracle over here and you're not helping!" Piper exclaimed, interrupting their conversation. Her bright blue eyes flashed at them dangerously. "Leave this room now or I will tell Johnny you were flirting with Hannah."

Dave dropped his mouth open. "You wouldn't dare."

Piper's lips flattened.

"Alright, I'm going." He took his little cup and headed for the door. Hannah followed.

Shawn's phone rang. He glanced at the screen and started to go the opposite way down the hall. "I gotta take this."

They walked down to the control room where they'd mixed his last album and sat on the couches there. Johnny had headphones on and was messing with the switches on the board.

"So, you got Piper a tutor?" Dave asked, his mind bouncing back to the newcomer. "How's that working out?"

Hannah wagged her head back and forth. "Piper doesn't like that she can't play basketball until her grades are back up. And I don't know shit about English so I couldn't help her."

"And you trust her? The teacher?" Dave had already forgotten her name. Big surprise.

"She's nice. A little dorky. Great references. Quinn doesn't trust her, but Alex does so I went with it."

Quinn was their "landlord" and also the CEO of his soon to be full-time security.

He didn't know Alex. And he hadn't met either one yet.

Hannah must've sensed the questions in his mind. "You'll meet them on Monday."

He sighed and sank back in the couch.

For the first time in weeks, he relaxed.

He finally felt like he was in a place that wasn't about to crush him at any moment.

The people here weren't trying to get something out of him, or expect the impossible, or even misunderstand his intentions.

This was good.

This was right.

No more girlfriends, no more distractions.

He could make his silly songs and just be…happy.

Chapter Three
Good Feeling

SABINE

It was a full moon.

That had been her first hint that that night was not going to be as normal as she'd hoped.

Though normal was subjective.

Maybe what she really meant was unsurprising. Yeah, that made more sense.

For the most part, she didn't mind a little chaos on her Saturday night so long as no one got hurt.

Besides, working the VIP section at Geekeasy usually meant she only witnessed the chaos instead of participating.

But when she'd walked in on her boss, Big Mike, taking a sponge bath in the sink of the employee bathrooms right before her shift started, she should have expected it to get weirder.

The night had been going fine. Nothing exciting, just the usual.

And by usual she meant predictable.

(Except for that unfortunate couple of seconds when her eyes met Big

Mike's in the mirror. But we're just going to move past that because what else is there to do?)

But everything else had been predictable.

And Sabine loved predictable.

It's what helped grow the reputation she'd cultivated among her students of being feared.

And loved.

That part was important too.

At nine, Big Mike stopped avoiding her and told her the VIP Lounge was hers. Someone had reserved it last minute and she already knew the drill. She'd signed so many NDAs by then that she could have given a seminar on them.

She was however surprised to see Sunshine Capone the moment she swiped her badge at the door.

Oookay.

This was the third time this week she'd run into him.

Now Sabine believed in a lot of ridiculous things. Things that often got her laughed at and didn't earn her any respect. Crazy things such as: true love, friends forever, and the perfect pillow (she hadn't found it yet, but she would never give up looking!)

Something she didn't believe in?

Coincidence.

"Good evening, gentlemen," she greeted with a warm smile, quickly scanning the room.

Sunshine was on the middle of three couches in a semicircle setting, watching the basketball game on the flat screen. Two other men about his age lounged in similar fashion on the furthest couch from her. Two people in suits, clearly professional security, stood at the doors. One by where she'd entered and the other at the door to the exit to the alley (VIPs had their own special entrance).

All in all, it was a smaller group than what she would have expected.

Sunshine Capone wasn't small potatoes.

She had looked him up online after their second encounter. If you could call it that.

Hopefully that information would help her land a big tip.

She liked big tips and she could not lie.

VIP tips often paid the rent. And with the holidays coming up and

Sabine's propensity to spoil her loved ones with gifts, she could use some extra cash.

"What can I start you out with? I should mention that the wings go fast, so if you want some, order sooner rather than later."

All eyes came to her as she spoke, and she hesitated when she glanced in Sunshine's direction.

Recognition flared in his gaze.

Involuntarily she smiled.

It was a slip for which she was not known. Sabine was quite capable of just being the hired help and perfectly invisible.

But then he smiled back, and she may have sighed just a bit.

"Uh," she stuttered, forgetting her next lines. "Wings and beer sound good?"

Sunshine sat up and leaned forward, trying to catch her eyes again.

He was in a gray hoodie again—possibly the same one from the other day—dark jeans, and white sneakers. His hair had been cut very short compared to the pictures she'd seen of him online. The tattoos on his hands stood out in stark contrast to his pale skin and she found her gaze darting from his hands to the sun at his throat to the rose near his eye.

Apparently, she had completely forgotten all of her training because when her gaze finally tangled with his again, she couldn't look away.

"Wait," he said, eyes sharp. "Are you…? Is it a small world?"

She coughed a small laugh and nodded. "Seems to be."

Please don't bring up the tube man incident.

"You know her?" the companion to Sunshine's right asked. He was in a white button down and dress pants. His sleeves had been unbuttoned and rolled up exposing strong forearms. The dark hair on his arms matched the jet black short-styled hair on his head. He looked like the kind of guy who was comfortable in a suit. Like her brother. Like the way she was comfortable in her "teacher" clothes. It was all just part of the uniform.

Sunshine shook his head. "We haven't been formally introduced but we keep running into each other."

"Really."

The flat declaration, not question, had Sabine's gaze bouncing to the companion who had narrowed his eyes at her in suspicion.

Someone else didn't believe in coincidence it seemed.

Before Sabine could even attempt to explain how and why, Sunshine beat her to it. Which was good because the words out of her mouth were probably going to be, "He took my shirt off."

"She works for a friend of mine."

"What friend?"

"Don't worry about it."

Sabine suppressed a smirk. The companion was less than pleased.

"No, I *will* worry about it because someone needs to worry about it. Now, missy, what's your name?" he demanded.

"Shut up, Max." The other friend entered the conversation.

Sabine let her attention be taken from Sunshine's sleepy smile to the companion on his left. He wore an off-white cable knit sweater that showed off his black skin. His head was shaved smooth and he had a perfectly groomed goatee. The sleeves were halfway pushed up his forearms revealing a gold watch on his right wrist. His pants were dark, she couldn't tell if they were jeans or slacks. His legs were bent in such a way that he looked tall, even sitting down.

Did she mention the sweater?

Cable knit.

It was gorgeous.

It looked soft and thick, but his muscles were so massive that even the thick sweater couldn't hide the bulging biceps and rounded shoulders.

For a second, she thought it was Terry Crews sitting in her VIP Lounge. Which, okay, yeah, she didn't get excited about celebrities.

But Terry Crews would have been someone to get excited about.

Spoiler alert, he was *not* Terry Crews.

He was much younger, probably in his mid-twenties. But just as beautiful.

"Don't tell me to shut up, Leslie. You know he's far too trusting."

"He's an adult man. You've gotta stop mother-henning him," Leslie warned like it wasn't the first time he'd said something about it.

"I will *not!*" Max snapped.

Sabine pursed her lips and raised her eyebrows.

Sunshine rolled his eyes and covered the smile on his mouth.

"Beer and wings, please," Leslie said pointedly. "Whatever you have on tap." His eyes narrowed at Max. "Dude, we have *armed* security. He's literally the safest he's ever been. You have got to chill."

Max huffed and slumped back onto the couch. "Fine." He lifted his eyes to Sabine. "Sorry about the missy thing."

"It happens," she replied with a wink. "I'll be back with some beer, and I'll put that wing order in."

* * *

DAVE

"Do I need to crush up some antihistamines and hide them in your drink?" Dave asked his friend Max after Sabine had sashayed out of the lounge.

Max sighed dramatically. "Are you suggesting that I need to be sedated?"

"You're a little more high-strung than usual is all." Dave eased back into the couch, his eyes on the television screen. "I have Benadryl in my bag in case you need it."

None of his teams were playing but that didn't matter. Watching professional basketball was both relaxing and exciting. In a nostalgic sort of way.

Even the guilt that tried to creep in wasn't strong enough to overpower his love for the game. That had always been as pure as anything.

"Yeah," Max agreed with a huff.

Max had been jumpy since he'd arrived at the door of Dave's condo the night before. Even Leslie, who had a high tolerance for Max's enthusiastic anxiety, was already weary.

Max thought for a minute. "I don't like you living up here by yourself. I feel like you're exposed."

Leslie crossed his arms over his chest and rolled his eyes. But he stayed quiet, pretending to watch the game.

This wasn't the first time Max had expressed such concerns.

When Dave had decided to move to Chicago after the Nora incident, he had been met with a lot of resistance.

But everything he'd been attached to in Texas was ashes now.

Literally.

It was time to start somewhere new.

Max had wanted Dave to move back to Long Island with him. Had set up numerous private real estate showings all over the five boroughs.

And as with anything Max did, they were all classy, high-end, and perfect for what Dave had talked about.

He was pretty sure Max had envisioned a true Taylor Swift-esque professional and creative renaissance by moving back to the city.

But it just didn't feel like New York was the place for him anymore.

He wanted a different adventure.

Hannah's pitch for Midwest Blindness—not being recognized even when you're recognized because Midwesterners assume you're not who they think you are—also helped.

He rubbed a hand along his jaw, still not used to his facial hair being gone. He'd shaved off his "signature" beard a couple days ago. He barely recognized himself in the mirror.

Not only that but his face had leaned out from the last time he'd been clean shaven. A mix of his ADHD meds and not having an appetite over the fire drama and he'd dropped weight. He felt it in his clothes and in his skin.

He didn't like it.

His doctor was going to be pissed, he realized, tracing the sharp line of his jaw with his fingertips.

"You've only been here a week and what? Already have a stalker? No, thank you." Max's Long Island accent wasn't as strong as it used to be. After years of doing business all over the world, he'd mostly dropped it. But when he was with friends, family, or when he was agitated, it would show up strong again.

Strong and nasal. Just like his ma.

"She's not a stalker," Dave replied with a soft smile.

"How would you know?" Max spat. "You never see the crazy until it's burning your house down."

Leslie chuckled and turned it into a deep throat clear to cover it.

"I'll have her checked out. Would that make you happy?" Dave offered, already knowing Sabine would pass the background check with ease. She'd passed Hannah's after all.

"Yes. Actually." Max agreed. "I would feel better."

Dave and Leslie exchanged a look that they had shared many times over the years.

Max's default setting was "tightly wound." To be his friend meant tolerating a lot of neuroses.

The door opened and Sabine returned with their drinks.

Max eyed her suspiciously.

Okay, time to end this.

"Sabine?" Dave asked, suddenly unsure he had her name correct. She tilted her head to listen. "I'm sorry, one of us should have mentioned this. My friend Max can't have gluten."

"Oh!" Her eyebrows arched and she looked to Max. "Would you like a cider or wine? We have several gluten free options. I can even make you something at the bar. I highly recommend the Alderaan Sunrise. It's like a tequila sunrise, but it has this burnt aftertaste that can be fun if you're able to ignore the guilt."

All three men blinked at her. Leslie covered his mouth which Dave knew was his way of hiding a smile. Max opened his mouth to say something and couldn't.

Dave chuckled.

Max flattened his lips, trying to stay upset. "A hard cider."

Dave narrowed one eye at his friend.

"Please," Max added begrudgingly.

"Not a problem. I'll be right back." She hurried to the door and turned back. "Oh! The wings are safe for you! You can eat them." She flashed one more smile and was gone.

"See? She's nice," Dave pointed out.

"So was Nora," Max countered.

Leslie snorted. "No, she wasn't."

Dave frowned because the point had quickly gotten away from him. "I'm not dating her. I just don't think you're being fair."

"I know that, you damn apologist," Max grumbled. "Can't you just let me be suspicious?"

Dave struggled with how to respond. He wasn't trying to drive anyone crazy. He just really hated misunderstandings.

Before he had settled on what to say next, Sabine returned with Max's drink.

"Here you go." She handed him the bottle. "This one is my best friend's favorite. She's also celiac."

Max took the bottle but kept that suspicious expression firmly affixed to his face. "Thank you. Not many people take me seriously."

Sabine rolled her eyes. "Tell me about it. She can hardly go anywhere. No one cares enough to be careful."

Max regarded her carefully.

"You know who he is?" Max asked point blank, nodding his head at Dave.

"Yes?" Sabine replied, confused.

Max leaned forward, bracing his elbows on his knees. "What do you know?"

"Oh my God, Max. You have got to chill. Just let the woman do her job." Leslie was nearing an end in his patience.

Sabine slid her hands into the front pocket of her apron and smiled at Max. "I get it. He's your friend. You're just being protective." Her eyes bounced to Dave's for a second before returning to Max with a playful gleam. "He's Sunshine Capone, the voice of a generation."

Dave groaned out loud.

Max grinned. All bitchiness dissolved in his brilliant, gleaming smile.

"Please don't call me that," Dave protested. "I'm just Dave. And I just want to eat wings, pizza, and watch some basketball with my friends." He glared at Max

"But that's what he is," Max agreed with earnest glee. "I came up with that."

"I like your shirt, by the way," Leslie changed the subject.

Sabine glanced down at her threadbare ringer tee with the Star Wars logo emblazoned across her chest. It was a faded cream color and the rings around the sleeve and collar were maroon. She was also wearing jeans that hugged her backside in a way Dave shouldn't be noticing.

Except he had noticed.

"Thanks. It's a favorite."

"Are you a fan of the movies or just of the shirt?" Leslie continued conversationally.

Dave knew where he was headed with this. Leslie *loved* Star Wars. Not the way other people loved Star Wars. But like the way people loved their children.

It was as uncomfortable as it sounded.

He would talk about Star Wars to anyone he could, anywhere he could. He barely needed a reason.

One time Dave had had to force him to leave a certain important White Party thrown by a certain important person because he got into a heated debate about whether Jar Jar was actually supposed to be the Phantom Menace.

"Huge fan of the movies," Sabine replied. "And the shirt is vintage. I found it in a bin in…" She trailed off like she'd decided in the middle of her sentence that she didn't want to reveal where she'd gotten the shirt.

"It's not the official uniform?" Leslie asked.

They hadn't explored the rest of the bar. They'd come through the back entrance with his security escort. Dave wanted to explore but he'd agreed with Leslie and Max's suggestion to let one of them get the vibe first.

Sometimes being famous was more of a pain than it was worth.

But he understood their reasoning.

It would be a shame if they had to leave early just because someone recognized him.

She waved her hand in a circle indicating the bar. Dave had already noticed the whole place was packed with geek and nerd memorabilia.

"This place is geek chic. We have a basic uniform of black shirt black pants for when we work the main floor or the bar. Big Mike lets me wear whatever I want when I work VIP."

"Let me ask you a question," Leslie said, hands resting on his knees.

Her hazel eyes flicked over the group of men curiously before coming back to Leslie.

"Which Obi-Wan is the best?" Leslie asked.

She took a deep breath and rolled her eyes to the ceiling in thought.

Leslie grabbed a beer and handed it to Dave before taking one for himself. Max took a drink of his cider and then frowned curiously at the label. He took another drink.

"Good?" Dave asked him.

"Are…are you sure this is gluten free?" Max asked, sounding concerned.

Sabine's eyes flicked to him. "For sure. Kara says it tastes too good to be true too, but it's never made her sick."

"Hmm." Max glanced around the VIP Lounge and Dave knew he was figuring out where the bathroom was just in case.

Sabine cocked a hip and narrowed one eye at Leslie. "You're asking me to choose between Sir Alec Guinness or Ewan McGregor?"

A smirk tugged on the side of Leslie's mouth. "And the animated Obi-Wan—"

"James Arnold Taylor?" she cut him off with a sassy eyebrow arch. "Do you include Seth Green on your list as well?"

Dave fought the grin but failed. Not everyone remembered or even knew that Seth Green had voiced the character on *Robot Chicken*. And not everyone could match Leslie in trivia knowledge.

"We generally don't include him." Leslie shrugged one shoulder, pretending like he wasn't completely delighted with her participation.

"Mm-hm, mm-hm." She nodded, tapping her chin with a forefinger. "Right, right, right."

Dave glanced from her to his friends.

Max may be overprotective and neurotic, but Leslie was the one who judged people's character based on what they thought of Star Wars. It was a ridiculous litmus test but it had yet to fail him.

It wasn't her answer that mattered. Every one of them had their own opinion on the subject.

What Leslie weighed was whether or not their answer was thought through and honest.

Sabine pinched her chin. "Ewan. Hands down."

The room erupted in both shouts of disgust and agreement.

Dave chuckled and waved for his friends to calm down.

"Okay," Leslie said, addressing her with a level stare. "Why?"

Dave shook his head. One of these days Leslie was going to meet someone who didn't think all his questions were harmless.

"Why?" Her eyes widened like the answer was obvious. "Obi-Wan in the original trilogy was cool and all, but he just didn't scream 'Jedi Knight' to me."

"He was a Jedi Master," Max corrected, crossing his arms over his chest. "Just saying."

Sabine's mouth twisted to the side as she attempted to hide her amusement. "Yeah," she replied slowly. "But he had to be a knight first, right?"

"Right."

"And I'm supposed to believe he just, what? Went full retired Boomer on Tatooine and let all those skills go?"

Leslie chuckled as Max rolled his eyes dramatically.

"Also," Sabine dipped her head to emphasize her next point. "Seeing Ewan McGregor on screen had an effect on my heart and body that I can't just ignore."

"Wait! No! That's not part of this!" Max sputtered. "You can't measure how good of an Obi-Wan he is based on how *crushable* you find him."

Sabine shrugged like she didn't care. "And I may not have agreed with all of the changes George Lucas made to the original trilogy, but if he wanted to digitally erase Alec Guinness and replace him with Ewan, I wouldn't be mad about it."

Max gasped, personally affronted at the suggestion.

Leslie was loving it, since he'd been Team Ewan from the beginning. Max turned wide, panicked eyes to Dave. "She doesn't know what she's talking about."

Dave had gone back and forth over the years. He loved all the renditions of Obi-Wan, truth be told. They were all winners in his book.

He sent a sly look to Sabine who happened to be looking at him at the same time. There was a definite tease in her eyes that sent a thrill through him.

She grinned widely at Max. "You're telling me that you can watch Ewan McGregor wield a lightsaber and *not* be completely ready to ruin your life for that man?"

"Exactly!" Leslie declared, pointing at Max. "That's what I've been saying this entire time. The fighting skills alone—"

Max and Leslie began arguing with one another in earnest. Sabine smiled and pulled her order tablet from her apron.

She skirted around the table and sat down beside Dave.

"Would you like to order anything else? The pizza is good. We even have a gluten free crust that I've been told is just as good as the real thing."

"Haven't you tried it?"

"I have. I just can't tell the difference. Kara swears by it. Says that it's the sole reason she keeps working here."

So her best friend was like Max. Happy coincidence that was. Winning Max over was pretty easy if you went out of your way to make sure he didn't get sick.

"Yeah, a couple of those then. Just pepperoni and something veggie."

She tapped the order into her tablet, and he took a second to look at her up close.

Her dirty blonde hair was pulled back into a messy and complicated braid. She had a short nose, flat chin, full lips, and dark eyebrows that made him think the blonde wasn't natural. Not that he cared. He had a feeling she could do whatever she wanted with her hair and still be beautiful.

Yes, he thought she was beautiful.

Don't everyone freak out about it.

Acknowledging her beauty seemed a given.

Like when people pointed out his face tattoos. Yeah, they were there. Vocalizing it didn't make you more perceptive than the rest of the world.

When she was finished, she looked up at him and smiled. She had a deep dimple on one cheek that did something to his chest. It tingled, like static electricity, but only in the area directly above his sternum.

Had that always happened with dimples or was it new?

"Anything else?" she asked.

"Why wouldn't you look at me?"

He hadn't really meant to ask but he hadn't been able to stop thinking about it.

The moment he'd pulled that sweater off her head, she'd taken one look at him and then…stopped. Stopped speaking, stopped looking. Like he was invisible.

Her lips parted and her eyes widened a fraction. A light blush touched the top of her cheeks and she shook her head once.

"Um." Her voice dropped lower, and her eyes flicked to his friends who were now listening intently instead of arguing. She set the tablet on her leg and opened her hands to explain. "I work for a lot of celebrities…they usually don't like it when I look *directly* at them."

"Seriously?" Dave had heard of things like that but none of those type of people were in his circle. So she didn't look at him because she assumed he was just like every other famous douchebag out there.

"I mean…" She folded her hands together and bobbed her head in thought, bottom lip curled in thought. "It's common enough that I just make sure I avoid eye contact. My job sort of relies on recommendations in the right circles."

"The tutoring gig you mean?" She couldn't mean this job. Being a server. But maybe she did. Hell, he didn't know anything about either job. His jobs before getting famous consisted of shoveling rocks (no, really) and fast food.

Her eyes lit from within at the mention of teaching and she nodded. "But it's not that big of a deal. It doesn't bother me."

"It bothers me."

He wasn't lying. The more he considered it the more he realized *how much* he was bothered.

So much.

She tilted her chin down just a bit and those lips of hers that were perpetually in an almost smirk twitched.

"Well, I won't do that with you again."

His eyes dropped to her mouth and then back to her hazel eyes. "People are just people. No one is better than anyone else. It's fucked up that they think they are. You shouldn't have to *avert your eyes* for some."

Her head tilted slightly to the left and she studied him with intelligent eyes. Seeing him in a way that made him second guess his previous statement.

"I think," she said slowly, diplomatically. "I think it's not about that. I think when someone reaches a certain recognizability, they don't want to be gawked at. It can make them feel *less* human. And more like a commodity."

Surprise rippled through him and he lifted his eyebrows.

Max stood and barked a laugh. "She just Uno reversed you, son!"

"Don't say son," Leslie corrected.

Dave coughed a laugh and sat back on the couch, stunned.

And delighted. He covered his mouth with a hand and slowly shook his head because dammit. She was right.

Wasn't that why he was hiding in VIP instead of exploring the bar? Wasn't that why he'd chosen Chicago? For the anonymity?

Not only that, but she'd defended the other side with sweet understanding. She hadn't jumped to being a victim even though he'd provided the avenue.

Oof. Another sucker punch to his assumptions.

"I'm not sure I follow." Sabine eyed the three of them.

"Dave looooves to play devil's advocate. It drives us crazy because he's always trying to give a good excuse for someone's bad behavior." Max arched a knowing eyebrow at Dave. "Like arson."

"A-arson?" Sabine questioned, with not a small amount of shock registering on her face.

Dave waved away her question.

Max took a huge bite of chicken wing.

"I just think assuming is dangerous and there's always more to a story." Dave shot a grin to Sabine. "It's not often someone gets me back."

"As in never," Max interjected around his mouthful. And coughed.

Max's eyes went wide and he coughed again.

No, he wasn't coughing.

He was choking.

"Can you breathe?" Sabine asked, standing.

Dave stood up too. He exchanged a worried look with Leslie who had his phone out.

Max shook his head and his eyes filled with terror.

Sabine moved swiftly toward Max. "Stand up, bud."

He did, and she ran a hand down his back once in a soothing motion.

Out of the corner of his eye Dave saw the two security guys step towards them. One had his hand by his mouth.

"I need you to lean forward," Sabine commanded, voice firm. Calm.

Max leaned forward, his face panicked, tears streaming freely from his eyes.

She struck him on the back with the heel of her hand one…two…three…four…five times.

Nothing happened.

Sabine circled Max's middle with her arms and positioned her fist on his abs. She thrust once…twice…and a chunk of partially chewed chicken flew out of Max's mouth and hit the flat screen.

Max sucked in a fresh breath and held his chest with one hand. He wiped the tears off his face with the other.

"Oh my God." He coughed a couple more times and then spun around to face Sabine. "You just saved my life."

She gripped Max by his biceps, scanning his features, all business. "Are you okay? Can you breathe?"

He took in several gasping breaths, testing his ability. He nodded.

"Good." She rubbed her hands along his arms, almost absentmindedly. "You should probably see a doctor to make sure you're not injured."

Max nodded and then suddenly wrapped both arms around her middle.

Max was not a hugger.

But he was hugging Sabine.

Leslie and Dave exchanged matching perplexed expressions.

Max set her down and then picked her up again. "You saved my life. You're like an actual Jedi."

Sabine snorted a laugh and patted Max on the back until he set her down again. She shook her head, her face pink with embarrassment. Or maybe Max had been squeezing too hard for her to breathe.

"I'm going to get some water for you, okay?"

She left the lounge.

"You guys, I almost died." Max had one hand on his chest and the other on his hip.

"Well," Leslie shrugged one shoulder. "We were all here. We weren't going to let you just choke to death and kick you under the table."

But Max wasn't listening. He pulled his phone out and started dialing. "Ma? You're never gonna believe this… Uncle Rob is there? Put me on speaker."

Leslie dropped his head back and closed his eyes. "We are never going to hear the end of this, are we?"

"Not likely." Dave chuckled.

Sabine returned with the water which Max took and then continued his phone conversation.

"I'm pretty sure he's calling everyone he's ever met," Dave explained to her.

"Do you want me to put the pizza order in then…?" Sabine asked, her mouth pulling to the side in question.

"Yeah. Yes, please." He smiled at her. Thankful she had been there, thankful she knew what to do, thankful she was so chill about the whole thing—and wishing he could say all that.

"Okay, I'll be back."

She smirked fully then and gave him a finger wiggle as she left.

"What's that?"

Dave glanced at Leslie who had a knowing smile on his face. "What?"

"That little smile you gave her. What was that?"

Dave rolled his eyes and crossed his arms over his chest.

"You think I didn't see it, but I saw it," Leslie pressed.

"I'm still allowed to smile, right?" Dave asked.

Leslie nodded once but his expression didn't shift away from that slightly amused one.

Dave got it. They thought he was ridiculous because he'd sworn off women. Actually, they thought he was ridiculous because he'd decided to be celibate. He'd tried to explain it but they really didn't see it the way he did.

Sex complicated things—for him specifically. He couldn't speak to anyone else's experience.

Don't get it wrong, sex was awesome. He definitely enjoyed it. And he had every intention of enjoying it again in the future.

But when he'd driven up his driveway and found the house on fire, he realized he needed to do something different.

He had a history of hooking up with women who were just as impulsive as he was. Which always felt amazing in the beginning.

But they had too much in common when it came to chasing the dopamine and mistaking sex for connection.

He realized sex made things confusing for him. It felt like love and it looked like love, but it had taken the place of critical thinking in his brain. He looked past red flags, he ignored his friends' warnings; he ignored his own warnings.

And because sex filled that part of his brain that desired connection and impulsivity, he'd just chase the dopamine until it was gone.

Literally a pile of ashes.

The women who were eager to sleep with him, move in with him, go on trips with him, they had impulse issues the same as he did. It was unreasonable to expect the relationship to do anything but fail. It wasn't built on anything stable.

So, he'd decided to try something different. No sex until he was certain he'd found *the one*. And maybe he wouldn't find her. Maybe *the one* was a fantasy. But the longer he went sticking to his convictions, the better he felt about himself and what he wanted.

The antidepressants had helped in that area too.

It was a completely new way for him to operate though, so he understood why Max was suspicious and why Leslie teased him. It would take some time to establish a new pattern.

At least that's what he kept telling himself.

"No, ma, I didn't see Aunt Silvia. Because I *almost* died. I didn't actually die." Max paced between Dave and the television.

Shit that had been scary.

But it was over.

It'd gone incredibly fast.

One minute he was flirting with the cute teacher, and the next Max was choking on a chicken wing.

Life in one breath and the end of life in another.

Dave shivered at his own dark thoughts.

Nope.

He didn't like that.

Luckily, distractions were never hard for him to find.

He pulled out his phone and opened the voice memo. He grabbed his beer, took a long drink, and then started to pour his thoughts into the receiver.

What felt like just a few seconds later, the smell of pizza invaded his thoughts. He closed the phone down and looked up to see Sabine eyeing him thoughtfully.

She arranged the pizzas carefully on the table and served slices to Leslie, Max, and Dave.

"How about the secret agents?" she asked when she was near enough to him that no one else could hear her.

Dave frowned in question.

She got closer and jerked her head just slightly towards the door. "Do they get…?" She held his pizza out to him.

"Yeah! Of course." Truthfully Dave hadn't even thought about it, but obviously they could have food.

Sabine smiled and dished up two more plates and took them to the security guards. They seemed surprised but pleased. It kind of made Dave feel like shit for not thinking of it.

They probably hated him.

See? This was why it was hard to hire people to protect him. He wasn't special. Not really.

He was just a dude who happened to be good at meeting the right people.

Sabine came back and started cleaning up their empties. Dave plopped his pizza down and waved at her. She tilted her head to the side in question.

"You should eat with us," he offered.

She seemed taken aback. "Oh, that's very sweet of you, but I don't eat with the guests."

Her gentle refusal hurt even though it shouldn't. She hadn't meant it to, she hadn't been rude or unkind. And yet he was sore.

And embarrassed.

"Are you sure?" he asked again. "We have all this pizza." He scooted over on the couch. "And all this extra room to sit down. You've been working so hard for us all night. You can sit down for a second."

Her mouth opened to protest but her eyes were sizing him up again.

She looked confused.

Damnnnn it.

He hated it when he confused people.

"No, Dave's right," Max spoke up around a mouthful (not having learned his lesson at all).

Sabine turned her attention to him, and Dave could swear she was thinking the exact same thing.

"Stop talking with food in your mouth," she said, incredulous.

Max swallowed and looked down, shamed.

"Aren't we VIPs?" Leslie asked.

Sabine shot him a smile.

"Then maybe you should have some pizza at the VIPs' request."

She adjusted the tray of empties on her hip and dropped her head back for a breath.

"Okay. Fine. I will have one slice with you. But then I have to get back to work. First," she arched an eyebrow, "I'm taking these down and I'll bring back refills, 'kay?"

The pressure in Dave's chest eased and he relaxed back into the couch.

She came back, ate a slice of pizza, and slipped into easy conversation with him and his oldest friends.

And four hours later, when they were shutting the place down, he had no idea how he'd lost track of all that time.

But his cheeks hurt from laughing, and his stomach was warm and full of food.

Chapter Four
Myself

SABINE

On Monday, she wasn't as surprised to see Sunshine—er, Dave—at the studio.

And if she were being completely honest (and she always was), she was happy to see him.

Though cautious.

On Sunday while she did her laundry for the week, she also did a little… research.

Yes, that's what it was. Research.

She started by watching his music videos, which led to award show appearances, which led to vlogs about his dating habits and motivations.

There were a *lot* of people who thought they knew everything about Sunshine Capone.

By the time she went to make dinner last night, her head was fuzzy with opinions.

None of them her own.

How was it that every single person on the internet described someone she hadn't met? None of the things they said matched with the guy she'd hung out with on Saturday.

It had given her a lot to consider.

So, she'd switched out her regular playlist for his music and found herself enjoying it.

A lot.

Which annoyed her.

Not because his music was annoying, but because she couldn't seem to decide one way or another what to believe.

And since she had been fooled by people in the past, she was a little more guarded when she walked into XY Records on Monday afternoon.

He was already in the lounge when she arrived. He was hunkered over the espresso machine and didn't hear her come in. He was in jeans again and a different hoodie. This one was emerald green.

She tossed her bag on the table and quietly approached him.

"Hm." He righted himself and cupped his chin in one hand as he studied what looked like a variety of coffee grounds in small glass bowls. "Maybe it's the water."

"What's the water?" she asked at his shoulder.

He jumped, startled, and spun around.

"Holy moly," he exclaimed.

Okay, so *that* was adorable.

She tried to fight the smile on her face, but she couldn't say why.

"Did I scare ya?" she asked, pumping her eyebrows once.

"Only in the literal sense." He smiled and scanned her up and down. Not in a creepy way, more like he was just observing her whole person. "How are you today? No attacking sweaters, I see."

Maybe it was because she'd been listening to his albums nonstop since last night, but now even when he spoke, it sounded like it was in rhythm. As if his words were perfectly cadenced for a specific purpose.

"Today has been uneventful. Just the way I like it." She took a step back before turning around. "What are you doing with that poor espresso machine?" she asked, unloading her binder and laptop.

"Making sweet, sweet love to it."

She looked over her shoulder at him with raised eyebrows. "Oh really?"

He chuckled at his own joke but otherwise didn't elaborate.

She sat down and went through her notes while he ran the espresso machine repeatedly. Sometimes she'd stop to watch him but all it looked like to her was that he was making numerous shots of espresso.

He never looked up at her, just kept working on whatever had his interest.

It was super cute.

"Do you drink espresso?" he asked, and she realized he was now standing very nearby.

"I have." She set aside her binder and turned slightly in her chair. "I'm not an aficionado or anything."

He rubbed his hands along the sides of his jeans. "Would you know if an espresso was bad or good?"

"Perhaps." She narrowed her eyes at him.

He seemed to be having an internal conversation. He nodded. "Right. Will you try this and tell me if it's good?"

He scooped up one of the cups and took two long strides in her direction.

She accepted the tiny cup of espresso, eyeing him warily.

"I didn't drink out of that one," he said, not taking his eyes off the cup until he was sure she had a hold of it.

She brought the cup to her lips and took a small sip.

Oh.

Took another, larger sip.

Oh.

"This is…" She frowned and held the transparent cup up to the light. She had no idea what she was looking for. An explanation as to its delicious flavor?

"It's good?" he asked, sort of bouncing on his toes.

"It's *very* good." She took another sip and eyed it again. "Why is it so good?"

"I don't know!" he exclaimed, shoving his hands in his hair and pulling them back out again. It made his hair stick out all over the place.

He paced back to the machine. "I have tried three different roasts from different companies today. I have tried tap water and bottled water. The result is always the same though."

"Delicious espresso?" she guessed, wondering if he'd make her another one.

"Unless…" He muttered to himself and began opening the doors below the sink area.

He resembled a mad scientist a little bit.

"How many espressos have you had today, Dave?" she asked, keeping her voice casual.

He spun around. "Why do you ask?"

She couldn't help it. She really tried though.

She smiled.

His eyes flicked to her mouth and back, and his lips also began to curve.

"No reason." She swallowed.

This was not the guy in the music videos and tabloid headlines. He wasn't calculated and manipulative. He wasn't egotistical and full of himself.

You know what he was? He was a bit of a dork.

"Do you want another one?" he asked.

"Yes, please."

He ran the machine again and brought her a new cup of espresso. She eyed the empties starting to pile up on the counter.

"Do you do this every day?" he asked, taking a seat at the table.

She assumed he was asking about the tutoring. Granted, a recording studio wasn't her usual workspace. But she could work anywhere.

"More or less." She angled herself to face him. "We meet every day for the first couple of weeks and then reevaluate the student's progress and see if we can cut back."

"How many students do you have?"

"At the moment I have three full time and one part time."

"And you work at the bar on the weekends." He nodded, as if cataloguing that information away. "Why tutoring and not teaching?"

"Oof." She checked her watch, Piper was late. She could probably give him a shortened version of her story. She crossed one leg over the other and tugged her dark gray skirt to cover the top of her knee. She was wearing opaque tights as usual, but the habit to cover her legs remained. "I wanted to be a more traditional teacher. But I couldn't pass any of the background checks." She chuckled at his expression. "That sounds worse than it is."

He narrowed his eyes playfully. "Are you a criminal, Sabine?"

"No. But my mom is."

Piper entered the room with a flurry of censored expletives. Which is to say, it was obvious which swears she was deliberately omitting.

"Stupid mother effing idiot sh-face." She stopped when she saw Dave and Sabine. She ended on a growl and flopped her backpack on the table. "Sorry I'm late."

Sabine eyed the eighth grader. "You okay?"

"No." Piper tossed her glossy dark hair over her shoulder. "I had detention today." She narrowed her eyes. "Me. Detention."

"First time?" Dave asked casually.

Piper sighed and rolled her eyes. "Yes. I don't get detention!" she yelled towards them but not really *at* them. "I didn't even do anything wrong!"

"Detention's not the worst thing," Dave said.

Both Sabine and Piper gave him the side-eye.

"What? I had detention all the time and look at me." He held out his arms like they were supposed to see him revealing all his success.

Piper grimaced and scratched the side of her neck. "You don't get it."

He really didn't get it.

But Sabine did.

Being blamed and held accountable for something you had no part in was… well, it was what she'd just been talking about.

"What happened?" Sabine asked, focusing on Piper.

"Some idiots were throwing clay in art class. And the rule is 'don't throw clay.' I was just doing my *stupid* sculpture and Josh Szippl hit me square in the face with a hunk of clay. I was mad so I threw it back. And that was the moment Ms. Beck looked up. I was the only one who got caught!"

"Wait." Dave blinked at Piper. "Say his name again."

"Josh Szippl."

"That's his real name?"

Piper rolled her eyes. "Yes. And usually, he's hilarious. Until he's getting me detention." She shoved her backpack aside and glowered at the table.

"Was Hannah pissed?" Dave asked, shooting Sabine a look.

If he knew Hannah the way *she* knew Hannah, then yeah, she was going to be pissed.

Piper's expression fell. "She doesn't know yet," she grumbled.

Big oof.

"How did your speech go?" Sabine asked, changing the subject. Nothing to be done about the detention now anyway.

Piper glanced up at her and some of the tension eased from her face. "Fine. I got an A."

Sabine sighed and kept her smile small. Too much enthusiasm and teenagers became suspicious.

"Of course you did." Sabine opened her binder and flipped to Piper's next assignment. "Let's go over your essay one more time, shall we? Then we can add another A to the pile."

Piper groaned. "I hate school. I'm so bad at it!"

"You are not bad at it. You'd just rather be doing something else."

"Maybe I'm not meant to be a scholar," Piper suggested looking down her nose at her laptop.

Before Sabine could reply, Dave spoke up.

"What are you meant to be?" he asked, sincere curiosity lighting up his features.

"I am meant to wreak havoc on the basketball court," Piper replied with smug self-assuredness.

Dave barked a laugh that had Piper shifting into a begrudging smile. Sabine narrowed her eyes at the both of them.

"That's a basketball reference, isn't it?" Sabine asked.

Piper shook her head at her, disappointment dripping from her expression.

But Dave gave her an understanding smile, and she again noticed the deep blue shade of his eyes.

Oh, he had nice eyes.

The kind of eyes a person could curl up and take a nap in.

Wait? Who said that?

"It's a commercial from the 90s. I'll show it to you some time."

Her brain paused on his statement at the same time he shot her a wink.

It wasn't the wink. It was the solid four second eye contact they shared immediately after.

Which caused a full system reboot.

A wink is like a wave. It's usually followed by the person walking away. It's a jaunty little farewell. It's cute and spunky and *meaningless*.

But he didn't immediately turn away.

He held her eyes for four whole seconds. As if he were waiting for her to agree or respond.

Which she could not.

Because a full system reboot was in progress.

Later, she was going to blame his nappable eyes. They were soooo soft.

Maybe this was what those vloggers were talking about. Maybe he was stealthy with his charm. Maybe it snuck up on you and caught you unprepared. Maybe the adorable dorkiness was just an act.

Maybe it was all Jedi mind tricks.

"Sabine."

"What?" she replied, blinking rapidly and sitting up straighter.

She refocused on Piper.

Piper stared at her and one side of her mouth came up high. "You weren't listening."

"What? Yes, I was," Sabine denied. "I was totally listening."

Sabine glanced around the lounge. Dave was gone.

How had she missed him leaving?

How long had she spaced?

Piper pressed her lips together, trying to hide her amusement and failing.

The door to the lounge opened and Shawn walked in.

"What's going on?" he asked, picking up on the energy in the room.

"Oh nothing. Just Sabine forgetting where she was in time and space."

"Reeaaally?" Shawn asked, drawing the word out. He parked an elbow on the back of Piper's chair and they both regarded her with twin expressions of teenage suspicion.

Sabine sighed. "I hope you're both in theater or drama class because you would be amazing at it."

"What happened?" Shawn asked, eyebrows bouncing.

"Oh, nothing much. Just a rock star winking at her."

"*Oooooh.*"

These two.

"Oh please. It would take more than that to throw me off."

"And yet." Piper grinned.

"This reminds me of the time I met Scotty Pippen."

Piper's eyes bugged out of her head and she leaned forward. "You met Scotty Pippen?"

No. She had not. In fact, it was one of two basketball players' names she knew. But that wasn't the point.

"Yes. And you know what he said?"

Piper shook her head.

"He said, get back to work."

Shawn chuckled and wandered away. Piper glared and rolled her eyes.

"Not funny."

Sabine smirked because she disagreed.

With Piper's attention back on her work, Sabine took the opportunity to glance over her shoulder.

But Dave was gone.

* * *

DAVE

He'd had too much espresso.

Caffeine didn't affect his mind the way it did others. If anything, it helped him think more clearly.

But it upset his stomach if he had too much.

Which he had.

It's why he'd jetted out of the lounge without saying goodbye to anyone.

And after what he'd done to the bathroom shortly after, he wasn't going to go back.

Besides, he had a meeting with Quinn Sullivan in…he glanced at his phone.

Shit.

He was supposed to be there right now.

He walked into the building and checked in with reception. The person there sent him up the elevator where he was greeted by someone else he knew he wouldn't remember.

He felt bad about that but it was true.

Names and faces didn't always store properly in his long-term memory.

The conference room they showed him to was empty.

Except for the espresso machine in the corner.

He stared at it wryly as his stomach gurgled a desperate warning.

Chicago was full of delightful temptations.

"Mr. Hansen."

He turned at the greeting and gripped the hand offered by the man with the snazzy suit and perfect teeth.

"Quinn Sullivan," the man introduced himself. He waved to a second individual with glasses and black hair who actually looked even less friendly than Quinn. "This is Alex Greene."

Right. Hannah had mentioned him.

Alex leaned across the table and shook his hand. "Nice to meet you. Big fan of how you told the system to piss off and decided to be successful anyway."

"Oh." Dave wasn't sure how to take that. Not a lot of people knew his history. The one that *wasn't* on the internet. But apparently Alex did.

All right.

"Sorry I'm late," Dave apologized.

Quinn's cool gaze narrowed slightly. "I understand that moving to a new location can have difficulties in the beginning."

Oh, that was nice of him, giving him an excuse. But that just made Dave feel worse.

"I'm just bad at time management," Dave confessed.

"Maybe that's something we can help with." Quinn did that casual cool thing that men who know how to be men do where he unbuttoned his suit jacket just as he sat down.

That was the number one reason Dave never wore suits. He had no idea how to do the button thing. He knew he'd overthink, make a mistake, and everyone would know what an idiot he was.

Which he was.

But he didn't need to help them out with it.

He tried not to feel underdressed in his hoodie and jeans as he sat down at the conference table.

"How have you found your accommodations so far?" Quinn asked, his blue eyes measuring and careful.

"Great." Dave shrugged. "Way nicer than I deserve."

Quinn slid a folder across the table toward Dave.

"This is the proposal I put together for your personal security. The two men I had with you over the weekend reported that you were polite and cooperative. For which I give my thanks. In there you will find a more detailed description of the services I am willing to provide. Personal security is not a part of my company anymore. Publicly. I do take on clients on a case-by-case basis with very specific expectations." He dipped his chin at the folder. "I suggest you read it thoroughly and have a lawyer look it over before signing it."

Quinn paused.

It was the kind of pause that was designed to get attention and add weight to his next words.

"You may want to pay special attention to the morality clause."

Dave swallowed.

"What's a morality clause?"

He was pretty sure he could guess just from the name, but he wouldn't be him if he didn't ask.

"It states that if you deliberately do anything to misrepresent my staff or company's ethos then our contract is terminated."

Alex snorted.

Quinn stiffened and he side-eyed the man next to him.

"You have something to offer?"

Alex lifted an eyebrow at Dave. "You won't need to worry about it. He's making it sound way worse than it is."

Quinn reared back in the most polite rearing back Dave had ever seen. "I disagree. I believe, based on Mr. Hansen's history and public persona, it is in a fact a *very* serious thing."

Shame rolled through Dave's entire body and he fought to sit still.

Alex rolled his eyes and snorted again. "So he's a had few romantic entanglements that ended in misdemeanors. I told you, I don't believe any of that was his fault. Not directly."

"Arson is a felony," Quinn replied tightly. "And three is a pattern, not a coincidence."

"Don't make *their* choices *his* choices. All of those women had a social history of instability and a criminal record. Long before they met Sunshine Capone." Alex turned his eyes to Dave. "Right?"

"Some people aren't equipped to deal with the life I have." Dave shrugged. "I understand your worry. I'm not planning on dating again for… ever?" He forced a humorless laugh. "I know that's not a practical long-term plan but it's what I have for right now."

After a beat of silence Quinn spoke again.

"Arson, Mr. Hansen. That's not just being unequipped."

"Are you asking me if I drove her to it?" Dave asked sadly.

"Did you?"

Dave ran a hand through his hair and let his hands drop into his lap, defeated. "She thought I had cheated on her. I didn't though. I would never do that. But she saw something online and believed the worst."

He'd hugged a friend. Someone he hadn't seen since high school. They'd run into each other outside of a restaurant in New York. She was an architect now. They had spoken for maybe three minutes as he waited for his car at valet. They hugged and parted ways. They didn't exchange numbers. They didn't promise to hang out.

Someone had taken a picture and posted it to Twitter, and by the end of the day, an entire scenario had been concocted that had never happened.

But Nora didn't believe him.

"You can't even tell me what you had for lunch. How am I supposed to believe anything you say?"

She'd taken one of his favorite basketball jerseys, lit it on fire, left it in the bathtub, and left the house.

She hadn't planned on burning down the house.

"Do you have a social media manager?" Quinn asked. "Because those are things that could be controlled."

"I'm not on the internet anymore," Dave said. "My lawyer hired someone to do all those things. And I'm really not dating anymore. I've taken a vow of celibacy," he tried to joke. It wasn't a joke, but they didn't know that.

They didn't laugh. Instead, they frowned in unison.

Dave shrugged. "I'll have my lawyer look at it. He loves paperwork."

Max did love paperwork. He lived for paperwork. If he could marry paperwork he would. And Dave was positive they would have a beautiful life together.

Meanwhile, paperwork made Dave break out into hives.

Figuratively speaking of course.

"May I ask, Mr. Hansen, why did you contact us?" Quinn asked. "There are numerous personal security firms throughout the nation that could provide you with similar protection."

"Hannah Lee James," Dave answered simply. "She told me that if I wanted something to be different, I was going to have to try something different. And then she gave me your card."

Quinn exchanged a look with Alex.

Dave couldn't read it, but they didn't tear up the contract, so he counted that as a small win.

Chapter Five
Use of Time

SABINE

"What are you going as for Halloween?"

Sabine looked up at Piper's question. "Nothing."

Piper screwed up her face in disgust. "Nothing?" she asked, like the word tasted bad.

Sabine shrugged. "I don't really like Halloween."

Piper reared back. "What?"

It didn't bother Sabine that Piper was confused. She'd been blowing people's minds with her disinterest in Halloween since the sixth grade.

"I'm going to require an explanation." Piper crossed her arms and leaned back in her chair. Clearly taking advantage of the interruption in her studies.

"An explanation for what?" Dave asked, entering the room. He tossed the basketball he was carrying to Piper who caught it with ease.

It had been three weeks since he'd first walked into the studio's lounge. Now, he was there almost every day that she was. She didn't know if he was there on the days she wasn't because she didn't ask. But she thought he probably was.

But he hadn't come back to Geekeasy since that first night. Though she'd signed up for extra VIP shifts just in case.

Not that she was trying to hang out with him. That wasn't it. She wasn't a friggin' groupie.

But after getting to know him a little she just wanted to make sure that he didn't get stuck with a server who might treat him…well, different than she would, she supposed.

Had she ever wanted to do that for any other VIPs?

Not that she could recall.

And that was why she didn't say anything to Kara about it. Because Kara would have (valid) questions that Sabine just didn't have answers for.

"For why she doesn't like Halloween."

"Wow. Didn't even know buses ran through here until you threw me under one, Piper."

Piper snorted.

Dave laughed outright.

"Why don't you like Halloween?" he asked, taking a seat on the sofa. Piper bounce passed the ball back to him.

"It's just an excuse for people to get drunk and be horrible." She scrunched up her nose. "I'll pass, thank you."

Piper fiddled with her pen as she thought. "I guess that can be true. But I really like the dressing up part."

"Yeah!" Dave jumped on that. "Costumes and candy for the win!"

Sabine smiled at their enthusiasm.

"Listen, I get it. I'm not saying other people can't enjoy themselves or that Halloween should be banned. I, personally, don't care for it."

Piper sputtered.

Dave narrowed his gaze and held the ball in his lap. "But Halloween is everywhere."

Sabine rolled her eyes. "Tell me about it."

"So what do you do instead? Lay on the floor with the lights off?" His eyes widened as a new thought occurred to him. "Do you at least hand out candy?"

You'd think she'd committed a crime against children with the way they were looking at her.

Her shoulders rose in defense. "I don't see the point. That's all."

"You withhold candy from children?" Piper blinked, more affronted than the time she found out that bananas were technically berries. That had been a wild afternoon.

"I'm not withholding candy," she defended. "They still get candy. Just not from me." She waved her hands in front of her, flustered. "Besides, the children of America have enough problems without me adding to their cavities."

Dave and Piper exchanged a look that Sabine had never seen before from either one of them.

"So that's it, huh?" she asked. "Halloween is the dealbreaker with you two? Now I'm what? Shunned?"

"Yes."

"No."

They answered at the same time. Piper being the yes.

"No," Dave reiterated, and he arched an eyebrow at Piper. He set the basketball aside and leaned forward, elbows to knees. "So, what do you do? On Halloween."

"Lock my doors and windows, and pray for dawn."

Dave stared at her. "It's not the Purge, babe."

Sabine covered her face with both hands. "Gah!" She dropped her hands. "This is why I don't tell people."

Dave's smile stretched across his face and she knew he wasn't making fun of her, not really. But fun was definitely being had at her expense. "I've never met someone who doesn't like Halloween."

Sabine pressed her lips together because she had already said too much. The only person who "got it" was Kara. And even that was more of a tolerance than a true understanding.

"I'm going to a party at Ana's," Piper decided to contribute.

Dave held Sabine's eyes for a moment, his mouth still doing that smile thing, and then he glanced at Piper. "Costume party?"

"Yes." Piper's face lit up. "I'm going as Maleficent."

Sabine's lips twitched. "You're going to rock that."

Piper smiled, pleased with the compliment.

"See? Costume parties are cool. I'd love to do that part. But you can't just do that. You have to suffer through the gross and drunk, and I'd just rather not." Sabine shuddered. "It's not like I haven't tried. I had a childhood. I did the things. I've just had too many bad experiences to make it worth it."

Dave's indigo eyes regarded her carefully. He sat back on the sofa and rubbed a hand along his jaw.

Shawn entered the lounge at that moment and Sabine breathed a sigh of relief. Usually, she didn't mind defending her dislike of Halloween. But for some reason, this time felt different.

Uncomfortable different.

Shawn created a small disruption by stealing the basketball and claiming he could dribble better than Piper. Who immediately got out of her chair and tried to steal it from him to prove him wrong.

Sabine spun Piper's laptop around so she could read through her essay.

It was good.

A lot better than she gave herself credit for.

But that was pretty common with the athletes she tutored. They had zero interest in academic work, saw it as a waste. Which was fine. It wasn't Sabine's job to convince them they were wrong. It was her job to get them to a place where their grades didn't interfere with their passions. And if they learned a little something at the same time then that was a beautiful bonus.

Shawn dropped into Piper's chair, breathing heavily.

"How's she doing, teach? Failing miserably? Ow!" Shawn held the side of his head where Piper had pulled his hair.

Sabine shook her head and clucked at him. "What have I told you about teasing her?"

Shawn stuck his tongue out but didn't reply.

"Did you tutor Shawn, too?" Dave asked.

"I helped him prep for the SATs."

"You took the SATs, Shawn?"

Shawn narrowed his eyes at Sabine, upset she'd told. "Yes."

"How'd you do?" Dave asked.

"I don't want to talk about it."

"He got a 1500," Piper informed the room.

"That sounds really high. Is that high?" Dave asked Sabine.

Sabine arched an eyebrow. She hadn't known Shawn's score before now. "It's high."

"Then what's the problem?" Dave asked, his attention back on Shawn.

"I said I don't want to talk about it." Shawn dove for the basketball and stole it. Piper chased him around the lounge.

Dave shot a curious look to Sabine who just shrugged. Shawn was very bright. But he was not happy about it.

"What if… and just hear me out before you shoot me down…" Dave leaned forward and braced his elbows on his knees. "What if you had one good experience?"

Sabine blinked, her mind scrambling to track down what Dave was talking about. This was not the first time he'd interrupted a thought with another thought and just expected her to be on the same page.

Sometimes she could follow the breadcrumbs back to where things had changed.

This was not one of those times.

She was going to have to ask.

"Can you please be more specific with your request?" she asked gently.

His eyebrows lifted like he just realized he'd given no context. "Oh, for sure. Sorry. I was still thinking about Halloween."

"Ohh." That tracked.

"I was thinking that if you had one good experience—"

She was already shaking her head.

"Just wait," he repeated. "What if we compromise?"

"We?" She arched an eyebrow.

"What if we dress up in fun costumes, hand out candy to kids, and still lock all the windows and pray for dawn."

She snorted a laugh because when he said it, it did sound ridiculous.

"I'm not having a party." Never again. She loved her loft. It was pretty and clean, and she wasn't going to invite a bunch of drunk assholes over to ruin her sanctuary.

"Of course, not a party." He shook his head like the idea was horrendous. "Just me, you, a bucket of candy, and the rosary."

"I'm not Catholic," she replied with a reluctant smile.

He shrugged one shoulder. "I haven't been Catholic in years so I'll just follow your lead then." He dug his phone out of his pocket and handed it to her. "Put in your information. I'll text you and talk you into it."

What was happening?

She took the phone and stared at him.

"You're serious?" she asked, not quite sure how far he'd take his ridiculous joke.

Because it had to be a joke.

Right?

"Yes. And you better have a good costume because I have a doozy. And I *will* make fun of you if yours sucks." He leaned forward and tapped on his phone screen. "Hurry up. I know you have to leave soon."

She shook her head once and darted a look to Piper and Shawn who were watching with fascination.

Sabine typed in her information in a dazed fog. This seemed like a bad idea.

So why was her stomach making little happy flips inside?

Dave took his phone back and stood. He held his hands up and Piper passed him the ball. He bounced it a few times on the wood floor. "I love the floors in this building."

"Johnny installed them himself," Piper provided.

Sabine's alarm on her watch went off and she gathered her things.

"Send me that essay—"

"I know, I know. You'll go over it tonight." Piper fluttered her eyelashes. "I'm not a total noob anymore."

Sabine rolled her eyes but smiled. She finished buttoning her coat and slung her bag over her shoulder.

She wanted to say something to Dave. But she was at a total loss and she had to go.

She didn't have time to lollygag like a moony teenager—which she was *not*.

"I'll see you," she said, giving a low wave.

"Tomorrow."

She glanced over her shoulder and he met her eyes.

"You'll see me tomorrow," he repeated, a soft smile on his lips.

She didn't know what to say so she didn't say anything. She just rolled her lips inward and nodded once.

And then she drove home with the dopiest grin on her face.

Oh, she needed a reality check.

Bad.

Superstars don't hang out with teachers.

Lost Track

She took a breath as she parked in her spot and caught a glimpse of herself in the rearview mirror.

Yeah, as fun an idea as it was, there was no way Sunshine Capone was going to spend the biggest party night of the year hanging out with her.

But if he did…

She had the perfect costume all ready to go.

Chapter Six
Something Just Like This

"Are you sure about this?" Kara hovered in the doorway dressed as a Thundercat.

Sabine straightened the shoulder pads under her cape and turned to look in the full-length mirror at her backside.

"Am I sure?" Sabine asked slowly. "No. But it's happening anyway."

"And you're sure it's not a date?" Kara asked for the one hundredth time.

Sabine huffed and went to her bed, picked up her phone, and handed it to Kara. "Read through those texts and you tell me."

Kara scrolled through the text conversation that Sabine had been having with Dave since last night. Kara chewed on her thumb nail, silent.

Sabine knew what she was reading because she'd been over it no less than five times herself. Which just made her feel like such an idiot.

The texts had been friendly, short, and innocent. He didn't flirt or ask for anything inappropriate. He hadn't even sent an emoji. Not one!

It was one of the most boring text conversations Sabine had ever had with a guy.

Which just made her like him so much more.

Wait. What?

No, she didn't.

Not like *that*.

Sure, she liked him as a human and as an artist. But she didn't *like* him like him.

"It doesn't seem like a date." Kara sighed and tossed the phone back on the bed. She crossed her cheetah print covered arms and tilted her head. "I can stay, you know."

Sabine rolled her eyes. "Don't be ridiculous. You love working on Halloween." Kara always dressed up cool and made mad tips. She didn't mind the drunks and the gore that came with the holiday. She also never tried to convince Sabine to join and Sabine never tried to convince Kara to skip it.

Sabine stuck another bobby pin in her braid to keep it pinned back.

Kara's phone pinged. "That's my ride." She moved to the front door and Sabine followed, her long black cape billowing out behind her.

"It's cool though, right?" Sabine asked, doing a twirl in her costume.

Kara's lips twitched and her eyes shone with that sweet adoration that can only come from a friend who loves you despite the choices you make.

"It's very cool."

"Yeah, it is," Sabine agreed quietly.

If nothing else, it had been fun to dress up. Even if Dave didn't show, Sabine was going to watch Star Wars and eat the candy by herself.

Kara put on her coat and hugged Sabine. "I'll be home by three."

"I will be waiting for you."

Just because Sabine understood that Kara liked Halloween didn't mean that she would relax until her friend was home safe and sound.

Kara left and Sabine went back to her room to put on the finishing touches. She was going to wait to put the helmet on until Dave texted that he was on his way up.

She put the gloves on, slid the lightsaber into the belt, and stared at herself in the mirror.

"I look so fucking cool," she whispered.

Her phone pinged and she caught her grin in the mirror before reaching for her phone.

So she was excited. So what?

.   .   .

DAVE: I'm in the elevator

Sabine slid the helmet on and rushed to the door.

She listened to the elevator arrive followed by footsteps down the hall.

He knocked and she opened the door.

She wasn't sure what she was expecting; both of them had kept their costumes a secret.

But his was not as elaborate as hers. If it could even be considered a costume. He looked like he was in his pajamas.

"What the hell?" she blurted, disappointment and embarrassment rushing through her.

Except she'd switched on the voice filter, so it came out sounding like James Earl Jones.

Dave's chuckle started small and grew larger. Until he was belly laughing in her hallway.

She took the helmet off and glared at him.

"Where's your costume?" she demanded.

"I'm wearing it!" He stood back and did a little twirl.

He was wearing pajama pants, a t-shirt, house slippers, and a long burgundy bathrobe.

She screwed up her face, unimpressed. "Are you supposed to be Hugh Hefner?"

He scoffed, offended. "No. I'm retired Obi-Wan Kenobi." He opened his robe to reveal the lightsaber on his hip.

Oh.

He fished a hand into the pocket of his robe and held out a wrapped candy.

"Butterscotch?"

Okay, that was kind of clever.

"Why did you laugh at me?" she asked, eyeing him critically.

His smile was immediate. "Because you're not tall enough to be Darth Vader." He pressed his lips together. "You look like Dark Helmet."

She pursed her lips, seeing the humor but not ready to admit it. "I find your lack of faith disturbing."

His reaction was to throw his head back, laughter bursting from him in deep, hearty waves, the hand with the butterscotch gripping his chest.

Unable to help it, unwilling to try, she watched.

The joy sprang out of him so unencumbered that she felt it ripple through her on its way into the universe.

Guys didn't find her funny.

Not really.

Her jokes and pop culture references were usually met with muted smiles and exasperated blinks.

Okay, girl, hold on tight. He is not for you.

She took a step back and he entered the loft.

"I looked up the trick-or-treat times online and there doesn't seem to be a set time." She closed the door and followed him into the kitchen dining area.

He gazed up at the high ceilings and around the open floor plan.

"It's usually sundown, isn't it?" he asked, running his fingers over the back of the dark purple velvet couch.

It probably wasn't as posh as the places he'd lived but she was still filled with pride. It was her living space. Hers.

And Kara's obviously.

But she had worked and paid for the nice things she had. No one could take that from her.

That might not mean anything to someone else, but it meant a lot to her.

Pushing aside thoughts of her childhood in general and her mom in particular, she stepped into the kitchen.

"Do you want something to drink? I don't have any espresso, but I do have Dr. Pepper."

She glanced over her shoulder and he was sliding onto the stool at the butcher block island.

"Dr. Pepper please."

"I don't even know if we'll get any trick-or-treaters," she said, setting the pop can on the countertop.

On cue, the doorbell rang.

Dave tilted his head and waggled his eyebrows. Her mouth dropped open and excitement tingled in her fingers.

Oh, this was happening.

They went to the door together.

"Wait. My mask." Sabine grabbed the helmet and slid it back on her head. Dave waited, one hand on the knob. She nodded. "Okay."

He grinned and opened the door.

"Trick or treat!" Two of the tiniest Avengers she'd ever seen held out cloth bags.

"You guys are so *cute,*" Sabine said, crouching down to be at eye level. But again, her voice changer was on, so it sounded like a grown man.

The children giggled.

Dave chuckled and tossed candy into their bags.

He closed the door and Sabine stood up, taking off her helmet.

"See? That wasn't so bad."

"I know what Halloween is, dummy." She rolled her eyes. "But you have to admit that unless you're home, handing out candy, Halloween after a certain age is way less fun."

He narrowed his eyes. "What age did it stop being fun?"

"Maybe that was just me then." She gave up. "Apparently I'm the only one in the whole world who dislikes this universally adored holiday. I'm the Halloween grinch. Blah."

His lips twitched like he found her amusing. "I didn't say that."

The doorbell rang again, and she sucked in an excited breath.

"Put your helmet on," he prodded, reaching for the doorknob.

* * *

The next ninety minutes were filled with so much fast-paced fun she was surprised when it was over.

The children who lived in her building were sweet and adorable, and she wanted to give them all the candy in the whole world. At one point a young Darth Maul asked to duel Dave and they had a lightsaber battle in the hallway where Dave died dramatically.

When the candy had been depleted and the trick-or-treaters had stopped arriving, Dave locked the door and turned off the entry lights.

"Now we can commence the praying for dawn."

"Ha ha," she mumbled, taking off her cape. She rolled her shoulders and stretched her arms over her head. "Capes are heavy."

He pretended to turn up the collar of his robe. "This is why bathrobes are best."

She snickered and pulled an arm across her chest, stretching her shoulders. With the cape and helmet off, it was less of a costume. Just black leggings and a black tank top, and black boots—which she removed next.

"I noticed you didn't bring your bodyguards with you tonight." She sat on a stool by the island and pulled one foot into her lap, rubbing the sole.

He flashed his lightsaber on his hip. "I brought protection." He watched her hands silently and then asked, "Your feet okay?"

She grimaced as she hit a tender spot. "Yeah. They will be. Those boots are a little small and my feet are all cramped up." She switched to the other foot.

"Hm." He turned his attention to the kitchen and started opening cupboards like he owned the place.

"Do you have popcorn?" he asked.

"I do."

When she didn't offer any more information, he gave her a look.

She wasn't sure she'd be able to describe it except it was flirty and exasperated all at once.

And she liked it way too much.

"And *where* is your popcorn, smart ass?"

She pointed at the one cupboard he hadn't gotten to yet next to the oven.

"Why are you making popcorn?" she asked, bracing her elbows on the butcher block.

"Because you have to have popcorn when you're watching a movie." He found the popcorn bowl and brought it over to her. "Two bags or one?" he asked, holding up the microwave popcorn box.

"Two."

He flashed her a smile that had her wishing she'd spent some time desensitizing herself to his face. Maybe she could have printed out photos from online and used them like flashcards.

Sure, at first glance he wasn't what someone might consider "attractive." But looks were such a small part of someone that she barely noticed those things.

He was enormously attractive in all the ways that counted.

His smile, his laugh, his sense of humor, his energy, how he treated children...

Oof.

Her heart was already way too fond of him.

He had not said or done anything to suggest he was interested in her *that way*. And neither had she, she was pretty sure.

But she'd always been very good at longing in secret.

"What movie are we watching?" she asked, knowing all of this was probably a bad idea and not caring enough to put a stop to it.

He flicked his eyes between her and the television in their living room. "Whichever Star Wars is your favorite."

"If you're running for office, you have my vote, sir." She slid off the stool, washed her hands at the sink, and then hobbled her sore feet over to the sectional. She sank into the soft, velvety cushions and picked up the remote control.

While the loft filled with the scent of fresh popped corn, she cued up *Empire Strikes Back* and hit play.

Dave joined her and placed the huge bowl of popcorn on the seat between them. They both put their feet up on the square ottoman in front of them.

The opening story scroll finished and the camera focused on the big Star Destroyer as it jettisoned probe droids out into space.

"Did you check the windows and make sure they were locked?" Dave asked quietly.

"Shut up," she muttered.

He craned his neck, looking around at the loft. "Can we lower these lights?" He focused on her. "Would you mind?"

She shrugged and shook her head. "I don't mind."

He got up and started messing with the lights. First the kitchen, then the dining area, then the living room. He flicked the lights in the hallway on and off several times. It took him at least five minutes of fiddling before he came back to the couch.

She had to admit, he'd found the perfect balance of light to see the movie better.

"Sorry."

She glanced over at him and frowned.

"About the lights," he explained. He grabbed a handful of popcorn. "They distract me."

"You don't have to apologize." She thought for a second about whether she should share what she was thinking. "I wish I was confident enough to ask for things that would make my life easier." She shrugged. "But I tend to just tolerate whatever is happening so I don't make anyone uncomfortable."

He squinted at the screen but she knew he wasn't really looking at it.

"I guess," he started. Stopped. Crossed one leg over the other. She noticed he had taken off his shoes. Something about that detail filled her with happiness. He felt comfortable enough to relax.

"I guess I'm so used to people being uncomfortable around me all the time anyway that I figure it's not going to make anything worse."

She had not expected him to say that.

She wanted to defend herself, but she took a breath first. He hadn't accused her of anything.

"Why do you think people are uncomfortable around you?"

He turned his head in her direction and rolled his eyes. "C'mon, you've met me, right?"

Her heart squeezed. She'd dealt with several students with a similar outlook and things started to click in her mind.

"Because you see the world differently than others?" she guessed.

He took in a deep breath and she watched his chest rise and then slowly release. His eyes trained on the screen.

"That's a really nice way of saying it," he muttered.

Oh.

She'd accidentally stumbled upon something sensitive.

She dug into the popcorn and held a handful close to her chest while she ate one piece at a time with her free hand. "For what it's worth, you've never made me uncomfortable."

He turned to look at her but she kept her eyes on the movie.

She tried to remain undisturbed but his words made her insides chaotic with frustration. Too many times she'd tutored kids who were neurodivergent and the hardest part about teaching them was getting them to realize there was nothing *wrong* with them.

Yes, they were different. But they weren't fucking broken.

She took a deep breath, trying to quiet her urge to get up and rant about the system and society and people being d-bags.

Here was this amazing, talented, *gifted* artist and somewhere along the way someone had made him feel *less than*. To the point that he pretty much assumed everyone saw him that way.

It was fucked up.

Her heart hurt.

And it was also angry.

But it wasn't her place to fix this. Not for him. He wasn't her student or her boyfriend. He wasn't *hers* at all.

Which…

She held her breath and swallowed hard. Just the idea of him being hers made her face get hot.

Oh no.

Dave's phone rang and she jumped.

He pulled it out of his robe pocket and held the screen for her to see.

It was his friend Max facetiming him.

"Should I pause it?" she asked, already reaching for the remote.

"Yeah." He swiped to answer. "Hey."

"Where are you and who are you with?" Max asked and it made Sabine smile. She hadn't seen him since the night they'd met and she'd saved him from choking on a chicken wing.

"I am with Sabine and we are watching Star Wars." He turned the phone so Max could see her.

"Hello, gorgeous," Max said brusquely. "You look amazing as usual. Have you two been out tonight at all?"

The tense tone of Max's question put Sabine on alert.

Dave sat up and leaned forward. "No. I came over about five-ish and we haven't gone anywhere."

"Good." Max sounded relieved. "Just do me a favor and keep doing that."

Dave chuckled and chewed on the side of his thumb. "You wanna tell me what's going on?"

"Not really. As long as you're in a safe place and you're not, I don't know, at a hockey game or anything."

Hockey game?

Sabine and Dave frowned at each other in unison.

"I'll be in town tomorrow and I'll explain more then," Max said. "Hope to see you again too, Sabine."

And then he hung up.

Sabine waited for an explanation but Dave just put his phone down on the ottoman and relaxed back onto the sofa.

"Is that a normal conversation with Max?" she asked.

He shrugged. "For the most part."

"You're not curious what's happening that he's adamant you not be a part of?"

Dave sent her a lopsided smile. "I'm always curious. It's my nature. But there are a few things I try not to stress out about. I let Max do that."

She nodded and pressed play again.

After a minute she tugged out her own phone. "I'm too curious to not at least do a search."

He put the popcorn bowl on the ottoman by his phone and leaned an elbow onto the cushion to be closer to her. She obliged by leaning his direction and holding her phone so he could see.

She began typing in Dave but he stopped her.

"Sunshine," he said. "No one really calls me by my actual name."

She glanced at him and corrected her search: Sunshine Capone + hockey

A video popped up immediately from CelebX. The headline said: Sunshine Capone causes chaos at hockey game.

"Should I click on it?" she asked, suddenly unsure.

"Hell yeah," he said. "Let's see what I did now."

She snorted and hit the link.

The video was taken on someone's cell phone and it wasn't very clear. But it looked like Sunshine — or someone that looked like Sunshine — was making out with a girl in the stands. A guy came up and grabbed the alleged Sunshine by the collar and punched him. Alleged Sunshine then shoved the guy and took off. A brawl broke out in the stands.

"Officials are still trying to piece together what happened at United Center," Sabine read out loud. "It appears that Sunshine Capone made a pass at an unknown woman. The woman's partner took offense and stepped in. Capone escalated the situation and then fled the scene. This story is still updating."

She dropped her phone with disgust.

"Seriously?" she asked. "Escalated the situation? The other guy threw the first punch! If anything, it was self-defense."

Dave took the phone from her and set it aside and looked her in the eye. "That wasn't me. I was here with you tonight."

"Right." She jerked her chin back. "I know that. I mean, obviously that wasn't you. But if it had been, they wrote the piece in such a way that you were the one responsible for all of it."

He lifted his eyebrows slightly and gave a sad smile. "Yeah."

So much made sense in that moment.

"This happens a lot, doesn't it?" she asked.

"It is the main reason I don't go on the internet anymore."

"At all?" she asked, surprised. Everyone was on the internet in one way or another. "But you have social media accounts," she said before she realized that she was admitting to looking him up…and maybe following him in a few places.

He shrugged. "Someone else runs those. A firm that Max found for me."

Her heart softened hearing that. "Max watches your back, huh?"

"He and Leslie have been with me since middle school. I had a few other friends for a while but…" He chewed on the side of his thumb again. "Success can change things. It doesn't always. But if someone has a problem with you, money makes it obvious."

His eyes grazed over her face and she realized they were still leaning towards each other.

"It's a rare person who doesn't look at me like a scandal, or a payday."

Oh.

"How do I look at you?" she asked, her voice just above a whisper.

"Like you see me," he replied. His gaze dropped to her mouth and then bounced back up to her eyes and he smiled. "Do you mind if I grab another Dr. Pepper?"

"Go for it," she replied, sitting back up and trying to compose herself.

The fuck had just happened?

He got up and bounded to the kitchen. "Do you want anything?" he called.

"A bucket of ice?" she mumbled to herself and then groaned. "Water, please," she called instead.

Here he was, making a friend, trusting her to not be like every other asshole trying to take advantage of him, and she was thinking he was going to kiss her.

Thank God he hadn't.

How awkward would that have been?

Her mind fled through a variety of possible scenarios, and they all ended in bad, bad uncomfortable outcomes.

But a friendship? That she could do.

She could rock the fuck out of being someone he could trust.

Chapter Seven
...Ready For It?

DAVE

He was going to have to buy her more Dr. Pepper, he realized as he took the second to the last can.

But he did that. Consumed sugar and caffeine until he'd depleted the entire supply. She would probably never invite him back.

He returned to the sofa, handing her the bottle of water he'd grabbed.

"Remind me to get you more pop," he said, settling back into his corner of the sectional.

She snorted. "Don't worry about it."

"Fine. Then I'll just remind myself." He picked up his phone and spoke into it. "Remind me to buy Dr. Pepper for Dark Helmet."

He glanced her direction and caught the eye roll.

After a beat he heard her mutter, "I'm not that short."

"You're shorter."

"What?" She sounded truly offended. "I am not."

"How tall are you?" he asked. "Because Rick Moranis is five foot six."

Silence followed and he turned to face her stunned expression.

She narrowed her eyes. "I call bullshit. How would you even know that?"

He shrugged one shoulder. "I know things."

The truth was, he knew it because he and Leslie had just had a debate the other night about how the best actors were tall. Dave was on the side that height didn't matter to greatness and Rick Moranis was his featured argument. He'd had to look it up and weirdly, the information stuck.

Sabine lunged for her phone that was still on the ottoman and began typing.

Dave noticed the popcorn and pulled it into his lap.

"You're right. He's five six."

"And how tall was Darth Vader?" he asked, watching the movie.

"Shut up." She reached over and stole a handful of popcorn.

"And how tall are you?" He smiled and she tossed a piece of popcorn at his face.

"Five three."

"Hm." Dave nodded, happy to be right. "How about that?"

Another piece of popcorn hit his face and he chuckled.

"It was still a cool costume," she muttered glumly.

Now he felt bad for giving her a hard time. He gave her a repentant look. "I'm teasing you. It was a very cool costume. You had me beat by a million."

She half-smiled but didn't respond.

They watched the movie, laughing together at their favorite moments and discussing weird bits of trivia they had both acquired over the years. When it was over, he asked her to start the next one.

"We can't just leave Han Solo with the bad guys," he said.

She narrowed her eyes at him. "Are you sure you don't just want to see Princess Leia in the gold bikini? You can tell me if that's the case."

Dave's stomach soured a bit.

He'd forgotten about the gold bikini scene.

He rolled his lips inward and debated whether he could tell her the truth. He'd tried to explain it to people before, and no one ever believed him.

But Sabine *listened* to people.

"I'm actually in the minority on the gold bikini," he started.

She tilted her head and waited.

See?

Listening.
Not scoffing. Not mocking.
Just waiting for more information.
He liked that a lot. So much.
In fact, it was probably her most attractive quality.
Outside of the obvious of course.
"Don't get me wrong, the gold bikini is hot. But she was a slave. She wasn't wearing it by choice, and that is waaay less hot. It kind of makes the entire thing gross, if I'm being honest."
Sabine's dark eyebrows dipped. "Are you serious?"
Maybe she didn't get it either.
"I can't separate the details. They all hit me at the same time. Gold bikini, disgusting bad guy, chained up against her will. The negatives outweigh the hotness, and it just makes me kind of queasy."
She stared at him. Probably trying to figure out if he was being honest or not.
And that was the thing, he *was* being honest. But it was too difficult a thing to prove. She would either believe him or not and there wasn't a damn thing he could do about it.
"Freedom is sexy," he decided to add when she hadn't responded.
Her smile seemed a little surprised and unsure.
"You really are one of a kind, aren't you?" she asked.
He swallowed, waiting for her to make fun of him or call him a liar.
But she just hit play and settled back into the couch.
The story scroll started, and she snickered to herself. "Freedom is sexy."
He allowed some of the tension to ease out of him.
Maybe she thought he was a weirdo. Maybe not.
She hadn't asked him to leave. In fact, when he suggested the next movie she readily agreed.
A knock at the door had both of them looking at each other with wide eyes.
"When is your roommate coming home?" he asked.
"Not until three." Her voice was just above a whisper and the color had drained from her face.
"Wait. Are you scared?" he asked, caught between being amused and indulging her fear and joining her there.

"Shh!" She waved at him to be quiet. She turned the movie's volume down.

Out in the hall were voices. Deep male ones.

Someone tried to open the door.

Okay, now that was just rude.

Dave didn't like fear as a general rule. If something frightened him, he tended to go towards it.

He was almost to the door when he heard Sabine sputter behind him.

"What are you doing?" She was backwards on the sofa, her fingers digging into the cushions.

"I'm going to see who it is," he explained.

"What if they're murderers?" she whispered frantically.

Dave shrugged. They probably weren't murderers. They were being very loud. They sounded like drunk idiots who got off on the wrong floor. But she looked too worried for him to point that out.

"Do you have a weapon?" he asked.

She hurtled over the back of the sofa and fell to the floor. She jumped right up and darted to the freestanding locker next to the coat rack.

He had wondered what that was for.

She pulled out a cricket bat and handed it to him.

"Ookay," he said, hefting the flat wooden piece of sports equipment. Of all the things he thought she'd have on hand, a cricket bat was not it. But he'd have to ask her about it later.

He moved to the door and felt something at his back. He stopped and slowly looked over his shoulder. Sabine was right behind him and she had hold of the belt of his bathrobe. Her hazel eyes darted up to him and she gestured for him to keep going.

Good grief she was adorable.

He bit back his smile and headed for the door.

He paused before opening it, looking through the peephole.

"Who is it?" she whispered at his back.

"It looks like a bunch of serial killers."

She sucked in a startled breath as he unlocked the door and opened it.

So she could see it was indeed, a bunch of serial killers. Five of them.

Dave braced his hand across the door jam, blocking entry to the loft.

"Freddy, Jason, Hannibal… is that Stuntman Mike I see back there?

Michael." He nodded at the very drunk men. "I believe you have the wrong apartment, sirs."

Sabine poked her head out from under his arm.

"It's not 3B?" Michael asked, taking off his mask and squinting at the numbers above Sabine's doorbell.

"Nope. You're at 4D," Dave explained slowly, pointing at the number. "You need to go one floor down and across the hall."

Freddie pushed forward and got very close to the number. He studied it for several seconds before shrugging and waving at the guys to follow him.

The serial killers scratched their heads and their junk, and got back into the elevator.

Dave waited until they were gone before turning to Sabine.

"I saved you," he said, amused at her theatrics.

She pressed her lips together and went back into the loft. He followed, locking the door again.

In the kitchen, she retrieved a bottle of water from the refrigerator and put it on the counter.

"You must think I'm ridiculous."

He held up his thumb and forefinger pinched close. "Just a little."

She sighed, her eyes drifted over his shoulder to the movie still playing, then back to him. "You don't have to stay. You can go if you want."

That is not what he wanted. Nor what he expected her to say.

"What about praying for dawn?"

She smirked. "C'mon. You don't want to be here babysitting me on the biggest party night of the year."

He frowned. "Yes, I do. This is exactly where I want to be."

She rolled her eyes.

"You must be confused," he went on seriously. "Let me remind you of what's happening here. We have Star Wars playing nonstop on a truly gigantic television screen." He swept an arm out to indicate the movie. "Drinks, snacks, lightsaber duels, moments of panic, followed by moments of absurd bravery. Why *do* you have a cricket bat, by the way? And did you bruise your entire body when you came over the back of the sofa?"

Her cheeks bloomed a wonderful hot pink but she was smiling again.

He really liked it when she smiled. The dimple showed up and did that static electricity thing to his sternum.

"But you're like —" she waved a hand indicating what he assumed was his whole being. "—a really cool, chill person. And I am…" She made a face that could only be described as intense self-reproach.

"Whoa, whoa, whoa, hold your horses. Who told you I was the cool one?" He held a hand to his chest. "Or that I was chill? What gave you that impression?"

She licked her lips and opened her mouth to reply but he wasn't going to let her argue her way out of this. One thing he absolutely hated was when someone amazing didn't realize that about themselves.

"I have had the best time with you tonight. You have made me laugh so hard. And not once have you made me feel like I wasn't welcome to be myself." He shrugged and tried not to let his emotions show too strong like they sometimes did. "I wouldn't want to be anywhere else."

She ducked her chin and lifted her eyes. "Even though I'm one door knock away from overreacting."

"You remember Max, yeah?"

She nodded.

"He's ten times more intense than you. He invented overreacting. And he's also one of the best people I've ever known."

She took a deep breath and let it out, signaling that she was letting it go.

"Okay, but the cricket bat," he said again, lifting it up and placing it on the island.

"It was my brother's. He played for a club in England when he lived there."

"You lived in England?"

"No." She shook her head. "My mom and dad split when we were little and my dad took André, that's my brother, with him to England. I stayed here with mom." Her expression grew cloudy and then she shook it off.

He had so many questions though.

"But he lives here now, and I stole his bat from him because I thought it was cool." She picked it up and took it back to the locker, tucking it inside.

"Do you have any siblings?" she asked.

"Nope. Never had the privilege. Just me and mom."

She tilted her head which he was figuring out was her way of letting him know he could share if he wanted but she wasn't going to push.

It was such a gentle way of communicating that it filled his chest with tender feelings. No wonder she was a teacher. She had a heart for it.

They made their way back to the couch but instead of facing the film, they faced each other.

"You were going to tell me about why you're a tutor and not a teacher. Remember that?"

She smiled. "Oh yes. Well." She tipped her head back and thought. "My mom is a con woman. That's the short version. The details are way more sordid and even I don't know them all. But essentially, she was an investor stealing money from clients and the SEC was closing in, so she stole my identity and tried to flee the country. They caught her."

Dave's mouth hung open.

Sabine nodded. "They did a documentary on Netflix about it."

"And so you can't be a teacher?" he asked, trying to process.

"Schools have limited background checks. Basically, if something gets flagged it's easier for them to just reject the application rather than paying for a deeper search. Celebrities and more affluent families pay for a more thorough background check. Which means they can see I'm in the clear and it's my mom who's the criminal."

"Where's your mom now?"

"Federal prison."

"Shit, Sabine, I'm sorry."

She shrugged. "Thanks but it's okay. It's *mostly* okay," she amended. "Sometimes I still get angry when I think about it, but she's paying what she owes and getting what she deserves."

Sabine looked around the loft.

"And I owe her nothing."

"What about your dad? Did he know?"

"Nah. When André told him what happened he came over and helped me get my name cleared and then he was gone again."

Dave knew a little about absent fathers.

"You and your brother are close?"

Her smile was soft. "Yeah. As much as we could be with an ocean between us. But he moved to Chicago a few years ago and we see each other as often as we can. He's a professor of archeology."

She brought her knees up and hugged them to her chest.

Great.

She was a teacher and her brother was a teacher. It became more and more obvious that she was way too smart for a guy like him.

Maybe that should have been a turn-off, but he was never one for being predictable. Instead, he found himself battling his intense attraction.

Funny, smart, kind, beautiful.

Never had he been so aware of a woman's *presence*. She filled the room, the entire loft.

Is this what celibacy did? Heightened his other senses?

Because it was intense.

He liked it.

"What about you?" She asked. "Tell me one of your scandals."

"Ah, I have so many, you see." He waggled his eyebrows.

"Did your last girlfriend really burn down your house?" she asked.

"She really did," Dave confirmed. "But that wasn't her fault."

Sabine stared at him. "How?"

"Some people have a hard time with what my life entails."

Sabine narrowed her eyes suspiciously.

"Nora…" He stopped and thought how best to tell the story. He didn't like how Nora kept getting blamed like she was crazy. She wasn't crazy. She made a terrible decision and now she was paying for it.

He sighed. "What you need to know about Nora is that we met at a party. I was already very drunk, so was she." Heat spread up his neck because this was not going to make him look good. But for whatever reason, he trusted Sabine to not hate him for it. "She was super hot and I wanted to kiss her. So I did. We were both very intense and it all moved very fast. She lives her life on social media. It's literally her job. So when she saw pictures of me hugging someone in New York, she assumed the worst. It didn't help that it was the first time I'd taken a trip without her. She saw the photos and called me." He grimaced. "I didn't handle the call well. I got very defensive and definitely said some things I shouldn't have. She hung up on me. And it made me mad, so I didn't call her back." He licked his lips. "I probably should have called her back."

"Did you cheat on her?" Sabine asked softly.

"No." Dave worried his bottom lip. "But truth is boring. It doesn't sell. And some people can't distinguish between something that is sensational-ized and reality. It wasn't her fault. She got caught up in an industry she couldn't begin to handle. Those photos were everywhere. Everyone was saying that I was cheating. Everyone."

"Are you seriously blaming yourself for a woman burning your house down?" she asked, incredulous.

"I like to give people the benefit of the doubt. Nora was a sweetheart. She didn't ask to have her heart dragged through the court of public opinion. If it had been true—which it wasn't—she'd have every right to burn my shit to the ground."

Sabine listened, inhaled slowly, and folded her hands on top of her knees.

"As noble as it is of you to defend her, she made her own choices too."

His lips twitched. "Now you sound like Leslie."

She arched a single eyebrow.

"Hey, not to change the subject but I have a question." He took a breath. He hadn't realized he was going to do this until the moment was upon him.

Oh shit. His hands were shaking.

"Have you ever tutored an adult?"

Her eyes softened and he *knew* she had figured it out.

"I have." She waited for him to get his shit together to actually ask.

He licked his lips and straightened his shoulders. "I never graduated high school."

Fuck.

There it was.

That huge shameful secret he never told anyone.

"You know what? I'm feeling hungry." He got up and circled around the sofa, heading back to the kitchen. "I think I saw some tater tots in your freezer. Can we make those?"

He turned to see her twisted over the back of the sofa to watch him. Her face a mixture of perplexed and patient.

"Dave, what were you—" She stopped when she caught the pleading look on his face. "Yeah. Let's make tots."

He thought he was ready to talk about that. But nope.

Maybe he'd be brave next time.

Instead of bringing up his education, she joined him in the kitchen where they made tater tots and he told her about how Max ate tots exclusively for an entire year on a dare.

They laughed, they ate, they watched more Star Wars.

Her roommate came home and she threw dollar bills at them as Dave and Sabine danced for tips.

It was one of the better nights he'd had in a long time. Free to be himself. Free to laugh and play and exist without the microscope of his own industry on him.

And when the sun came up and Kara had gone to bed, Dave and Sabine were still awake.

"We made it," he said, pointing at the sun coming up through the windows. "It's dawn."

She smiled and pulled a fluffy blanket closer to her face. "I survived one more Halloween and the legend grows."

He snickered and crawled across the couch to join her. She lifted the blanket and he squeezed in between her and the back of the sofa. He rested his head in the crook of her neck, his arm around her middle, and she covered them both.

"Do you want me to leave?" he asked, knowing he was too close, knowing that leaving would be smart. But she was warm, and he was tired and happy. He didn't want to let go of everything he felt in that moment.

"Shh. We sleep now."

She exhaled slowly and he could tell she was already out.

Moments later he joined her.

Best. Halloween. Ever.

Chapter Eight
I'm Gonna Be

DAVE

He wasn't sure how long he slept but he woke up to the sound of crunching.

Slowly he became aware that someone was watching him.

He peeled one eye open to see Kara standing at the back of the sofa holding a bowl of cereal, staring at him.

She spooned another bite into her mouth and chewed, not taking her eyes off him.

He squeezed his eyes shut and then rubbed them with a hand. When he opened them again, she was still there. He sat up and looked around the bright loft.

Sabine was nowhere to be seen.

"Kara? Right?" he asked the tall blonde.

She narrowed her eyes at him and then pointed her spoon.

"Last night was fun, huh?" she asked.

"Yeah," he agreed. "It was awesome."

"You sleep okay?" she asked into her bowl.

"Oh yeah." Warmth spread through his chest at the memory of Sabine's soft body under his. He'd slept like a damn baby.

He couldn't remember the last time he'd slept that well.

Like he didn't have a care in the world.

She nodded and her bright smile evaporated into a threatening scowl. "I don't know what your plan here is, but Sabine is the greatest human on earth. If you hurt her, I'll haunt your dreams. You'll never know peace again."

She scooped another spoonful into her mouth and smiled again but with dead eyes.

A chill raced down his spine.

"Hey, you're awake!" Sabine came out of the bathroom. She glanced between Kara and Dave. "What's going on?"

Kara shrugged and turned away from Dave, going back to the dining room.

Dave got to his feet. "What time is it?" he asked, picking up his phone. "Oh, it's late. I should go."

He actually had no idea what time it was. Yes, he'd looked at his phone, but all he saw were several missed texts from Max and he panicked.

"Do you want food before you go?" Sabine asked, her hazel eyes bright.

Her braid had come mostly undone. Soft strands framed her face, her clothes were rumpled, and her face was fresh and rested.

Wow.

Just.

Wow.

"I think I'll just use your bathroom and then take off, if that's okay." He made his way around the sofa and went down the short hall.

He did his business and washed his hands. As he was drying his hands on the pink towel, he noticed the butterfly wallpaper.

Huh.

He'd been in the bathroom a few times the night before but he hadn't been paying attention.

One wall was covered in butterfly wallpaper. The towels were matching light pink. The bathmat was butterfly shaped.

Next thing he knew he was pulling aside the pink and yellow shower curtain and smelling Sabine's shampoo.

Yep, that was it. That was the scent that had tangled into his dreams all night.

Sonofabitch, she smelled good.

Like flowers and sunshine.

She smelled like a damn meadow and he really, really liked it.

"What the hell are you doing?" he asked, putting the bottle back. He missed the shelf and it dropped into the bottom of the tub.

"Shit."

He picked it up, tried to put it back, dropped it again.

"Why am I so bad at snooping?" he hissed. He reached for the bottle again and then decided to just leave it there.

When he left the bathroom, Sabine and Kara immediately stopped talking.

Cool.

They were probably discussing what a weirdo he was and why he was loudly rummaging through their bath essentials.

"Well." He clenched his hands into fists, relaxed them, and then shoved his hands into the robe pockets. "I better get going. I had a lot of fun."

He ducked his chin and went to the door.

Sabine hurried to meet him there.

"Thanks for hanging out," she said, almost shy about it. "And for saving me from the serial killers."

"Anytime," he replied tightly. He couldn't meet her eyes.

They were too pretty and too honest, and he knew he'd say something stupid. He needed to just get the fuck out of there.

"Okay, well…I'll see you?"

He didn't respond. He just pressed his lips together and dipped his head. And then he left.

It wasn't until he got to his car that he took a full breath.

Why was he acting like such a dipshit?

Everything had been so easy last night. What the hell had happened to him that morning to make him rethink every decision he had ever made?

He should apologize for being weird.

He pulled out his phone to text her and the string of texts from Max distracted him. There was also a missed call from his publicist and one from his manager.

It was going to be a workday apparently.

He started the Range Rover and set his phone in the hands-free cradle on the dash.

He'd start with Curtis, his manager, and work his way through the list.

* * *

Dave's stomach growled for the fourth time in as many minutes and he finally took his headphones off.

"What are you making and when will it be done?" he asked, approaching his kitchen.

Yes, it was his kitchen but he only ever used the microwave and the refrigerator.

Max wiped his hands on a nearby towel and sent him an exasperated look. "You've never been very patient. Gourmet takes time."

Dave snuck around Max and got a cider out of the fridge. He peeked over Max's shoulder into the pan on the stove. "That looks good."

"Obviously," Max replied. "Go sit down."

Dave slid onto a stool at the breakfast bar where Max had set placemats and silverware.

A moment later, Max set a plate filled with chicken, mushrooms, and cheese in front of him.

"Mushroom Asiago Chicken," Max declared triumphantly. "Gluten free, obvi."

Dave smirked. "Obvi." He took a bite and dropped his head back in bliss. "Oh wow."

"Good?" Max asked, sitting down on the stool beside him.

"Like you have to ask."

Max shrugged. "Still nice to hear."

"I know getting diagnosed celiac really sucked at the time, but it has been a huge benefit to me." Dave took another bite and was again transported to a world where nothing else existed but cheese and his taste buds.

"You're not wrong," Max agreed. "You would've starved to death years ago without me."

Dave chuckled. "I'm not completely incompetent."

"No. You'd just be subsisting on frozen pizza and cereal." Max shook his head like the idea was appalling.

"I do that anyway when you're not here." Dave decided to razz him just a little. "I like cereal."

"Don't I know it. I took the recycling out when I got here." He wiped his mouth with a napkin. "I'm going to make a 'this is what done looks like' list for you before I leave."

"Oh, that'd be great."

A "this is what done looks like" list was one part photo album, one part chore list, and one part checklist. Dave tended to avoid doing what others might consider automatic. He couldn't picture what "finished" looked like in his head, and then the task would quickly become overwhelming. Which led to a lot of avoidance.

Having a list gave him a clear idea of what he needed to accomplish, thereby making regular daily tasks doable. Instead of terrifying.

"What happened to your previous list?" Max shook his head. "Never mind. I'm sure it was destroyed in the fire."

Dave didn't really know for sure. He hadn't gone back yet. The house had been cleared for him to return to gather his belongings. And he would. Eventually.

But he was putting it off for as long as he could get away with it.

"Did you talk to Curtis and Gloria today?"

"Yep. Told them I wasn't at the hockey game." Dave took a drink of his cider. "But they said they'd already figured that out when they tracked my cell. I forgot I had turned on Find My Friends with Curtis."

Max made a face. "That sounds invasive."

"Sometimes it's just easier than having to answer my phone all the time. You know how much I hate being taken out of the moment." Some moments, like last night, he wanted to stay in it.

He needed to text Sabine.

He should've texted her already. He kept forgetting. Was it too late to text now? Had he missed the window?

"Did they catch the guy from last night?" Max asked, pulling him back to the present.

"I have no idea. That's not my department."

They talked throughout their meal, resting easy in each other's company.

Times like these and Dave wondered if maybe moving to Long Island to be closer to Max would have been the better move. He knew Max thought it would've been. But he still showed up to support the decision Dave made.

Dave knew the friendship he had with Max wasn't typical. They both just happened to be wired in specific ways that spoke to one another.

After dinner, Dave helped Max clean up and then they worked on the "this is what done looks like" list together.

That had started some time in high school. Max would remember the exact date, but all Dave had were impressions of memory. He was still trying to go to school full time because he didn't want to stop playing ball.

He'd been to a few doctors and one of them had diagnosed him with inattentive ADHD.

Dave had been so mad.

It had felt like the most unfair and unbelievable conclusion.

His mom hadn't really known what to do. He knew she'd done her best, but he hadn't made it easy on her either.

He'd get mad and throw fits, frustrated that *this* was just how it was going to be. His brain was a battlefield. He was expected to live with a constant war of thoughts piling on top of one another until they spilled over.

He'd fought it.

He thought he could negotiate his way out of it.

And when that didn't work, he'd avoid, avoid, avoid. Running away from anything that confronted him with reality.

He'd finally told his friends about his diagnosis. He'd had kept it a secret for as long as he could, afraid they'd treat him differently.

But they hadn't.

They'd just accepted him and moved forward with the information.

Dave had had a harder time moving forward. He'd have a couple of small victories and then one setback, and it would cause him to slide back into despair.

But his ma wasn't around for whatever reason (he couldn't remember the details), and he had to get himself up and to school. Every day it got harder and harder.

Max and Leslie took turns picking him up in the morning.

Max also came over to the house on the weekends and would clean and do laundry.

He never, not once, complained about it. In fact, he seemed to really enjoy putting things back in order.

Even though it made Dave feel like he wasn't doing something right.

It couldn't be normal, to have your best friend cook and clean for you.

Looking back, Dave could see the telltale signs of depression.

Hopeless was an emotion he didn't wish on anyone.

Thankfully, even though he'd started missing school more days than he went, he had still been going to see his doctor. After some years of trial and error, they found the right combination of anti-depressants and ADHD meds to help him.

He'd had to adjust over the years to keep up with life changes but finding something that had helped him feel less helpless had been a game changer.

At the time, Dave had had no idea that Max had been trying to figure out ways to help him get organized.

Until one day Max had come over with this book he'd found in the library. Something about living with ADHD.

Dave had already decided he was going to drop out of school, but the binders helped him be able to do the basic things he needed to get done so that Max and Leslie could pursue their own dreams.

And that had given Dave the courage to chase his own. Because he no longer felt trapped by his limitations. He had the tools to help him get the things done that everyone else found so easy to do.

Dave took pictures of the clean kitchen, the refrigerator, the inside of the cupboards and printed them out on the printer Max had already set up. Max typed up lists and laminated them.

Yes, he had a portable laminator that he carried in his luggage.

And a label maker.

And every color of dry erase marker in existence. Even though Dave only used the green ones.

If Dave had to make a binder it would take years and never be finished.

With Max, it took a little over an hour.

Though, Max had the system down. He used the same checklists and customized to location.

When they were finished, it finally felt like home.

Well, Dave's home.

A binder in every room and one for his car.

"How long do I have you for this time?" Dave asked, turning on the game console. "Did you…?" He made a slow circle in the living room. "Did you unpack in here?"

"Of course." Max shrugged. "I also unpacked your bedroom."

"I hope you know that you're a damn catch, Max." Dave sat down on his leather couch and wondered if he should get a velvet one instead.

He still hadn't texted Sabine.

He glanced at his phone. It was probably too late now.

"I'm here for the week. Then I have to be in L.A. for a few days but I'll come back after that." Max handed him another hard cider and joined him on the couch.

Dave handed him a game controller. "Super Smash?"

"Like my life depends on it."

He loved having Max around.

Despite his need for independence, he was very social. When he went too long without his people, he got sad.

Maybe he should try to convince Max to move to Chicago.

Ha.

Yeah, right.

Chapter Nine
Gold Rush

SABINE

In the parking lot of the recording studio was a black Range Rover, a silver Camaro, a nondescript Toyota, two pickups, and a black Honda Civic.

She didn't know what kind of car Dave drove. Or if he drove a car. Maybe he had a service.

No.

He seemed like the kind of person who'd want to leave whenever he wanted. Freedom and all that.

It had been three days since he'd left the loft and she hadn't heard from him. Not a text, not a phone call, nothing.

But they'd had such a great time together so she didn't think he was avoiding her or anything.

Right?

Unless that entire night had gone differently for him.

The memory of him throwing his head back laughing washed through her and she smiled. No. It hadn't just been her. He'd had a good time too.

She gathered her bag and headed to the back entrance of the studio.

"Who's there?" Nikki called down the hall.

"Sabine Debois," she replied.

Nikki was the studio manager. Or at least that's what Sabine had deciphered after months of casual observation. She was blonde, perky, high energy and if Sabine was correct, she was a secret genius hiding in plain sight. But they hadn't interacted much, so Sabine couldn't be sure.

Nikki came around the corner, eyebrows furrowed.

"Your last name is Debois?" Nikki asked suspiciously.

"Mm-hm."

Nikki eyed her up and down. "Do you have a brother?"

Shock must've radiated on Sabine's face because Nikki pressed her lips into a grim line.

"Do you know André?" Sabine asked.

Nikki's pale cheeks flamed red. "No." She took a deep breath. "Can you help me with something for a second?" She turned and went back from where she'd come.

Sabine followed her, more curious about why she'd obviously lied about knowing André than anything.

They went down a hall and then through a door that opened into a huge room with thirty-foot ceilings. The windows at the top let sunlight in and filled the recording space with warmth.

A drum kit was set up in the center and other instruments were scattered around the perimeter in various stands and cases. Sabine took it all in and quickly followed Nikki up the metal staircase.

That led to a smaller room with leather couches and a bank of sound engineering equipment against a glass wall that overlooked the larger room they had come from.

"Can you snap your fingers?" Nikki asked, fiddling with equipment Sabine couldn't begin to identify.

"Y-yes." Sabine set her bag on the couch and took off her coat.

"Great. I have this track that needs a little something extra and the dude's finger snaps are entirely too aggressive. Johnny thinks that I can just soften it in mixing—and he's not wrong—but the less I have to mess with, the cleaner the sound in the end. Okay."

Sabine followed Nikki's instructions and snapped her fingers near the microphone in time with the backing track Nikki played.

It probably didn't take more than five minutes but when Nikki added it to the song she was working on, Sabine got a rush hearing her fingers mixed into it.

"That's so cool!"

Nikki grinned and flipped some switches then made some notes on a tablet.

"That is all I need from you, teach."

Sabine gathered her things and hesitated by the door. "How do you know André?" she finally asked.

Nikki flinched but didn't turn around. "I used to know him. A few years ago. But I don't know him anymore."

Oh.

If that didn't tell her more than enough, nothing would.

"Sorry," Sabine muttered and hurried from the control room.

She hadn't spoken to André in a couple weeks. But they never discussed their respective dating lives anyway. And yeah, she was assuming Nikki was an ex of some sort.

People generally didn't get that guarded unless their heart had been involved.

She made it to the lounge and heard laughter on the other side of the door.

Speaking of hearts…

Dave was standing in the middle of the couch, spinning a basketball on the tip of a finger, his friend Max was leaning his back against the counter holding a cup of espresso, Shawn was sitting at the table with Piper.

As soon as Piper spotted her, she bounded across the room.

"I got an A+!" the teenager hollered. She grabbed Sabine by the hands and jumped up and down. "I get to start in Thursday's game!"

Sabine's heart doubled in size and she did a little hop of excitement. "That's great!"

Piper dropped her hands and did a lap around the room. "I've been waiting all day to tell anyone so I could tell you first." She stole the ball from Dave who gaped and then pouted. She bounced it across the room, doubled back, dribbled it between her legs and passed it back to Dave without looking.

Dave caught it; his expression clearly impressed.

"Girls got skillz with a z." Max chuckled.

"I am so proud of you," Sabine said, catching Piper by the shoulders.

Piper beamed. "I've had a really patient teacher."

Sabine felt the emotion creeping into her throat and she tried to clear it. It was so not cool to cry in front of teenagers. She just blew out a breath and nodded.

"I'm gonna tell Hannah now," Piper declared and darted from the room.

"Well done." Shawn applauded. "I wasn't sure she'd ever get to play again, and let me tell you, she has been really annoying. You've saved us all."

Sabine rolled her eyes. "It's my job."

"You must be pretty good at your job," Max remarked approaching her. He wore a navy-blue suit today but the jacket was draped over the back of a chair.

"I do my best," she admitted.

"I'm going to hug you because that's how I greet those who've saved my life." Max wrapped his arms around her, and she let him.

"How are you, Max?" she asked after he'd let her go. "Did you get checked out after the whole…?" She touched her throat.

"I did. Thank you for asking. Everything was fine. No permanent injuries." He stepped back and slid his hands into his slacks.

Sabine turned her smile on Dave who was holding the basketball under one arm, his eyes bouncing between the two of them. They landed on her and stayed, and his smile did something to her insides that she didn't know if she'd ever felt before.

From a smile.

"Hey," she said.

He hopped off the couch and for a second, she thought he was going to hug her too. But he stopped short and just gazed down at her.

"Hey."

"How did Halloween go?" Shawn asked.

Sabine broke her eye contact with Dave and went to the table to set her stuff down. "It was a really fun night." She pulled out a chair and sat down. "At least, *I* had fun," she amended.

"I had fun," Dave declared. "I had so much fun that I slept most of the weekend to recover." He pulled out the chair across from Sabine and sat down.

"It's true," Max confirmed. "I can vouch for that."

"Max," Sabine said as something occurred to her. "What do you do for a living?"

"I'm an entertainment lawyer."

"Well, that's awfully convenient," she pointed out. And then immediately felt like an ass.

Max's eyes darted from Dave to Sabine and back again. "You haven't told her?"

Dave shrugged and started to spin the basketball on his finger again. "It didn't come up."

That made sense. From what she'd put together, if something didn't come up organically, he probably would have no reason to ever mention it.

"Okay, so Dave, Leslie and I all made a plan in high school. By that point in our friendship, it was pretty obvious that Dave was going to do something extravagant with his life."

Dave snorted.

"I wanted to go into law anyway, Leslie was leaning toward communications."

"Isn't it hard to work with friends?" Sabine asked even as she realized that she'd be able to work with Kara no problem.

"Working with family is hard," Max clarified seriously. "So, we all pushed each other to be the best. When one of us shines, all of us shine." He grinned.

"That's kinda cool," she mused out loud. Turning to Dave she asked, "Did you always know that you'd be a superstar?"

His expression flattened and he caught the ball in his hands again. "Still don't."

"What do you mean? You know you're incredibly famous, right?" she asked, teasing him.

He rolled his eyes.

"He has a hard time feeling successful," Max provided. Dave shot him a scowl. "What? Is it supposed to be a secret because you're terrible at keeping it."

Dave barked a laugh at his friend. "You're not wrong." He folded his arms around the ball and rested his chin on it as he gazed across the table at Sabine. "I just don't feel successful, I guess."

She rested her chin in her hand, elbow propped on the table. His eyes bounced around the room, happy, dark blue, and guarded. They landed on her and gentled.

"What does successful look like to you?" she asked softly.

His expression grew distant and then his gazed sharpened on her again. "You're doing that thing. I'm not gonna fall for it."

She jerked her chin back. "What thing?"

"That thing where you look into my soul and get me to start spilling all my thoughts and feelings." He stood and palmed the basketball while pointing a finger at her with the other hand. "I'm onto you though."

She chuckled and decided to play along. "Whatever you say, Sunshine Capone. But someday all your secrets will be mine."

He pursed his lips, his eyes sparkling with amusement. "That's exactly what I'm afraid of."

Sabine shook her head and caught the carefully blank expression on Max's face as he rubbed the back of his neck. Max's eyes bounced between Dave and Sabine. He dropped his hand and stepped to the doorway.

"Shawn, I have some documents I need to go over with you." He left the room.

Sabine shot a look to Shawn who blushed.

"He's helping me navigate the industry," Shawn explained shyly.

"So you're doing the thing?" Sabine asked, her heart skipping a small beat for the young musician.

"I might be doing the thing," he replied noncommittedly as he headed out the door.

"Did you set that up?" she asked Dave.

"Huh?" Dave turned around, the sound of the espresso machine having drowned out her question.

She folded her arms and leaned back in the chair. "Shawn and Max, did you set that up?"

Dave glanced toward the door and back to her. Something about his expression turned introspective and serious, and she should have braced.

"I am more aware of my privilege than most people think I am. Without the people in my life, I wouldn't be anything." He picked up his espresso and took a sip. "If I have the opportunity to share that with someone who deserves it, I will."

Shivers raced over her arms and she tugged her sweater sleeves down to cover them. Meanwhile, warmth started to creep up her neck.

Why did every single conversation with Dave get her all discombobulated?

It was as if he refused to be defined by normal standards and kept reinventing exceptions.

She licked her lips. "You're incredibly talented…and brilliant—if I'm being honest. What makes you think any of that is other people's doing?"

One side of his mouth tugged upwards, and he leveled her with that dark blue, direct gaze. "I'm a high school dropout, Sabine. I need someone to tell me when to take out the trash. I have never been on time for one thing in my life. I am a difficult person to be around on a good day. I know exactly how lucky I am to have Max. To have Leslie. To have Hannah and Johnny. Nothing I have would exist without the patience and work of others. So if my success can make the people I care about rich, then I'll choose that every time."

Sabine stared at him, her heart hammering in her chest. Absently, she realized she was rubbing her earlobes in an effort to calm down.

Someone along the way had taken this brilliant, creative person and made him feel *bad* for his gifts. Made him feel *apologetic* for them.

Her anger churned deep in her chest and she breathed slow. In and out. In and out.

"I should have offered," Dave cut into her thoughts. "Do you want an espresso?"

"No, thank you," she replied. "Dave, you're…"

He waited—his expression open, unguarded. But all the words that she wanted to say to him somehow seemed inadequate to what she wanted to convey.

She exhaled, defeated. "You're awesome."

He grinned, his energy back up to what it had been moments ago.

He crossed the lounge and sat down across from her again. "So I was thinking," he began, like it wasn't the beginning but the middle of a thought she hadn't heard the rest of. "What if I hired you?"

"What's that now?" she asked, trying to let go of what had been bothering her and grab hold of what he was presenting now.

He held the espresso cup on the table in between the fingertips of both hands and turned it in his grasp. "You said you've taught adults before."

"Yes."

"What if I hired you?" He looked up from the cup and smiled tentatively.

"To help me get my GED?" He cleared his throat. "Or whatever the Illinois equivalent is."

Oh. *Ohh.*

"You don't have to hire me for that. I'd gladly help you figure out how to get all that done." She straightened in her chair and rested both her elbows on the table.

His expression closed down just enough for her to notice. "No, I'd rather hire you if that's all right."

She didn't want to push. Except she'd spent just enough time around him that she knew if she didn't push, she'd never get the answer. Though on the other hand, she had no idea what would happen if she pushed. He could get angry. Shut down the conversation altogether. But if that was the case, she'd rather know that now rather than start their friendship off by walking on eggshells.

Because that's what they were, right? Friends.

"I would feel awkward being paid for something I would gladly do just because you asked me to," she said softly.

His jaw pulsed. "I don't want you to do it because you feel sorry for me."

Her eyebrows shot up. "I do *not* feel sorry for you, superstar."

His lips twitched and he relaxed a bit. "I'm a little sensitive about…" He shrugged. "I have ADHD. The inattentive kind. It makes things… tricky." She folded her arms on the tabletop.

She had suspected as much but it was nice to have it confirmed.

"You don't look surprised," he remarked.

She smiled. "Not surprised. But thank you for trusting me with that."

He sighed. "Are you sure you still want to help me?"

Oh man, if she ever got ahold of the person who had shamed him for the way his brain worked, she was going to… Well, she was going to go to jail.

The certainty she felt over it was startling.

"I'm looking forward to it, babe," she said honestly.

He flashed a relieved smile and her heart squeezed.

Piper interrupted their moment and Sabine took a breath. She was going to have to remember this for next time. Being with Dave, having his undivided attention, it was… overwhelming wasn't the right word. It was more than being with anyone else, but not in an uncomfortable way.

It was like being lost in a blanket fort and not caring because the snacks were endless and the company was sparkling.

"Piper, I forgot!" Dave declared excitedly. "I wrote something for you."

Piper slid into her chair and eyed Dave. "What do you mean?"

"That guy that got you detention, I wrote you something about it."

"You're kidding," Piper barked a laugh. "Well, let's hear it." She crossed her arms over her chest.

Dave pulled his phone out. "Gimme a second. I need to remind myself." He covered his mouth with a hand as he gazed at the screen on his phone.

Sabine and Piper exchanged equally excited looks.

"Okay, here goes…

Slippery like a bandit,
and unfunny if I'm candid,
his morals are famished,
his friends are left stranded,
he's bluffing too hard,
he's not playing what he's been handed.
He's a class A shart,
A fucker at large.
Maybe I went too far.
It's just his name rhymes with nipple,
It's obvious and simple,
sometimes I got too many words,
like a kid with a kindle,
like the muse of a fiddle,
like a hey diddle diddle,
and I ran away with this tune.
when I find something so funny,
I don't know what to do,

Szippl has a weakness,
but only in one spot,
It's on his chest and its round,
ok there's two,
—and they're dots

That one went to plural,
like a hoe's thought to THOTS,
hard fought,
pockets of tots,
until I'm Dynamite,
I'll get it right,
Pedro has this fight.
did I mention
I'm not voting for
Josh Szippl's detention"

"OHH!" Piper hollered, covering her mouth with one hand and punching the air with the other. "That's incredible!"

Dave was glowing.

Absolutely preening.

"Are you going to record that?" Piper asked, excitement radiating off of her.

He snorted a laugh. "Pretty sure that wouldn't be too good for my brand, releasing a diss track on an eighth grader. Nah, honey, that was just for you."

Piper threw her arms around Dave's neck and his face turned an adorable shade of crimson. He darted his eyes up to Sabine and they were shining.

* * *

"Whatcha thinkin' about?" Kara asked, snapping Sabine out of her little daydream.

She sent a small smile to her friend and stirred the chili one more time.

"Is it a certain rock star with face tattoos, perhaps?" Kara teased.

Sabine sagged slightly. "He's really cool."

Kara smiled but it was heavy with knowing.

"He wrote a diss track for a boy that got Piper detention and it was weird and dumb and it just made Piper's entire day." Sabine pulled a teaspoon out of the drawer to her right and dipped it into the chili. She tasted it and tossed the spoon in the sink. "And he asked me to help him get his GED." She reached for the red pepper flakes and glanced at Kara.

"And then you told him your rates, right?" Kara asked, warning in her voice.

"No." Sabine added the red pepper to the chili and put the lid on. "He was adamant that he pay me though. Even though I volunteered."

Kara looked a little impressed. Not a lot. She was being careful.

Unlike Sabine.

"Do you think he's being really elaborate in his efforts to get in your pants and subsequently in the tabloids?"

Sabine chuckled. "No. He's just a really nice person. I don't think he's into me like that." She adjusted the pin holding up one side of her braid. "Besides, I'm not really his type." It was a confession she needed to say out loud. She had to hear it. She needed to say it to drive home the reality of it.

"What do you mean?" Kara asked with a concerned frown.

"I mean," Sabine said, hating the truth. "He's fun and impulsive. He lives a wild life compared to me." She shrugged. "And I'm the boring teacher girl. I think we can be friends easily. But I don't think you need to worry about his intentions. Not with me."

"Does that make you sad?" Kara asked.

"A little." Sabine shrugged again and swallowed the bitterness in her throat. "But I can be a really good friend."

It shouldn't bother her to know she wasn't rock star girlfriend material.

But she wasn't really anyone's girlfriend material.

She'd get asked out, sure, but it always fizzled quickly and the guys all said the same damn thing.

I think we're better as friends.

And then they'd marry the next girl they dated.

"This is fine," Sabine said, pushing back from Kara. "This is more than fine; this is good. Now you know you don't have to worry."

"You're a kickass friend," Kara said forcefully.

"I know. Thank you," she said, tossing a smile over her shoulder.

She did know.

And there were way worse things she could be.

Kara grunted like she was still unsettled by what Sabine had shared. But Kara was protective of Sabine. She always had been. And Sabine was protective of her. It worked out well for them.

It wasn't like Sabine had experienced a huge heartbreak.

Not really.

Just a bunch of tiny fractures that over time had made her heart a little more sensitive to rejection.

Which was weird because when she thought about Dave and how he saw the world and the people around him, she just knew… If he ever loved her, it would be different.

Different from what anyone else knew of love. It would be confounding and hectic and absurd.

It was best if she never found out what different love felt like.

Chapter Ten

You

SABINE

"That A+ was a short-lived victory." Piper slouched into her chair.

"We get to build on it. And they're letting you play, right?"

"Yeah." Piper perked up a bit. "I made two three pointers in last night's game."

"That sounds impressive," Sabine replied with a smile.

Piper rolled her eyes. "You really need to learn more about basketball." She straightened up in her chair. "Especially if you're hanging out with Sunshine now."

"You call him Sunshine, huh?" Sabine asked, packing up her binder.

"Eh. I go back and forth." Piper closed her laptop. "But seriously. Basketball. Go to a game. Turn on ESPN occasionally."

Sabine put on her coat. "You think there's going to be a pop quiz?" she teased.

"No. But it's important to take an interest in your partner's hobbies." Piper's electric blue eyes widened like she just realized what she'd said. "You know what? Never mind. I'm sure you know what you're doing."

Sabine opened her mouth to ask at least three questions when Dave came into the lounge.

"Hey, should we have a study session?" he asked.

It had been a whole week since he'd brought up her helping him get his GED. She'd gotten the information she needed and texted him to let him know they could start whenever he wanted.

He said he'd get back to her.

And a week had passed and he hadn't brought it up.

Until now.

"I would love to do that, but it's grocery day. I have to go shopping. And then go home and make dinner." Kara would be proud of her for not rearranging her day to accommodate Dave. No matter how much she wanted to.

"I like groceries," Dave said. "Do you need company?"

She flicked her eyes to Piper who was trying to watch them while also packing up her own stuff.

"I don't *need* company, but I wouldn't mind it."

He grinned and shoved his hands into the front pocket of his hoodie and his expression changed. First it was thoughtful, then excited, then downright mischievous.

She eyed him and waited for Piper to clear out before she lifted her chin at him. "You look like you have a secret."

He didn't even try to hide his delighted smile. He came close, only a foot away from her, his hands still in his hoodie pocket.

"Have you ever been just a little bit drunk when you've gone grocery shopping?" His eyes sparkled with mischief.

Sabine bit down on her bottom lip to keep from smiling, and then realized that she didn't care if he saw her smile. "I can honestly say I have never done that."

"Okay," he took a step closer, his voice dropping even lower. "I have two tiny bottles of gin in my pocket. I saw them at the gas station, and they were too adorable to leave behind. Anyway, we could each drink one."

"Those are called nips," she supplied.

"Oh my God, that's even cuter. A nip. I love it." He fished two small bottles of gin out of the front pocket of his hoodie and showed her. "It's what? A shot and a half?"

"Something like that." She took one of the bottles and narrowed one eye at him.

"It's the perfect amount to get buzzed on an empty stomach. And then it's over." He made it all sound so innocent.

"Unless you're a heavy drinker and then you might not even feel it," she pointed out skeptically.

"I never drink. I don't have the time. What about you?"

She narrowed both eyes then, trying to figure out if he was being truthful. "I don't—"

"It's so fun. Just this once."

Every cell in her body rebelled against that idea. He was talking about public intoxication and just *slightly* breaking the law. And maybe it was because she'd watched her mom use every excuse under the sun to justify all of her illegal activity.

But Dave was bouncing on his toes, his eyes lit up making their usual indigo color more of a faded blue. He was like a wild wind blowing through her mind and she was trying to cling to her calm and predictable ideations.

He made that impossible.

"And before you get worried about driving and things like that, we can drop your car off at your place, and my security will drive us."

"Your security?" she asked, her mind trying to keep up with his.

"I barely use them so why not use them to do fun stuff? You have a list, right?"

"A list?"

"For what you need. Because we should really have a list. Otherwise we won't have anything stopping us from buying junk."

"You've really thought this through." She shouldn't be smiling. It was encouraging him. She could see it. And his excitement fueled her amusement, and they were hyping each other up.

He wagged his head back and forth. "I try to do my thinking before my drinking. I'm not a fan of preventable consequences."

"Are you a fan of any consequences?"

What was she doing? She was getting swept up in his energy and matching it. This was dangerous.

Or was it?

Yes! This was so out of her normal routine she should just politely decline and get her groceries.

Alone.

And sober.

In more ways than one.

"Please say yes," he interrupted her thoughts. He leaned just a fraction closer, hardly a noticeable amount. "I really want to do this with you."

She wasn't going to admit out loud how great that sounded. Being picked to do something that sounded fun for the sake of being fun? She'd always been taught that fun should have a purpose. Otherwise, it was a waste of time, money, and life.

But she was watching Dave get more and more excited about a seemingly ridiculous idea and she wanted to be a part of it.

With him.

Anyone else and she'd easily say no.

And maybe that's what made it feel a little dangerous. Because her reservations turned into dust in the face of his enthusiasm.

"Okay."

He stopped bouncing on his toes and a hesitant smile touched his lips. "Okay?"

"Yes," she confirmed with a resolute nod. "Let's do it."

* * *

"What are you making for dinner again? I know you told me, but I wasn't listening."

"At least you're honest about it," she snickered. "For dinner tonight I am making spaghetti with meatballs."

"Right." He snapped his fingers like he remembered, and she smiled again.

She'd been smiling nonstop since they'd left the studio.

He'd ridden with her to her loft where she changed out of her teacher clothes and into jeans and a hoodie since that's what Dave was wearing.

His security team met them and took them to her grocery store.

They were two different people than had accompanied him to the Geekeasy. A man—Darius—who had a smile like a Disney Prince and perfect hair to match. And a woman—Dallas—who was taciturn and looked lethal.

Sabine had to force herself to stop staring at Dallas because the woman could probably kill her without Sabine even realizing she was in danger.

Which meant she was already in danger.

It was thrilling.

"And this is where you shop every week?" Dave shoved his hands in the pocket of his hoodie and gazed around the store like he had never been inside one before.

"Where do you do your grocery shopping?"

He shrugged. "I have a service." He picked up a box of vegan cookies and read the back of it. Then he put it back on the shelf.

"Because you're so famous?" she teased, pushing the cart down the next aisle.

He made a noise and shook his head. "Most people don't recognize me, and those that do, don't approach."

She turned to look over her shoulder at Darius standing by the entrance of the store. Dallas was somewhere nearby because Sabine could feel eyes on her. "Right. You're just like the rest of us."

He pulled her hoodie strings, slightly closing her hood around her face.

"What are you doing?" she laughed.

He gazed down at her, amused, happy, thoughtful. "Are you giving me a hard time?"

"Maybe," she conceded, shoving her hood back. "But you have to admit, your life is just a little out of the ordinary."

"I admit nothing." He winked and turned around.

That fucking wink.

Her brain sputtered to a stop and she sighed.

This was all fun and games for him. And yeah, she was having fun too. But her heart... Oh, her heart was ringing a warning bell deep inside her chest.

She liked him.

She really, really liked him.

* * *

"What on earth is that noise?" Dave asked when the elevator opened on her floor.

Sabine snorted. "Uh, banjo. I think." She struggled with her keys and the sack of groceries in her arms.

Why had she sent away his security? She should have let them carry the groceries because she had seriously underestimated how buzzed that one nip was going to make her.

"Are you sure? Because it sounds like Gilbert Gottfried falling down a flight of stairs."

That was it. That was the last straw.

She'd already gotten the giggles a few times during their shopping trip, and it had been threatening to completely dominate her all evening.

That one last comment did it though.

He was too funny and she was too happy.

The giggles took over and she sank to the floor of the hallway in slow motion.

"Oh no, she's going down," Dave said, his own voice pitched higher than usual and full of amusement.

She snorted on the inhale and hugged the loaded brown paper bag to her chest like it could somehow help her regain her composure.

His deep laughter joined hers and they spent a good three minutes just laughing at each other.

Finally, he reached for her keys.

"We need to get some food into you. I had no idea you were such a light weight."

She struggled to her feet just as he found the correct key and opened the door to the loft.

They went inside and deposited their bags on the counter. She took off her hoodie and tossed it over the back of the couch.

"Would you like some water?" she asked, because she was going to drink a gallon. It was either that or open a bottle of wine and keep drinking.

Which was oh so tempting.

"Water would be great." He began to unpack the bags and set the foodstuffs on the counter. "What do you need for dinner?"

She handed him the glass of water with one hand and separated the ingredients for the meatballs with the other.

"Go sit over there." She pointed at the stools on the other side of the island.

"So bossy," he muttered with a grin.

The banjo playing continued—undeterred by their laugh fest in the hallway.

"I bet that gets annoying."

He didn't have to specify what he was talking about.

She stuck her tongue out and grabbed her phone. "I usually tune it out with music." Once she had the app open, she handed it to him. "Here. You pick."

"You have a lot of Taylor Swift on here."

She shot him a warning glare but he missed it. "She makes me feel things."

"She makes us all feel things," he agreed.

His comment pleased her, and she found herself smiling at him. He glanced up and caught her but she wasn't sorry.

"What?" he asked, mirroring her smile.

"Guys usually give me a hard time about Taylor."

His expression turned thoughtful. "Sometimes guys are just uncomfortable with feeling things."

She wanted to hug him, and give him a high-five, and take a blood sample to see if he was a real person or if he was manufactured in the Lab of Perfect Things.

But instead, she took a deep breath and got back to making dinner.

After a second, music began playing through the loft speakers.

Daft Punk. Nice.

And not surprising.

"I'm making you a playlist," he said. "Just some essentials that everyone should have." He looked up suddenly. "Your speakers are throughout the entire loft?"

She nodded.

"How did I not know that?" He left the stool and started inspecting various corners and vents throughout the loft.

She chuckled, drank some more water, and reflected on the past few hours.

Was it really only Monday?

Had a Monday ever been this fun?

Sabine jumped when she turned around and Kara was standing in the kitchen.

"Is he here?" Kara asked just above a whisper.

Sabine just nodded, suppressing the smile that wanted to take over when she thought about Dave and their grocery adventure.

She'd texted Kara from the back seat while his security had driven them to the market. Kara had been adamant that Sabine do the ridiculous thing.

Kara came to stand very near her, her expression glowing. "How was it? Was it as fun as I said?"

Sabine answered with a giggle and Kara hugged her.

"My little rebel. I'm so proud of you."

"You even have speakers in your bedroom—oh, sorry. I didn't mean to interrupt."

Kara let Sabine go and lifted her chin at Dave. "Mr. Capone."

His eyes bounced between them. "Dave is fine."

"Dave," Kara said with an emphasis that Sabine didn't understand. "Would you like a glass of wine? You are staying for dinner I assume."

He looked to Sabine for his answer, but she just shrugged.

"Yeah?" He frowned, cleared it. "If you're having some, I will."

"Pink okay?" Kara asked, opening the fridge.

"I have no preference. I don't drink wine."

Kara closed the refrigerator door and set the chilled bottle on the counter. "You must have wine sometimes. With your girlfriend, perhaps?"

Sabine made a noise in her throat that was part growl, part cough.

"I don't have a girlfriend," Dave replied easily. His neck was bent as he studied Sabine's phone screen. Presumably working on that playlist.

Kara shot a look to Sabine that was pure mischief, and Sabine almost burst out laughing. The only downside to having a best friend who was brilliant and sly was that she was brilliant *and* sly.

Kara poured three glasses of wine. She pushed one toward Sabine and carried the other two around the island. Taking a seat next to Dave, she handed him a glass.

"What are you doing?" Kara asked.

"Making Sabine a playlist."

Kara made a face at Sabine who just rolled her eyes and kept cooking. Whatever.

Kara could think and speculate all she wanted but Sabine knew the truth: Dave had never expressed any kind of romantic interest.

Sometimes…well, sometimes he almost did. But she wasn't clueless. She knew what it was to be flirted with and he always came to the line but never crossed it. There was nothing to wonder about because he'd done nothing untoward. He hadn't even hinted at it.

And while the initial emotion that came with that knowledge was disappointment (who didn't want a rock star to flirt with them?), what followed was sweet appreciation. And fondness.

The man just wanted to be friends.

And there was something so refreshing and charming about it that she hoped she never did anything to ruin it.

She made dinner, bopping around to the playlist Dave made while Dave and Kara talked. When dinner was done and they all sat down at the table together, Sabine looked around and smiled.

This could work.

She could be friends with a superstar and still maintain the normalcy of her life.

Thankfully her mom would be in prison for a long time yet. Because this would have her looking for any and all angles to make money off of it.

Heartburn threatened to disturb her peace and she set it aside.

"This is so good," Kara said around a mouthful of food. "My diagnosis was almost the end of happiness for me. But Sabine took it upon herself to convert all my favorite foods for me. She's a G-D national treasure."

"My best friend Max is celiac," Dave said. "He cooks for me all the time. In fact, I probably wouldn't eat anything outside of cereal if he didn't stop in every couple of weeks."

Sabine's heart lurched at that.

"You don't cook?"

Dave shrugged. "It's a lot to keep track of. I start out with the intention of making something and end up eating all the ingredients while I'm trying to focus on preparing it. And then I'm sad and full. It's easier to skip the whole thing."

Sabine laughed despite the tragedy of what he'd said.

Kara was nodding. "No, I get that. Sometimes the effort just isn't worth the outcome."

"I love cooking. Especially for people who love eating. Being appreciated is my love language." Sabine took a bite of her food.

Both Kara and Dave smiled brightly at her, and she paused.

Hm. She catalogued that similarity to go over later.

"What are you doing for Thanksgiving?" Kara asked.

Dave thought. "Max and Leslie will be in town. I think Mama Capone might fly in. Max usually makes a turkey with all the fixins. Oh!" His eyes widened and he sat back in his chair. "You guys should come for Thanksgiving!"

A half smile crept up Kara's face and she exchanged a look with Sabine.

"Well," Sabine started. She rubbed her hands on her napkin that was draped over her thighs.

"We should do Thanksgiving here," Kara blurted.

"What?" Sabine frowned at her bestie.

"That's a better idea than mine because my place doesn't have the room. I realized that after I said it out loud."

"Sabine and Max can make a gluten free Thanksgiving. And you and I can drink pink wine," Kara held her wine glass up and Dave toasted her.

"This holiday is quickly getting away from me," Sabine said, giving up and going back to her food.

"Would that work for you, dimples?" Dave asked, his voice soft and sweet.

And he called her *dimples*?

Sabine inhaled and didn't dare look at Kara. She knew what she'd see there, and she didn't need that kind of encouragement racing through her pink wine saturated veins.

"That sounds fun. I can't wait."

Chapter Eleven
Space and Time

DAVE

He paused outside the door and listened.

She was inside the loft singing along to… Taylor Swift?

Of course she was.

He waited another second, trying to identify the song.

"Superstar."

He was not going to read into that. But he did wait until the song was over, just listening to her sing through the door like a weirdo. The alternative was to go in and embrace the fanboy he was by holding up a lighter and swaying back and forth.

She would probably assume he was making fun of her.

He would never.

He rang the bell and she squawked in surprise. He chuckled because he knew she wasn't expecting him.

The music paused and she opened the door, frown firmly affixed. Her eyes widened when she saw the bundle he'd set on the floor.

"How many pies is that?"

"*That* is three. And these make five." Max joined him. He'd been delayed in the parking garage due to a phone call he'd gotten when they'd arrived.

"Five pies?" she asked. "Why on earth would you make five pies?"

"Why?" Max asked, suddenly suspicious. "How many did you make?"

"I made three," she said, voice soft.

"Eight pies," Dave broke the stunned silence. "I'm not complaining."

Max scoffed. "Of course you're not complaining. You have the metabolism of a hummingbird."

Sabine shrugged and stepped back to let them in. "Set them on the buffet."

They entered the loft and Dave was enveloped by the smell of fresh baked goods.

They set their pies on the buffet amongst banana bread, pumpkin bread, and two other pies.

"I'm just waiting for my pecan to set and then I'm done with today's baking." Sabine returned to the kitchen. "Can I get anything for either of you?"

"Water would be great," Dave said, joining her in the kitchen. "I can get it." He touched the small of her back as he maneuvered around her. He opened the cupboard and grabbed a glass. "You want water, Max?"

"That would be lovely. Thank you, David."

Dave frowned at Max over the top of Sabine's head. "David?" he mouthed. Max smirked.

He filled both glasses in the fridge door and slid onto the stool next to Max at the island.

"You were right, this is a much better location for hosting a meal." Max took a drink of water and looked around the kitchen and dining area. "Your condo would have fit us, but you don't even have dishes yet. Or a table."

"You don't have dishes?" Sabine asked, putting on oven mitts.

Dave shrugged. "I left Texas with what I had on me. I haven't really been back to see if…ah, it doesn't matter."

Sabine darted a look between Max and Dave but didn't reply.

She opened the oven and removed what looked and smelled like a pecan pie. She set it on the cooling rack on the stovetop and removed the hot mitts.

"Maybe we should have discussed pies when we started planning this thing." She turned worried eyes to the buffet where the other seven sat.

"I'm glad you didn't. I promise they won't be wasted." Dave nodded confidently. He was a master at eating pie.

Her mouth curved up slightly on one side.

"I doubt it would've mattered on my end. I always make five pies." Max pulled out his phone and opened his notes app.

"You're joking."

"I never joke about pie."

"It's true. He's won ribbons."

Sabine looked impressed.

"But just to avoid any more surprises, let's go over tomorrow's preparations."

Sabine slapped a spiral notebook on the island and leaned on her elbows.

Max nudged Dave in the ribs and grinned. "Look at that. She's analog. Like you."

Sabine shot a shy smile to Dave that hit him directly in the chest and left him a little dazed.

Sabine and Max went over their lists and plans, and Dave faked following along. But they could have quizzed him immediately after and he'd have come up blank.

It didn't matter. He wasn't in charge of planning for a reason.

That reason being he sucked at it.

Also, planning was boring.

Like…if he had to name the most boring things in the world, planning would be at the top of the list. And then he'd obviously not finish the list because fuck that noise.

All he had to do was show up and eat.

Which he could do.

His phone pinged and he glanced at it.

Oh. His ma's flight had landed.

"Mama Capone is coming after all," he announced, replying back to her.

When all that followed was silence, he glanced up.

"Is she now?" Max asked carefully. He forced a small smile. "Well, that's very generous of her."

"It is," Dave agreed. "I wasn't sure if she'd be here. Sometimes she has other stuff going on," he explained to Sabine. "You'll like her."

"I'm sure I will," Sabine replied with a smile and her eyes bounced to Max.

"Yes," Max confirmed tightly. "You will like her. She's a likable woman that Mama Capone."

Dave stood, sliding his phone into his pocket. "I'm going to use your restroom."

* * *

SABINE

The door to the bathroom closed behind Dave and Sabine zeroed in on Max.

"What's going on, Max?" she asked quietly.

Max's mouth flattened into an unhappy line. "Mama Capone is… well, she's unreliable if I'm being honest. But you'll understand when you meet her." He glanced at the bathroom and dropped his voice further. "She travels. A lot. She took off when Dave was sixteen and never really came back." He tilted his head and smiled to himself. "That was when I took over as a caregiver in Dave's life. I think I did all right."

Sabine shook her head, trying to keep up. "So his mom is…flighty?"

Max rolled his eyes. "In a sense. But I always got the impression that she just didn't like the responsibility of being a mom." He squinted as if that explanation didn't sit right either so she waited.

He took a deep breath. "Right after Dave was diagnosed, she took off. And she doesn't really acknowledge that he is the man he is." His face pinched in frustration. "You'll see what I mean. If she even shows up tomorrow."

But Sabine understood pretty well what Max was saying. It wouldn't be the first time she'd had to deal with a parent in denial of their child's neurodivergence.

Though it would be the first time it happened with someone she cared for way more than one of her students.

That distinction hit her like a punch to the gut.

She cared for Dave way more than she cared for a lot of people.

"Listen," Max broke into her thoughts. "I'll share all the tea when I come over in the morning." He stood and pocketed his phone. "Do you have a French press?"

"Uh, yeah. Yes. I do." She blinked at him, hoping she appeared as chill as she had a moment ago.

"Have the coffee ready at five a.m." Max lifted just his eyes to the bathroom door as it opened. "We will *discuss*."

"Is it time to go already?" Dave asked, clapping his hands together.

"It is!" Max's voice was bright and happy, and Sabine wondered how much Max hid from Dave about his true feelings. Then again, she did that with Kara too sometimes.

Was the codependency bad if both parties were happy with the outcome?

"I'm coming back in the morning to cook. You can sleep in."

Dave nodded but when he looked at Sabine, she could swear he didn't want to leave yet.

She didn't want him to leave either but what could she do? Beg him to stay?

She could beg him to stay.

No.

No.

That would be weird.

She would just see him tomorrow.

And meet his mom tomorrow.

It was a good thing they weren't romantically involved otherwise tomorrow would be incredibly stressful.

Yeah.

Good thing.

Chapter Twelve
Willow

SABINE

"**G**ood Lord, woman! What possessed you to buy a thirty-pound turkey?"

"It's twenty-seven pounds."

"Does that make you feel better? Shaving off that three pounds as if it'll somehow make this bird fit into your standard size oven."

Sabine made a face. "Do you think anyone will notice if we just—" she shrugged her entire body— "don't have a turkey?"

Max turned to face her. Probably so she could feel the full weight of his judgment.

"You wonder if they'll notice there's no turkey. On Thanksgiving."

Her lips twitched, threatening to smile and spoil the fun she was having.

Normally Sabine wasn't one to share her kitchen. She liked her space and "too many cooks" was a common phrase for a reason.

But Max's intensity and attention to detail had her in stitches.

He was sooo easy to fluster. And if she thought for one second that he was legitimately upset she would stop. But he was going to be this intense either way, so she may as well have fun with it.

Just a little.

He'd arrived exactly on time at five in the morning with a canvas bag of cooking accessories and a garment bag. He was wearing khaki pants and a long sleeve tee which he said was in case it got messy.

Meanwhile she'd been in what she called "wake up wear." Gray and red flannel pajama pants, fuzzy socks, red tank top.

Then he showed her how to properly use her French press because apparently, she'd been doing it wrong.

That was when he spotted the massive turkey chilling in the sink.

"Oh!" She remembered something. "I have this countertop roaster we could use!" She spun around, eyes searching for Kara.

Kara was also in her pajamas—turkey themed, orange, red, and yellow—and sitting at the island, her chin propped on her fist, hair in a tall pineapple, sleepily watching them.

"Do you know where we put that roaster?" she asked.

Kara rubbed an eye with the heel of her hand. "Um. I think it's in the storage unit. Upstairs."

"Right." As soon as she said it, the memory of Sabine shoving the box to the back of the storage unit sprang to mind. Ugh. She was going to have to put real shoes on.

"You think it'll hold this monstrosity?" Max asked, smacking the turkey resting in the sink.

Sabine stared at the bird, not sure at all. "We have to try."

"Yeah, we do," he agreed with a grumble.

"Not it."

Max and Sabine looked at Kara who cradled the coffee cup in front of her.

"Not it," she repeated.

Sabine stuck her tongue out at her.

Max glanced back and forth between them. "What? Is your storage unit in the depths of hell?"

Kara made a choking sound.

Sabine pressed her lips together and looked between the bird and the oven, rethinking her idea. She really didn't want to go into the storage unit.

But it was obvious the turkey would never fit in the oven. Even if they took out both racks and shoved really hard.

She didn't have a choice.

She turned back to Kara. "Can I borrow your goalie mask?"

Kara nodded once and slid off the stool.

"Goalie mask?" Max asked, incredulous. "I thought she was a nanny."

Kara came back and handed over the mask. "I play on an amateur rec team."

"And you're the goalie?" Max asked, still confused. "What kind of rabbit hole have I fallen down?"

"What? The women in your world don't fight their own battles?" Kara asked innocently.

Max's chin jerked back. "That's not what I…" He glanced between the two women like he was caught in a trap. "I am all turned around."

Sabine snickered. Even early in the morning and before a full cup of coffee, Kara was an expert shit giver. "She's messing with you."

Max huffed but visibly relaxed.

Sabine slid her shoes on and then her coat.

Time to face the inevitable.

She doubled back and drained the last of her coffee. The hot liquid cascaded down her throat and landed with a splash in her belly. She imagined it reinforcing her resolve and giving her courage.

It's not that she was afraid. She wasn't. Or at least, she wouldn't call it fear.

But maybe it was fear. Who knew at this point?

It had started out as fear and now it was more of an unpleasant fact.

She tucked the mask under one arm and paused at the door.

She turned to face her friend and Max, pressing her mouth into a grim line. "Wish me luck."

Kara saluted.

Max shook his head and flung his hands out in exasperation. "Fine. You've perplexed me. I'm coming with you."

He put his shoes back on—they were nice loafers, probably expensive— and then his coat. "Do we have to go outside? Is that why the coat?"

"Yeah." Sabine opened the door out into the hallway. Max followed.

"Safe journey, pilgrims," Kara called just before the door shut behind them.

Sabine walked beyond the elevator to the stairwell. "Our storage unit has roof access," she explained. Cold air greeted them in the stairwell and she tugged her coat close to her neck. Maybe she should have put a sweater on over her tank top. Even though the storage unit wasn't far, and the unit itself was temperature controlled, it was freezing the entire journey there and back.

If they made it back.

She snorted at her own dark joke. She didn't share because she was pretty sure Max wouldn't have appreciated it.

But Dave would've laughed.

As stressful as it seemed at first to have everyone come over to the loft for Thanksgiving, she was stupid excited to spend any amount of time with Dave as she could.

He was so *fun*.

It probably wasn't the most prudent idea for her heart. Oh well.

They trudged up the stairs, the only sound their feet hitting the cement steps as they traveled in single file. When they reached the top, she stopped and glanced at Max. She peered out the small window in the top half of the door.

She didn't see anything.

But she'd been fooled before—just last summer when she thought she'd try sunbathing on the roof and had wound up having to get a tetanus shot and three stitches.

"Zip your coat all the way and put your hood up," she instructed.

Sabine put on the goalie mask and then raised her hood over it. She tugged and pulled the fabric around the mask and secured it with the hood's strings.

Max frowned but did as he was told. "What's out there?" he asked.

"Sometimes nothing. Sometimes hawks. Sometimes feral cats," she said simply. She sighed a resigned sigh and noticed Max's pale face. "It's okay. Just stay close and I'll protect you," she promised. Then she shoved open the door to the roof and stepped outside.

Freezing wind whipped around them and sucked her breath from her lungs for a moment. She checked her immediate surroundings, saw nothing, and hurried across the rooftop to the storage unit, Max right behind her.

Just as she got to the door that would lead them to the row of storage units, she heard a garbled yowl from behind them.

"Sabine?" Max called, worry in his voice.

She struggled with the keypad, her fingers already frozen from the cold air. She felt Max at her back, crowding her into the door.

"Sabine?" he called again, right on top of her.

So was the yowling.

Their lives were in danger.

She needed to get the lock open otherwise they were going to become cat food.

She glanced over her shoulder and saw it. The demon eyes in the black void that served as a face.

"That's the one that got me," she said.

"What?" Max asked, his body vibrating against hers. He was pressing against her to the point she could hardly maneuver her arms to work the lock and handle.

A strangled laugh escaped Sabine's throat even though she knew it wasn't appropriate.

Max made a noise that sounded like a mix between a flailing Muppet and a drowning man. She sucked in a breath that wanted to become a laugh.

She would not laugh.

She would not laugh.

She would not laugh.

Max was legitimately terrified.

As well he should be.

Laughing would be wrong.

She typed in the code again and the lock disengaged.

She shoved the door open and Max shoved her through it.

She tripped in the narrow hallway and turned in time to see Max slam the door closed behind him and press his back to it, eyes wild.

"What the hell was that thing?" he demanded.

"That was the cat." She was deep breathing, keeping her laughter at bay. But Max was making it more difficult by the second.

"I have seen cats." Max sliced a hand through the air. "I've held cats. That was a-a-a-a *cougar!*" Max shouted.

That did it.

A huge laugh burst out of her and she sank to the floor. She sucked air but it was whisked away by more laughter. It was like the laugh was punishing her for trying to hold it back for too long.

Max stalked away from the door and raked a shaky hand through his hair. He spun around, eyes wide. "How are we going to get out of here? How will we ever get back? I left my phone inside your loft. I can't even call the authorities." He shuddered as he exhaled, completely ignoring the fact that she was wheezing on the floor.

He crouched down to look her in the eye. But that was difficult because she was still wearing the hockey mask. He grabbed the mask on either side of her face and held his forehead against hers.

"Is this where we die?" he asked.

Dead serious.

Sabine's laugh had turned squeaky and incoherent. It sounded like crying. She pulled the mask off and wiped at the tears that had spurted from her eyes.

Max took one look at her and began to pace. "Oh, Sabine, you are useless."

She slumped to the side, still gasping between giggles.

She waved at him. "It's fine," she said. "I'll protect you." Admittedly, she didn't sound very convincing.

He made a disgruntled noise in the back of his throat, hands on his hips as he stared down at her. "What is the matter with you?"

Probably too much adrenaline and caffeine on an empty stomach.

She struggled to her feet and patted his shoulder. She schooled her features and was proud of herself for succeeding. "It's going to be fine. C'mon."

She led the way to her storage unit, Max followed.

"It's the hawk that really scares me," she explained over her shoulder. "I'm afraid that thing will take my eyes out." She shuddered at the thought.

"This is a nice building," Max pointed out. "It can't be cheap to live here. Why is this even happening on your rooftop? It doesn't make any sense."

"Hm. As far as I can tell, one of the other residents tried raising chickens on the roof at some point. There's still some sort of pen in one corner and a little shed. It must've attracted predators."

She slid the key into the lock of the storage unit and opened the door. She flicked the light on and grimaced.

This was going to take a minute.

"I'm not sure when the cat started coming around. Kara thinks it made an alliance with the hawk."

"If the chickens are gone, what keeps them here?"

Sabine stepped over a storage tub and slid a stack of boxes to her left.

"Someone is feeding them." She grunted as she hauled the storage tub with the Christmas tree toward the front. She would need this in a few days anyway. She paused. Should she bring the Christmas decorations down now?

No.

Max was already freaked out enough.

She'd have to come back up later.

Alone.

Still…

She pushed the holiday tubs towards the front to make it easier for herself later.

"Who's feeding them?!"

"What?" She frowned at his tone. "Oh, I don't know. But sometimes I find empty food containers up here."

"You need to report them to the building management."

She snorted. "I have. They don't care."

"What?" He sounded so disgruntled she almost laughed. "How could they not care?"

She stood straight and put her hands on her hips. "Well, I think they *care*. But not enough to do anything about it." She shrugged. "Besides, if I could get them to fix something for me, it would be the undead banjo players, not the feral beasts of the roof."

He shook his head at her. "I do not understand you at all, Sabine Debois."

"I can live with that," she replied smiling. "Here." She hefted the box with the roaster in it and handed it to him. "You carry this."

She stepped around the new stacks she'd created with her digging around.

"What will you do?" Max asked, the fear resurfacing in his eyes.

She turned off the light, closed the door, locked it, and faced him.

"What I promised. I'm going to protect you."

She paused at the door to the roof and cracked it open.

"I don't see it," she muttered, trying to bend her eye around the corner. She glanced over her shoulder at Max who was clutching the large roaster in his arms. "I'm going to fling the door wide and I want you to run, fast as you can, to the other door. It doesn't need a code, just go inside. Do not stop."

She unzipped her coat and fluffed it up around her body and lowered the hockey mask.

He swallowed. Sweat shone across his brow and she withheld a smile.

"You can do this, Max," she encouraged.

He nodded.

She took a deep breath and pushed the door open hard. Max bolted past her, his loafers slapping against the concrete. Sabine came up behind him, her eyes darting around the perimeter for the cat.

"REOWWW!"

"AHHH!"

A black object came around the corner of one of the chimneys and bounced on its feet. Max yelled but didn't stop running. Sabine sprinted in the direction of the cat and opened her coat wide. The wind caught it and it puffed around her. She threw her arms out to the side to increase her size.

Then she pulled her lips back, bared her teeth, and hissed.

The cat bounced back, its hair raised, its teeth showing.

Sabine hissed again, really giving her throat a thrashing. She waved her arms in the air.

"RWARWWW!" the demon cat warned, bouncing at Sabine.

"RWARWWW!" Sabine yowled back, flapping her arms and jumping up and down.

The cat hissed, its tail pointing straight into the air, its ears flat against its head.

Sabine charged at it, wondering which one of them would flinch first. If she got much closer, she was going to need stitches.

Again.

And the ER was not where she wanted to spend the holiday.

Not when Dave would be here in a couple hours. She wanted to be here when he ate her pie. She wanted to have pink wine with her friends and tease her brother about Nikki hating him.

She had too much to live for!

She hissed as loud as she could and the cat darted back around the chimney.

Sabine dashed to the door where Max had made it safely inside and didn't look back.

The door slammed behind her, but she didn't stop until she'd cleared the entrance to her loft.

Max was there to catch her.

His arms went around her waist, her arms went around his neck, and their nervous energy exploded out of them both in laughter.

"You were amazing!"

"No, *you* were amazing!"

They released each other, then hugged again, slapping one another on the back and continuing with their mutual congratulations.

"You'd think you'd been to war and back with the way you're acting," Kara said when they'd let go of each other again. "Here," she handed Sabine a cup of coffee.

"Oh, you're an angel," Sabine said, taking the hot cup with one hand and removing the hockey mask with the other. She sipped the hot beverage and the heat traveled down her throat to her belly. "It's cold out there." She shivered. "Also, you're going to want to sanitize that thing. I spit in it." She made a face. "Like a lot." She tossed the mask in the corner by the shoes.

"I like it here." Max was also cradling a cup of coffee, a happy grin on his face. "You two are insane."

* * *

Leslie arrived an hour later and Max put him to work peeling potatoes.

She'd been around Max a few times but hadn't been able to spend any time with Leslie since that night they all met at Geekeasy.

And for some reason that caught her by complete surprise, she wanted Dave's friends to like her. They didn't have to be besties or anything, but it was important that they be able to exist peacefully with one another.

At least that's what she kept telling herself.

She needn't have worried.

Leslie and Max fit into Sabine and Kara's rhythm with ease. Leslie acted like he'd been to the loft a hundred times and Sabine's apprehension settled.

Especially after Leslie got Kara to confess which Obi-Wan was her favorite.

Their discussion had Sabine thinking about her initial answer a few weeks ago. She wasn't about to jump up and tell the room this, but she'd changed her answer.

Her favorite Obi-Wan was the one that had spent Halloween with her handing out candy and making her laugh.

Hands down. Best Obi-Wan of them all.

"When did you tell Dave to be here?" Leslie asked.

Sabine, standing at the stove stirring the onion and celery, looked over her shoulder.

Max replied. "I told him to be here by ten."

"We're not eating until two though," Sabine interjected. Not that she didn't want him to show up early. Why was she arguing?

Max lifted his eyes to her. "He's always late. I told him ten. He should be here by noon."

She tried a light laugh. "You don't think he can be on time?"

Leslie and Max exchanged a look of shared sympathy.

"He'll be late." Max's eyelashes fluttered and he looked at Leslie again. "Oh. And Mama Capone is coming. Allegedly."

Leslie rolled his eyes.

With all the excitement from that morning, Sabine had forgotten about Max's promise to spill the tea about Dave's mom.

Kara poured fresh coffee into the cups on the island. "Who's going to fill me in on the hot goss?" She shot a wink to Sabine.

Leslie sat back from his hunched over potato peeling position. He exhaled loudly and then reached for his coffee.

"Mama Capone, or Cherry as she'll ask you to call her, is a vibrant, likable, adventurous woman." Leslie's dark eyes grew sad as they lost focus.

Sabine waited for more but none came.

"So what's the issue? You guys clearly don't like her," she prompted. If there was something she should know, she wished they'd just get it over with. "What, is she a Nazi or something?"

Everyone shot matching looks of disgust at her. Kara tsked and shook her head.

"Sorry I brought up Nazis. I got nervous and tried to be funny," Sabine apologized.

"It's not that we don't *like* her," Leslie explained with a frown.

"We don't like how she treats Dave," Max added.

Leslie nodded. "Yeah, that's pretty much it."

Ugh. This process was excruciating. Either commit to the gossip or keep your mouth shut, that's what she thought.

"Is she mean?" Sabine asked. If they weren't going to say it, she was going to start guessing.

"No."

Leslie and Max exchanged a look. Again.

"Is she bossy? Controlling? Vindictive? What?"

"No, not really," Leslie said, looking to Max for help.

Sabine's annoyance reached its limit. She turned off the burner and moved the skillet to a cool one. She wiped her hands on the towel and faced the two men.

She cocked a hip, crossed her arms, and pulled out her teacher voice. "Boys, say what you're not saying."

When they remained silent, Kara snorted. "You two are terrible at this."

Sabine's lips twitched with a hidden smile because Kara was right.

"Okay," Leslie declared, waving a hand. "It's like this. It's not that she's deliberately bad or mean or anything. She's just not a good mom."

Kara coughed on a cashew. "That's so ambiguous."

Sabine glared at them. "More information," she demanded.

Leslie sighed, his big muscles stretching his maroon sweater to dangerous levels. "She was a single mom. My mom was a single mom. It's hard. But with Dave it was a different kind of hard. My mom had help because we lived near family. But Cherry didn't have anyone. At all. No friends, no family. It was just her and Dave. And Dave had certain… challenges growing up."

Sabine rolled her eyes even as her heart squeezed. "Right. The ADHD. I know."

Leslie pressed his lips together and took a breath. "At some point when Dave was in high school, she decided she was done."

"Done," Sabine repeated, narrowing her eyes.

"Done being a mom," Max continued the story. "She started to act more like his friend, or a wacky aunt."

"No discipline, no boundaries, no expectations whatsoever," Leslie picked up the thread. "And then one day she just left."

"Costa Rica the first time, right?" Max asked Leslie who agreed.

Sabine swallowed and waved a hand to get their attention. "You can't just abandon a child. That's illegal," she pointed out.

"Yeah." Leslie shrugged. "If someone turns you in."

"His teachers didn't notice?" She was a mandatory reporter. She knew how this shit worked.

Max's gaze turned dark. "Like I said, wacky aunt. She gave permission to withdraw from school when he turned seventeen."

The fuck?

Even the parents of the students she tutored who struggled with their children's neurodivergence still cared about their education. Hence why Sabine was their tutor.

What kind of a parent didn't care whether their child was adequately educated?

"Wait, wait, wait." She was waving both hands now like it would help make sense of any of this.

Leslie, anticipating her line of thought, started nodding.

"In Texas you can drop out if you're enrolled in a GED program *and* your parent gives permission. He was enrolled, she gave permission." Leslie made a face. "You think she ever cared to check if he completed that GED?"

Like the Magic Eye pictures that she used to stare and stare at for hours to find the image, there was a slight shift in her perspective and Dave's insecurities came into stark focus.

He'd been living his life with all of this hanging over his head.

"But you can't say anything to him about it." Leslie shook his head like he was giving a dire warning.

"What?" she asked, still trying to sort through all the information that seemed more emotional than factual. There was a lot of conjecture and assumption being hurled around.

"Dave loves his mom. Like, a stupid crazy amount. He accepts her as she is, and he doesn't like it when people judge her." Leslie shrugged one massive shoulder.

"That's why you two are weird about it," Sabine guessed. Because if they said what they thought, Dave would defend the person they saw as not worth defending.

But that wasn't their judgement call, was it?

Dave was allowed to love his mom whether his friends thought she deserved it or not.

Max and Leslie both grunted. Sabine and Kara exchanged a look.

On one hand, Sabine was glad to have the heads-up. It explained Max's discomfort. She could better anticipate any issues that might arise. Also, it didn't seem plausible that Dave would be able to say the things his friends just had.

On the other more weighty hand, she wanted to stick her hands in her hair and scream at the top of her lungs.

Because there was so much about this situation that was fucked.

And it made her nauseous.

What had she gotten herself into?

When it was just her and Dave, it was as if the rest of the world just… faded away.

No one and nothing else mattered.

But there was (and it sounded like always would be), a sense of dread just in the back of her mind. Parts he withheld, parts he hid. Details that maybe didn't matter.

But maybe they did.

She realized she was still staring at Kara.

Kara, the first person in her life who loved her despite her shortcomings. Whose friendship had changed the bitter course of her heart many years ago.

Because who was Sabine to judge someone's family life? The thought would have been humorous if it wasn't so true.

And the best way to deal with truth?

Name it.

Give it a name, call it out, don't let it be a shameful secret hiding in the dark. Welcome it into the light and deal with the reality of its existence.

"Well, families can be complicated. My mom is in federal prison and I can count on one hand how many conversations I've had with my dad." As soon as the words were out, the pressure that had been building in her chest released. Kara's mouth curved into a knowing smile. "We do what we have to, to survive. It's better that Dave loves his mom than the alternative."

Max scoffed. "But she's just the worst."

"Someone who chooses love is the best kind of person. Every time." She wiped her hands on the towel again and cleared her throat. "Now, someone needs to help me baste."

* * *

DAVE

. . .

"And she comes flying past me, hissing like a crocodile! And once again, Sabine Debois saves my life." Max slapped his thighs with his palms.

"I'm sorry I missed it," Dave said. He brought the can of Dr. Pepper to his lips and paused. He didn't recognize the slithering emotion in his chest, and he didn't like it.

"And then," Leslie broke in, "The turkey is thirty pounds, right?"

"Twenty-seven."

"Shh, you. I'm telling a story." Leslie shot a wink at Sabine, and that slithering in Dave's chest moved again.

Sabine crossed her arms over her chest and rolled her eyes. But the smile on her lips belied her irritation.

Dave had arrived not that long ago, and his friends had not been able to stop talking about how amazing Sabine was. How cool, and smart, and fearless, and *fun*.

God, they'd had so much fun without him.

Because he'd slept through it.

As usual.

"And she's refusing to let one of us help her," Leslie continued. He placed a hand on his chest. "You know, the ones with the muscles. She has to clean and prepare it on her own. I walk into the kitchen to see her in mid-wrestle with a raw turkey. And it looks like the turkey is winning."

"Raw poultry is very slippery," Sabine interjected.

"And before I can reach her, the turkey shoots out of the sink, and she steps back like a professional wide receiver and *catches* the raw turkey in her open arms. But it's too heavy and it knocks her on her ass."

Dave darted a glance to Sabine to verify, and she nodded, annoyed.

"It also knocked the wind out of me," she added begrudgingly.

"This is the turkey we're going to be eating?" Dave asked.

"Oh yeah. Max and I got it in the roaster when she went to wash up."

"I had to shower again. Couldn't exactly prepare the rest of the food with my salmonella breastes-es." Sabine's lips quirked with her joke as the rest of the room laughed loudly.

She got up from the couch and went back to the kitchen. Dave followed her and took a seat at the island, his back to the television. Where everyone else was drinking ciders and watching football.

"You need a new drink?" she asked when she saw he'd followed her. "I have pink wine," she offered with a twinkle in her hazel eyes.

He shrugged. "I'm good."

He watched her take the lid from the roaster and baste the enormous turkey thoroughly. She put the lid back on, checked the temperature setting, and leaned her elbows on the butcher block, those hazel eyes anchoring him to the moment.

"Don't have a team playing football today?" she asked, lifting her chin toward the television.

"I'm not a huge football fan," he confessed. It wasn't usually something he liked to admit. Because of the assumptions.

She raised surprised eyebrows.

"It's not the football," he amended. "Football is a cool sport. I just can't watch it on TV. Too many ads and interruptions. It gets…overwhelming. Hard to focus. I'm afraid I'll miss something important or hurt someone's feelings."

She hummed in understanding. "That's very self-aware of you."

He felt his entire body sigh.

That was the power of Sabine's attention on him.

Those eyes, that smile, her voice, her mouth saying words that no one had ever said to him.

That's probably why he always found himself blurting out the truth when she was around. Because something inside of him recognized it was safe with her.

Hell, even his friends felt safe around her. He couldn't ever remember a time they liked one of his girlfriends.

Not that Sabine was his girlfriend.

She wasn't.

They weren't.

Vow of celibacy.

Not that he assumed she would just sleep with him. He wasn't assuming that at all.

Oh shit.

He really hoped it only seemed like she could read his mind and she wasn't *actually* reading his mind.

Except if she could read his mind, then she'd be able to see his intentions weren't nefarious.

And he wouldn't have to worry if she understood.

Except he'd still worry about that.

Because that's what he did.

He blew out a nervous breath. "My friends seem to be highly enamored with you," he pointed out the obvious.

She snorted, her eyes bouncing over his shoulder to where they sat. "I keep saving Max's life. He has a Wookie life debt now."

"I really am sorry I missed it," he said softly.

Her eyes returned to his, confused. And then they softened as she realized what he meant. Because it never took her long to figure out what he was saying.

It was the kind of easy connection they'd had right away.

He'd never had that.

Ever.

With anyone.

Not even Max, who tried harder than anyone in his life to make sure Dave was understood and taken care of.

With Sabine it was effortless.

It was like Sabine could look into his eyes and see right to the heart of him.

"Don't be sorry," she argued, her nose scrunching up adorably. "There was no reason to—"

"No," he stopped her. "It was you. That's reason enough."

She licked her lips, her eyes bouncing between his. She took a breath like she was going to say something. Or maybe ask him a question he knew he didn't have an answer for yet.

And a timer went off somewhere behind her. Saving both of them from the unexpected.

And the irrelevant.

"Oh! I meant to ask you but I keep forgetting," Sabine said closing the oven door. "What's up with the basketball at the studio?"

He took a deep breath and heaved a loud sigh as he formulated his answer. "It's a spherical ball, used in the game known as *basketball*. They range in size from very small to quite large, depending on their specific purpose. Traditionally they were made of leather, but they are also made of rubber and synthetic materials. They have an inner bladder that's filled with air. They're—" He caught the hot mitt she threw at his face.

"Smartass," she muttered.

But she was smiling, and the dimple was out so he didn't think he'd really upset her.

Max opened the refrigerator. "Is he telling you about his basketball facts?" He reached in and brought out two more ciders. "He knows everything about basketball. He used to sleep with one."

Dave crossed his arms over his chest. "What do you mean, 'used to'?"

Max opened the ciders and went back to the living room.

Dave's gaze slid back to Sabine. "Was that not what you meant with your question?"

"I meant why do you always have one at the studio? Is there a secret basketball court under the studio I'm not aware of?"

"Oh." He nodded. That question made sense. "No. I wish. How cool would that be?" He should ask Johnny about putting in a basketball court. "I found a gym in town that lets me come in whenever I want to shoot hoops." He watched as she pulled a bottle of pink wine out of the fridge. "You know what? I do want some of that pink wine."

She grinned and grabbed another wine glass. She poured both glasses.

"What gym is it?" she asked.

Dave pulled out his phone and called up the webpage he'd bookmarked. "Weight Expectations."

She did a little hop and squeaked. "That's my gym."

He knew he was smiling at her like an idiot but she was too cute sometimes. "Really?"

She nodded. "That's so cool!"

It was pretty cool. Maybe they could go together sometime.

See? And now he was looking for more opportunities to hang out with her.

Because she was that awesome. That's all it was.

Feelings, emotions, attraction, none of that played a factor.

And then a handsome man entered the room and Sabine threw her arms around him.

And Dave's stomach fell to the floor.

Chapter Thirteen
Get Me

DAVE

"Dave, this is my brother André."

The handsome man was her brother.

That both eased his mind and frustrated him.

Because he had absolutely no business wanting Sabine to be anything other than a friend. He'd just reiterated those facts to himself.

But then she'd hugged someone much more attractive than Dave (objectively speaking), and Dave had almost cried.

No, really.

Sure, he was shaking hands with André and smiling but inside he was still recalibrating.

"Nice to meet you, André." Dave clasped the offered hand.

André was tall, much taller than Sabine. He had dark hair, verifying what Dave had always thought Sabine had under her lightened locks. And matching hazel eyes. He wore a red V-neck sweater that hugged his torso like it was tailored.

Maybe it was.

What had Sabine said about their upbringing?

"Pleasure to meet you," André replied in a slight British accent. Dave remembered something about her brother being raised somewhere else. Right? Or was that a movie he'd seen?

Sabine introduced her brother to Max and Leslie, and all three immediately slipped into easy conversation.

Dave was proud of his friends. They had worked hard to establish the careers they had. It only made sense that they'd fit comfortably into the places he just…didn't.

"Sorry about that," Sabine said, returning to him. She slid onto the stool beside him and clinked her wine glass against his. "What's going on with you?"

"What do you mean?" he hedged, facing the kitchen again and giving his back to the things that made him uncomfortable.

"I mean," she dropped her voice. "You're very quiet today. And I noticed."

"Sometimes people are quiet," he replied, that old defensiveness kicking in. He forced a smile to try to cover it.

Sabine's smile was immediate and warm. And she didn't push. She just drank her wine, sitting beside him, not pestering. Though he doubted he'd ever see her as a pest. She could pepper him with questions for hours and he'd soak up all her attention the way grass soaked up sunlight.

And that should have settled him.

But he was decidedly *un*settled.

He couldn't stop thinking about how much fun his friends had had with her. And not with him. It was as confusing as it sounded. Was he jealous?

How stupid would that be?

He wasn't a jealous person.

Never had been.

Max and Leslie were his friends. And Sabine was his friend. (The hottest friend he'd ever had, but whatever.)

Separate parts of his life were mixing when he wasn't around, and it made him uneasy. How could he make sure everyone still got along if he wasn't there to smooth everything over?

Except they had gotten along just fine. So well in fact that Dave was sad he hadn't been able to be a part of it.

But if he'd been there, he'd have been so preoccupied with making sure everyone was getting along, that he wouldn't have had the fun that they did.

Was he a wet blanket?

No.

He rejected that notion immediately.

He was the rebel, the renegade, the one that got everyone in trouble.

But that wasn't the entire picture either, was it?

"I am just now realizing that I may have some control issues," he said out loud. To Sabine.

It was the kind of statement that should probably stay inside but it was too late for that.

She rotated slightly his direction.

"Why do think that is?" She tilted her head to the side, and his vision was drawn to the wide opening of the collar of her sweater. It exposed the tops of her shoulders and her entire collarbone. Skinny black straps disappeared into the sweater and he wondered if it was the same silky tank top she was wearing the day they met.

He didn't remember people's clothes very often. But he remembered that tank top.

"I just want everyone to get along," he said with a sigh. "I hate misunderstandings."

"Do you think you're capable of smoothing out all misunderstandings?"

"Yes," he replied evenly.

Her eyebrows twitched higher. He'd surprised her.

He peeled the label on the cider. "Logically, I know that's not realistic." He looked back up at her. "But I still think that way."

"It's okay to be misunderstood," she said, her voice soft, careful.

Everything inside of him hardened at her words. She didn't get it. How could she?

He shook his head, disappointment flowing through him. "Nah. Misunderstandings lead to misery."

"Or," she touched his arm, calling his eyes back to hers. "Misunderstandings are a place to learn more."

Again, everything inside him rebelled against that idea. But she looked at him with such calm assurance that he couldn't help questioning his own convictions.

"People don't want to learn more," he argued, still holding tight to his irritation.

"Don't I know it," she agreed. Then those hazel eyes—those fucking swirls of green and brown and gold that made him feel like the dumbest, most important piece of shit in the world—scanned his face. She was looking at his tattoos.

And for the first time since he'd started tattooing his face, he wished he hadn't.

"I think the rose is my favorite," she said finally. "But the bird is a close second."

"Why is the rose your favorite?" he asked, shoving aside his insecurities and focusing on the curve of her collarbone and how much he wanted to touch it.

"It's classic." She shrugged, her sweater dropping just a little more off her shoulder.

"Do you have any tattoos?" he asked, craning his neck like he was looking for what he suspected didn't exist. "I haven't seen any."

Her lips twisted to the side as she glanced away.

"Wait. That looks like you have a secret," he teased.

Her cheeks bloomed hot pink and she shook her head. She covered her mouth with her hand and avoided eye contact.

Oh. She had a tattoo that was either embarrassing or in a personal location.

Or both.

Now that was a distracting thought.

"Tell me." He tugged on her sweater sleeve.

"Okay, but you can't make fun of me." She arched an eyebrow at him.

"Never," he promised.

"I have a rose on my hip…" She dipped her chin and lifted just her eyes to him. "And a Jamiroquai tattoo on my butt." Her cheeks turned an even hotter pink before she covered her face with both hands.

Dave couldn't move.

Such was the information she'd just given him.

Slowly, deliberately, he reached for her arms and gently pulled her hands away from her face. Her sweater was even softer than he'd imagined, and he encircled her wrists with his hands.

Her smile, all embarrassed and shy, was quite possibly the hottest thing he had ever seen.

"You said you wouldn't make fun of me," she reminded him.

He took a calm breath, completely enamored with the woman in front of him.

"Don't take this the wrong way," he said, still holding her wrists in his hands and looking directly into that gorgeous green and gold swirl, "But I am completely in love with you."

* * *

SABINE

"Mama Capone!" Max said loudly from the area of the front door. "Dave! Your mom is here!"

Dave broke eye contact with her and let go of her simultaneously. The sudden disconnect was disorienting enough that Sabine forgot for a second that it was her loft and she should probably greet the newcomer.

Because she was still hanging on to that last thing he'd just said.

He had just said that right? She hadn't imagined that entire interaction.

Right?

Her eyes darted to Kara who was frowning at her.

Sabine just shook her head and shrugged.

Don't take it the wrong way?

What?

How?

What?

"Sabine, this is my mom."

Dave was back in front of her.

Sabine had not moved at all in however much time had passed. Minutes? Hours? A week? What day was it?

"Hi," she said to the woman standing beside Dave. She slid off the stool to her feet.

"This is Sabine. This is her place." Dave draped an arm around the smaller woman and hugged her to his side.

Dave's mom was somehow not what Sabine had pictured and yet made complete sense.

She was taller than Sabine but shorter than Dave. Her eyes were a lighter

145

blue than Dave's. She had brunette hair without a trace of gray that she wore in loose, beachy waves.

But it was the orange snakeskin bellbottoms that drew the eye. She had paired the bellbottoms with a white gauzy top and layers and layers of necklaces and huge silver moon earrings.

She looked too young to be Dave's mom but that was probably the point.

"You can call me Cherry," his mom replied with a brilliant smile. "I'm just in from Tulum and I didn't bring anything for this weather. I love your loft." She took a step back, her vision taking in all that was Sabine and Kara's dwelling. "I love it when they convert old warehouses. Is that Leslie?"

"Cherry!" Leslie greeted, calling the woman toward the living room.

Sabine's eyes bounced from Leslie to Max to Kara to André to Cherry but not to Dave.

The timer went off.

"Oh." Sabine held up a finger. "I have to baste."

"Hey, you okay?" Kara asked, voice hushed.

Sabine continued to baste and nodded. "Sure. Fine. It's all fine." She put the lid back on the roaster and leveled a look at Kara. "Remind me that it's a bad idea to drink too much."

Kara's lips twitched. "I will do no such thing. You're a blast when you're wine drunk."

"You're no help."

Kara shrugged. "Should I make it a holiday pour?"

"What are you two whispering about out here?" Max joined them, pushing his sleeves up to his elbows.

"You have Timothy Dalton eyebrows," Sabine said, finally figuring out why he looked so familiar to her.

"I don't know how I feel about that," Max replied self-consciously.

"You should feel good about it," Kara reassured him. Then to Sabine she said, "What happened?"

Sabine looked from her best friend to Dave's best friend. "I can't tell you," she said slowly.

Kara's eyes narrowed slightly, and she glanced at Max.

"What did he say? Did he say something mean?" Max asked, disappointment clouding his features.

"No." Sabine shook her head. "Nothing like that."

Should she tell them? *Could* she tell them?

Just the very idea of repeating the words made her face heat.

"Is it hot in here? Should I open a window?" She left the kitchen and went to the balcony off the dining room. She opened the door, stepped outside and closed the door behind her.

The cold wind cut through her clothes and her skin but she still couldn't think clearly.

And now she was standing outside in freezing temperatures.

Great.

She could imagine the questions when she went back inside.

There were so many *people* in her home. Whose idea had this been?

Oh right.

Dave's.

Dave and his "dimples" remark.

"Aghhhh!" she shouted into the wind. "This is stupid!"

She sucked in one more breath, willing the cold to freeze her soul until the end of the day. Then she went back inside.

"Are you okay?" Leslie asked, concern evident in his tone and expression.

"Fine." Sabine's eyes connected with her brother's. André was wearing a small smirk and he arched an eyebrow at her. She straightened her sweater and squared her shoulders. "Just had to scream into the void for a moment, that's all."

* * *

"Who's the boy?"

Sabine glanced up as her brother joined her in the kitchen. The place she'd been hiding out for the past hour.

"Which one?" she asked, knowing full well which one.

Max and Leslie were dressed like André—in sweaters and slacks. Dave was in jeans and a hoodie.

"The one who looks at you like his next breath depends on it."

Sabine glared at her brother. "We're not close enough to have that kind of a conversation."

He barked a laugh. "Is that your way of telling me off for being busy?"

"Busy?"

"It's been an intense semester," he admitted. "I should have called more."

She shrugged, letting it go.

He sidled up next to her and bumped her shoulder with his. "Is he the reason you had to scream into the void?"

She chuckled despite herself. "Maybe."

"You get that from our father, you know. He screams into the void often. Most especially when his forwards aren't living up to his very reasonable expectations."

She snorted. "Is it still the void when half the country can see it on television?"

André hummed and slid his hands into his pockets.

They stood side by side in the kitchen for a minute, looking out at the rest of her guests having a lovely time. Cherry was telling some sort of story with graceful hands and animated facial expressions.

From this distance, Sabine could see the "whacky aunt" vibe that Leslie had mentioned.

She was quite captivating.

And elegant in a wild sort of way.

Sabine touched one of her braids where it disappeared into the knot at the back of her head and then glanced down at her wool socks that poked out from the hem of her favorite pair of jeans. They were her favorite because they were the most broken in—super soft and frayed in all the right places.

She watched as Cherry leaned over and touched the Peter Pan collar of Kara's dress. The dress was super cute—baby blue with white scalloped trim at the sleeves and neck. The hem hit Kara mid-thigh, making her legs look a mile long.

Sabine's heart did a sad, slow slide to the floor where she kicked it under the oven with her wool socks.

"Are you going to see him for Christmas?" she asked, referring to their father.

André rolled his eyes. "Are you?"

She chuckled.

"So me, you, and a batch of cookies?"

"Absolutely."

"Oh hey," she said, frowning. "Do you know someone named Nikki…?"

She made a face because she didn't know Nikki's last name. "She works at a recording studio?"

André straightened and sighed. "Nicole. Yes. I-we-dated…" His voice trailed off and he studied the floor intently.

"So she's an ex?" Sabine didn't meet all the women André dated, only some. She figured when he was serious about one, he'd let her know.

"Yes and no." André made a groaning noise in the back of his throat like a car dying. "Did she mention me?"

Sabine crossed her arms over her chest and angled her body toward him. "Sort of. She heard my last name and asked if we were related. When I asked if she knew you, she said no."

André grimaced and raked a hand through his hair. Sabine remained perfectly still. André wasn't one to get flustered.

He blinked at her, at the floor, cocked his head to the side, and rolled his eyes. It was like he was having an intense internal debate with himself.

"We were engaged," he said so quietly that she thought for a second she'd misheard him. But his shame-filled eyes darted up to hers and she sucked in a breath.

"Engaged!" she repeated.

"Quiet," he hissed, forcing a smile over her shoulder. "Yes, engaged." He stepped closer to her. "I didn't tell you because it's not my proudest moment."

She put her hands on her hips and tapped her foot.

He scratched the side of his neck and shifted on his feet.

"I took her to meet dad and he said… he said things that dad says and got into my head."

"You took her to London to meet our father but never thought to mention her to me?"

"It's complicated, Sabine," he said, sounding distressed. "It was intense and fast, and we were in Europe for other reasons when I proposed." He held his hands out in front of him, palms down. "I didn't handle it the way I should have."

"What happened?"

"We got back to the city and I…" He dropped his head back and squeezed his eyes shut. He righted himself and sighed. "I ghosted her."

Sabine stared at her brother. Her wonderful, sweet, smart, idiot brother.

"That was about two years ago."

Sabine gave him a slow blink.

Today had been full of surprises, and the turkey hadn't even been served yet.

"I think it's time to open more wine."

He nodded and went for the fridge.

* * *

"Are you doing Saint-Tropez for Christmas this year?" Cherry asked from the head of the table.

Sabine and Max exchanged a look.

Cherry had been dropping hints throughout the day that Chicago wasn't where she thought her son should be spending the holiday. That perhaps Dave should be someplace warm with people who weren't people he got to see all the time anyway.

She hadn't come right out and said it, but it was obvious that she thought a traditional Thanksgiving was boring.

"I have a friend." Cherry stopped and smirked. "Well, we're more than friends. Anyway, he has a yacht. I spent President's Day there."

"Ah, yes," Max remarked. "The sexiest of all the holidays."

Cherry slid her eyes in his direction but didn't respond.

Max had gotten into the pink wine and his comments had started to get louder as the day had progressed. On one hand, Sabine was a little worried Max was going to cause trouble for Dave. On the other, Max was increasingly hilarious.

And Kara, that little chaos demon, just kept the man's glass full.

"Max," Kara stood up. "Do you think you could teach me how to properly load the dishwasher?"

Max stood up, chagrined. "How are you a functioning adult and you don't know how to load the dishwasher?"

Kara waggled her eyebrows at Sabine and sashayed her way to the kitchen.

Oh.

Kara and Max?

It wasn't the worst idea.

"You're a teacher?" Cherry asked, addressing Sabine.

"I'm a private tutor," Sabine replied, her gut twisting in on itself.

150

"Dave could never get along with teachers," Cherry said, the smile on her face not matching the implications of her statement. "They were always convinced there was something wrong with him." She tilted her head and smiled sweetly at her son. "But he just needed room to breathe."

"I think it's neat that both of you are in education," Leslie broke in, nodding his head at André. "How did that happen?"

"Is it true what they say?" Cherry asked. "Those who can't do, teach?" Again, she was smiling but not really.

André, more practiced at social situations like this, leaned back in his chair and put on his professor face. "I *do* and I teach. I teach archaeology at Wheaton. And I have a small paleontology class this semester as well. But next summer I'm joining a dig in South Dakota."

"Oh, you got it!" Sabine exclaimed. "That's awesome." He'd told her he'd applied to a private company that did excavations but she hadn't heard any update.

André smiled at her reaction and then sobered again, addressing Cherry. "Sabine's been teaching since she was small. She's always seen the world in a complex way and taken it upon herself to make sure everyone could see the full picture. She has the heart of a teacher."

Sabine blushed and looked down. She reached for her wine. She wasn't sure she was as cool as her older brother made her sound, but it was nice to hear.

"I'd agree with that," Dave spoke up.

She glanced at him, and he sent her a soft smile.

"She helps me see things in ways I hadn't before."

Oh.

That felt…

Incredible.

She should not add that to how he'd told her he loved her because that was a lot to process in one day. But oops, there she went, throwing all of it into the same pile and then staring at it like a lovesick dope.

"You're going to dig up dinosaurs this summer?" Leslie asked André who nodded.

"That's so cool!" Dave said, sounding more than a little enamored. "Dinosaurs are awesome."

André chuckled softly, and Sabine smiled at her older brother. She was very proud of him. Professor Debois…who had ghosted his fiancée. Oh, she was just going to strangle him later. When there weren't quite so many witnesses.

"Who wants pie?" Sabine asked, shoving away from the table.

A chorus of "me" went around the table. Except Cherry who stood and pushed her chair in.

"Actually, I should be going. I have an early flight and I need my beauty sleep."

"Wait. You're leaving?" Dave asked.

"I'm heading to Lisbon tomorrow."

"Tomorrow?" Dave repeated, his face scrunched in a frown. "Didn't Gloria get ahold of you?"

Sabine was missing something. She looked to Leslie for answers but he'd gone silent and just stared at the table with sad eyes.

"I told you, remember? I'm going to Lisbon for two weeks. I can't stay here in the cold climate. It makes my body hurt." She wrapped her arms around herself as if there was a draft.

Which there was *not.* Sabine had gone through the loft with an infrared gun to be sure every crack and crevasse was sealed.

"But—" Dave frowned harder. "I thought—"

"Cherry," Max interrupted sternly. "The NMAs are at the end of the week. You were to be Dave's date."

To her credit, Cherry looked stunned and remorseful all at once.

"Oh, my goodness. I completely forgot. I'll cancel." She dug into her purse. "I'll fix this."

But she was still heading for the door.

"Gimme a hug, baby." She waved Dave toward her and hugged him tight. "I'll fix this, yeah? I need to make some calls and I'll get ahold of you tomorrow."

Dave hugged his mom again, and something about it made Sabine's chest ache. Like he didn't want to let her go.

A few minutes later, the hurricane known as Cherry, had departed.

And Dave had retreated to the sofa.

Alone.

André bumped her with an elbow. "I'll bring you both pie."

She smiled her thanks and joined Dave on the sofa.

"Did you get enough to eat?" she asked.

He nodded.

"So traditionally we now eat pie and watch *National Lampoon's Christmas Vacation.* Are you up for that?" she asked.

He smiled at her and took a deep breath. "She's not going to cancel her plans."

"You don't know that. She might. Who wouldn't want to go to an awards show? I'd much rather do that than go to Portugal."

He smirked, and she knew he knew she was just trying to make him feel better.

But she didn't know what else to do.

He loved his mom. And she wasn't going to talk shit about a woman she didn't know.

"You'd go with me?" he asked.

"For sure!" she declared. "Not even a debate. What does Portugal have?" she scoffed.

"I'm taking pie orders," Kara called from the buffet.

Dave draped an arm over the back of the sofa as he turned around. "I'll take a slice of each different kind."

Kara lifted her eyebrows but didn't argue. "And what about you?"

"Pecan, please." Sabine smiled brightly.

Kara and Max served up the pie, Leslie refilled wine glasses, André got the movie started.

Dave moved closer to Sabine on the couch, until their thighs were pressed against each other. When the pie was eaten, he pulled a fluffy blanket over the both of them and snuggled against her.

"I am thankful for you," he whispered in her ear as he wrapped his arms around her and settled in.

And before Clark Griswold lost it on Santa and the eight tiny reindeer, Dave had fallen asleep.

Chapter Fourteen
Delicate

DAVE

"How was your Thanksgiving?"

"I think, just judging by the dopey smile on his face, that it went well?" Johnny said when Dave hadn't answered.

Dave didn't even care. He shrugged, keeping his smile right where it belonged. He glanced to his left and tugged his love beanie down over his eyes.

Hannah James' smirk grew a fraction and she snorted. "So why are you hanging out here? Looking for guidance from your elders?"

Johnny chuckled before getting up from his chair. He slid his fingers through Hannah's hair on his way past her and out the door. "I have to switch out those pedals."

Hannah closed her eyes and her face relaxed at his touch.

Dave wondered at that. How did something like their friendship grow into what they had? Was it an accident? Was it purposeful? Did someone pave the way?

He'd been there, er, here, when Johnny and Hannah had "started." It

155

seemed so small and uninteresting to him. The music they'd made that week had been far more exciting.

But that just goes to show that people only see what they want to see.

Or, in Dave's case, he'd chased the dopamine.

"Are you happy?" Dave asked.

Hannah tilted her head to the side and her face softened. "Yeah. I really am."

"Good for you." Dave offered a fist bump which she accepted though she looked amused. He sat back in the couch cushions and crossed his arms over his chest.

"What's going on, Dave?" Hannah asked.

"Nothing," he answered honestly. "I wish something was going on, but…" He made a face and shrugged.

"Do you have anything you want to talk about?" she asked slowly.

He shot her a lopsided smile. "Did that feel as uncomfortable to ask as it sounded?"

She scrunched her face. "Sorry. That obvious, huh? I'm trying something new."

He chuckled. "I appreciate it. But no, there's nothing to talk about."

She rolled her lips inward and nodded.

"Are you going to the NMA's next week?" Dave asked.

Hannah jerked her chin back. "Fuck no."

Dave laughed. "Yeah. I wish I was strong like you."

"What's that supposed to mean?"

"You just live your life. On your terms. No one makes rules for you."

Hannah frowned. She sucked in a breath and paused. She licked her lips. "Dave. You can do whatever you want."

He rolled his eyes. "No, I can't. Not really. When I do what I want, people get confused and I hurt their feelings and… Ugh. It's too hard to explain."

Hannah chuckled darkly and he narrowed his eyes at her.

"If you go, and you see Coach Riley, ask him how his nose is."

He chuckled. "I don't know if I'll remember, but if I do, you got it. And I have to go. My… management team is adamant that I go and make a public appearance."

"Right." She nodded. "Still repairing your image after the house fire."

"I'm supposed to take my mom and wear an actual tuxedo and everything." He rolled his neck, trying to fight the tension building as he thought about the event. "I agreed to perform and present."

Hannah whistled low. "That's a lotta bullshit."

He laughed again because he agreed. And it felt good to laugh with someone who knew what he was talking about.

"What are you working on lately?" she asked, swiveling the stool she was on to face the control board.

"Nothing solid. I'm supposed to be writing and recording the third album. That's the only reason Curtis hasn't been around. I told him I needed space to make it work." He widened his eyes and filled his cheeks with air. "But I have not been doing anything."

"Nothing?"

"Well…I'm always writing. But it's not anything I can use. It's mostly me venting my frustrations."

She spun back around and lifted her chin. "Can I hear some of it?"

He thought about it. "They're mostly voice notes. They won't make any sense."

Hannah rolled her eyes. "No, I get that. But let's work through it. Sometimes you have to take the lid off to see what else is inside."

He eyed her, intrigued by the challenge in her tone.

How had he gotten so lucky as to have the coolest people in the world on his team? It didn't make sense. It was like he'd stumbled into fortune again and again. He hadn't earned it. He didn't deserve it. And yet he knew, just by looking at her, Hannah would go to bat for him for literally any reason.

He opened his phone and picked the one he'd taken after his most recent phone call with Curtis. "You gonna give me a beat or what?" he asked, lifting his eyes to Hannah.

She covered her mouth and started beat boxing. He shook his head because Hannah Lee was absolutely at her hottest when she was beat boxing.

"But when I leave,
I got no team,
Supportin' like enemies,
How to think, how to act, who to be, how to be,
What's what, and that's that,
Throughout the map,

It's
—You ain't right kid,
—You ain't shit,
Get the fuck up so I can kick you again.

Now I ain't you and I ain't psychic,
I think you think you're helpin'
But you actin a dickhead,
I'm frustrated too but I don't make it your business,

I'm going to do what I do and you'll be a witness,
I slip but I finish,
I fell but, get this,
I have a team at home,
And fire I can't quench,
I will continue,
I will not forget,
The support from my girl that I can't help but win,
She keeps me on target like Katniss,
She's my arrow, I can't miss,
I don't need you for clout,
You spin me out,
Fill me with doubt,
Divide like partitions,
More walls and divisions,
Nellie Bertram leaves me in stitches."

He sat back in the couch and laughed at his own absurdity. "That's it. That's what I got."

Hannah clapped her hands and Johnny—who had returned sometime during that—joined her.

"Are we working or playing?" Johnny asked.

Someone else asking that question and Dave would've bristled. But there was a reason he had found his producer. He didn't want to press record with anyone else. Johnny Torres was it. Probably the best in the business. And that was because he respected his artists.

"Just playing."

Hannah's bright smile turned sneaky and she cleared her throat. "Who's ah, who's your girl?"

"What? I don't have a girl." Dave's face flamed hot but he didn't know why. He didn't have a girl.

"You said *'support from my girl that I can't help but win, she keeps me on target like Katniss, she's my arrow, I can't miss.'"*

He narrowed his eyes at her and she met his gaze unflinching.

"You just memorized that bit, huh?"

"It was catchy," she said seriously.

A minute passed, neither one looking away. Dave finally shrugged one shoulder. "It's just a verse. It fit."

"Uh huh."

Truth was, he knew exactly what girl had inspired that rhyme. But he couldn't explain how it was just because she was kickass and awesome and had nothing to do with whatever Hannah was trying to imply.

Nothing whatsoever.

His phone, still in his hand, rang.

He held Hannah's stare as he answered.

"Hey, ma."

"Hey, baby." The apologetic tone in her voice had his insides collapsing in on themselves.

She wasn't coming.

"I thought I could get back in time for the show but Ricardo's plane has run into some trouble and we're too far away from any major airports."

She said more things.

Nice things.

Apologetic things.

Flattering things.

Dave wished he was the type of person that didn't chase everyone away.

"It's okay, ma," he said. "Have fun. Be safe."

The phone dropped onto the floor after the call disconnected and he didn't retrieve it.

"Curtis is going to be pissed. So much for the perfect PR moment." He snorted and dropped his head back. "Maybe I should fake strep throat or something."

"Orrr," Hannah said. "You could go with a friend."

"Are you volunteering?" he asked with a scowl.

She scoffed. "Gross. No, I mean, go with a friend. Like Max or Leslie or Sabine or someone." She shifted her eyes away and Dave knew that if he were a different person, he'd pick up on whatever she was trying to hide. Or imply? Or hint at.

But as it stood, he couldn't read her mind and it frustrated him.

"Just say what you're not saying," he grumbled. "I can't decipher code."

Hannah's cool blue eyes narrowed to dangerous slits and she pursed her lips. "Ask Sabine to go with you. You guys seem to get along and you know she won't be overwhelmed by a bunch of celebrities. You might have a good time."

Huh.

That *was* a good idea.

"You think she'll go for it?" he asked, a memory tickling in the back of his mind of her saying that she'd choose an award show with him over going to Portugal.

But people said shit all the time.

"What song are you doing?" Hannah asked.

"Uh, they're honoring The Supremes so they asked me to do a cover of 'You Can't Hurry Love.'"

"You're not doing one of your own? That last album was a banger. They didn't want you to do one of those?"

Dave made a noise in his throat. "I'm still doing it *my* way. The only thing the same is the chorus. The arrangement is all new and I wrote new verses."

Hannah made a face and pressed her lips together.

"Did you already record it?" Johnny asked, casting a side-eye to Hannah.

"Yeah. They had to approve it ahead of time. I flew out to L.A. and did it in an afternoon."

Johnny ran his tongue over his teeth and faced the sound board.

"What?" Dave asked.

"Nothing." Hannah rubbed her palms on her thighs. "Just business stuff. You should ask Sabine. I think you'll have a good time."

She made it sound so simple. *Just ask Sabine.*

Of course, they'd have a good time. They always had a great time when they were together. That wasn't the problem.

The problem was that it might look like it was more than just two people hanging out.

And he'd been lectured by his manager, his publicist, and even Quinn Sullivan that anyone he dated would have to be vetted thoroughly beforehand.

And that was a commitment he couldn't make.

Not for himself and definitely not for anyone else.

But he and Sabine had a nice friendship. Maybe if he was clear this was a friend thing it would be okay.

She hadn't implied she was interested in anything more and neither had he—he'd been very careful.

Also, Hannah was right. Sabine would be super cool about the red carpet and anyone they had to interact with. She was probably better suited for that size of an event than even Max.

Okay… okay.

He bent over and retrieved his phone. He called up their last text exchange and smiled. It was a terrible joke about Spaceballs.

She was the best.

DAVE: mom bailed. Are you busy on Saturday?

He looked up at Hannah and tried to ignore how he could feel his pulse in his fingertips.

"She might have to work," he said, thinking out loud. "She works weekends at this nerd bar. She might not want to miss out on tips. Not for something like this."

Hannah didn't look convinced.

His phone pinged.

SABINE: I'm free on Saturday

"She said she's free on Saturday." He exchanged a smile with Hannah.

"Who's dressing you?" Hannah asked.

"Catherine is meeting me at Leslie's."

Catherine always dressed him. She was a costume designer in Hollywood, and she was the only one who he trusted to not make him look like someone he wasn't. She dressed him for big events, photo shoots, music videos—all of it.

"You need to let her know she needs to bring something for Sabine."

"You think?"

"I do think. And I think you need to give Sabine's number to Catherine so she can get her measurements."

Dave frowned at Hannah. He understood what she was saying but it didn't make sense. Not really.

"Won't Sabine want to wear her own clothes?"

Hannah pressed the fingertips of one hand to her forehead while crossing her chest with her other arm. "Oh, sweet motherfucking shit balls," she muttered. And then directly to him she said, "Please trust me on this. Provide a dress for her. Shoes, jewelry, hair, makeup—all of it."

"Okay," he agreed, alarmed by Hannah's reaction. "I can do that."

"Do you have an assistant?" she asked. She dropped her hand from her forehead to cup her opposite elbow.

"Sometimes," he admitted. "But I drive them crazy and they usually quit after a couple weeks."

"You don't say." Hannah took a deep breath and forced a smile. "It's gonna be fine. I'll walk you through it."

Chapter Fifteen
Homemade Dynamite

It's not a date, it's not a date, it's not a date.

She reminded herself a thousand times as she stared at the perfume on her dresser.

She wanted to smell good.

Why she had fixated on smell of all the things she could have fixated on, she had no idea. But for some reason, how she smelled had gone to the top of the list of things to worry about.

So much so, that the night before she'd had a dream where her perfume had caused everyone at the awards show to go into anaphylactic shock.

She basically had two options.

Okay she had three.

A super sexy, warm scent, that was definitely more of a "night" perfume.

A bright, fresh faintly floral scent that she wore daily.

Or nothing.

She grabbed both bottles and shoved them into her bag. She would ask the stylist person when she got there.

A stylist.

Catherine.

Sabine didn't know her last name. Just that some unknown number had begun asking her very personal questions a few days ago.

A heads-up would have saved her the panic attack. But Dave hadn't thought to tell her.

Honestly, Sabine felt silly for not figuring it out sooner.

She rushed out the door and to the elevator. She checked her phone for the time. Damn it. Her ride was probably waiting.

She hated being late.

By the time the elevator released her onto the main floor, she was sweating.

Dave's security man, Darius Masoud, was waiting by the door. He greeted her with his brilliant smile, and she hopped into the back of the black SUV.

If Darius was picking her up, then that meant Dallas was getting Dave.

"How's your day, Mr. Masoud?' she asked him.

"It's been uneventful, Miss Debois."

"You can call me Sabine," she reminded him. For the tenth time.

"Please call me Darius."

"I suppose that's fair." She sighed and looked out the window at the city as they drove through town.

To the private plane that was going to take them to Los Angeles.

If she thought about it, she would throw up.

When Dave had asked her if she was free on Saturday, she really should have asked more questions.

But no.

She'd jumped at the chance to be there for him.

Literally.

Her phone had pinged with his text and she'd jumped on her bed for a full two minutes before she'd responded. Partly because she needed to expel the energy she wanted to use to hunt down his mom and coochie punch her. And partly because she wanted to be that person for him. The one he called when he needed someone.

And if that didn't say stupid crush, nothing did.

As it was, she did not ask questions.

On Tuesday someone named Gloria called her and asked for her bio. "I just need a sentence or two. For the statements."

Then she received several emails of documents that needed her electronic signature. Most of them NDAs.

Then a man named Curtis called her and made sure she understood that under no circumstances whatsoever was she allowed to think of this event as a promise, date, courtship, or otherwise romantic entanglement. That she was Mr. Capone's guest and would have certain privileges that would immediately be revoked if she even so much as thought about Mr. Capone in a romantic way. He had a document for her to sign about that as well.

At which point she finally broke down and called Dave. For the first time.

They had texted often enough that she shouldn't have been as nervous as she was to call him.

But calling was different from texting.

Texting was saying, "hey, not to bother you but when you get a minute here's a question." Calling was more like, "answer me now."

Which was a lot pushier than she liked to be.

Especially with a cute boy.

Wait. Who said that?

Anyway, he'd answered and that's when she'd found out about the private plane and the fact that she needed the entire weekend off, not just Saturday night.

Again, she blamed herself.

Any Google search would have told her that the NMAs were in L.A. Common sense would then dictate that they would have to leave sometime before the event started.

She really had no excuse for why she was so taken off guard.

After a very evasive conversation with Big Mike about why she couldn't work that weekend, she'd packed a bag.

Well, Kara had packed the bag. Sabine had paced.

The small airport came into view and Sabine peered through the front window.

"I had no idea this airport even existed," she muttered.

"There are actually twelve active airports in the Chicago area," Darius informed her.

"Oh." Silly her, she only knew of the two major ones. A thought occurred to her. "Are you coming with us?"

"Yes. Dallas and I will be accompanying you this weekend."

For some reason that eased some of her nerves.

"Good. I'm glad." She looked forward to Dallas's calming presence. It steadied her. Plus, having security there made it feel less… intimate.

Darius flashed his Disney prince smile. "Nervous?"

Sabine blew out a breath. "Yes. But not for the reasons you might think." She gazed at the jet waiting on the runway. "Have you ever liked someone more than you know you're supposed to, but still can't talk yourself out of it?"

Darius put the SUV into park and chuckled softly. "Maybe someday I'll tell you about the time I fell in love with a thief."

She swung her eyes around to him. "What happened?"

He grinned again, all teeth and blinding beauty. "I married her."

Damn. She hadn't seen that coming.

Darius took her bag and his, and gestured for her to go to the jet. He handed their bags off to flight personnel and joined her at the stairs.

"Whoa," she muttered, entering the main cabin. "I feel like Tony Stark."

The interior looked about how they all looked in the movies. And yet, it still seemed unexpected. It was all white leather and wood accents. It looked like what she'd expect a yacht to look like, not a jet.

But maybe there was only one design for the super-rich.

A long leather couch was against one side facing a television. Four chairs sat in facing pairs near the pilot's cabin. Four more chairs and a table were tucked into the back corner next to a doorway which narrowed into a hallway with more untold things. Probably a gold toilet.

If she had a chance during the flight, she was totally going to check it out.

Dave emerged from the narrow hallway and his mouth split into a grin when he spotted her.

He was in jeans, as usual. But unusually, he wasn't wearing a hoodie. He was in a plain white t-shirt and she could see the tattoos that snaked around both of his arms and disappeared up his sleeves. She couldn't remember if she'd ever seen him without long sleeves, but she didn't think she had.

At least not in person.

"You made it!"

"You beat me," she said, surprised.

"That's because Dallas was in charge of me today," he answered ruefully.

Dallas tipped her head silently at Sabine in greeting. Darius joined her in one of the big chairs near the front of the jet.

Dave waved Sabine to the chairs with the table. "I have food for you." He grabbed a blue hoodie and tugged it on over his head.

Her stomach growled, and she was pretty sure he heard it because he smirked as he sat down.

"Nothing fancy. I just picked up some sandwiches on the way over." He watched her take a seat across from him and let the flight attendant take her coat. "I like your sweater."

She glanced down. She was in one of her standard cardigans that she wore for work and a short navy skirt. It wasn't scandalous or anything, but it was shorter than she usually wore. She paired it with opaque black tights. They were still in Chicago after all.

But the light burgundy cardigan did have little pink bows where the buttons went. She touched one of the bows and smiled.

"I like fun things." She shrugged.

The flight attendant closed the door and informed them they'd be taking off in five minutes.

Sabine's stomach churned with anxiety and she gripped the arms of the chair.

"You've flown before, right?" Dave asked, eyeing her hands.

"Just commercially."

"This is way smoother. You'll like it."

The engine whine increased, and she braced as the jet taxied down the runway. She sucked in a breath and held it as the jet lifted into the air. Dave watched her, an amused expression on his face.

"Are you okay?" he asked.

"Hm-mm," she nodded tightly.

His amused expression spread into a smile and she closed her eyes. She needed to focus on *not* throwing up.

The takeoffs were the hardest part for her. After that, she usually did much better.

The jet began to level out, but her stomach was still climbing into her throat.

She relaxed her grip on the armrests and patted them gently.

"I like your jet. Do you have a matching yacht? Do they come in pairs?" she asked, trying to joke around despite the tremble in her limbs.

Dave scoffed and passed out the food.

"It's not mine. It belongs to the label. If I had one of my own it would not look like this."

She smiled, the knot in her stomach loosening slightly. "Oh yeah? What would yours look like?"

"For starters, it would not have wood paneling. Fucking hate wood paneling."

She chuckled, surprised by his answer but delighted all the same.

Because it was a nice reminder of who she was with and why she'd said yes to a crazy weekend. This was Dave. Her friend. Who went drunk grocery shopping with her and wore a lightsaber with his bathrobe.

"Hey," he said, suddenly serious. "I'm sorry this week was so chaotic. Hannah chewed me out pretty good for not being clearer with you. I'm not a details guy. But I'm trying to get better."

"Oh," she said, startled by his candor. "It's okay."

He shook his head and rested his hand on the table. "It's not okay." His hand clenched a napkin. "I really appreciate you doing this for me. I need to be better at taking care of my inner circle."

Her eyebrows raised at that. "Inner circle, huh?"

"Shut up," he muttered, and took a bite of his sandwich. But she could swear there was a hint of pink on his cheeks.

"I just..." He frowned, obviously still not thinking it was okay despite her saying it was. "Sometimes I forget that not everyone sees what I see. Especially the people closest to me. I should have planned better." He scratched the sun tattoo on his throat. "Or maybe I should try to get another assistant. I am *not* good at planning."

Sabine rested her hand over his on top of the table. "Hey." He met her eyes. "Thank you for the apology. Next time I'll call you sooner if I have questions." She shrugged and removed her hand. "We both learned something in this."

He watched her carefully, like he was trying to decide if he should agree with her.

"You're a really great person," he said. "Like, top tier human."

She shook her head and swallowed another smile.

She'd been reading up on inattentive ADHD so what he was saying made more sense to her than it probably would to someone unfamiliar with it.

But she wasn't about to tell him that.

What if he misunderstood her intentions?

All she knew was that there was something she could do to learn more about him and she'd gone after it.

She'd done the same when Kara had been diagnosed celiac.

It was in her nature to care for her people with all the talent she had. And her talent was education and application thereof.

"Will Curtis be joining us?" she asked, focusing on her own sandwich and hoping her tone didn't reveal her aversion of the man.

"No. Why?" Dave put the sandwich down and wiped his mouth with a napkin. "You gotta thing for Curtis?" he asked, a tease in his eyes.

She rolled her eyes but had a hard time hiding her smile. "Right. That's it."

He chuckled and sat back in his chair.

"We might see Curtis." He rolled his eyes. "He wanted us to stay at his place this weekend but I passed."

Sabine's nose scrunched up in distaste all on its own, and Dave must've noticed because he barked a laugh.

"Exactly what I was thinking. Did you have to talk to him a lot?" he asked, expression guarded.

"Oh, just enough for me to absolutely know without a doubt that you and I are friends, just friends, and nothing but friends. I'm surprised he didn't ask me to produce proof I'm taking birth control."

Shut up, Sabine. Why had she said that? So stupid.

Dave choked on his sandwich and she focused on her own food.

"I'm sorry about him," he said after he'd recovered.

"Let me guess, it's not his fault?" she asked with an eyebrow quirk.

"I'm not easy to manage."

That was it.

Sabine put her sandwich down and narrowed her eyes at him.

"Stop that."

"Stop what?"

"Stop blaming everyone else's poor choices on yourself. They're not children, Dave. They're responsible for their own decisions. Not you."

His mouth opened and he started to speak and stopped.

She took that as an opportunity to say more.

"People fuck up. They make mistakes and choices and break things. It's not on you to apologize for them and smooth it all over. All you have to worry about is you. Stop taking on the emotional burden of other people. Especially people who would never do the same for you."

His eyes darted to Darius and Dallas sitting too far away to hear her. But it really helped solidify her belief that he cared far too much what people thought of him.

"And while I'm at it," she added. "Stop apologizing for who you are." She sucked in a breath because her emotions rose into her throat out of nowhere and she didn't want her voice to tremble. "You're awesome. End of." Her eyes burned and she clenched her jaw. "You are exactly awesome."

She nodded matter-of-factly at him and resumed eating her sandwich. This time staring at the table between them.

What she didn't say, but was right on the tip of her tongue, was she loved him. Exactly as he was. In all shades he showed up in life.

And that was something she could never tell him.

After a few minutes he cleared his throat and reached across the table.

She looked at his outstretched hand and froze. He wiggled his fingers. She glanced up at his face and the pleading she saw in those indigo eyes had her ready to walk through fire for him.

She set her hand in his and he curled his fingers into hers.

"Thank you." He swallowed and squeezed her fingers briefly. He looked like he wanted to say more but didn't know how.

"You're not mad I yelled at you?" she asked with a small smile.

He lifted his eyebrows. "Never."

After a beat of staring into each other's eyes, he squeezed her hand again and let go.

But he took a tiny piece of her heart with him.

* * *

"Welcome! Welcome!" Leslie greeted them in the circle driveway of the house they pulled up to hours later.

"Leslie!" Sabine jumped from the SUV and hugged the tall black man. She tried to squeeze his muscles with her hug but knew she didn't make a dent. "I didn't know you'd be here!"

"Well, it is my house," he explained with a soft laugh. He curled an arm around her shoulders and steered her towards the door. "And when you go to New York, you'll get to stay with Max."

"*If* I go to New York," she corrected.

He hugged her to his side. "I know what I said." He let her go in the entryway of a beautiful one level home.

Darius examined the security system and Dallas stalked through the house like a silent predator. Leslie didn't seem to mind. Or maybe he didn't even notice things like that anymore.

"We do have one small problem," Leslie said when Dave had joined them, setting his bag down in the entry. "I'm storing some equipment for a client and it's taking up two of my spare rooms. And with your security team here as well, you and Sabine will have to share a room. Hope that's okay." Leslie turned without waiting to find out if it was okay or not and led them down the hall.

Sabine shot a glance at Dave who seemed unconcerned.

But all she could hear was Curtis's insistent voice telling her that this was unacceptable.

She was going to be fired from the entourage on her first mission out.

Was that a thing?

Was she mixing her metaphors?

She didn't know, she'd never watched the show.

She should have watched the show! Maybe it would have prepared her.

She jogged to catch up with Dave and Leslie who were discussing dinner plans.

"Maybe I should stay at a hotel or something. I have some points on this app and I think if I stay one more night, I get another night for free."

Both men stopped walking and turned to face her.

Leslie regarded her with what looked like barely tethered amusement.

"No, babe." Dave took her by the elbow and continued walking. "You're staying with me."

Ack!

They weren't listening.

She'd signed so many documents!

It wasn't like they were back at the loft. This was a big deal with big deal consequences. He was essentially working, and she was supposed to be the companion that made him look good for the media.

Curtis and Gloria had both told her that Dave's reputation was on the line and if Sabine did anything to violate all the things she's signed, she was a walking dead woman.

The door was open at the end of the hall and Dave continued inside while Leslie stopped at the door.

Sabine turned in a circle.

One bed. And a small couch. More like a settee.

"Do you have an air mattress?" she asked Leslie hopefully.

He pressed his lips together and shook his head once. "Nope."

"Sabine," Dave said, exasperated. "It's a California King. There'll be three feet between us. I don't sleep much anyway. The bed is basically yours. And we've slept on the same couch together multiple times. What's going on with you?"

She exhaled a strangled sigh. "But Curtis was very clear—"

"Yeah, that motherfucker doesn't run this house," Leslie interrupted her. "He's not my manager and he's not yours." He held her gaze. "Remember that."

Leslie slid his hands into the pockets of his slacks and faced Dave. "Catherine said she'd be here in a couple hours. Dinner will be delivered at six. I will see you both tomorrow."

"Where are you going?" Sabine asked.

"I have a date." He booped her on the nose and then left.

"Are you scared I snore or something?" Dave asked.

She clenched her fists at her sides and turned around.

He was setting up his things on the table next to one side of the bed.

A small spiral bound notebook, two bottled waters, two prescription pill bottles, a phone charger, and what looked like a green lava lamp.

Were those snacks?

Interesting.

She shook herself out of it. She couldn't get distracted by his adorable quirks.

"What if *I* snore?" she asked, still trying to quell the fear that Curtis was going to come storming in the door and arrest her.

He sniffed a laugh. "It won't bother me. I can sleep through anything." He straightened and gave her a thoughtful glance. "I guess I never considered it being weird. I've slept in the same bed as my friends lots of times. Does it really bother you?"

That made sense she supposed.

"I think Curtis just got in my head," she admitted. "I have a complicated relationship with authority."

His mouth softened into a sweet smile and he held his arms open. "C'mere."

For a hug?

Oh.

She would love a hug right about now.

She slid her arms around his waist and pressed her cheek to his chest. He wrapped his around her shoulders and rested his chin on her head.

They held one another for several long breaths and she felt her tension ebbing away.

"This is nice," she said, eyes closed and basking in his warm embrace.

"Mm-hm," he agreed.

This she could do. Dave and his patient smiles and his laugh and his hugs and his silliness. But the things that came along with Sunshine Capone were more stressful than she had anticipated.

Still, they were both him. She couldn't have one without the rest.

Leslie and Max seemed to cope with both. Maybe they could give her tips. She thought about Leslie's comments earlier and wondered if maybe he was already trying to give her tips.

Dave let her go and stepped back. "Catherine will be here soon and I wanna shoot some hoops before she gets here." He went to his bag and pulled out some shorts and a white t-shirt. "Would you like to join me?"

Sabine grimaced. "I don't actually know how to play basketball."

He flashed her a dazzling smile. "I can show you."

* * *

The rest of their day was way more relaxed.

Even when Catherine came over and had them pick what they were going to wear the next day, it had seemed normal and fun.

Dave had done his best to show her how to shoot a basketball but there had been more laughing than teaching.

For dinner they ate on Leslie's back patio overlooking the Hollywood Hills and Sabine could see it—the appeal of this kind of life. On its surface it was simple and elegant. This was the kind of life her mom had believed she was entitled to: wealthy, easy living. Maybe that's why it made Sabine uncomfortable.

That's what she was thinking about when she should have been sleeping.

The bed was comfortable, the blankets soft, the ambient noise pleasant. She couldn't even tell Dave was on the other side of the bed. He had remained perfectly still and silent since they'd laid down an hour ago.

But she was awake, hands folded over her stomach, staring at the ceiling.

Dave rolled over in her direction and she sucked in a breath.

"Sorry. Did I scare you?" he asked softly.

"I thought you were sleeping."

"How can I sleep with your loud thoughts taking up the entire bed?"

He was teasing, she could hear it in his voice. But it just made her feel guilty.

"I'm sorry. I can go find—"

He put a hand on top of hers. "Just talk to me."

She took a deep breath. He picked up one of her hands and held it.

"I was thinking about my mom, of all things." It felt weird to say out loud. "How if she knew where I was right now, she'd probably try to take that too."

His fingers flexed against hers.

"She can't have this."

Sabine snorted and rolled her eyes. "Obviously. The paperwork from Curtis alone would stop her."

"No." He scootched a bit closer. "This." He squeezed her hand. "You. These moments we have that are real and simple and perfect. She can never have anything close to that. Thieves never can."

She blinked as her eyes burned. Well, that was unexpected.

"And maybe it's not my place but I'm just gonna say it. If she tries to mess with you ever again, I will make her regret it. No. No. Strike that. She won't get a chance to regret it because she won't get a chance to mess with you." He scooched closer. "Just thinking about anyone trying to hurt you makes me a little crazy inside."

She sniffed a laugh. "Thanks."

He moved his thumb over the back of her hand. "You aren't allowed to go anywhere, I've decided." The teasing was back in his voice.

"Oh really?"

"Yeah. You're very ergonomic."

Her laugh bubbled out of her. "What?"

"Yep." He sounded so very sure of himself. "You fit right by me."

"What are you talking about?" she asked, her giggles shaking the bed.

He scooched closer, bringing his body flush against hers. He snuggled in close to her neck. "See? You fit right by me."

Sabine sighed, completely exasperated by him and also so appreciative of his adorable antics. Her body finally relaxed with the heat of his nearness.

Which was confusing for so many different reasons. Shouldn't his nearness make her nervous?

But he'd snuggled her many times since they'd first met and his hands had never wandered. His intentions had never been dubious.

She always felt safe with him.

She resolved that he would always be safe with her as well.

And that was her last thought before she fell asleep.

* * *

DAVE

He felt Sabine's body relax, and soon after her breathing evened out.

And he wasn't upset at all that his mom had bailed.

Not. At. All.

Chapter Sixteen
I Don't Care

DAVE

His phone rang and he glared at the screen before answering it.

"What up, Curtis?"

Leslie stuck his tongue out and held his hands up for Dave to pass the ball to him.

"What are you doing?" Curtis asked.

Dave bounced the basketball to Leslie.

"Just shooting some hoops with Les." He walked to the back of the court and watched Leslie dribble to the hoop for a layup. "What do you need?"

"How did rehearsal go this morning?" Curtis asked.

"Fine." Dave shrugged and paced towards the pool and back again.

"Will you and your guest be on time tonight?"

"Should be." He stopped and gazed up at the blue California sky. "Is there something you're not saying?"

"The background check came back on her and there are some red flags."

Dave rolled his eyes. "Yeah, I know about her ma. It's not something you need to be worried about."

"You said that about the last one too," Curtis muttered.

Dave clenched his free hand into a fist. "We've talked about this, Curtis. You don't get to choose my friends."

"I know, I know," Curtis sounded stressed. "But this is a huge event and she's going to be a person of interest the moment she steps out of that limousine."

Dave frowned and paced back the way he'd come.

"You're going to have microphones shoved in your faces all down the carpet. You haven't done an interview since *Flash Cache* came out and the entertainment sites are salivating over your appearance tonight."

Dave's stomach churned and his pulse picked up.

"I'm not trying to choose your friends. But you both need to be prepared for the assumptions that are going to happen when you show up together. I tried to prep her as best as I could over the phone. I think I could have made my point better had you brought her here when you came to town. But—I get it—I do. You need your space and to have as close to a normal life as possible. I'm not complaining. Your freedom means better music and that's what I can sell. But we're getting close to showtime and I need you to be prepared for what's coming."

Fuck.

He had a point.

"Now, if she's a person of romantic significance to you we can make something work."

"Please stop trying to force me into something."

Curtis swallowed his protests and just settled for a loud grumble.

"We're friends. End of story. She's cool. You'll see." He held his palm out to Leslie for the ball. "I need to go. I'll call you next week."

He hung up without waiting for Curtis to reply and tossed his phone onto the table nearby.

Leslie passed the ball and they continued their one-on-one game.

* * *

"Are you ready, dimples?" He rested the back of his head against the wall and slid his hands into his pockets.

He loved what Catherine had come up with for him. Yes, it was a tuxedo, but she'd put her own brand of Sunshine on it.

Black pants, forest green jacket, black shirt, diamond encrusted bowtie, wingtip shoes.

It was so deliciously gangster.

He'd shaved his face smooth and gotten a haircut. Even he could admit he looked pretty ballin'.

He had no idea what Sabine had picked to wear. Catherine said she'd given her a couple choices that matched what Dave was wearing.

She'd also mentioned that Sabine had been a joy to dress and to call her for the next event.

That wasn't surprising. He was figuring out that everyone loved Sabine as soon as they met her.

"I need help." Sabine's soft voice came through the door. He was reminded of the day they'd met. She needed help then too.

He decided then and there he always wanted to be in a position to help her.

He pushed away from the wall. "Well, come out here and I can help you."

The door opened and for a minute he was stunned silent.

She stood before him in a silver floor-length gown that looked like it was made out of satin. Or pure liquid. Because it flowed and cascaded over every curve and slope of her body. It had thin, barely-there straps at her shoulder, and a plunging neckline that he stared at way longer than was polite. A thigh-high slit up the side showed her shapely legs. Her shoes were strappy silver numbers that made her several inches taller.

Her hair was down and in loose waves at her shoulders, and her makeup was smokey.

She had her arms behind her back.

"Oh my," he said, doing another slow up and down.

That was it.

He had no words. She'd rendered him speechless.

"Wow."

Her words brought his eyes back to her face.

"You look incredible," she said, stepping into the hallway. She reached out with one hand and adjusted his bowtie. "Such a baller."

That's what he'd thought too.

But he was nothing compared to her.

Her smile was blinding, and he stopped breathing for a second.

He tried to swallow but found it difficult.

"Can you help me?" She turned around to show him her completely bare back. And thank God she couldn't see his expression because he would not have been able to hide his thoughts.

Which were lustful.

And not the way he should look at a friend.

It wasn't like he'd completely forgotten how gorgeous she was. But he'd been able to compartmentalize a lot of it. It was a tactic that had served him well over the years. A special compartment for everything. The compartments didn't intersect or blend unless he reorganized them in his head first.

Her exposed back blew up all of his compartments.

"I have this chain thing I'm supposed to hook…" In her fingers dangled a sparkly strand of jewelry. "But I can't get it."

He inhaled slowly and reached for the chain. She let go as soon as he had it and dropped her arms to her sides.

Her skin looked unbelievably soft. He wanted to touch it. To run his fingers from her neck, down her spine, to where the dress *barely* covered her bottom.

Black tattoo ink peeked out of the border between skin and dress.

That's right.

She'd said she'd had a Jamiroquai tattoo on her butt.

That had been a tidbit he'd stuck into the "too sexy to think about" compartment. Right next to the way she danced with her arms over her head when she thought she was alone, and the way her neck smelled when he hugged her.

His head filled with curse words and variations thereof.

"Can you see where the catch is?"

He twitched at her soft question.

"Catherine showed me how to hook it, but I couldn't manage. Now I'm worried we'll be late."

"We won't be late," he said, his voice thick.

He tried to swallow again. And again, it was too difficult.

He frowned at his own distractibility and shook his head to help focus.

Okay, where was this hook?

He found a small loop on the opposite side. That must be it. He clipped the sparkly chain to it and then made sure it laid correctly along her lower back. It was a diamond bow positioned just on the curve where her ass sloped into her back and it matched his tie.

God bless Catherine.

His fingers skimmed over her warm skin and lingered. "You have dimples back here too," he said without thinking.

She glanced over her shoulder like she was trying to see what he was saying.

He touched one of the dimples with a finger. "Venus dimples." He winked at her. "I thought this chain would serve more of a practical purpose but it does not." *Except to make me want to touch her right there.* "How is this dress even staying up? It defies logic."

She turned around and his hand slid free of her skin. She looked up at him with worried eyes. "Is it stupid? Should I wear something else?"

"No." He shook his head, and even though he knew better, he cupped her cheek with his palm and looked directly into those hazel eyes. "It's perfect. You're the most beautiful woman I have ever seen."

She smiled, her cheeks turning hot pink.

"But for real," he pressed. "How is this staying up? Is it magic?" He dipped his head, bringing his face closer to hers. "You're magic, aren't you? It's okay, you can tell me. It would explain a lot, actually."

And then something happened. Something that was going to be burned into Dave's memory for the rest of his life.

Sabine, still smiling, licked her lips and dropped her eyes to his mouth.

He took a deep breath while taking a large step back. His hand slid free of her face and he scanned her up and down again.

"You don't wear your hair down often. Did you lighten it again?" He needed to get the walls of his compartments repaired. Quickly.

She touched the ends of her freshly lightened hair and smiled self-consciously. "Catherine's team did the hair, the makeup." She held her hands up, palms facing her. "My nails."

"You look incredible. No one is going to understand why you're there with me."

Her eyebrows dipped. "No."

"No?" he repeated, lips twitching.

"We're not doing that tonight. We're taking a break from all the negative self-talk. Got it?" An eyebrow arched in challenge.

How was he supposed to tell her that he'd do whatever she said?

"Okay," he agreed, with a single nod and a slow blink.

Her expression softened and he reached for her hand. She slipped her smaller one into his and he couldn't remember ever feeling so anchored.

* * *

SABINE

They'd spent a lot of time together as Dave and Sabine, but this was really the first time she'd been able to experience Sunshine Capone.

The moment they'd stepped out of the limo he'd come alive. Bright smiles, waving to everyone, gracious with his fans.

Instead of proceeding to the red carpet, he went over to the ropes where crowds of fans had gathered to catch a look at their favorite artist. Over and over, he signed things, smiled for pictures, took selfies.

At one point he was facetiming someone and singing one of his songs.

Who did that?

She looked around at all the other celebrities arriving and the answer was no one. No one did that.

When he rejoined her, he took her by the hand and led her to the red carpet. He waved a final time to his fans.

"I just realized I have never spent any time with Sunshine Capone," she said.

He grinned down at her and she felt it in her toes.

"Let me know if it's too much and we can go."

"Don't be ridiculous," she muttered, squeezing his hand. He absolutely meant what he said and she knew it. But there was no way she was going to miss seeing him in his element.

The red carpet was about what she expected.

Tons of people. Everywhere.

Her training kicked in and she didn't look anyone in the eye, keeping her vision in the areas *around* where their faces were.

They were at their second photo op when she felt the slippery fabric of her dress start to slip to the side of her chest. Her hand still in Dave's flinched and he turned to look at her.

"I have to fix my dress," she whispered under her breath.

He glanced down to her cleavage and then positioned his body directly in front of her.

Oh.

He was blocking the cameras.

She quickly tugged the dress back into place and smoothed it down. Oh, it wasn't as bad as she feared. It wasn't often she went out in public with this much showing. As in never. But she was still covered. No side boob, no nip slips. Catherine had equipped her perfectly.

"Okay."

"You good?" he asked.

That was when she realized he was standing impossibly close. His fingers tugged slightly on a strand of her hair and she glanced up into his beautiful indigo eyes.

And she smiled.

His eyes were always the happiest, softest place to land.

All she could do was nod and he pivoted back to be by her side.

He had just turned his back to all the cameras and didn't care for a second that he was being rude. As if it was her carpet walk not his.

He took her hand and tucked it into the crook of his arm, patted it, and smiled down at her.

They moved down the carpet and he didn't let go of her the entire time.

A well-dressed woman with a microphone and a cameraman waved him over and he happily tugged Sabine along. She stopped out of view of the camera and he hopped onto the platform for the interview.

The woman with the microphone eyed Sabine like she was trying to place her. Someone said something in her earpiece and she focused on Dave.

"Sunshine Capone," the woman greeted. "Nominated for two awards tonight including best hip-hop album, how are you feeling?"

"Honestly, I forgot I was nominated." He laughed. "But it's cool. It's always cool to be nominated."

"You look amazing. Very dapper. Who are you wearing tonight?"

"Catherine Anne put it together. I think she said it's one of hers."

That was accurate. Sabine remembered. He glanced over his shoulder as if to ask her to verify, so she nodded. He waved a hand like he wanted her to join him.

She frowned and shook her head.

This was his moment.

"No tour this year? Maybe next year?" The interviewer asked.

Sabine wished she could remember her name. She leaned around to see the emblem on the microphone.

CelebX.

Ugh.

Fine.

The people who wrote the online articles probably weren't the same people who did the in-person interviews.

Probably.

Maybe.

Hopefully.

Tabatha!

That was the interviewer's name.

Dave faced the speaker again and drew out his answer.

Sabine schooled her expression. Everyone knew why he hadn't toured with the last album.

Girlfriend drama.

"Maybe next year," he said with a flirty smile. "Have you seen my date?"

He turned to the side and held out a hand to her.

Oh boy.

She took his hand he helped her step onto the small platform. He let go of her hand and slid his along her lower back, playing with the diamond bow with his fingers. He shot Sabine a sly smile. "This is Sabine. She's one of my best friends."

"You're just friends?" Tabatha asked, sounding unconvinced.

"No, we're *best* friends," Dave corrected.

"Wow, best friends. As his friend, what do you think of his nomination?" Tabatha tilted the microphone toward Sabine.

"It's well-deserved." She smiled over at Dave. "I think it's incredible that he shares his gifts with us. He's brilliant and amazing, and I'm so glad I'm not the only one who sees."

His gaze softened on her and she faced Tabatha again.

"He really is talented. Sunshine, I heard a rumor about you," the lady said with a coy smile.

"Uh oh," Dave laughed, and pulled Sabine just a bit closer to his side.

Don't worry, babe, Sabine told him mentally. *I have no problem tripping into the camera if she asks anything uncomfortable.*

Where had that come from?

Huh. How about that, she wasn't lying. If this interview got weird, she'd just drop to the ground and faint. She had no problem looking like a fool to save Dave.

"I heard you can make something up on the spot without any preparation. Is that true?" Tabatha asked.

His body relaxed just enough for Sabine to notice.

"I don't know. Maybe that's true." He shrugged, the light dancing in his eyes.

"Could you do it now?" Tabatha pressed.

"Now?" He pinched his chin. "I don't know."

"C'mon, something quick. Just a few lines."

"You have to give me a subject."

"Your date. Say something about her."

Oh no.

Abort! It's a trap! She screamed through her eyes. If he understood her, he ignored it.

He angled toward her and her heart thundered in her chest. His lips moved silently for a few seconds and he nodded to the beat only he could hear.

"Okay, okay, check this out…

She's a whole vibe in a dress,
Girl's got values to address,
I'm honored by her hand in mine,
But it might as well be inside my chest.
She's quick on her feet,
Her mind knocks the wind out of me,
Like a force to be reckoned with,
She holds the course and I'm never wrecked.
She's a dark horse,
A life source,
Harder to enforce than endorse,
Keeps me on my toes,
Helps me laugh away my woes,

my bff for life,
you can't have her, get your own"

People nearby began clapping but Sabine was staring at him.

She hadn't been lying when she said he was brilliant, but she'd never experienced the full effect of his talents.

Her entire body shivered, and he grinned because she was certain he felt it.

He leaned in and brushed his lips across her temple.

The lady said more flattering things but Sabine couldn't hear them through the roaring of her pulse in her ears.

He wasn't just talented; he was *very* sweet.

And talented.

Both.

Who knew that was such a potent combination?

Something tumbled from her chest to the ground and she was pretty sure it was her heart.

It was falling.

Falling.

Falling.

Dave tucked her hand in the crook of his arm and tugged her further down the carpet. He glanced down at her.

"That's it," she said, dead serious. "That's the competition. You just won all the awards."

He threw his head back and laughed.

Not just any laugh, but the one he'd done the first night they'd hung out. Where it looked like all of his energy was in the laugh, and his knees weakened because his steps faltered, and he put his free hand on his chest like the laugh was exploding out of him.

It was her favorite of his laughs.

She wanted that laugh in her life for the rest of it.

Sure, he was laughing, but she wasn't joking. As far as she was concerned, his talent exceeded all others.

They made it through the rest of the gauntlet without stopping to talk to anyone else. Though many people with cameras and microphones tried.

"I didn't do any press after the last release," he said in her ear as he steered her through the venue to their seats. "Curtis warned me they'd be bloodthirsty."

"Why did you choose that one?"

He shrugged, following their liaison through round tables of well-dressed celebrities and production crew. "I like to throw them a bone every once in a while."

When they arrived at their table, Dave waved away the liaison and held her chair out for her to sit down. He took the seat next to her, pulling the chair much closer to hers than it had been.

He sat down, let his eyes roam over the room as it filled with people and then settled his gaze on Sabine.

It felt like such a deliberate action that her heart responded with a little shiver.

Something about the slow perusal of his eyes through people he knew, people he worked with, collaborated with, should probably network with, and he chose to focus on her.

He leaned closer to her and draped an arm over her chairback.

"How are you feeling?" he asked, looking her in the eye.

"I feel good," she responded quickly. But truthfully, she was a little overwhelmed.

He handed her the glass of water at her place setting and watched her take a sip.

"How are you really feeling?" he asked, voice soft and low, meant just for her.

"Nervous," she confessed. "But I don't have a reason." Her gaze flicked through the room but couldn't settle on any one thing. So much glitz and glam that it all sort of blurred together. "I think I'm afraid that I'll have to talk to someone famous and forget who they are and then offend them. Like, what if it's the President or something and I just completely blank on him. And then I'll make you look bad and I don't want to do that ever."

"Dimples." He took her hand and her attention.

She stopped looking around the room and focused on him. He brought her hand up to his mouth and pressed his lips to her knuckles and remained there for several seconds.

"You can't make me look bad. That's not possible. And don't worry about remembering anyone. I am *terrible* at names and they keep inviting me to these things anyway."

She smiled, her nerves relaxing. She propped an elbow on the table and rested her chin on her fist. He was still holding her hand and she didn't hate it.

In fact, it was anchoring her to reality, filling her with calm assurance.

"So," she said, remembering what she wanted to say since the red-carpet interview. "I had no idea you could do that. Make something up like that on the spot, that is."

His lips twitched and he shrugged one shoulder. "It's my brain. Moves fast."

"I'm going to say something you already know but I haven't told you yet."

His eyes darkened to a deeper blue, almost navy, and he shifted closer to her.

"You're insanely talented," Sabine said seriously. "I wasn't kidding when I said that you win all the awards. There's no competition. They should just call it the Sunshine Capone award and send everyone else home."

He chuckled, his cheeks turning a light pink, and looked around the room briefly. He focused on her again, his smile cute and self-conscious.

"Well," he licked his lips and pumped his eyebrows once. "It was a little like cheating. She asked me to say something about you. The rhymes write themselves."

She dropped her head back and laughed. When she righted herself, he was watching her with a sort of wonder on his face.

"You think I'm joking?" he asked. He dropped his voice and held her hand near his lips again.

"Has no idea
she hits like a dart
An energy drink to my heart
Caffeine, taurine, and smarts
The chill in my veins
The sun in my name
Can't complain, all the same
Leading me out of the dark"

. . .

She bit down on her bottom lip because she had no words.

He grinned and kissed her knuckles again.

But she felt it in her heart.

* * *

DAVE

He didn't win anything.

His performance went fine. Not that that had been on his mind. Performing was cake for him. He saw artists freak out all the time over silly shit like missed cues and clunky effects.

But he just went out there and did his best and if it went to shit then it went to shit.

It was the afterparties that spiked his anxiety.

Everyone else seemed so at ease at those things.

He wasn't. More people meant he had more of an opportunity to say or do something confusing.

But Curtis had asked him to go to one afterparty. A specific one hosted by the label.

He'd promised Sabine just an hour and then they could go get some food and sleep.

After all, their flight left at four in the morning. Which was six to her internal clock because of the time change. She'd be up for 24-hours without even a nap to sustain her. He couldn't ask her to keep Sunshine hours.

Though, for the first time ever, he wasn't as nervous about being at the afterparty. It was as if having Sabine with him changed his entire perspective. Even if everyone else in the room misunderstood him, she wouldn't.

"Yo, Sunshine!" Chizeled—his friend and sometimes collaborator— grabbed him in a bear hug. They slapped each other on the back.

"I didn't know you were here!" Dave said, happy to see the rapper.

"I dipped out of the show early." Chizeled rubbed a hand over his chest as he glanced through the crowded venue. "Are you here with someone?"

Dave nodded and pointed out Sabine.

She was still in that fucking ridiculously hot dress, standing at the bar with Zara Lorna playing lemon mouth.

Because of course she was.

"You're here with Zara?" Chizeled asked.

"No, the hot one," Dave corrected. He watched as Sabine shoved the lemon wedge in her mouth and Zara's eyes went wide.

"Damn. How long you been dating?"

Sabine spit the wedge out and the bartender removed it. Then she high-fived Zara and the bartender. The bartender grinned. Not at Zara Lorna, the award-winning songstress with the number one song on every streaming platform out there. No, he couldn't take his eyes off Sabine, the tutor from Chicago who dressed like Darth Vader to impress a boy.

"What?" Dave asked. "Oh, we're not dating. We're just friends."

Chizeled laughed and Dave tore his eyes away from Sabine to look at his friend. "What?"

"Right. Friends. Okay." Chizeled laughed again, harder this time. "You're full of shit."

"No, really," Dave defended. "She's just a friend. I'm not dating anyone."

Chizeled eyed him carefully, still not convinced, but he let it go. "When do you have some time? I have a track that needs some specific Capone type massaging."

"I'm in Chicago these days. You can come see me whenever you want."

"You have a studio there?"

"Yeah. A good one."

"Sweet. I'll call you."

They slapped hands and backs and parted.

Dave went to the bar and even though he knew he was playing with fire, he slid his hand along Sabine's lower back. She turned bright eyes over her shoulder to greet him.

"Hey!" She looped her arm around his waist.

"Lemon mouth?" He shook his head at her.

"Sunshine," Zara greeted with a curt chin lift.

"Zara," he responded, tipping his head to the side. "Congratulations on the award. It was well deserved."

Her expression softened a touch. "Thank you."

"He loves that song," Sabine spoke up. "I swear he's made up twelve different remixes for it."

Both Zara and Dave turned wide eyes to her.

"I didn't know you had heard those." Further, he didn't know she had picked up the differences between each one.

"I listen to everything you say," Sabine said with a snort that sounded like "duh."

He chuckled and slid his hand to her hip where he applied pressure so she'd lean more fully into him. "Oh, Sabine, you are hammered," he said around a smile.

She just shrugged. "We did shots."

"Did ya?" He pressed his lips to her temple. She was too cute.

"I've always thought that a collab between us would be a good idea," Zara said, drawing his attention away from Sabine's smile.

Dave wasn't sure if he successfully hid his shock or not. "I would love that. Truly."

Zara glanced at Sabine and then back at Dave. "Lemon mouth?"

"Yes!" Sabine patted the bar. "May we please have a lemon wedge, Henry?" she asked the bartender.

Dave was pretty sure Henry would run naked through a shopping mall if Sabine asked him to.

She took the lemon wedge, turned in Dave's arm, and held it up for him.

He held her gaze and opened his mouth.

She bit her bottom lip and put the wedge in his teeth. He bit down and closed his lips around it

Sabine and Zara started counting out loud, their voices gathering volume the higher they counted.

When Dave's eyes were watering and he couldn't feel his gums anymore, he took the wedge out.

Sabine stuck her tongue between her teeth with a squeal. "You're way better at that than me. I can't hang."

The DJ running the music called for dancers on the floor and the song that began playing was "Animal" by Neon Trees. Sabine grabbed Zara's hand and took off for the floor.

Dave eased his elbows onto the bar, as he faced the dancefloor.

And he just watched her.

Her arms over her head, dancing like she wasn't surrounded by the most important people in the industry. Just radiating joy and freedom and all the things he loved about being alive.

If there was ever going to be someone who could do this with him, live this life between lemon mouth shenanigans and reaching for the stars, it would be Sabine.

He'd known it for a while but having her here, immersed in the rest of his world, it was more than obvious.

Maybe the vow of celibacy was working. Because he was thinking more clearly than he could ever remember.

He knew decision time was coming.

Either ask her to cross that line, take a risk with him—the kind of risk that could be the ruin of them both.

Or maintain course.

Friends forever.

Lovers never.

But the way she moved, the smile on her gorgeous face, the blush on her cheeks…those things made him want to risk it. He wanted to touch her skin, kiss her lips, and make her sigh his name.

That's why he left the bar and crossed the room.

He slid his hands onto her hips just as the song changed to something else. One he didn't recognize. She looped her wrists around his neck and smiled up at him.

"Are you having fun?" she asked.

He nodded, his pulse pounding through his body. He stared into her eyes, willing her to read his mind. To know what he was thinking and maybe then he would never have to say it.

He ran his hands from her hips up to her ribs and back down.

And thought the words as hard as he could.

And hoped she could read his mind.

Chapter Seventeen
Off My Face

SABINE

It was the intense pressure in her bladder that drove her out of the most comfortable sleep she'd ever had.

She rolled out from under the heavy arm on her belly and dropped her feet to the floor.

Her floor.

In her bedroom.

In her loft.

She stood up and blinked against the gray light filling her room.

Dave was in her bed.

Shirtless.

Well, at *least* shirtless.

She couldn't see the rest of him because the sheets were pulled up to the middle of his back. He was sleeping on his stomach one arm extended onto her side.

It had been his arm pressing into her bladder.

She rushed to the bathroom and glanced at herself in the mirror on her way to the toilet.

She was wearing underwear and a t-shirt.

Not her own t-shirt.

It was definitely a man's white undershirt. It came to her mid-thigh.

Flashes of the night before came back to her.

Dancing until they shut the place down. Getting tacos at a food truck with ambiguous signage. Drinking tequila like it was water. Barely catching their flight on time.

She was thankful they'd packed ahead of time at Leslie's suggestion. She'd been able to change out of her dress and into sweats before Darius and Dallas made them leave.

On the plane they hadn't rested or slept at all. Instead, they'd spent the ninety-minute flight playing quarters, telling stories, and chugging water.

Back in the city, she'd offered to have him sleep there for a few hours before going home in the afternoon. Or whenever they woke up.

And instead of sleeping on the couch like *he offered*, Sabine had asked him to stay in her bed with her.

She groaned, remembering how he'd been very polite with his desire to stay on the couch and she'd made a fuss about hating to asleep alone.

She *did* hate to sleep alone but that was a *secret!*

She washed her hands and frowned at herself in the mirror.

Wow, girl, you're a mess.

She washed her face, brushed her teeth, and reapplied deodorant.

On one hand she wanted to stay awake, make some food, take a shower, pretend like she was on top of her life again instead of…

Well, instead of reality.

Which was that she had a slight hangover, she was exhausted, had blisters on her feet from dancing in high heels, and a hot guy in her bed. Maybe she could snuggle back under his arm and sleep away all her insecurities.

Side note: when had she started thinking about Dave as being hot?

That was something she'd have to talk about with herself later.

She left the bathroom and went back to her bed.

Because she was only so strong.

Carefully she lifted the covers and slid back inside. Dave lifted his head and gave her a sleepy smile.

Her heart flipped over.

Oh no.

It wouldn't be so bad if she didn't remember with perfect clarity how amazing he'd been to her all weekend. He'd made her laugh so much that her stomach still hurt. And his ease and lack of anxiety when he was on stage really upped his hotness.

Then there'd been the dancing, and the intense eye contact, and his small touches all night long.

She was in so much trouble.

He rolled the opposite direction and got out of bed. He was in boxer briefs. Black ones.

Whoa, Nelly.

She curled around her pillow and closed her eyes.

He grabbed her foot on his way around the bed and gave it a little squeeze.

If she had her days right, it was midafternoon on Sunday. Kara was at work already and wouldn't be home until late.

They could spend the rest of the day doing nothing.

Maybe she'd order pizza or something.

But for the moment, all she wanted was sleep and to live a little longer in the fairytale that had begun the day before.

She tried to not notice the water running in the bathroom longer than just handwashing. She tried to tell herself he wasn't freshening his breath for any particular reason. She tried not to feel the butterflies thrumming in her stomach.

A memory flashed through her mind from two months ago when she'd first met him. A vlogger had spoken at length of his charm and charisma and how his unassuming nature just made it easier to land models and actresses. That his MO was always the same, befriend, flirt, whisk away to places unknown, rob them of their hearts and minds, and then discard them when he'd emptied them out. Leaving shells of broken women in his wake.

She closed her eyes against the words and forced them to the back of her mind. Because that wasn't Dave. That was someone who had never even met him, dissecting him for clicks.

The bathroom door opened and she forgot about the vlogger.

"We are not in California anymore." He ran into her room, closing the door behind him, then jumped onto the bed. "It's so cold here." He pulled the covers back and crawled inside.

"I don't know what you're talking about, I'm very warm." She rolled her back to him.

"That's because you're a little heater. C'mere." He wrapped both arms around her and buried his face in her neck. His legs tangled with hers and after a second, their bodies were touching in every possible way.

And Sabine's heart was pounding.

She needed to calm down.

This was something they had done many times. The snuggling and the affectionate touches, those were common. Though they'd never done it in their underwear. In her bed.

Her bed was her sanctuary.

She didn't allow anyone else in her bed unless there was imminent threat of marriage.

Maybe threat was the wrong word.

"Can we stay here all day?" he asked.

"Mm-hm." She rubbed his forearm where it was pressed to her middle. "I don't work until tomorrow. You can stay all day." She left off the "if you want." Because it seemed unnecessary.

He lifted his head and she glanced over her shoulder to see him narrow those sleepy eyes at her.

"Are you sick or anything? Do you need water or painkillers?" he asked.

"I'm pretty good, actually. Tequila doesn't hurt me the way vodka does." She reached a hand around and traced a finger over the rose near his eye. When her eyes came back to his, they were darker than before.

"Sabine," he said, his voice husky. His eyes dropped to her mouth and stayed for a beat. His fingers on her stomach splayed wide and he tightened his hold. Then he lowered his mouth and brushed his lips over hers.

He slid his hand from her stomach up to her side and then down her hip. His lips found the spot behind her ear and pressed kisses from there down the line of her neck.

Her body reflexively arched into his.

The hand at her hip guided her to her back until she was looking up at him. He was propped up on one arm while his other hand still lingered on her. Everywhere. All over her skin. Featherlight touches. As if his fingers were cataloguing every curve and plane on her body with deliberate accuracy.

His hand moved to her ribs, caressing her body through the shirt she was still wearing. He watched his hand move down her side until it curved around her hip and over her ass, and then back again. Slowly, he ran his hand up to her ribs again, this time under the shirt, stopping just below her breast.

His gaze came back to her and he brushed his lips over hers again.

He put his head on her chest, his ear pressed to her heart and held her tight.

She tried to breathe.

He had to be able to hear her heart racing. It wasn't like she could hide it. Instead, she brushed her fingers through his hair and down his back. She used both of her hands to touch him in soft ways. His shoulders, his arms, his forehead.

His hand roamed down her side, kneaded her hip, moved down to her thigh. He hooked behind her knee and brought her leg over top of his. Now she was twisted at the waist, lower half facing his, upper half pinned down with his head on her heart.

He continued moving his hand all along her skin, her legs, her stomach, her back, her hips. He really liked her hips. He would pause at her hips and hold them in a firm grip before moving on to softer touches.

He lifted his head a bit and pushed the shirt up her stomach to just below her breasts. He licked his lips and then pressed them to the skin of her belly.

She must've let out some sort of sound because he lifted his eyes to her. He watched her then as he lowered his face and placed open mouth kisses all over her exposed stomach. From her ribs down to where the hem of her panties began. His hands were everywhere. Soft, gentle, soothing. Her legs, her hips, her sides. All the while, watching her reactions.

He raised onto his knees and her eyes skated over the tattoos on his torso she had never seen up close before. There was not one inch of bare skin. It was all black ink and swirls of design.

"Is this okay?"

She flicked her eyes back to him.

His hands rested on her hips in that possessive way again, but he was waiting for her to answer. "I just want to kiss your body. That's all."

She nodded, unwilling to break this moment by saying something stupid.

He let his gaze roam down her body and his hands followed wherever they landed. He turned her hips slightly and brushed his fingers along her lower back before following those touches with his mouth, licking the small dimples he'd noticed yesterday.

He tugged down her panties just enough so he could see her tattoo back there and then his mouth went there too.

A small groan escaped him and he pressed his forehead to her hip as if trying to steady himself. His hands fluttered over her legs, up and down both thighs as he shifted her onto her back again.

He lowered his head and pressed his lips to the top of one thigh, then the other. His hands, fingers splayed wide, like he was trying to touch as much of her as he could at once, stroked up her legs and then down to her calves.

Never in her life had Sabine felt so delicate. Or desired.

He kissed the instep of her foot, the inside of her ankle, her calves, the back of her knee. Then he switched to the other leg.

He murmured some words into her skin she couldn't understand but she got the feeling they weren't for her ears. Words of pleasure and appreciation spoken onto her body.

He made his way back to where he'd started, placing open mouth kisses all along her hips and stomach. He pushed the shirt up, exposing her breasts. But he didn't go right for them. Instead, he resumed those slow, open mouth kisses along her ribs and center of her chest.

She squirmed under his ministrations.

Arched into his touches.

Never had her body felt so alive as it did when his hands were on her.

It was the fact that this was *Dave.*

His hands, his mouth, his focus.

It was all so careful.

Unhurried.

Deliberate.

All at once, heat enveloped one erect nipple and she sucked in a breath.

He groaned again, cupping her breast and flicking his tongue over the peak. Then he moved to the other one and did the same.

She writhed beneath him, her hands on his shoulders, wanting him to never stop but also wanting his mouth on her mouth. She wanted his tongue sliding against hers in a way that felt desperate and needy.

He raised his head, his sleepy eyes grazing over her face. He slid his palm along her jaw and curved his fingers around her neck where he applied slight pressure, making her tilt her head back.

Then he lowered his mouth to her neck, kissing, licking, nipping the column of her throat and under her chin.

He tugged the shirt back down over her body and brushed his lips over hers in a soft caress. He studied her face for a beat, satisfied with what he saw, smirked, grabbed the covers and flicked them over the both of them.

He settled in again with his head over her heart, and his arms wrapped around her.

Was that it?

She waited, unmoving for a couple minutes.

He took a deep breath and let it out.

That's when she realized he had fallen asleep.

Well shit.

He had said he'd just wanted to kiss her body. He'd done exactly that.

Now she was more turned on than she'd ever been in her life and he was sleeping.

Cooooooool.

How had that even happened? One minute he was asking her if she had a hangover, the next he was gathering intimate knowledge of her erogenous zones.

And she'd noticed the erection he was sporting. It wasn't that he hadn't been enjoying himself.

And he hadn't even properly kissed her on the mouth!

Nothing about this made sense.

Confusing, unexpected, dastardly.

That was Dave.

How weird was she?

Because she was super into it.

* * *

DAVE

He woke up alone.

Which was good because he had a very noticeable erection and if Sabine had still been beside him, he would have asked for more than kissing. He wasn't sure he could resist her twice in a row.

Not with how she touched him and responded to his hands on her.

Fucking hell.

He rubbed his face with his hands while thinking about basketball stats.

Fuck, he was turned on.

It felt like he'd had a raging hard-on for 24 hours.

Kissing Sabine all over her glorious body had not helped. Neither had the small noises she made or the way she shifted beneath him.

He should have never found out how her skin tasted.

It wasn't just her body that he wanted. It was all of it. Her smiles, her jokes, her soft looks and touches.

He'd woken up that afternoon wanting nothing more than to slide inside her sweet softness.

And he'd told himself that he could have just a little taste. Just touch her, feel her move, get a closer look at her tattoo, lick her back dimples…

He told himself that wasn't the same as sex.

It was safe.

Yeah, no.

Her body was now going to be starring in every fantasy he'd ever have for the rest of his life.

She had to be so confused by him at this point.

That thought deflated him instantly.

He didn't want to hurt her or confuse her.

He was confused enough for the both of them.

He needed to figure out what he wanted. For both their sakes.

Because right now, with her body fresh in his mind, he was ready to commit to forever. Take all the vows and never look back.

But that was crazy.

Right?

Voices filtered through the bedroom door and he knew he was going to have to face her sooner or later. It wasn't like he could just get dressed and sneak out the window.

But he didn't have any answers.

And she'd have questions.

Fuck, she had a *right* to her questions. *He* was the one with all the mixed signals.

He craned his neck around to look at the tall windows. Was that a fire escape?

Maybe he could just disappear into the night like Batman.

He slid out of bed and put on his sweatpants while examining the latch to the window. It looked like it opened easily enough. He could just climb onto her dresser, open the latch, and step onto the metal staircase.

Except it was Chicago. Also known as the frozen tundra.

He'd die before he made it to the ground.

On the other hand, it would be cold enough that his erection definitely wouldn't come back.

While he contemplated whether dying on the side of a Chicago building was an honorable death or not, the bedroom door opened.

"Oh, you're awake!"

He turned to find Sabine's bright smile at the doorway.

"We have pizza if you're hungry," she offered, motioning with her thumb over her shoulder.

She'd showered and her hair was in the twin braids that seemed to be her brand and she was no longer in his shirt.

Why did that disappoint him so much?

"Sounds good," he replied, voice tight. He tried to clear his throat.

She narrowed her eyes at him and tilted her head. "Were you thinking of jumping out the window just now?"

He pursed his lips because he didn't want to answer that question.

She laughed and for some reason he loved it.

Who was he kidding? He loved everything about her.

Every. Damn. Thing.

Instead of admitting that though, he just crossed the room and rolled his eyes at her. "Shut up."

After he was done in the bathroom, he joined Kara, Max, and Sabine in the living room. They were sitting on the couch with a couple pizza boxes on the ottoman.

"Sleeping beauty," Max greeted.

"I didn't know you were in town," Dave said, taking the empty seat nearest Sabine. He leaned forward and grabbed a couple slices while he slid his other hand along her thigh. He sat back and ate with one hand, keeping his other on her.

"I haven't left. I'm actually looking at getting my own place in your building."

"Really? I thought you said you'd never leave New York."

Max smirked and his eyes drifted to Kara. "I'm not leaving New York. But since I'm here so often I might as well have my own place."

They ate, they watched movies, they laughed.

They laughed a lot.

And not once did Sabine make him feel weird about what had happened between them earlier.

Dave couldn't stop picturing it. What if this could be his life? Quiet nights in, his friends relaxed and happy, Sabine within arm's reach.

Fuck.

He wanted Sabine within arm's reach.

As a friend *and* as a lover.

He'd never wanted both in the same woman before.

Max made moves to say goodbye for the night, but Dave didn't want to go.

"What's going on? Are you and her…?" Max asked a valid question.

Dave rubbed the back of his neck. "No. I mean…no," he settled on that for an answer. Because they weren't. Not yet.

"Then you don't need to stay here, right?" Max pointed out.

"Right." Dave agreed but he also didn't care.

"If you're not in a place to make a declaration, you shouldn't be spending nights. It's confusing," Max reminded him gently.

"Yeah. Okay." Dave took a deep breath and nodded.

Max was right. As usual.

Sometimes Dave needed it spelled out for him. He needed to be reminded that just because he saw things one way, didn't mean it was the *right* way. It definitely wasn't the only way.

He gathered his things and shoved them into his bag. While he did so, he recalibrated his emotions and expectations.

He wanted to be her friend so much.

She was funny and smart and wasn't annoyed with him yet. When they went places together, she made it fun and people thought better of him because of her.

His attraction to her was going to ruin all of the good they had built.

Because friends don't kiss all over each other's bodies.

Or go on giggly late night taco adventures.

Honestly, he didn't know what kind of relationship those aspects existed in. He'd never done those things with a girlfriend either.

Maybe he'd figure it out eventually.

But he wasn't going to figure it out at the expense of Sabine's heart.

He grabbed his bag and met her at the door.

"Hey," he said, getting her attention.

"Very serious face, I see," she teased, coming to stand close to him.

He gazed down into her beautiful eyes and tried to keep his smile from being too large. "I'm going to be busy working for the next couple of weeks."

"Me too." She blew out a breath. "My students have semester tests and finals to prepare for, so my calendar is very full in December."

Now why did her saying that bother him? Wasn't that what he'd just been trying to tell her?

"Just because you don't hear from me doesn't mean I'm avoiding you. Or that I forgot about you," he continued, staying on course.

She flashed him a bright smile. "I know. Same goes for me."

See? There was no one like her. He could tell her things and she *got it*. He didn't have to explain it ten different ways until it made sense. She heard him, and whether or not the words made sense, she seemed to have the cypher required to decode it.

Which just solidified what he'd already decided.

He needed to figure out what he wanted and stop wasting her time.

She was too important for him to be such a dipshit.

"Ahh, I like you." He heaved a sighed and then wrapped her in a hug. "Thank you for being the best." He pressed a kiss to her forehead, lingered for a beat, and finally left.

He was unlocking the door to his condo when he thought, *maybe I'll ask her to go to Saint-Tropez for Christmas.*

Chapter Eighteen
Intentions

DAVE

He made it three days.

Three days without seeing her, talking to her, hearing her laugh.

It had felt more like three months.

Which, okay, yes, time passed differently for him.

But his feelings were his feelings, and apparently Sabine owned every single one of them.

But he still needed to maintain distance. He knew it as surely as he knew that his next album was going to have a very specific feel to it.

If only because he needed to make sure his feelings were what he suspected they were. Without the distraction of his attraction.

It was strange though.

He thought he'd been in love a few times in his life.

What he felt for Sabine was familiar...but different too. Bigger, more intense, calmer. How did that work? Hell if he knew. You figure it out.

On day four he walked into a tattoo parlor and got something he said he'd never do: a tattoo for a woman.

Everyone knew that getting a tattoo for a significant other was a kiss of death, a curse, bad luck. He had mocked many of his friends for doing the same.

"Good?" the artist asked as Dave examined the stencil on his skin.

Words scrawled along his inner wrist on the left arm.

the force is with her

What if it was a curse?

What if getting something written on his skin for Sabine accelerated the end of everything?

Would he immediately cover those words with dark ink to block out the heartbreak?

No.

Because no matter what happened next, no matter how the rest of their lives progressed, he didn't *want* to forget this feeling.

He wanted to be reminded that it was possible to fall in love.

Which was why he'd chosen to put it on his wrist. So he could see it every day for the rest of his life.

"Yeah. Let's do it."

* * *

He made it another three days before he finally couldn't take it anymore.

The elevator doors opened and Kara stepped onto the floor.

"Motherfucking shit fuck!" Kara hissed, grabbing her chest with a hand and staggering back a couple steps.

"Sorry." Dave muttered, getting to his feet. "I didn't mean to scare you."

"What the hell are you doing in the hallway? I nearly had a shit hemorrhage." Kara glared at him.

"I just…" He shrugged because he didn't know what else to do. By the time he'd figured out he wanted to see her, it was the middle of the night. He got to her door and sat down in the hallway as he debated whether to knock, call, or go home.

Hours had passed and he hadn't yet decided.

Kara regarded him critically. She gestured with her head for him to follow her. "C'mon. I'll make you tea."

"Are you sure?" he asked. "I don't want to wake her up."

She shoved her key in the lock and eyed him. "We're not waking her up. But it's time you and I had a conversation."

He hesitated in the open door. Did he want to have a conversation with Kara? Sure, she'd been cordial to him but those had all been times Sabine had been there too. That one time they had been alone she had kind of threatened him.

Not kind of.

She had definitely threatened him.

He had successfully avoided being alone with Kara since.

She went inside and he stayed in the doorway, debating whether he wanted to die in the loft or if he had a better chance at survival in the hall.

She stepped around the corner and waved at him impatiently.

Okay.

Time to be brave.

He closed the door behind him and then joined Kara in the kitchen. She puttered around, filling a kettle with water, plugging it in, turning it on, getting mugs out. Dave slid onto what he'd begun to think of as "his" stool at the island.

"Were you at work?" he asked, uncomfortable with the silence.

She glanced at him over her shoulder. Friendly was not how he'd describe her expression. "Yes. At Geekeasy. I have tomorrow off though."

"Don't you also nanny?" he asked, hoping he didn't sound like an asshole.

He *felt* like an asshole.

And a little like a stalker.

"Yes. I nanny on the weekdays. So what was your plan, homeboy? Were you gonna sleep in the hallway and hope she didn't trip over you in the morning?" She moved the cups to the island.

"I didn't have a plan. I just missed her." He shook his head. That sounded stupid even to him.

"You don't think ahead too far, huh?" she said rather than asked. She brought the kettle over and poured water into the cups. She set the kettle down on the countertop and tipped her head to the side, studying him.

"No." He huffed a humorless laugh. "My brain is like three very-eager-to-help eight-year-olds. It's a lot of ideas and enthusiasm. But my intentions are good."

"What *do* you want from this thing with her?"

Good question. His gaze drifted away and he lost focus. There was so much to cover with what he wanted. And what he *should* want and what he *could* want.

She patted the butcherblock in front of him, getting his attention. "I can tell this is going to be a long chat. I'm going to change my clothes and we'll sit on the couch."

She padded down the hall and he brought his steaming cup of tea with him to the purple velvet sectional.

A purple couch.

Dark purple. Almost black.

And velvet.

He took a seat and rubbed the fabric with his free hand.

She even had cool furniture.

He played with the string of the tea bag as he waited for Kara to come back. This might be his first cup of tea ever. Was he supposed to leave the tea bag in this long?

Kara came back, her makeup gone, her hair in a topknot, wearing an oversized Yankees baseball tee and pajama pants. She grabbed her tea and joined him.

She curled into the opposite corner of the couch and faced him.

"I'm gonna be straight with you," she began, keeping her voice hushed. "When you first started coming around, I was hella suspicious. But Sabine was adamant that you weren't trying to get in her pants, so I didn't chase you away."

Dave smirked into his tea.

"But now you're here all the time. And she likes you."

His eyes came up sharply.

"Like, really likes you." Kara didn't look pleased with this revelation. "This is not brand-new information. Don't look so shocked." She took a sip of her tea and added, "And you like her too."

His lips twitched but he didn't deny it.

It was why he was there in the middle of the night, wasn't it?

Dave tipped his head back and gazed at the night sky out the tall windows.

"I have friends," he said. "I have really good friends. The kind of friends people would die for. I could go to them and talk to them about what's going on in my head but…" He licked his lips and took a deep breath. "She's on a whole other level."

Kara didn't respond. Which Dave appreciated because he was just now putting some of the scattered pieces into place.

"I keep thinking that if I could just hang out with her, everything would make sense. I know how it works for most people. I know they can close the book on the day, go to sleep, and pick it back up in the morning. And I don't want to get in anyone's way. I don't want to turn her life upside down." He glanced to the side. "Or yours," he added. "I just can't put it away yet."

"What would help you put it away for today?"

He shook his head. "I…don't know."

"She leaves for work pretty early in the morning." Kara pressed her lips together like she was contemplating several different avenues of thought. "I don't think this is solvable in one night."

Not exactly news to him. Also, not the first time he'd felt utterly exhausted by the way his own brain worked.

"Is it easier to be able to make decisions?" he asked, frustrated.

She arched a sardonic eyebrow and snorted. "I don't think love is ever easy, babe."

He rolled his eyes and they landed on her. "Babe."

"Babe."

"C'mon, babe."

"No, babe." She smiled and reached for his empty mug. Closer now, he could see the compassion shining out of her tired eyes. "I think you should get some sleep. Go sneak into Sabine's bed. She won't mind."

"But won't that be confusing?" he asked, even as his soul reacted in quiet jubilation. Just the thought of being near Sabine, even in sleep, was enough to quiet the turmoil for a moment.

Kara shrugged and stood up. She looked down at him. "She misses you too, dummy."

She took their dishes to the kitchen and left him on the couch to make his own decision.

Maybe Kara didn't hate him after all.

Or maybe she was giving him just enough rope to hang himself.

That thought immediately flooded him with guilt. That wasn't at all what Kara had intended. She was fiercely protective of Sabine.

Kara and Sabine's relationship reminded him of what he had with Leslie and Max, and he realized he didn't really know the story behind that. Sabine knew all about Leslie and Max's history with him but he couldn't recall being told much at all about Sabine's past.

Was that why he was hesitating?

Because she was?

Sometimes it seemed like she was all in but if he really examined their interactions, she had been… careful.

Oh. Discomfort washed away and was replaced by delighted shivers.

Because he *understood* that.

She wasn't going to throw her heart in his face and get angry when he dropped it. That wasn't her at all.

He'd been so focused on his own damn self that he hadn't taken the time to uncover everything she kept carefully hidden away.

Meanwhile, she'd peeled back his layers and not only accepted his confounding personality traits but seemed to delight in them.

Didn't she deserve the same, if not more?

Yes.

YES.

He had wanted a resolution. Something that felt like he'd closed the day.

And there it was.

* * *

SABINE

Her alarm went off and she slapped at her phone on the bedside table.

Holy fuck it was hot in here.

Why was it so hot in here?

She threw the covers off herself and the air cooled her heated skin.

Movement to her right stopped her. She frowned at the ceiling, blinked, and then propped herself up on an elbow and looked at the figure beside her.

Dave?

She tugged the covers away from his sleeping face and stared.

What?

When?

Also, *what?*

She rubbed her face with a hand.

Yep. That was Dave. Burrowed into her covers like a kid, his mouth slightly parted and his hair sticking up all over the place.

She sat up and tried to piece together what was going on but she… couldn't.

She'd definitely gone to bed alone last night. She glanced down at her pajamas—sleep shorts and an oversized t-shirt—not her cutest. So, yeah. Definitely gone to bed alone.

She snatched up her phone and checked her messages.

Nothing.

She checked recent calls.

Also nothing.

She had no memory of letting him in last night.

But she must have… right?

The toilet flushing had her eyes swinging toward the open door.

Kara.

She slid out of bed and closed her bedroom door behind her.

The bathroom door opened and a sleepy Kara jumped when she saw Sabine scowling at her in the hallway.

"Did you let Dave in last night?" Sabine whispered.

Kara smirked and patted Sabine on the shoulder.

That was it.

No explanation.

Kara went to her room and closed the door.

Okay.

Sabine went back to her own bedroom and crossed her arms over her chest, watching the award-winning lyricist sleep in the sheets she had bought as a gift to herself for her birthday.

He didn't move, clearly undisturbed.

Her phone beeped its warning that she needed to shower and get going.

Even if he woke up right now, she didn't have time to ask the questions she had, let alone wait for the answers.

Shaking her head in frustration, she hurried to her closet and grabbed her clothes, shoes, and bag. She left him to sleep and closed the bedroom door behind her.

While she ate her breakfast, she scrolled through social media and entertainment headlines, looking for any kind of hint why he would have showed up at her place. Because that had to be it, right? He had to be feeling attacked or alone or something to make him come to her.

Right…?

Or…

Or maybe he missed her as much as she missed him?

No. No, that was silly.

Chapter Nineteen
I Think He Knows

Her first student that week was a fifteen-year-old social media influencer whose life had exploded in both good and bad ways. Her parents had agreed to letting her convert to home study after her school had failed to protect her from stalkers showing up on school grounds.

Sabine knew the basics of her students' personal lives but she didn't think it was pertinent to know too much. More information could be distracting. And Sabine didn't want there to be any obstacles to her teaching. It was easier to think of them as students, not "influencers."

She was their teacher. Her job was very simple in that respect.

She didn't get involved in their lives outside of their lessons and she didn't share personal information about herself.

So it was quite jarring when Sally sat down at the table and slid her tablet across the table to Sabine—on the screen was a picture of Sabine in the dress she'd worn to the NMAs.

She frowned at the screen, blinked a few times, licked her lips.

"That's you," Sally said after Sabine had not responded for enough time that it was weird.

"Yep," Sabine replied. What was she going to do? Deny it?

"You were at the NMAs." Again, Sally stated instead of asked. Sally cleared her throat and cocked her head to the side. "Let me be more specific. You were at the NMAs *with* Sunshine Capone. And then you were put on no less than four lists of 'Best Dressed' from that night." Sally blinked at her.

Best dressed, huh?

Sabine tried not to smile but failed. Sally narrowed her eyes at her.

"Okay," Sabine said, understanding that there would be no moving forward until she gave Sally something. "You may ask me three questions and then we have to get to work."

Sally leaned forward eagerly. "Are you and Sunshine dating?"

"No." Though he was currently asleep in her bed. *That* detail she would not be sharing with the teenager. "We're just friends."

"Who dressed you?"

"Catherine Anne." Sabine glanced down at the screen again. Wouldn't they have included that in their best dressed blurbs?

Sally made a noise in the back of her throat. "But she only works in costume design. She doesn't do celebrities. Or teachers."

"I don't know what to tell you. Da-er-Sunshine said she dresses him, and she told me what to wear. I just showed up."

"Mm-hm." Sally didn't sound convinced but she moved on. She swiped on her tablet and another picture of her showed up. This time she was dancing with Zara Lorna at the afterparty.

"Are you and Zara Lorna friends?"

"We just hung out at the afterparty. I don't have her phone number or anything."

"Is she going to collaborate with Sunshine Capone?"

"You've hit your three-question limit," Sabine said with a chuckle.

Sally snapped her fingers. "I was hoping you weren't counting."

"I appreciate your interest in my personal life, but I really don't have any exclusive information to share. I'm still the person I was before you saw this picture."

Sally's eyebrows dipped and she slid the tablet back her direction. "Do you not know how cool you are?"

Sabine barked a laugh. "Excuse me?"

Sally's face relaxed into a stunned expression. "Oh my god, you don't know. That's hilarious." She picked up her tablet and started swiping and tapping furiously.

Sabine sighed and patted the table. "Okay, we really do need to get to work."

"Just…one…second…" Sally chewed on her bottom lip. "Done." She set the tablet down and reached for her laptop.

Sabine eyed the tablet, a question on her tongue. Did she want to know what the internet was saying about her?

No.

She really didn't.

And not because she was afraid of them saying something, but because she knew who she was. She didn't need to see how a stranger had parsed her identity down to tidbits.

Between students while she inhaled soup she'd bought at a deli, she decided to send Dave a message.

SABINE: Hey. You were sleeping when I left but I feel like we need to talk about why and how you were in my bed this morning.

DAVE: absolutely. Will you be at the studio later today?

SABINE: yes

DAVE: we will talk then

Why didn't that make her feel better?

* * *

DAVE

"Dave, sweetheart," Nikki said coolly, poking her head into the control room where he was going over his idea with Johnny. "Why is there a pop icon in my lobby asking to see you?"

"What?" Johnny spun around on his stool.

Nikki crossed her arms over her chest and stepped into the control room. "Zara Lorna is here."

Johnny blinked slowly. "Again…what?"

Dave took a breath and eyed his producer who looked like he was about to faint but also a little like he wanted to strangle someone.

"Okay, this is what happened." Dave quickly spilled the story about the NMAs, Sabine making friends with Zara, and their quick conversation about collaborating. "I didn't really think she was serious." Dave ended with a shrug.

Johnny closed his eyes and flexed his hands into fists and opened them a few times. "Always tell me these things. Even if you don't think it'll go anywhere."

"You got it," Dave agreed easily. What else was he going to do? Argue about how Johnny wanted to run his studio? "Then you should know that Chizeled will probably be calling too."

Johnny closed his eyes and inhaled slowly.

"So, should I bring her back?" Nikki asked, pointing over her shoulder with a thumb. "She's alone. No entourage of any kind."

Johnny glanced around the control room and ran a hand through his hair. "Let's meet in Studio X. It's brighter and looks better than…this."

Dave looked around at the cozy control room and shrugged. Whatever Johnny saw as a problem, Dave didn't. Though he'd been told he didn't view his surroundings with the same kind of eyes others did.

But he did know that Studio X was gorgeous. Easily the most impressive room in the building. He understood Johnny wanting to put his best foot forward with the pop star.

Zara entered the studio and Dave recognized the look of awe that crossed the singer's face.

Yeah, moving to Studio X had been the right call.

"So this is your big secret?" Zara said, sliding her hands into the back pockets of her jeans. She nodded at Dave and then at Johnny. "I'm impressed."

Dave introduced Zara to Johnny. "This is his place. He makes the magic. I just show up late and sometimes rhyme about it."

"What brings you to Chicago?" Johnny asked. He looked cool. He looked so cool he was nearly ice. But Dave had known him long enough now that he could see Johnny was vibrating with excitement.

"I'm actually here for a photoshoot and thought I'd see if Sunshine was around to show me his remix ideas for 'Good Intentions.'"

Johnny lifted his eyebrows but didn't otherwise show that he was taken off guard. "Are you ready to show her those things, Sunshine?"

"I could be ready for that," Dave agreed easily.

* * *

SABINE

She'd finished up her lesson with Piper and checked her phone. She hadn't heard from Dave since their last text exchange. And he hadn't come into the lounge at all either.

To say she was disappointed was an understatement.

But Dave had never failed to show up for her before. He'd been late a few times, but he'd never pulled a no-show.

Shawn burst through the door and grabbed the top of his head with both hands.

"Oh my god, Piper," he said, his voice just above a whisper. "Do you know who's here right now?"

Piper cast him a withering glare. "Why do you need so much attention? Who isn't loving you?"

He dropped his hands, unaffected by her reproach. "Zara Lorna."

Piper froze. "What?"

"Zara Lorna is downstairs, right now, in Studio X recording mad vocals with Sunshine."

Piper dropped her bag and darted from the room, Shawn following close behind her.

Well, that explained where Dave was.

Sabine shouldered her bag and draped her coat over an arm before following the younger two down to Studio X.

Johnny was in the control room, his head bobbing to the beat playing. On the other side of the glass was Dave, dressed in his usual hoodie and jeans. And on the opposite side of the room singing into a microphone was Zara Lorna, pop star.

Sure, Sabine and Zara had played lemon mouth and danced with each other like they were old friends. But that was like a dream version of Sabine's life.

This was real.

And it was really freaking cool to see.

Dave sang his verses, rapping them out with ease and that special rhythm she'd come to think of as his own. Zara added in her soft vocals overtop and they sounded amazing together.

Goosebumps skittered along Sabine's arms as the sound cascaded over her.

He really was so good at what he did.

Pride and admiration and something that felt a lot like affection filled her chest.

Her disappointment from earlier disappeared because this was important too.

Dave spotted her through the glass and first he smiled, bright and beautiful. And then his eyes widened and he pulled out his phone.

He waved at Zara and Johnny simultaneously, and left the recording area.

"I had no idea what time it was," he said as he slid his arms around her. He stopped from hugging her fully and gazed down into her face. "I'm sorry."

She rested her hands along his arms and looked up into his sincere expression.

"It's okay," she croaked out. How was she supposed to be upset when he apologized immediately and without prompting?

Then he hugged her.

He wrapped his arms around her and lifted her to her toes.

Dave gave good hugs.

He held her for four seconds longer than a regular hug before putting her down. But he didn't let her go entirely.

"Hi," he said, his gaze all over her face, landing briefly on her mouth before settling on her eyes. "You're beautiful."

"You're forgiven," she said around a giggle.

He grinned, pleased with himself. They were interrupted by Nikki and Johnny moving some equipment around and muttering about buzzing.

"Can you give me a hand?" Johnny asked Dave.

He let her go and joined Johnny in the bright recording room.

Zara moved in and gave Sabine her own hug. "I was hoping I'd get to see you," the pop star said.

They stepped back, out of the way of the bustling activity.

"So things with you and Sunshine look…interesting." Zara was fishing and Sabine laughed out loud.

"Interesting is an accurate word for it."

"We still staying friends or are we upgrading to more than friends?"

Sabine swallowed a smile. "I don't know. I mean, I love him, but—"

Zara's eyes widened just noticeably and she grasped Sabine's elbow. "You mean you like him."

Woof. Is it hot in here?

She hadn't meant to say that.

Or had she?

Was it a slip of the tongue or a slip of her thoughts?

"Yeah, yeah, of course." Sabine blinked and waved her hand like she could wipe away what had just happened. "I like him."

Zara narrowed her eyes at Sabine like she didn't believe her. "Hey, gimme your number. I'm out of here tonight but I have to be back in a few days for a thing. I want to see more of you."

Sabine watched from outside her body as she exchanged contact information with the woman who won Artist of the Year three years in a row.

What was her life anymore?

If Zara had kids this would make sense. But it looked like Zara Lorna wanted to hang out with Sabine? For the sake of hanging out?

"You know I'm a teacher, right?" Sabine asked, not wanting to spoil whatever image Zara had of her but not wanting to mislead her.

Zara giggled softly. "I know."

Dave rejoined them and Zara waved goodbye.

"So we're going to try to get this finished before her flight. Can I call you later? It might be very late." To his credit he looked conflicted. She was pretty sure that if she said she needed him, he'd drop everything and go with her.

But that would be ridiculous.

She tugged on one of his hoodie strings. "We can talk tomorrow." She pushed up on her toes and kissed his cheek. "Go be amazing."

The way he looked at her was part adoration and part disbelief.

But it was all Dave.

* * *

DAVE

. . .

She left the studio and he thought maybe she took a piece of him tucked inside the pocket of her cardigan. It was the gray one with tiny purple unicorn buttons. She probably thought no one noticed. But he had.

Zara playfully punched his shoulder.

"Do you need to go?" she asked, laughter in her eyes.

He rubbed the spot she'd hit, not that it hurt. "Nah, she said I should stay and do this." He took a breath.

Had a woman ever encouraged him the way Sabine did?

He couldn't ever remember if anyone had.

They liked the things his occupation could provide for them, but they seemed irritated that he had to be gone so often. Not just on tour, or at the studio, but if an idea hit him, he would leave whatever party or event they were at so he could get the ideas down. His writing interrupted a lot of his relationships.

A thought occurred to him and he focused on Zara. She tilted her head like she knew this wasn't going to be a small question.

"You're in a pretty serious relationship, right?" he asked. He wished for the first time in his life he paid attention to the gossip rags.

"Hmm," Zara hummed. "Are you asking for advice, padawan?"

His mouth split into a wide smile. "Nice." Of course, she was a Star Wars fan.

Zara sighed and looked around the control room. She waited for them to be alone again before she spoke.

"What if you take her out for dinner?" Zara suggested.

"Like a date?"

"Not *like* a date. An actual date." She blinked at him. "I know this awesome Italian restaurant here in town. If someone recognizes you it would be a patron not a pap. It's a small, easy way to make moves into the public without sacrificing your privacy."

"But," and he felt like this was obvious, "We're not officially dating."

If looks could melt, Dave's head would look like that guy at the end of *Raiders*.

"If you ask her on a date, and she says yes, you're officially dating. It's not that complicated." She patted his shoulder and walked away. "Let's get this done, I have a plane to catch," she called over her shoulder.

Hm. Maybe he'd been overthinking it.

It wouldn't be the first time.

He pulled out his phone, drafted a text, deleted it and started over.

Shit.

This was harder than he expected.

How do you ask a woman you really like, and maybe even more than like, to have dinner with you in public, while also not coming across like you're *telling* her to have dinner with you?

He wanted her to feel free to say no.

But when he tried putting that into text it sounded like he didn't want her to say yes.

"Zara!" he called, going back into the studio. She started this.

He needed help.

He needed so much help that he was rethinking asking her at all.

* * *

SABINE

"So you're really not going to tell me what you two talked about last night, huh?" Sabine asked through narrowed eyes as she held her glass of wine up to her lips.

Kara shook her head but she maintained that mischievous look in her eyes. "I told you everything."

"You dick," Sabine said, chuckling. "All you said was you made him tea and talked about me."

Kara shrugged. "All true."

"I hate you."

"No, you don't." Kara stretched her long legs out on the couch and pointed her toes. "Should we talk about him? Specifically, how you feel about him?" She arched an eyebrow at Sabine.

"I…I don't know."

Kara snorted. "Liar."

Sabine studied the pink liquid in her glass. "I don't know what else to say."

Kara sighed and they sat in silence for a few minutes.

"I think if I knew how he felt maybe it would make it easier for me to know what I feel."

"Bullshit."

Both girls giggled.

"How am I supposed to know anything? Honestly? You want to know how I honestly feel?" Sabine sat up and set her glass of wine on the ottoman.

"No, I want you to lie to me some more." Kara rolled her eyes.

Sabine clasped her hands in her lap. "I've never known anyone like him. Let alone *dated* someone like him. He's sweet and sincere, and funny." The pressure in her heart squeezed a bit as she thought about him. She didn't allow herself to think about him too much because sometimes that pressure in her chest felt too big to carry. Inexplicably, her eyes began to burn. "He doesn't ask me to be or act like anything. He just lets me be who I am. And I *like* who I am when I'm with him. He makes me feel like…myself."

Kara tilted her head, her eyes shining with emotion. "Maybe that's all you need to know."

Sabine bit the inside of her cheek and blinked away the moisture in her eyes. "His life is very big." The words felt thick in her throat.

Kara nodded.

"And he hasn't made any declarations. I don't feel comfortable considering whether or not his life is one I want to join with mine. It feels so presumptuous."

Because a conversation about intention felt like such a commitment. Which she knew he wasn't a fan of. He hated being boxed in.

"I'm worried that I've been trying to play it so cool I've led him to believe that I'm cool with casual."

There it was.

She'd finally found the words.

"And how I feel for him is *not* casual." She swallowed and swiped at the single tear that had finally escaped. "But we've known each other for just a couple months. That's not long enough for anyone to know what they want."

Kara shrugged. "I don't know about that," she said cryptically.

Sabine narrowed her eyes at her best friend.

Kara finished her glass and stood up. "Refill?"

Sabine blocked the way by sticking her leg out. "After you tell me what you mean by that."

Kara cocked a hip and her lips twitched. "You said it yourself, babe. He's not like other people. Time moves differently in his mind. You're just going to have to talk to him."

Sabine let her leg drop back to the floor as Kara's words sank in. She was going to have to ask Dave how he felt. And if what they were doing was not casual.

The idea made her want to pack a bag and fly to Europe and hide for at least a year. She could probably stay at her dad's place for free and he wouldn't even know she was there.

Because what if it was all in her head?

What if she was the only one with feelings bigger than friendship?

But the way he'd touched her body and kissed her skin had not felt like a "just friends" thing. She wished she would have been brave enough to ask him about it sooner.

But what if her asking about it brought it to a sudden end?

"I'm going to have to be brave," she said.

Kara sat down again, closer this time. She put a hand on Sabine's knee. "You *are* brave. You've forgotten because sometimes you do that. But I'm always going to be here to remind you."

Sabine's phone pinged and both women looked at it.

She picked it up and read the message from Dave.

She read it three more times.

"What?" Kara asked.

Sabine shoved the phone at her. "Tell me what it says because I don't trust myself."

Kara eyed her and took the phone. Her eyebrows went up as she read it to herself and then she read it out loud. "Would you like to go out to dinner with me tomorrow night?"

Kara nudged Sabine with her foot.

"Are you going to reply?"

Sabine stopped chewing on her thumbnail. "Is this a friend thing or a date?"

Her phone pinged again and they both looked at the screen.

DAVE: this would be a date date. You can say no.

Kara snorted. "You two are hilarious."

Sabine's stomach felt like it was on a roller-coaster. She closed her eyes to try to reduce distractions so she could think. When she opened them again, Kara was typing a reply into her phone.

"What are you doing?" Sabine reached for her phone but Kara held it out of reach. "Annnd, send." She tossed the phone to Sabine. "I told him yes and asked what restaurant so that I can help you pick out clothes."

Sabine gaped at her friend.

"What? You were taking too long, and you know that boy was hyperventilating over his word usage. I work tomorrow night anyway so you have no plans. Boom."

Her phone pinged again, and she opened it to find a link to a local Italian restaurant.

Kara sprang to her feet. "Time to try on dresses!"

Sabine stared at the text thread for a moment as her heart processed what her brain was still comprehending.

He'd asked her on a date date.

An "in public" date.

Yeah, they'd been in public before at the NMAs, but this wasn't an event that required her to sign four thousand documents.

This was deliberate and weirdly normal.

It was real.

The loft speakers started playing Lizzo's "Juice" and Kara danced back into the living room with dresses dangling from both hands.

"Start with the red one," Kara said, tossing it at Sabine.

Sabine caught the silky dress and laughed.

Her soul exhaled pure joy.

She jumped up and began stripping.

She had a *date* to prepare for.

Chapter Twenty
At Least For Now

DAVE

About a year ago, Max had taken Dave with him to buy what he called, "Adult man clothes."

Dave humored him because it was Max. And there wasn't much Dave wouldn't do if Max asked him to. Mostly because Max never asked.

Which was how Dave owned the Tom Ford charcoal three piece suit he was wearing. He'd forgone the tie and decided to leave his white button up shirt mostly open so the sunshine tattoo on the center of his throat served as a focal point.

He loved all (most) of his tattoos, but that one was his favorite.

And for the first time in maybe his entire life, he was not only on time, but early.

He spun the long stem rose in his fingers as the elevator doors opened.

For as nervous as he had been during the asking portion of this date, he wasn't nervous anymore.

Because it was Sabine.

And when he was with Sabine, everything just made sense.

Tonight he was going to tell her all of it.

His vow of celibacy, how he felt, and what he was hoping for, about the binders.

You know, or maybe not. Maybe they'd just have dinner and see where it led.

Deep breath.

Okay, maybe he was a *little* nervous.

He knocked on the door.

After a few minutes it opened and his smile dissolved.

"Are you crying?" he asked, taking in her glossy eyes and the red splotches on her cheeks.

"Oh, Dave," she said, putting a hand to her head. "I'm not ready. I'm so sorry."

He stepped through the door and wrapped his arms around her shoulders. Seeing her cry made his stomach turn inside out and his heart queasy. "It's fine. What happened?" He cupped her face with a hand and looked into her eyes as more tears spilled over and ran down her face.

She swiped at them. "It's nothing. I just need a minute and I'll be ready." She spun away but he caught her hand.

"Sabine," he said seriously.

She turned back to him just as her face crumbled.

And then he was folding her into his arms. She clung to him and tiny little hiccups made her body shake. He held her close to his chest and rested his cheek on the top of her head.

What on earth had happened?

He'd been texting her most of the day and nothing had come up. He'd seen her briefly at the studio before he'd gone home to shower and get ready. Everything had seemed fine.

"Tell me what happened," he urged, rubbing a hand in slow circles over her back.

"It's stupid," she said, pulling away again. She wiped at her face and hurried into the kitchen.

He followed and found her trying to clean her face with tissues. He set the rose down on the counter and she saw it. She inhaled and her lips pouted, and fresh tears streamed down her cheeks. She caught them with the tissue.

"Is it something I did?" he asked.

She huffed a surprised laugh and grabbed more tissues. "No, of course not."

He worried his bottom lip, trying to decide between forcing her into another hug or calling Kara.

Sabine walked over to the island and picked up an official looking letter. "It's stupid," she said again. She didn't hand him the letter but tossed it back onto the island.

He snatched up the offending letter and frowned as he tried to understand what it was saying.

Ms. Debois, thank you for applying... blah, blah blah... Unfortunately, you did not pass the required background check...

He glanced at the sender. It was from the city.

Fuck.

"I don't even know why I applied. This is what always happens." She took a stabilizing breath and blew her nose into the tissue. "Let me go shower. I can be ready fast."

He scrubbed a hand over his face. "No, babe." He tried to figure out the best way to say what he was thinking but there were too many options.

Fuck it.

He was just going to start talking and hope for the best.

"I'm canceling those plans." He held her eyes and shook his head. "Let's stay here, get some food brought in—you like Chinese?—and talk mad shit about local government."

Her lips trembled with the beginning of a smile. "But you look so handsome and I was really looking forward to our date."

That's all he needed to know. And he didn't even need to know that but hearing that she had been looking forward to their date felt incredible.

He took the steps necessary to bring himself closer to her and carefully tucked her hair behind her ears. He didn't let go of her and she tilted her head back to look up at him.

"Sometimes plans change," he said. "We can go out tomorrow. But I think tonight, we should stay in."

Her eyes shone but it wasn't the helpless tears from before. "Okay," she whispered.

"Okay." He pressed a kiss to her forehead. "I have to make a call."

She took a breath and he let her go. He watched her walk down the hall before pulling out his phone and letting his security know they could go home. Then he called the restaurant and canceled his reservation.

* * *

"I wasn't even going to apply." Sabine stuck her chopsticks into her to-go container.

Dave wasn't coordinated enough to use chopsticks, but he'd still tried. Until his hunger outweighed his desire to succeed and he'd gotten himself a fork.

She hadn't given him a hard time about it either.

"I was downtown getting the things I needed for you…you know, your GED thing, and I saw that they were hiring for part-time teachers for adult classes at the community college." She took a bite and chewed like she was annoyed at herself.

She swallowed and dug around in her container again. "And I guess I thought I was hot shit for a minute because I went home and filled out the application."

She'd been ranting for the better part of an hour.

Dave had to admit, she was hilarious when she was pissed off. And when she was hilarious, she was even hotter.

How that worked out, he couldn't explain. It was a fact he was just discovering for himself.

Also, it had been the right call to cancel the reservations.

This was what she needed.

If he'd let her get all dolled up and they'd gone out, she would've kept all this inside and felt obligated to put a mask on for the public.

He didn't want that.

When they did go out, he wanted to know she was just as much present for it as he was.

He always wanted her to be free to express herself. Even if she was having the worst day ever.

They were sitting on her velvet sectional facing one another, their legs stretched out between them. She'd changed from her teacher clothes into a soft pair of gray yoga pants and a long sleeved light pink sweater. Her hair was out of the braids and hung in messy twists just past her shoulders.

He hadn't changed for the obvious reason that he didn't have anything else to wear.

Though he did consider it when she offered a pair of Kara's yoga pants.

He'd taken off his jacket and vest and rolled his sleeves up.

The suit pants kept trying to ride up in a very uncomfortable way but he ignored it.

Or did his best at it.

She glanced up, a new thought hitting her. "And why is it that I have to apply online but they have to send me an official letter in the mail to let me know I'm not good enough? Couldn't they email me? Why waste the paper? So stupid. The whole system is rigged.

"And I'm not even mad they rejected me. Not really. They're just doing what they do. I'm mad at my mom for making this such a sucky part of my life." She rolled her eyes, her mouth turning down. "This is how it's going to be forever too, and I know it. I will always have to work for rich people who can afford to get higher-end background checks." She huffed. "Damn it, that makes me sound so ungrateful and judgey. I love being a tutor. I like working for the families I work for. But sometimes I wish I had a few more options." She stuck her chopstick in the container and looked at him plainly. "The community college would have been so neat, you know." Her voice took on a wistful quality. "Adults continuing to learn because they *want* to. It's awesome. I would've loved to be a part of that.

"But yeah, mom, thanks for making sure your life of crime will have a lasting effect on the rest of my life." She made a throaty growl. "Did I tell you that I secretly think she only had me so she could eventually try to steal my identity?"

"What?" he said, laughing even though it was *not* funny.

Sabine rolled her eyes. "It's true. My mom is actually the worst person I have ever known."

He shifted uncomfortably, fighting back the urge to start defending a woman he'd never met.

"When I have kids, I'll never make them feel like that. I'm going to love them. No matter what they look like or what they want to be. I'm going to do all the fun stuff, too. Glitter will *not* be a forbidden substance in my house."

"She didn't let you have glitter?" Dave asked. Of all the things he'd heard about Sabine's mom, that one struck him as the oddest. Who didn't like glitter?

The look Sabine gave him told him that that wasn't even the weirdest thing.

"She was always mad at me for liking little kid things. Like mermaids and face paint. One time she found a Barbie a friend had given me, and gave me a huge lecture on maturity and how I wouldn't be taken seriously if I played with toys. I was six."

"Is that why you have fun buttons on your cardigans?" he asked.

Her laugh sounded like a rich bubble of released tension. "You noticed those?" She nodded. "Yeah. I replace the buttons on my clothes with fun ones that I find." She shrugs. "It's like I'm still rebelling even though it really doesn't matter anymore."

"I fucking adore you," he said without thinking.

She blushed but didn't call him out on his bullshit.

Which only made him love her even more.

What the hell was his problem?

It was like he kept standing on the cliff face of commitment going, "I'm not ready!" And in the next breath yelling, "Geronimo!" and leaping into the unknown.

He really needed to decide how to or even if he was going to tell her he loved her.

And yeah. It was love. He loved her. He'd loved her for a while now but he sure as hell wasn't ready to tell her that. Not until he knew if she wanted him to love her or not.

And yes, it was exactly as ridiculous as it sounded.

"What about you?" she asked. "Anything you'll do differently for your kids? Unless you don't want kids," she included at the end.

"I do want kids," he said carefully. "I want the whole thing. Eventually. I used to think having kids would be terrible. For the kids."

Her eyebrows dipped but she didn't interrupt.

"Because I struggled so much. I was afraid of that for someone else. What if I was just as bad a dad as I was a son, you know?" Whoops. That got serious. He cleared his throat and tried to lighten his tone. "But I think maybe if I have the right partner, I might have a shot at being a decent dad."

"You'll be a great dad," Sabine said with a serious frown. "And I suspect you were a delightful child."

He rolled his eyes but she wasn't done.

"Dave, you took one look at my weepy face today and showed up. You didn't get uncomfortable that I was crying. You didn't tell me to stop. You just stayed with me and let me feel how I felt. Not once telling me how I *should* feel. That's A+ emotional support skills."

He chuckled. "I think that's my first A+."

"I'm serious," she said.

"I know." He held her gaze and then nudged her with his foot. "Emotions don't freak me out. If anything, it's refreshing. I'm an emotional guy. It's nice knowing I'm not the only one."

She narrowed her eyes like something just made sense to her.

"That's why you like Taylor Swift."

He smirked but didn't deny it.

"Should we try to go out tomorrow?" he asked.

"I'd really like that," she said.

He glanced up and the gentle look she was giving him was almost enough for him to confess all of his hopes and dreams and beg her to stay with him forever.

Yeah, he had it bad.

He'd never felt this intensely about a woman.

And they hadn't even slept together yet.

Well, they'd slept—never mind.

He knew he was going to have to tell her about the celibacy thing. He just didn't know when.

Maybe if she knew, she wouldn't be interested in dating him.

The more he'd thought about it, the more it made sense to *him*.

But every time he'd tried putting it into words, he couldn't.

Explaining why he needed to keep his head clear was more difficult than he'd imagined. And he'd had a hard time explaining his thoughts his entire life. But this little issue was deeply personal.

And impossible to describe.

But this was Sabine.

Maybe she'd understand.

Maybe he'd tell her next time.

Chapter Twenty-One
What a Man Gotta Do

SABINE

Dave stayed until she was yawning because it was way past her bedtime.

He kissed her forehead at the door and promised to see her the next day.

She would have protested him leaving if it hadn't been a school night. But it was, and she was responsible for teaching children, so she needed her rest as much as they did.

Still, it was hard to say goodbye.

Especially when he'd been so great about everything.

She hadn't meant to be crying when he'd shown up but sometimes emotions demanded to be felt. And her rejection letter had triggered a bunch of them.

And he hadn't been scared off.

The opposite in fact.

So, when she saw him at the studio the very next afternoon before their second attempt at a date, she couldn't stop smiling.

Piper noticed.

"My personal life is none of your business, Miss James," Sabine said.

"Right." Piper studied her for a beat. "If you guys have babies, will you please name your first born after me?"

Sabine's mouth fell open.

"It's only fair. You wouldn't have met if it wasn't for me. I deserve some credit. Most of the credit. Actually, a trophy would do. A big one. Like they use for championships." Piper packed up her laptop and zipped the bag shut.

Sabine shook her head. Piper smirked like only a teenager can, slung the bag over her shoulder, and left.

She passed Dave on her way out.

"You owe me big time," Piper said over her shoulder.

"I'm sure I do," Dave replied. "Send the bill to my manager." He came into the lounge, spotted her, and smiled.

God, she loved that smile.

"Are you done?" he asked.

"Mm-hm. I was just getting ready to go home and get ready."

He pursed his lips and sucked in a breath. "What if…?"

"What if what?" she asked, eyeing him suspiciously.

"How much do you trust me?"

* * *

And that's how she found herself walking into a building she had never been in before.

She didn't spot the name on the outside. Dave was walking too fast for her to get her bearings.

To be clear, he wasn't hurrying. His legs were such a length that walking with purpose for him translated to jogging for her.

And he was holding her hand, so there was that.

Honestly it was the hand holding that was the most distracting.

She liked it a lot and was trying to come up with ways to get him to hold her hand more often.

They went through a neat lobby with a reception which they bypassed, into an elevator.

"Where are we going?' she asked him in the elevator.

He smiled down at her and put a finger to his lips like it was a secret.

Hello, butterflies.

When the elevator door opened, they were greeted by Dallas.

And by greeted, she meant Dallas was there and motioned for them to follow her.

They were led to a conference room and left alone.

"What's going on?" she asked, still not sure where they were.

"Do you want an espresso?" he asked, going straight for the machine.

"Yes." She crossed her arms over her chest. "Are you going to answer my question?"

"No."

She snorted and turned around in time to see two men join them.

"Ms. Debois," the taller one greeted her. He held out a hand for her to shake and introduced himself as Quinn Sullivan and the other man as Alex Greene. Apparently, they were part of Dave's security team.

That explained why Dallas was there.

It didn't explain why Sabine was there though.

They all sat down at the table.

Quinn and Alex on one side, Sabine and Dave facing them.

Dave sat a cup of espresso in front of her.

She contemplated downing it like a shot but didn't.

"Sabine Debois," Quinn started. "Your mother Adrienne Debois stole hundreds of thousands of dollars from several of my current and former clients."

And Sabine's guard went up.

"I'll tell mom you say hi," she replied flatly.

If Dave brought her here to make her pay for her mom's sins, she was not going to be smiling at him for a while.

Dave reached over and took her hand.

"I understand she stole your identity for a short time as well."

Sabine didn't reply. She just blinked at the man in the suit.

Head of security, huh?

Did she fail the background check for dating Sunshine Capone? Was that the new thing he was doing since his last girlfriend turned out to be an arsonist?

Quinn studied her. "You've altered your appearance slightly. You used to look more like her."

"Well, when you get arrested in front of your friends at the Statue of

Liberty you take the hint." She'd lightened her hair by several shades and had gotten a new nose.

"I understand that you applied to be a teacher at the community college. Can you speak about that?"

Sabine cast a look to Dave who nodded his encouragement.

"Yeah. I applied, and they said because I didn't pass the background check, they wouldn't be hiring me."

"You make a decent living tutoring, no?" Quinn asked, his eyes on the paper in front of him.

Was he looking at her tax returns?

"It's not about the money," she found herself saying. "I like teaching."

She licked her lips and glanced to Dave again. He hadn't taken his eyes off her.

"Teaching is a part of who I am. I like leading people to the places where they can take over their own lives. I believe education is the fastest and best way to unlock someone's freedom." She glanced at Dave again. "I'm not a brave person by nature, but I like surrounding myself with brave people." She looked back at Quinn and Alex. "And people who want to learn are the bravest people. In my opinion."

Quinn's lips twitched and he made the slightest motion for Alex to take over.

"Dave asked us to scrub your record. We should be finished in a few days. You'll be able to apply for any job anywhere you want, and Adrienne Debois' criminal record will not be attached to you in any way."

And for the second time that day, her mouth fell open.

Dave squeezed her hand.

After a beat she found her voice. "You can do that?"

"I have people who can do that," Quinn not really clarified. "But it can't be public knowledge. This was a personal request that I decided was worthy of... bending some things."

Was what they did not entirely legal?

She didn't want to know.

She cleared her throat and swallowed. "I would be happy to sign something that says I will be quiet for the rest of my life."

Quinn passed her the file folder and a pen.

* * *

DAVE

Was it dumb that he brought a rose again?

It wouldn't be a surprise this time around.

Nah.

He'd bring her roses before dates for the rest of their lives.

He knocked on the door and he should have held his breath.

Because when she opened it, she took it away.

Wow.

It was all he could think as he took her in.

She was in a knee length red dress that came in tight at her waist with a red satin ribbon tied in a bow. It flared out at the bottom when she moved. Her shoes were also red and he didn't know what kind they were but he could see her toes.

Her hair was down and curled, her makeup soft and simple.

Her smile bright and just for him.

"Would you please go on a date with me?" he asked.

She laughed and the sound traveled through him like sunlight.

She took the rose and he took her hand.

If someone were to ask him later what he liked about their first date, he would have said "her."

Because that's what made the entire evening.

Just her.

Her eyes, her smile, her stories about teaching, her ability to light up entire city blocks with her joy.

They went out to dinner, where they ate and talked and laughed. They laughed a lot.

And then he took her dancing.

Well, actually he took her to a local show. One of his friends was in town doing a small club tour.

They had to come into the venue through a special entrance but she didn't seem to mind.

When the song was a slow one, he pulled her to her feet and into his arms.

They danced to three, four, five songs in the shadows. He never wanted it to stop.

She asked him questions about his tattoos as she touched them in the dark.

The sun on his throat, the bird on his face, the words above his eyebrow.

And when the show was over and he walked her to her door, he didn't want to go home.

Because he'd found his home in her eyes.

"Do you want to come in?" she asked, unlocking the door.

Yes.

He did want to go inside.

But if he went inside, he wasn't going to want to leave.

"It's a school night," he reminded her, taking her hand.

She turned into his body and tilted her chin up.

His gaze went from her eyes to her lips and held. He licked his lips and watched her pupils dilate.

He curved one hand around her hip and dipped his head. His lips brushed against hers and he closed his eyes.

Her hands came to his shoulder, then the back of his head.

She parted her lips and he swept his tongue inside. She tasted like the mint she'd eaten in the car. Her mouth was hot and slick, and he slid a hand into her hair and palmed the back of her head, cradling it as he took the kiss deeper.

A little whimper spilled from her into his mouth and he greeted it with a groan.

Holy hell.

Had lips ever felt like this?

Tasted like this?

He backed her against the door and she pressed her entire body against him.

All he could think about was needing to get closer to her, needing to get rid of the barriers between them. He needed to touch her everywhere. Kiss her everywhere. Taste her everywhere.

He.

Needed.

Her.

He moved his mouth over her jaw and down her neck. His hands went from her hip, up her ribs, to just below her breasts. He brushed his thumb over the peak of one of them, and she moaned into his mouth.

And then the door opened.

He caught her before she fell into the apartment, holding her close to his body.

"Really, people?" Kara said, sounding irritated. "Some of us have to work in the morning." She turned around and sauntered back into the loft.

"Sorry, Kara," Sabine called.

"Yeah, sorry, Kara," he said too.

He grinned at Sabine still in his arms. "You make me a little crazy."

She looked completely unrepentant.

He pressed another hard kiss to her mouth and then let her go.

"I'll see you tomorrow?" he asked.

She nodded.

He took in her mussed hair, her kiss swollen lips, the brightness in her eyes.

"Fuckin' perfect," he muttered. He lifted his chin at her. "Get out of here before I force you to run away with me."

She snickered and backed into the loft and closed the door.

Yeah, he needed to talk to her about a lot of things.

Probably sooner rather than later.

Chapter Twenty-Two
I Can't Be Myself

After the best date of Sabine's life, Zara came back to town.

And she basically set up shop in the studio.

As such, Dave had started working round the clock.

Sabine wasn't exactly sure what they were all working on. She was going to ask. Just as soon as she could see him again.

Okay, it wasn't like they hadn't spoken at all.

He had texted her a few times. And they had smallish conversations at the studio. But she wasn't comfortable asking him about all the things she didn't know in front of his colleagues and coworkers.

How inappropriate would that be?

And then there were the nights he snuck into her bed without her knowing.

He'd done it two more times that week.

And of course she didn't have time to wake him up and talk to him before having to leave for work.

At least that's what she told herself as she pressed a featherlight kiss to his temple before hurrying out the door.

Here was the truth.

She loved waking up to him in her bed.

He was soft and snuggly, and he smelled like fresh air and expensive aftershave.

And she was dangerously close to falling in love with a guy who may have zero intention of handling her with care.

And by dangerously close, she meant, probably, definitely was in fact in love with him but unwilling to have the final thought pass completely through her brain and/or say it out loud.

Except for the one time she'd said it to Zara Lorna.

But not since then!

But it was there; a consistent pressure in the back of her mind. Reminding her steadily that she had not-casual feelings for him.

In fact, she had very large, wanted-to-kiss-him-and-do-other-things-with-him feelings.

So on Friday, when she had to work her shift at Geekeasy, she was only somewhat surprised when the VIP Lounge was occupied with Sunshine Capone, Max, Leslie…and Zara Lorna.

And Zara Lorna's entourage. Which appeared to be two models and two more bodyguards.

She had not been given a heads up before she'd gone up the stairs to the VIP Lounge. As such, she stood and stared for a solid sixty seconds before anyone else noticed she was there. And the first person to notice her?

Dallas.

The second was Darius.

Truthfully, Dallas had probably spotted her before she'd taken the first step up. That was her job after all.

She could do this.

She could be professional and affable at the same time.

Still.

Her stomach felt like the bottom had dropped out and she was not quite in a freefall but also not safe.

Of all the celebrities she'd been around in her multiple lines of work, she'd never been unsure of her ability to do her job.

But in that moment, she was unsure.

And she couldn't say why.

Just that everything felt off balance.

Why hadn't he said that he would be here?

She squared her shoulders, pressed her lips into a thin smile, nodded once at Dallas and Darius, and approached the group.

"Good evening, everyone," she greeted, hearing more enthusiasm in her voice than she currently felt. "What can I get you all started with?" She winked at Max. "Cider?" She allowed her gaze to slip through everyone else, reverting back to the no eye contact rule. "Beer? Cocktails? Are we thinking about food tonight or just drinks?" She pulled out her tablet as she spoke and called up the order menu.

"You really gonna act like we're not besties?"

She flicked her eyes up at Max's question. He was getting to his feet and she couldn't stop the smile that spread across her face. And then he was hugging her.

He pulled back and studied her with his dark eyes. "Where have you been? I've been in town for a few days. I thought for sure I'd see you at the condo."

Condo?

Dave's place?

She'd never been invited.

Instead, she shrugged. "I've been busy working."

He nodded once, not entirely believing her. But she wasn't lying. She really had been working all week.

And then it was Leslie's turn to hug her.

"Gorgeous girl," he said against her temple as he crushed her to him. "I missed you more than I thought possible. Did you know that my house is so quiet since you left that I've started to leave music playing constantly? I need your energy in my life." He hugged her again and she choked out a laugh.

And then Leslie was shoved aside as Zara squealed, did a hop, and then threw her arms around Sabine.

Yes. She was being hugged by a pop star.

"I asked Sunshine if you'd be able to come out with us tonight and he said you were busy."

Did he now?

Sabine lifted her eyebrows. "Well, I am working so…"

"You're kidding." Zara took another look at Sabine and her tablet. "You work here?" She looked back and forth between Dave and Sabine. "Is this real?"

Sabine finally let her eyes connect with Dave's.

Oh.

There it was.

That sleepy, peaceful place where she always felt safe.

He smiled, but it was small and uncertain. He squeezed the back of his neck, and he did not stand up to greet her like his friends had.

That was fine.

And she was fine with it.

Just.

Fine.

"I thought you were a teacher," Zara said.

"I am." Sabine wagged her head back and forth. "But it doesn't pay as much as I like to spend, so I work here most weekends."

Zara's eyes sharpened on her and her expression grew thoughtful.

Sabine inhaled and forced a bright smile.

"So what can I get for everyone so I can earn those tips I expect you all to drop on me tonight?"

She took orders from everyone and purposefully left Dave for last. She made her way around the room, pretending not to notice how she had to look *up* at the two models to get their orders. They even smelled pretty. Like flowers and fairies and mystical faraway lands.

When all she needed was Dave's order, she skirted the perimeter and made sure everyone else was thoroughly distracted.

"How about you, superstar?" she asked, taking a seat beside him on the couch.

"I feel like I haven't seen you in a month." His voice was rough; he reached for her and stopped. He tried a smile. "We need time. You and me."

Annnnd she was goo.

See? This was why they needed to have a conversation about all the things. Because when it was just them, it seemed way too effortless and simple. It wasn't confusing until she started trying to figure out where she fit in his life.

Somehow bringing drinks to his friends didn't fit into her long-term ideas.

Dave tucked a piece of hair behind her ear and his fingers lingered on her neck. "Is this okay? Should I have taken them somewhere else?"

Sabine didn't know how to respond. The thought of someone else bringing him drinks and getting hugs from Max and Leslie left her feeling ugly inside.

Jealousy, she realized. That's what she felt.

Ew. No.

"I just wanted to see you and I knew you were working tonight." He dropped his hand, but his eyes stayed, searching her expression.

Oh.

"I just wish we could have a conversation where one of us wasn't at work," she said, telling the truth.

He nodded solemnly. "Can I make sure you get home tonight?"

Her lips tugged up on one side despite herself. "And maybe stay the night?"

He bit down on his bottom lip and pumped his eyebrows once. "Maybe."

She exhaled a frustrated groan and closed her eyes. When she opened them, his expression had switched from playful to concerned.

"I'm driving you crazy, aren't I?" he asked.

If she said yes, would he understand that it wasn't *him*, it was just the circumstances?

She took a breath. "What do you want to drink? I'll put this order in… and we'll see how you feel about coming over later."

"Dr. Pepper," he replied quickly.

She cracked a smile. "Do you want rum in it or anything?"

"Nope. I don't want anything clouding my thoughts."

His tone sounded meaningful, and she glanced up quickly.

"I know how I feel," he said solidly. "And I'll be here to take you home tonight."

Her insides fluttered and she swallowed.

And then she left to put the order in.

And he was still there when her shift ended to take her home.

Chapter Twenty-Three
Anyone

DAVE

They crossed the threshold of the loft and Kara gave him a stealthy salute before disappearing down the hall.

So this was it.

They were alone and he was going to tell her all the things.

All of them.

Any minute now.

Sabine collapsed on the couch and closed her eyes.

"Those models can really get after it," she said sleepily. "They weren't even a little wasted at the end."

"Yeah, I think they went to a club that was still open down the street." He sat down in the opposite corner of the couch, facing her.

"Am I old or do I just not have the proper constitution for that kind of life?" she asked.

He patted his lap. "Gimme your feet."

She eyed him warily but swung her legs around and placed them in his lap. He immediately took one in both hands and began rubbing it.

A groan escaped her and she sunk further into the cushions.

"There is nothing wrong with your constitution. Those ladies live a lifestyle most can't keep up with. They probably won't sleep until tomorrow night."

"That does not sound healthy." She peeked one eye open. "That feels amazingly good."

He cracked a smile. "You have small feet so it's not hard."

"My feet are the national average, thank you very much," she retorted sounding slightly miffed.

"Sensitive about your tiny feet, are you?" he teased.

She tried to yank her foot away, but he held onto it. "Oh stop. You know I love your feet."

She snorted but relaxed again.

He rubbed her feet, taking turns between them, until she was loose and at ease. He moved his hands up her calves, rubbing the tight muscles there. And wondering how he was supposed to segue to what was on his mind.

Carefully, he crawled up her body until he was lounging in between her body and the couch.

She adjusted to make room for him and placed her hands on his chest. Then smiled up at him.

"Hi," she said softly.

He tucked a stray tendril of hair that had escaped her braid behind her ear and stroked his thumb over the apple of her cheek. "Hi."

She exhaled a contented sigh that rolled through his entire body.

Several nights that week he had snuck into her bed, determined to wake up with her in the morning. Only to find she'd been just as stealthy as him when she'd left for work.

But now they were both awake and together…and all he wanted was to stare at her.

"This is nice. I like being this close to you when we talk," he said, voice low.

"Should we talk about things?' she asked. The tone was light but her eyes were guarded.

He nodded. "What do you want to talk about first?"

"Hmm." She pretended to think. "What are you working on at the studio?"

Oh, she wanted to talk about that? He loved talking about what he was working on. He shifted slightly so they were both a little more comfortable.

"So Zara writes her own stuff, right? But after we recorded that remix, she's been sending me these ideas for more collabs. And we started writing and sending shit back and forth. And now we've got some ideas we're thinking about putting out as an EP maybe. Or maybe more. I don't know. It's not like anything I've ever worked on and it's kind of thrilling. I've never worked with another artist that's so focused but also so open to options. She writes incredibly fast."

He took a deep breath and pulled Sabine closer.

"That's about it."

"I like it when you talk about what you're working on. Your eyes get all happy and bright." She grinned up at him.

"I wish Curtis was half as encouraging as you are."

Her eyebrows dipped. "Is he not on board?"

Dave growled. "That's one of the reasons I was so out of it tonight. I'd just had a call with Curtis. He wants to come out for a meeting of all the things he thinks are the most important things in the world."

She smirked at his bitchy attitude.

"He's not wrong. I just hate how he acts like schedules and organization are so critical." He knew they were important. But he didn't want to have the little slice of peace he'd found disrupted already. And that's exactly what would happen. Curtis would come to town, meet Sabine, and *make a plan*. The man couldn't help himself.

Every damn thing was scheduled out with that guy. Dave wouldn't be surprised to find out that Curtis scheduled his daily bowel movements.

Curtis's phone call also reminded him that he needed to talk to Sabine about his life. Everything that came along with being in it and being a part of it. She should have the full picture before he asked her to get on the craziest ride in town.

"I didn't tour for the last album. I doubt I'll be able to get away with that again." He worried his bottom lip. "Touring is great, don't get me wrong. But it also takes me away from people that mean a lot to me."

Her smile was soft and held promise. "Maybe people could come see you on tour."

His gaze dropped to her mouth. "You think people might do that?"

"I think," she whispered. "If people cared about you and you made it clear you wanted them there, they would try their hardest to show up for you."

He licked his lips. "Are you my people?"

"If you'll have me."

He bent his mouth to hers and she met him there.

He kissed her slow, taking his time.

Deep, languid kisses.

His tongue, her tongue, heat and promise.

Like time wasn't anything.

Like they had forever.

"You have the most beautiful eyes I have ever seen." He brushed his lips over hers; watched the shy smile that happened there. God, he could look at her for hours.

"You truly are the most gorgeous person I have ever encountered." He traced the shell of her ear with a fingertip. Dipped his fingers into her soft as silk hair.

Everything about her was soft.

Her skin, her heart, the way she looked at him.

"What the hell are you doing looking up at me with eyes like that?" he asked gruffly.

"Tell me where I should be looking," she whispered back.

"At someone more worthy."

Her lips parted at his words. And even though he knew he should leave her to find someone else—someone less complicated and more predictable —he wasn't going to. Not ever.

He lowered his head and took her mouth again. This time with more urgency in his kiss. He ran his hands over her body, touching what he could while he could.

Her hands went into his hair.

His mouth moved to her jaw. She craned her neck back to give him better access. He slid his hands under her t-shirt and in one move, it was off and on the floor. He placed open-mouthed kisses along the top swell of her breasts. She arched, lifting her chest closer to his mouth. He curved both hands around her waist and held her against him. Her legs opened and he settled between her thighs, pressed against her center.

"Can I touch you?" she asked, her fingers skating along the edge of his shirt hem.

"Please do," he encouraged, going back to her neck with his mouth.

Her greedy fingers ran under his shirt just as he slid his tongue into her mouth again.

And then it was all hands and mouths and movement.

He held onto her like he was afraid she could disappear at any moment.

And maybe that was why he said what he said next.

Because of the hint of desperation in his kisses, or the way her touch felt like coming home.

"Come with me to Saint-Tropez," he murmured against her neck.

She tensed. Her hands paused their delightful grabby-ness. "What?"

He raised his head and gazed down at her flushed cheeks and kiss-swollen lips. "Come away with me. For Christmas. We can get drunk and lay in the sun, and I can kiss you all over this glorious body." He demonstrated by kissing the tops of her breasts one at a time. Then he grinned at her.

Her smile was hesitant. Which caused a spike of alarm in his chest. Had he done something wrong?

"Oh, superstar," she whispered. "I want to say yes so bad."

"Then say yes," he tempted with a cheeky grin.

She licked her lips and took a breath like she was trying to find the right words.

Which, again, spike of alarm.

She reached up and ran her fingers lightly over the tattoos on his face.

"I like you," she said softly, like it was a confession. "I like you in a very big, very not casual way."

His heart began to thunder in his chest. "I like you too."

"But you just asked me to go to Saint-Tropez with you for Christmas." She shrugged one shoulder, sadness shining in her eyes.

"How is that bad? What am I missing?"

"That's where you take every girlfriend. And then two weeks later there's some sort of giant, dramatic breakup, and it's over."

He blinked rapidly. That couldn't be true? Was that true? There was no way that was true.

"And I'm going to show all my cards here, but I don't *want* it to be over." She took a shaky breath and pressed a hand to his chest. "I don't know how you feel. But I know how I feel. I can't keep doing the casual, flirty, friend thing. I want more."

He wanted more too.

He wanted all of it.

That's what he'd been trying to say by asking her to go away with him. So he decided to say as much. "That's what I want too. I thought it would be easier for us to connect if we got away. Just us. And then we could see if this is what it seems to be."

She studied him thoughtfully, and he tried not to feel desperate. But for the hundreds of times they'd so easily been on the same page, this felt…off.

"Don't you want to come away with me?" he asked, searching her face.

She nodded. "I do. Badly. I want nothing more than to run away with you and never look back. But I can't do that. People are depending on me to show up for them. And if we jet off on a whim, and it doesn't work, I've blown up my entire life."

He was hearing her words, and most of them were making sense, but it still felt like heavy rejection. Like she wasn't saying no to the trip, she was saying no to him.

"I don't want to say no. I want to say yes." She ran her fingers through the hair at his temple. "But I need to be able to say no to this."

He pressed his lips together and took several deep breaths. "Let me have a moment to think, okay?"

Anyone else—hell, even Max or Leslie—and he'd have felt bad for asking for that moment. But deep inside he knew that Sabine would never disparage him for taking an extra beat to think it through.

Which helped him get to his conclusion fast.

He could see it. What she was saying. His hurt was still right up front trying to throw a tantrum but he didn't want to be that guy. He needed to be able to see her perspective. She spent a lot of time seeing things from his way. He could do the same for her.

She wasn't saying no forever. She was saying that she couldn't upend her life because he was feeling impulsive.

Which made sense.

His impulses often got him into trouble, and rarely got him what he actually wanted.

But when he slowed down, delayed his gratification—like the morning he'd spent time with his mouth all over her body—he ended up with more of what he wanted.

And he definitely wanted more of Sabine than just a holiday.

"Okay," he said, nodding. "I don't remember the breakups happening in that order, but I trust your memory more than mine. I can see why that would be something you wouldn't want to be a part of." He blew out a breath and exposed even more of his soul. "My feelings for you are not casual. I'm not interested in rushing through this."

She tried a hopeful smile. "Yeah?"

He couldn't resist her when she was looking up at him like that. "Yeah." He lowered his head and kissed her soft and slow and sweet.

"Would you like to stay the night?" she asked between breathless kisses.

He braced his hands on the cushions by her ribs, and raised himself up and gazed down at her.

So beautiful.

He wanted her.

Bad.

But she'd just reminded him why he needed to break the patterns he had. Because she mattered. Because what they were building mattered.

"I have to tell you something," he said.

She visibly braced and he almost laughed.

"I know how that sounded. It's not bad. Not like that anyway." He sat up and brought her with him. He leaned over and grabbed her shirt off the floor and handed it back to her.

He took comfort in her confused and disappointed expression.

"I've thought a lot about how to bring this up and I've decided there's just never going to be a good way to say it."

She tugged her shirt back over her head and gave him her full attention.

"The day Nora burned my house down I took a vow of celibacy." Immediately he cringed. He waved a hand at her surprised expression. "Not like in an official way. I sound like an asshole. No. I just promised to myself, to stop having sex until…"

She dipped her head like she was prompting him to finish that statement.

And that was the problem. He didn't have a clear ending to that sentence.

"Until I know I've found the one, I guess."

She sat back, thoughtful.

Not upset or judgmental. Just thoughtful.

She deserved more context.

"I've used sex a lot in my relationships to hide from real intimacy," he said. "And just like what you pointed out with me and Saint-Tropez, I have some patterns that would be better broken. For everyone involved."

"How will you know?" she asked. "That the time has come?"

He swallowed. That was a good question. Was he sweating?

"I'm still figuring that out," he admitted carefully.

Her eyes went soft, and a smile touched her lips.

Did she know?

Did she suspect that he was already stupid in love with her?

He was all in.

But if a trip to Saint-Tropez freaked her out, then him telling her he wanted to be with her forever would send her fleeing into the night.

No.

He could wait until she trusted what this was.

Because he wasn't sure how they'd found each other. Maybe it was complete chance. Maybe it was fate. Maybe he'd finally done something right and the universe had smiled down on him.

But she was it.

She was the missing verse, the perfect rhyme, the steady rhythm to his traveling thoughts.

She had a way of bringing him back to center. Back to himself.

He had no intention of losing her.

* * *

Morning came, and as always, he was surprised.

Time seemed to sneak up on him. The sunrise felt like a rude interruption.

They hadn't left the couch. Instead choosing to stay close and speak in hushed tones about favorite colors and songs and stories.

Small things.

Intimate things.

And then the sun was there, and Sabine had drifted to sleep in his arms.

He stayed as long as he thought he should, and then he slipped out. Not before leaving a note, though.

His car wasn't at her loft, so he had to call a service.

By the time he'd returned to his condo, the sun was committed to the day, and he was starving.

Max lifted his eyes over the rim of his coffee cup as Dave stepped through the door.

"Did you make food?" Dave asked, slipping off his shoes and tossing his coat to the side.

Max's eyes followed the coat's descent. "You have a closet for that, you know. And yes, I made food." He came off the stool where he was seated and went to the kitchen, filling a plate for Dave.

Dave picked up his coat and hung it up. Because Max was right. And also, if he didn't hang it up, Max would keep mentioning it until he did.

He took the plate of food Max handed him and sat down at the counter. Max joined him.

"I'm surprised to see you so early. I thought for sure you'd be having breakfast with Sabine," Max remarked casually into his coffee cup.

Dave nodded, chewing the mouthful of breakfast sausage. He swallowed, wondering if he could tell Max what was on his mind. Not *could*. Did he *want* to tell Max. That was a more accurate statement.

On one hand, he told Max everything.

But on the other…he kind of liked having something that was just his for a moment.

Max was fishing, that was obvious. But he wasn't pushing. Not yet.

"What did I do for Christmas last year?"

Max's eyebrows dipped. He finished swallowing his coffee and set the mug down on the counter. "You don't remember?"

Dave shrugged. "Not really. I know you were with your ma, and Leslie went home too. I don't remember what I did."

"You were on a yacht in the south of France."

"Saint-Tropez?"

"Possibly. Probably."

Dave thought about that and ate some more. He propped an elbow on the counter. "I asked Sabine to go to Saint-Tropez with me for Christmas."

Max went completely still.

Dave watched him from the corner of his eye.

"She said no."

Max visibly relaxed.

Dave angled his body towards his friend. "That's good?"

Max inclined his head slightly. "I would consider that good."

Dave narrowed his eyes. Still trying to understand it. "Why?"

Max got off the stool and walked around the counter to the coffee maker. He poured himself a new cup and refilled Dave's. Placing the carafe back on the warmer, he leaned his back against the counter and crossed one ankle over the other.

"She likes you."

Dave rolled his eyes. This was not new information.

"Yeah, and I like her, and we're not in middle school. Tell me what you're not saying."

Max eyed him and it tried Dave's patience. He was exhausted. Physically, emotionally, mentally. He had not slept all night and it was catching up with him. He had also just spent hours learning new things about someone he cared about. And on top of that, he was really trying to not revert to old habits of running away.

He was beginning to fray at the edges of his capabilities.

It must've showed because Max relented. He sighed, his shoulders dropped, and he set his coffee cup down.

"When I say she likes you, I mean she likes *you*. Dave. She's fine with Sunshine Capone and his life. But she *likes* you."

Dave frowned. Again, not new information.

Max looked heavenward and muttered under his breath. "You're really going to make me spell it out."

"Rude."

"I'm not insulting you," Max replied, irritated. "Up 'til now, the only girls you've dated have liked Sunshine Capone. They liked his money and the gifts and the trips to Saint Bart. But they didn't give a single shit about Dave Hansen."

He stopped there. Letting his words rattle around in Dave's head.

Had he really been that slow on the uptake? He hadn't noticed that they didn't really know anything about him. They never even asked.

"Leslie and I know you. We know that Dave and Sunshine are essentially the same person and yet not. Sunshine is a brand. A brand you created and developed and…" Max blinked, shrugged. "Frankly, it's brilliant. He's you but he's also someone you can put away and not have to be." He smirked. "And Sabine likes all of it. I don't mean that in a juvenile *ooh, she liiikes you*. I mean," he leveled his eyes at Dave, serious and happy at the same time. "She likes you. You. She. Likes. You."

Ohhh.

"There it is." Max shook his head and picked up his coffee cup again. "But I do have to wonder, why haven't you had her over here yet?"

Dave's guard went up again like a reflex. "How do you know I haven't?"

Max rolled his eyes. "Dude. I'm actually a semi-intelligent person. It's very obvious you haven't had a girl over. At all."

"Because."

"That's a good reason. *Because,* " Max mocked him.

"Why do you and Leslie like her so much?" Dave asked, not caring that he sounded suspicious as hell.

Max's lips twitched. "Because she cares about you. And she's fun and sweet and she's very likable."

"You didn't like Nora," Dave pointed out. "And she was all those things."

"That girl had crazy pouring out of her and you were the only one who didn't see it," Max retorted. "When I saw it come across my Google alerts that Nora had set the place on fire, I can't tell you how *not* shocked I was. She told me that if you ever cheated on her she would burn your life to the ground." He lifted his eyebrows. "Crazy always tells you their plan."

Dave schooled his features.

"You didn't like Mandy."

"Mandy stole my car and drove it into a pool." Max blinked at him.

"But you didn't like her before that," Dave argued, trying not to laugh.

"Because when I met her, she asked me if you were always so boring."

"Mandy thought I was boring?" That was the first Dave had heard about it. Why did that sting?

"This is what we're discussing? Right now? Okay." Max inclined his head again. "Remember Cassandra? The night I met her she was stealing a bottle of liquor from behind the bar."

Dave winced. He remembered. But at the time he thought it had been a one off, not a character trait.

"Do remember what she was arrested for?" Max asked but didn't wait for the reply. "Felony vandalism. She spray painted SLUT in big red letters on the side of a boat that wasn't yours."

"She thought it was mine."

Max didn't look amused. "And if it *had* been yours, you would have never pressed charges."

Dave opened his mouth to protest but Max wasn't wrong.

Hmm.

Max downed the rest of his coffee like it was whiskey and slammed the mug on the counter. "Please, for the love of all that is holy, don't let Sabine get away. You have been in love with that girl since the moment you laid eyes on her."

Dave smiled because he agreed, but still felt the need to argue. It was his nature after all.

"You weren't there the first time I saw her."

Max flattened his expression. "Please. I saw the way your entire soul lit up the night she appeared as our server. Why do you think I was so suspicious?"

"You're always suspicious."

"Touché."

They fell into a quiet thoughtfulness for a few minutes. Max took a deep breath and let it out.

"She's good to you. She's good *for* you."

Dave smiled softly at his oldest friend. "Yeah. She's it. I don't want anyone else. Just her. I want the whole thing too. Marriage, babies, ugly-ass white tennis shoes and tucked in shirts."

Max's eyebrows lifted into his hairline. And for once, the lawyer was speechless.

"I know, I know," Dave said, holding his hand out. "It's too soon for that. But..." He swallowed the tightness in his throat. "That's where I'm headed. I don't know how long it'll take to get her there, but I can wait."

Max took a careful breath. "You're not great with patience."

"You're not wrong," Dave replied regrettably. "I may need a few reminders along the way." He took a sip of his coffee and changed the subject. "By the way, I want to start putting my money to good use. I want lots of options. Schools, clinics, sports, kids, all of it. I don't know how to even start organizing those kinds of things."

Max's expression lit up. "I can make a binder for that!"

Chapter Twenty-Four

Bleeding Love

DAVE

"**A**re you busy?"

Nikki raised just her eyes and blinked at him. Her hands were currently wrist deep in an amplifier.

"That's a yes?" Dave clarified.

Nikki sat back on her heels. "I suppose it depends. If you need a ride to the airport, then yes, I'm busy. If you accidentally bought too many tacos, I am available."

He grinned. "Tacos sound like a good idea. We should order some. But I just need an opinion."

She tilted her head to the side, interested.

"I have plenty of those."

He was counting on that.

He turned to leave, hoping she'd know to follow.

She did.

Normally he would have asked Johnny or Hannah to come listen to what he and Zara had cooked up, but they had left abruptly for a meeting. Or something. He had only been half listening.

Nikki had a great ear though and Johnny would have asked her opinion eventually.

She followed him to control room X.

He hit playback on what he and Zara had been working on and then waited.

Nikki sat down at the board and adjusted some settings.

"It's fine but what if you added a…" She did the magic button thing and Dave nodded like he knew what she did different. He didn't.

Like, he could hear how it was changed, but he had no idea what thing she'd done.

"Oh!" Zara leaned forward and began singing over the beat.

"I thought you two were just doing one song," Nikki said, flicking through the work they'd created the week before. "There's more than one song here."

"I'm trying to decide which ones to put on the next LP," Dave explained.

"Sure," Nikki replied. "Or you could pick your five favorites and do an EP. A Sunshine and Zara collab."

His eyes met Zara's and she looked interested. "Or… We could do two EPs. Where we switch off the lead. And then we could use more of what we've written."

"There's a lot here." Nikki clicked through the files in the computer. "Can I play with these a little?"

"Of course," Dave agreed. That's why he'd gone to find her.

Zara's phone pinged and she glanced down at the device in her hand.

Dave pointed to the file he wanted Nikki to hear and she clicked on it.

"Hey, Dave…"

The tone in Zara's voice was wary, and both he and Nikki looked at her.

"Don't freak out."

Dave eased his body into a relaxed posture. Being told not to freak out was one of his most disliked phrases. Mostly because it assumed he was going to freak out which wasn't something he generally did. But also, it implied he viewed things the same as others. Which he did not.

"Mandy is stopping by the studio. She's just coming to pick me up before we go back to the hotel. I promise she won't stay long. And she won't cause a scene."

Mandy?

For some reason Dave couldn't place the name.

And then he did.

Mandy his ex. Who was friends with Zara.

He shrugged. "Okay."

Zara's eyebrows dipped and Nikki swiveled slightly on the stool to look at him.

But he didn't know why.

He and Mandy hadn't been together in two years. He hadn't even seen her around. Why would he freak out?

Nikki spun back to face Zara. "This is a drama free recording studio," she said, warning in her voice.

Zara held up her hands. "She will be on her best behavior. My security is here—" She gestured over her shoulder in the general direction of where one of her bodyguards sat in the lounge area. "There won't be drama."

"Honestly, it's not me that you should be worried about," Dave said with a short laugh. "It was Max's car she wrecked."

"What about Max's car?" Max asked, entering the control room.

"Oh look, Max is here," Dave said.

"This is the hang out place, isn't it? The place where we all hang out?" Max asked.

Nikki looked like she was at a loss. "Sure."

And then the light of his life entered the small control room.

Well, she stopped in the doorway.

"Hey," Sabine said, a crooked smile making her dimple pop.

Dave opened his arms and flicked his fingers, beckoning her toward him. She shook her head, but the smile grew a fraction.

"Fine. Then I'll come to you." Dave stood and went to hug her, but she retreated into the hallway.

Maybe this was better because now they didn't have an audience.

He curved a hand around her waist and another at her neck and backed her against the wall.

She sighed against him, dropping her bag on the floor before encircling his waist with her arms.

"Hi," he said against her lips, trying not to smile because smiling made kissing more difficult. But he really liked kissing her and smiling at her at the same time.

She kissed his mouth and his chin with little pecks between tiny happy noises she made. They were something in between a giggle and a hum.

This girl.

Absolute perfection.

He captured her mouth with his, and when he slid his tongue against hers, she tightened her arms around him.

He pressed her against the wall and wondered for the thousandth time how he'd gotten so lucky. She was soft and smelled like wildflowers and freedom. And he could get lost in her for hours. Days. Weeks. Whatever.

"Let's get out of here," he murmured to the skin of her neck.

"Aren't you working?" she asked, followed by a soft giggle.

He sighed because she was right, but he wished she wasn't. He ran his hands up and down her sides, loving the feel of her.

"Do you have plans for dinner?" he asked, kissing the tip of her nose.

"Would you like me to include you in my dinner plans?"

"Yes."

"Then you're included."

Easy as that.

"Can you stick around for a few minutes while I finish up?"

She wagged her head back and forth. "I can stay for a little bit."

"Okay, if you have to take off, just go. Don't worry about me. I'll be right behind you."

* * *

SABINE

Watching Dave and Zara make up what was sure to be a hit song out of thin air was amazing. It was like watching a magic show as a child and knowing there were things happening you didn't understand but not caring and just loving the exhilaration of it all.

She was also able to watch Nikki work. Something she hadn't been able to do and she was fascinated by the blonde's fast fingers and critical ear. She heard and understood things Sabine would never be able to catch. She was captivating.

And to think how close Nikki had been to being Sabine's sister-in-law. It was a strange realization. It left her with more questions than usual, and she had no idea who to even ask. Sure, she could ask André, but he wasn't talking. He hadn't even told her that he and Nikki had been a couple. And Nikki really didn't seem like she would spill her guts to the little sister of the guy who broke her heart.

Sabine was assuming there was heartbreak. How could there not be?

Engaged? Ghosted?

It had heartbreak written all over it.

Plus, there was the small fact that Nikki acted like Sabine *wasn't* the little sister of her former fiancé.

Though what was the alternative? To become besties?

Uh, no.

Zara waved and Sabine glanced over her shoulder as a leggy brunette entered the control room.

Sabine recognized her…

"Sup, Mandy?" Max asked, voice flat.

"Max," Mandy replied. She ran her tongue over her teeth and forced a smile. "Can I be in here or are you going to call the cops on me?"

Cops?

What?

Max shrugged, like he was considering it. "That depends. Do you feel the urge to steal a car coming on?"

Oh.

Ohhhh.

Mandy's eyes bounced around the room, hesitated briefly on Sabine, before she rolled them to the ceiling and sat down on the couch furthest from Max and Sabine. She picked up a guitar magazine from a nearby table and paged through it.

Mandy Moulin—model, B-movie actress, and one of Sunshine Capone's ex-girlfriends.

You know how people are always saying that celebrities aren't as pretty in real life and everything is engineered and photoshopped into perfection?

Yeah, no.

Mandy was breathtaking.

She was wearing high-waisted baggy jeans that no one—but *no one*—could get away with. Unless they had mile long legs and a minuscule waist like Mandy did. Her shoes were thin high heeled black boots with pointed toes. Her top was a soft, chunky knit grey sweater. She wore thin gold hoops in her ears, and her hair was pulled back in an effortless ponytail that hung between her shoulder blades. And her makeup was so subtle, it may as well not have even been there.

High cheekbones, pouty lips, striking blue eyes, framed by inky lashes.

Sabine had to remind herself to take a breath.

She did not get distracted by celebrities.

But Mandy Moulin was hella distracting.

Sabine glanced to her left and caught Max's eye. Max glowered and made a face, clearly not impressed.

Though that probably had more to do with Mandy stealing his car and driving it into a pool back when she and Sunshine had been dating.

Damn, she wanted to know more about that story.

Should she be worried that Dave was into her when she didn't have a criminal record? Or maybe all his girlfriends had been like her—minding their own business when a rock star had crashed into their lives and turned everything upside down?

Sabine sat back in the couch cushions and wondered if she could be driven to things like grand theft auto or arson.

Probably not.

Not with her mom setting that example for her. Going to jail always seemed very much around the corner.

Did that mean Dave would get bored with her?

Sonofabitch.

See?

Now she was questioning his feelings for her when she hadn't been given a reason to. She was her own worst enemy

Max's phone rang and he shoved to his feet.

"Go for Max." He stepped out of the control room.

That left Sabine and Mandy and Nikki alone. But Nikki was wearing headphones so she was basically not there.

Sabine pressed her lips together and tried to casually look at the time on the clock. The clock being on the wall just above Mandy's head.

They made eye contact and Sabine tried a small, non-threatening smile.

Mandy's lips tugged up on one side and she slid her gaze up and down Sabine's person like she was just now seeing her.

Sabine folded her hands in her lap and leaned her elbows on her knees.

Dave caught her eye through the control window. A huge smile lit his face and he gave her two thumbs up.

God, he was cute.

She sniffed a laugh and shook her head.

Mandy made a noise that sounded like a snort and a groan at once.

Sabine didn't want to know the model's opinion so she pretended like she heard nothing.

"So you and Sunshine, huh?" Mandy asked after a minute, still paging through the magazine.

Sabine took a careful breath and swallowed, neither confirming nor denying.

Was it hot in here?

"It must be pretty new. He's still happy to see you," Mandy mused out loud. Not caring that Sabine hadn't said anything.

Mandy set the magazine down and lifted her eyebrows at Sabine. "That changes. He gets distracted easily."

Sabine rolled her lips inward and contemplated how best to proceed. Because Mandy's tone didn't sound snotty or condescending. It was factual. Like she really thought she was doing Sabine a favor.

Mandy picked up the magazine again and reclined on the couch. "And when it's all over, two years later, you still won't know why you couldn't keep his attention."

Her words twisted around Sabine's heart.

"I'm sorry," Sabine said softly. "That sounds like it really hurts."

Mandy's eyes flicked up to her.

"Not as much as it used to." Mandy started, then stopped. She sat forward again. "I just want to warn you. No one warned me."

Sabine nodded, that made sense in a weird way. Women looking out for women and all. And maybe she would do the same if the positions were reversed.

"Don't lie, Mandy."

Sabine looked up to see Max had returned and was standing in the doorway, his expression dark.

"I warned you several times." His jaw flexed under his skin. Sabine had never seen him look so serious. Or so perturbed. "I told you he had his own work, and he didn't have time to chase you all over every runway. Didn't see you in Milan, by the way. Are you still on probation?"

Mandy's mouth flattened. "Maybe if you didn't baby him, he'd finally be forced to act like an adult." Her eyes flashed and darted back to Sabine. "Is he still making chore lists for him? Cleaning up his messes?" She went back to Max. "He hates how you try to parent him you know. He told me so."

Max sighed, unaffected by Mandy's mean words. At least, that's how he wanted to be viewed. But Sabine could feel the negative energy zipping through the room.

"I always find it fascinating how dynamic personalities can bring out different aspects of those who care about them," Sabine said calmly. Max and Mandy turned their attention to her with matching frowns. She tucked her hands under her thighs and continued. "I think we can all agree that Sunshine brings out big feelings in everyone around him."

Max's lips twitched and his gaze dropped to the floor.

Mandy eyed Sabine suspiciously.

Sabine's attention was drawn back to the window. Dave's expression looked worried as he viewed what he could see of the control room. Sabine smiled to reassure him.

And while she was confident in what she'd said—Sunshine *did* bring out big emotions in those around him—she couldn't help but wonder about Mandy's warning. Not because she thought that Max or Dave would intentionally mislead her. But there was enough truth in what Mandy said for Sabine to take note.

She'd never been invited to Dave's place for example. Was that because they weren't there yet or because Dave was worried he'd be judged?

Max sat down beside Sabine again and carefully changed the subject to benign things. They visited quietly; Mandy mostly forgotten in her corner of the room.

Sabine excused herself to use the restroom. On her way back to the control room, Zara and Mandy passed her in the hallway as they were leaving.

Mandy stopped, getting Sabine's attention.

"I get it. You're the cute teacher girl who's patient and understands him. It makes sense. But just remember, all of us thought we were the exception at one time."

"Babe." Zara tugged on Mandy's arm. "Let it go." She shot an apologetic smile to Sabine. "Sorry."

Mandy huffed and strode down the hall where Zara's security took over and escorted her to the back door. Zara watched until her friend was gone and she faced Sabine.

"Listen, you and Sunshine have something that's all yours. Don't let the opinions of others interfere with it. Trust me." Zara squeezed Sabine's arm with a smile and then she was gone.

Sabine stood in the empty hall for a few minutes, trying to get her thoughts and feelings in order.

That's where Dave and Max found her.

"Dinner at your place?" Dave asked, sliding his hands around her waist and placing a kiss on her cheek. "Can I ride with you?"

She rested her hands lightly on his arms. "I'd be honored. What about you, Max? Joining us for dinner?"

Max ran a hand through his hair and smiled. "Not tonight. Thanks anyway."

"Max has a flight to catch," Dave supplied, pressing soft kisses to Sabine's neck below her ear.

"See you two later," Max called over his shoulder as he left the building.

"Ready to go?" she asked Dave.

He paused, staring into her eyes with a soft expression on his face.

"Yeah," he replied, voice just above a whisper.

But she got the distinct impression he had more to say.

She waited, but he didn't add to his reply. Instead, he helped her into her coat, and they left the studio together.

* * *

DAVE

After dinner, they were snuggling on the couch, the movie they had started forgotten in favor of tender kisses and soft touches.

He was on his back, Sabine sprawled on top of him when she looked down at him and asked a question he wasn't prepared for.

"How come you never ask me to come over to your place?"

He tucked her hair back behind one of her ears even as his stomach clenched. She watched him, waiting patiently for an answer. The question must seem so simple to her.

It was not a simple answer.

All previous relationships had been conducted very differently to this one. For starters, he'd never been friends with a woman first. He'd always gone straight from attraction to making out to all the rest.

This thing with Sabine had been slow from the start.

But in a hot way.

With her, he was Dave. It was her world not his. He was still finding out how he fit into her space without taking it over.

It was quiet and safe.

Still, he understood where the question was coming from.

"Would you like to see my place, dimples?" he asked.

"As long as you're not hiding a secret family or anything, yeah," she said with a soft laugh.

He licked his lips. Not a secret family. But there were things he didn't want her to see. His lists and binders and reminders. Things he'd need for the rest of his life just to function.

When they were together in her place, he could ignore the details of his own life. He could pretend that he had everything he needed.

But how long could that have possibly lasted?

Maybe that time was up.

He wished there was a way he could know how she'd react to those things before inviting her over. So he could brace himself. Or prepare for the rejection.

Just the thought of her trying to convince him that he didn't need the binders made him break out into a cold sweat.

She noticed.

"What's going on?" she asked softly, her hazel eyes clouding with concern.

He tried to force a smile but he was pretty sure it looked more like a grimace.

"My life…my mind…" He swallowed. It was so damn hard to explain. How do you tell someone you care about that you're never going to be able to "get over" how your brain is wired? That at his best he was still going to need a certain amount of patience?

"Hey," she said, calling his attention back to her. "It's okay. No rush. I love you no matter what." She pressed a kiss to his lips and then rested her head on his chest, facing the television.

He wrapped his arms around her and focused on the movie. Or tried to.

She loved him.

Was that the first time she'd said it?

He didn't say it back.

I should say it back.

But she might change her mind when she sees the rest of me.

And then he wouldn't be able to unsay it.

Was he being fair to her by keeping her away from all his flaws?

No.

But inviting her over to see them up close felt like asking for trouble. Why mess with something that was going so well?

Soon.

He'd have to let his guard down eventually.

And then what?

And then…

He closed his eyes and tightened his hold on her. Because he couldn't even begin to imagine what might happen if she finally saw all of him.

Chapter Twenty-Five
Hoax

"What are your plans for the holidays?" Sabine asked, closing her laptop.

Piper shrugged. "I think we're going over to Aunt Carmen's. It's what we usually do for holidays now."

"Are you looking forward to the break?" Sabine asked, knowing the answer.

Piper had worked her ass off to get her grades back up. But Sabine had it on good authority that Piper was more than a little excited to not see her tutor for a month.

Piper flashed a smile and slid a red envelope across the table to Sabine.

"See you next year!" The eighth grader called, heading out the door, dark hair streaming behind her.

Sabine picked up the envelope and tucked it into her bag with the others she'd received that day.

"What about you, Max?" Sabine asked. She'd seen a lot of Max over the past couple of weeks. When he wasn't at the studio, he was at the loft.

Though neither he nor Kara had declared they were dating, it seemed like they were at least considering it seriously.

"I am heading home to Long Island this afternoon. Ma does not tolerate her kids being abroad for Christmas. Any other holiday we can miss. Not this one." Max flashed a grin and checked his watch. "What about you?"

Kara left for Mexico yesterday with the family she nannied for. She wouldn't be back until after the 1st of the year.

But that was okay because Sabine had the same plans she did every year.

"My brother comes over and we make cookies and watch movies."

"No other family?"

Did she want to reveal how much of an orphan she was?

Eh.

"Mom is in jail and dad is…busy." That was the easiest way to explain. If it wasn't soccer, the man didn't care. And yes, she deliberately called it soccer just because she knew how much he hated it. He'd probably have Christmas dinner with the family of one of his star players.

"Will Dave be joining you this year?" Max asked.

That was the question, wasn't it?

She had mentioned to him that he was more than welcome to hang out with her and André. But he hadn't said whether he wanted to or not. Or if he had anything else happening.

Since she'd declined his invitation to Saint-Tropez, he didn't seem like he wanted to talk about the holiday.

"We'll see," is all she said to Max, aiming a bright smile at him. "I'm headed down to watch him work for a minute. You coming?"

Max's phone pinged and he glanced at the screen. "Yeah. I'll be down in a few. I need to make a call."

She finished packing up her bag and draped her coat over her arm as she went down to Studio X.

Mandy Moulin had been in the studio all week with Zara. Sabine had done her best at avoiding the model.

And maybe Sabine was missing something, but she just didn't under-stand the friendship. Though, to be fair, she'd spent limited time with Zara. Still, Zara was cool as hell. And Mandy seemed… Sabine stopped herself. She'd had one interaction with Mandy, and she knew enough about people to know that wasn't the entirety of a person.

Plus, Dave had had feelings for her previously.

Those didn't spring out of nowhere.

Still, Sabine found her shoulders tensing as she walked into the control room.

Both Johnny and Nikki were manning the controls today as Dave and Zara worked their magic.

Mandy was on one of the couches, scrolling through her phone.

The music played through the speakers and was also pumped through the control room so Sabine could hear it clearly.

They sounded amazing together. Sabine secretly hoped that this was just the start of many more collaborations.

"Chills." Nikki held her arm out toward Sabine to show her the goosebumps along her skin. "Literal chills when these two get together."

Sabine grinned and Mandy sighed.

"He never wrote me any love songs," Mandy muttered.

"Maybe it's just working with Zara. Artists influence each other," Sabine said, guessing. Mostly because Mandy's comment made her uncomfortable and she didn't want the other woman to feel bad.

Mandy chuckled softly.

"No. He's different."

Sabine twisted her head around to lock eyes with the model. Mandy's expression wasn't guarded or hostile. She was open. Thoughtful.

"Look," Mandy said, seemingly resigned. "I'm sorry for what I said when I was here the other day."

Nikki slowly spun on her stool to see better what was happening behind her. Johnny pretended he didn't hear anything. Or maybe he wasn't listening; he had headphones on.

Mandy's eyes bounced between the two women nervously. She licked her lips and rolled her eyes.

"I was jealous." Mandy grimaced like the words tasted bad in her mouth. "Sunny is a different kind of person." She lifted an eyebrow at Sabine. "You know what I mean. He's not…" She shook her head and sighed. "He's weird, okay?"

I'll show you weird.

Sabine clenched her teeth.

Getting into a fight with a supermodel the day before Christmas Eve was not on her list of things to do.

She knew Mandy wasn't trying to be insulting, but it didn't take much to set off Sabine's protective side when it came to Dave.

"And you seem to really *get* him." Mandy twisted her lips to the side. "I didn't. I still don't. He's very confusing." She made a face. "I'm not crazy."

Nikki snorted and Mandy glared at her. But it was half-hearted.

"I'm not. I know I didn't handle the breakup in a very mature way. And that's all my lawyer wants me to share until a few more things are settled." Mandy folded her hands in her lap and her expression relaxed. "I'm glad you get him."

"Thank you. I'm glad I get him too," Sabine replied soberly.

Max entered the room and Mandy picked her phone back up.

Even if Sabine and Mandy could learn to co-exist, Max and Mandy would only ever achieve respective hostility.

"Can I get a ride?" Max asked Sabine. "I wouldn't ask but the services are all backed up because of the holiday. My flight leaves in a few hours."

"Sure," Sabine agreed. She didn't have anyone expecting her.

She waved at Dave through the window before following Max outside.

They hadn't made plans to meet up later, but she knew this was their final day of recording until January. He'd probably call her or text her later.

Or, more likely, he'd just show up at the loft.

She loved that.

Which was odd because she had never been a fan of drop-ins. But Dave being in her space felt so natural.

Like he belonged there.

And after what Mandy had just said about her "getting" him, she was feeling pretty confident.

One might even say overly confident.

Which was her only excuse for why she thought it was a good idea to do what she did next.

* * *

DAVE

He was feeling especially good that evening when he left the studio.

They had recorded one more track and Johnny was talking like this album was going to be even better than their last. Which said something because the last one had been his best one.

At least according to pretty much everyone.

The holiday lights decorating the city filled him with the kind of hope that only came along every once in a while.

Life was good.

He had an album that was almost complete, that he was proud of; a place that was beginning to feel like home, and a girl waiting on him.

Not just any girl, but one he could see himself building a life with.

He had the perfect gift for her for Christmas and he couldn't wait to give it to her.

Happy.

He was happy.

Happier than he could ever remember being.

He parked the Range Rover in the underground garage and wasn't really paying any attention as he made his way up to his condo.

Maybe if he'd been more aware of his surroundings the next few moments wouldn't have felt like stepping off the side of a skyscraper into the unknown.

He opened the door to his condo and spotted the back of Sabine's head.

Initially he was happy to see her, and then he realized where he was. Where she was.

"What are you doing here?" he asked, sounding weird to his own ears.

Sabine's shoulders straightened like she was startled, and she spun to face him. Her mouth opened and closed, and she pointed over her shoulder.

His eyes scanned the area around her and noticed the binder open.

His mouth went dry and his stomach dropped. Bile started to gather in his throat, and he swallowed several times.

Was he sweating?

"Were you looking at that?" he asked, taking a step toward her.

"I was just—" Her round eyes were everywhere, and her face was red.

"Okay, I got it." Max entered the kitchen. "Oh hey, Sun. I'm just headed out. Almost forgot my laptop." He lifted the bag that presumably held the aforementioned laptop.

What was happening?

He had asked her to wait for him…

"You brought her here?" Dave asked.

It sounded like an accusation. It *was* an accusation.

Max glanced back and forth between Dave and Sabine. "Yeah…? She was giving me a ride to the airport." He took another step, analyzing the tension rolling off Dave. "She hasn't been here yet?" Max asked slowly.

Dave didn't reply.

Because Sabine knew.

She knew he wasn't ready to have her see all of this yet and she'd come without him anyway.

Shame touched with betrayal rolled through him and he felt sick.

And she had seen one of the binders.

Without him there to explain any of it.

Everyone always thought they knew better.

"Dave…" Her voice cut through the fog in his head, and he realized his eyes were closed.

He opened them but didn't look at her.

He didn't want to see the pity and the confusion.

He hadn't prepared himself.

He hadn't prepared *her* for the misunderstanding that was his life.

He swallowed the bile back again. She was going to run away. She was going to make fun of him. She didn't understand. And she didn't think he was smart enough to explain it to her.

"Why did you come here?" he asked, unable to stop himself.

"I-I wasn't thinking. I'm so sorry." She took a step toward him and he backed up.

He didn't know her. Not in this moment.

He shrugged, trying to build a wall between them. His insides curled in on themselves. "Well, now you know. Not only am I an idiot who couldn't finish school, but I also can't clean up after myself without an instruction manual. I'm just a child after all. I need constant supervision. Are you satisfied now?"

"Dave, it's not as bad as it looks," she protested.

And that was it. That's all it took. The way she said his name with pity. Like he was something broken.

But she didn't know.

She couldn't know because it was his head and not hers.

No one understood that this was how it had to be.

He finally met her eyes. "That's because you can't see it the way I do. And you never will."

She jerked her chin back. "That's not fair," she protested on a whisper.

"Leave," he said, directing his eyes at the floor.

Several quiet moments passed before he felt her step around him and leave. Max stopped at his shoulder and heaved a sigh.

"Think about this," Max tried, voice low. "Really think."

But Dave didn't want to hear all the reasons he didn't understand how other people saw things.

"Don't," Dave said, so soft he wasn't sure Max actually heard it.

He must've though because a minute later and they were both gone.

* * *

SABINE

She drove to the airport on autopilot. Her mind a tangle of regret and confusion.

So this was what it felt like to instantly regret something.

"He'll get over it," Max said into the silence. But he didn't sound convinced.

"I think we both did a bad thing," she said, focusing on the traffic without really seeing it.

She cast a glance at Max and his jaw was tense.

"Did you know?" he asked.

"Did you?" she countered.

Because it had become abundantly clear that both Max and Sabine had overstepped. Not only that, but they had taken advantage of Dave's trust and had put him in a position that Sabine never wanted to see him in again.

"Do you think differently of him?" Max asked accusingly.

"Of course not," Sabine scoffed. "Was this some kind of a test?" she almost yelled at Max.

He didn't answer, and if she hadn't been driving, she would have shaken him by the shoulders.

"Were you testing me?" she asked again. Demanded, more like.

She kept glancing over at Max who looked more and more guilty.

"I needed to know!" Max confessed. "I needed to know if you could love him the way he deserves. He wasn't supposed to catch us."

"Oh my God!" Sabine yelled, her heart ripping in half. And she'd walked right into it. She'd been so confident in her own ability to do the right thing when it came to Dave that she'd made the worst choice possible.

She squeezed the steering wheel until her hands hurt, and it still didn't ease the ache in her chest.

"It was his step to take. Not yours. Not ours." She shook her head, her stomach tight and unyielding. Her eyes burned and she blinked back the tears gathering.

The look on his face. The absolute betrayal she saw there.

Not anger.

Not rage.

Just complete devastation.

Wounding Dave hadn't even crossed her mind as a possibility. It's not something she'd sought out and yet she'd managed to do just that.

And now he was hurting, and she was the one who'd caused it.

She needed to pull over, she couldn't see well enough to drive.

Spotting a parking lot for a clinic, she turned in and parked. Then she turned in her seat to face Max.

"Max," Sabine said, breathing through the pain. She hurt in places she'd never hurt before. "I love him." She swallowed the lump lodged in her throat and blinked furiously. "I love him so much. I don't care that he has to have binders. I don't care that he didn't graduate. I don't care about any of the things you think I could reject him for." She held her hand on her chest, like it would keep her heart from falling apart. "I. Love. Him."

Max still eyed her like he wasn't sure.

And she finally saw what it looked like on the outside when she would get protective with Kara.

"You know how sensitive he is about this!" she yelled at him. A fresh surge of anger welling up.

"So do you!" Max yelled back.

They both settled back in their seats.

"We both handled that very badly," she said to the windshield.

Both of them had let Dave down. And neither one even meant to. Relationships were stupid hard.

"Has he told you he loves you?"

She licked her lips, frowning. "What? No, not really." She thought back to Thanksgiving. "He said it once. But it was hard to tell if it was something I should take seriously." Tears flowed freely and she stopped wiping them away.

But hadn't he been saying it in his own way for a long time now?

Every chance he got, he made her feel adored and special and cared for. Wasn't that love?

"Do you know why he can't make plans?" Max asked.

She shook her head. Sure, she understood it as something he disliked because he wasn't good at it. It just wasn't one of his strengths.

"He doesn't make plans because he *can't* make plans." The muscle in his jaw twitched. "It's like the future is a myth. All he has is today and some-times tomorrow."

Sabine weighed that against her experiences with Dave. "It always feels urgent when we're together," she admitted. "Not like he's hurrying us along, but like he's grasping onto the moment."

Max lifted a shoulder and nodded. "He is. The moment is all he has. He can't picture what done looks like. His brain isn't wired that way. Not even for things that you and I find easy. Like where we want to be in five years, or what to buy at the grocery store."

Max sat back in his seat and sighed. He pressed his lips together and stared out the front window for a minute.

"He knows, logically, that there are finish lines out there. But Dave can't see past tomorrow. And yet, it's all eternity to him."

Something heavy shifted in her chest as those words slid into place.

"What do you mean?"

"I mean…" Max turned his face to her again. "When he tells you he loves you, he loves you in this moment, yes. But for him those moments never end. He loves you, no stop. It's continuous. Like gravity."

Her heart hammered helplessly in her chest.

"How do I fix this?" she asked.

Max gave her a sad smile. "I wish I had the answer. But we're in new territory with you." He chewed on his bottom lip, gaze growing distant. "I really didn't think he'd catch us. Fuck, I'm stupid. He's never had someone like you. The other women, when he was done, he was done. Just closed the door on the relationship and moved on."

Sabine caught a sob in her chest and pressed her fist to her mouth. The idea of Dave walking away from her—from them—was too heartbreaking to process.

"I love him so much," she whispered, not trusting her voice to work. "I'll fix it."

She wiped her hands on her skirt and breathed deeply. She drove Max to the airport, her mind swirling with how to apologize so that Dave knew she was sorry. But mostly she just wanted him to know that he was amazing.

Max exhaled and unclipped his seat belt as she swung into the terminal's curb and stopped. "I'll call him when I land and explain what happened. I'll tell him it was my fault."

"Max, if you talk to him before I do, tell him I love him and I'm sorry."

Max held her eyes for a moment. Then he got out of the car, got his bag, gave her a nod, and disappeared into the airport.

Sabine cried all the way home.

Chapter Twenty-Six
As I Am

DAVE

It was snowing.

It had started snowing right after she'd left.

Dave had stared out the window watching the fluffy white flakes swirl in between the buildings before making their way to the street below.

And with the arrival of the snow came the cold, empty feeling of guilt.

For as long as he could remember, his emotions had always felt *bigger.* He had no way of comparing them to someone else except to witness how others behaved.

He cried easier, got angry faster, laughed louder and longer.

His emotions seemed correct in the moment, but they also felt *very* intense. Sometimes overwhelming.

His medications helped him regulate those things for the most part.

But every once in a while, he'd get knocked on his ass.

Intense contrition smothered his other senses until he crumpled under the weight of it. He lay down on the floor of the living room and stared up at the ceiling. His hands rested on his stomach and he listened to the silence of his life.

He'd made her leave.

Told her to go.

Because he didn't want to hear all the reasons for why.

That's what he'd wanted. He had wanted to be able to explain things. Smooth over any misunderstandings. And he'd been denied that.

So he'd denied her the same thing.

Was that irony?

He hated it.

He wished he could go back and give her a chance to…

Hm.

But that's not how things worked. Going back was never an option.

His phone pinged several times and he rolled over to pick it up.

The first text was from Max. He didn't read it.

He got off the floor and went into the kitchen to get a glass of water. He passed the red binder on the way and shame sucked the air out of his lungs again.

He looked back at his phone as another text came through. And then the screen lit up with Sabine's face because she was calling him.

He dropped his phone and tried to catch it with his foot like a hacky sack. But he kicked it and it hit the corner of the wall.

He went to retrieve it and the screen was shattered.

That sucked.

What was he supposed to do after that?

He didn't have another phone.

There was nothing in the binders about what to do if he busted his phone during a holiday when everyone who did regular things for him was gone.

Because not only could he not function like a normal human being, but he was too famous to walk into a store and get a new phone set up. It would be a circus.

And a circus was fine when he was in the mood for a circus.

Which he was not.

All he wanted was to be able to… think.

He drank the water and went back to the living room where he sank back into his misery on the floor. He didn't deserve to be comfortable.

He deserved the floor.

He woke up sometime later and the sun was up again.

Time was weird for him, but he was pretty sure it was Christmas Eve.

They could've been on a yacht, drunk and tan, but no, she had to be perfect. She didn't want him for his money. She just wanted to be with him.

And he'd overreacted.

He knew he'd overreacted, but he couldn't figure out where he'd gone wrong. Every time he tried to re-examine the moment he'd walked into his condo, all of his thoughts swirled and piled on top of one another. Every single one acting like it was the most important one, until he was overwhelmed and exhausted.

More than once he reached for his phone to call Leslie or Max and then remembered his phone was busted all to hell.

How was he supposed to fix that?

How was he supposed to talk to Sabine about all the things he couldn't even begin to put into order in his mind?

He needed to talk to her.

She was always so…calm.

He closed his eyes and pictured her. She'd smile and her dimple would pop, and she'd duck her head and tuck her hair behind her ear even though it wasn't loose to begin with.

And she'd make him feel less stupid.

She always treated him like he had something to say.

She never made him feel like he was too much.

But then the black wave of shame returned and pushed him further into himself.

A memory surfaced of before he'd dropped out of school. Before the binders. Before his mom had left. He was still in grade school, but he couldn't be sure of his age.

"Can't you just leave me alone?" his mom had yelled through her bedroom door.

Dave had chased her there again because he had too many questions. The questions never stopped. But he learned to stop asking them.

She would get overwhelmed and hide from him.

He hated that.

The hiding.

It was one of the major reasons behind his music. He loved making things that were weird and seeing other weirdos bond over their similarities.

He reached for his phone again and sighed.

This wasn't working.

He needed to leave, maybe go for a drive.

No.

He needed to talk to her.

He had to try.

* * *

SABINE

"Is it a bad sign that I look forward to the broken cookies more than the unbroken cookies?" André asked, slathering frosting on the head of a snowman and then taking a bite.

"I am not the one to ask," Sabine replied taking off the hot mitts and reaching for her wine. "I think we might be the broken cookies."

He eyed her while sorting the cookies onto their respective plates. "Okay," he said like he'd settled something in his mind. "Where's the boy so I can kick his ass?"

She snorted even as her eyes burned and the familiar hole right through the middle of her widened just a bit more.

Yesterday, after she'd gotten home, she had been hopeful.

She'd texted Dave. She'd started with apologies. Then she'd tried to call. She left enough messages that his inbox filled up. After that, it didn't ring through anymore.

So she'd stopped.

Instead, she'd braved the feral cats on the roof and brought her decorations downstairs.

Not even the wild animals would give her the time of day though.

She'd set up her tree, tried to get in the holiday spirit with some Bing Crosby and Frank Sinatra. Until they were drowned out by the evil banjo demons across the hall.

By the way, they had been playing for *months*. She was starting to think they weren't even *trying* to get better. She was convinced that they *liked* how badly they played.

About the time she finished the first bottle of wine she switched her playlist to Islandic Death Metal and opened the door so as to better flood the hallway with noise.

Dave never called her back.

And now it was Christmas Eve.

And it was just her and her brother.

Eating cookies and frosting out of the bowl.

She'd tried to act like she was fine. But she couldn't stop thinking about Dave being all alone across town. That's not how it should be.

"I know I'm not great at the comforting, that's really Kara's territory. But do you want to talk about what happened?" André asked carefully.

What happened indeed.

Maybe this would be good. She could talk about it out loud and see if she was really as fucked as it felt like. In fact, André might have some insight into it that she hadn't considered. Maybe he could give her an idea she hadn't tried yet. Because she was one more glass of pink wine away from trying to climb the side of the building into Dave's apartment. Where she would undoubtedly be arrested.

Sabine refilled her glass and braced her back on the counter. "Okay. Some pertinent information. He has predominantly inattentive ADHD."

André's expression turned thoughtful and he came around the island to get himself a wine glass.

"Which, when he told me, I wasn't surprised or anything. It made sense. But he's…sensitive about it."

André poured a glass and nodded his head. He crossed one arm over his middle and mirrored her posture.

She blinked as the details surrounding her time with Dave started to swirl together in her mind. Some things created more questions while others dismissed earlier concerns.

"Like," she said, trying to grasp at some of the things that moved too fast for her to catch. "He told me he didn't graduate high school, and asked me to help him get his GED, and then every time I brought it up again, he changed the subject." She frowned at her brother.

"Did he feel embarrassed maybe?" André asked.

She shrugged. "I mean, yeah. But when I realized he didn't want to talk about it anymore I stopped asking. And then…" She sighed, took a long drink of her wine and set the glass on the counter. "Okay, so he has this friend, you've met him. Max."

André nodded his head.

"Max has made these, um, these binders for Dave. They're fantastic. Truly. Dre, you don't even know. I wish I could show you because it would blow your mind. But these binders are full of all the information that Dave needs to do daily tasks. Like, the one I saw in the kitchen had photos of what the cupboards look like when everything is put away. A photo of the inside of the refrigerator. A photo of the kitchen as a whole. It's like Pinterest but in a three-ring binder." Her voice got louder and faster as she spoke, because the binder was fucking brilliant. "And then there's a laminated checklist. Like put away milk, dishes in dishwasher, things like that. And there are different tasks for different days. Like Monday, take out the trash, Tuesday, refill the water filter." She stopped, her heart pounding as she thought about how incredible the binder was.

"And I'm pretty sure he has a binder for every room. There's probably one in his car too."

André's eyes narrowed. "That's a really good idea. I have a few students who could benefit from something like that."

"Right?" Sabine declared. "That's what I was thinking. I mean, I know that the executive functions in an ADHD brain don't allow for them to picture what 'done' looks like. And I can read about it and study it all the live long day, but I only have a *piece* of what he deals with. I can do my best to understand but he is so very aware of how he's different. He lives in a neurotypical world and he's doing his best to fit in but..." She huffed a laugh and her heart tightened. "He's so amazing when he doesn't fit. And he has no idea."

"So what happened?"

She dropped her head back and groaned.

"I saw the binders before he was ready to show me. Max invited me up to his condo to get something and Dave walked in and thought the worst."

"The worst? What? Like you and Max were..." He made a face.

"God no." Sabine scrunched her face up in disgust. "No. See? That's what someone else would think but that's not how Dave's mind works. He..." She sighed. Because this was where it all fell apart.

She knew he was hurt. That he was embarrassed. But until he *told* her how he felt, she was just guessing.

And she didn't feel comfortable guessing about how his mind worked. She wanted him to explain it to her.

She wanted him to trust her enough to explain it to her.

But she'd violated that trust by leaping ahead when he'd clearly asked for more time.

"He's different," she finished helplessly.

"Why do you think he reacted that strongly?" André asked.

This was one of their similarities. Even though they'd been raised by opposite parents and had grown up in different parts of the world, they both loved to ask questions. They *wanted* to understand. They delighted in the discovery. And they especially loved it when they could facilitate discovery in someone else.

"I think it has something to do with his mom not being able to deal with his diagnosis."

André made a face. "But he's hugely successful. Clearly, it's not held him back."

Sabine rolled her eyes. "Dude, we both know better than anyone how tricky mommy issues are. We are fully functional adults, and we still struggle in our relationships."

"Touché," André toasted his wine towards her.

She knew André struggled with abandonment issues, and she had trouble with trust. No one in this world had been spared.

All people were just walking wounds trying to find home and happiness.

"Anyway," she went on, a little sadder now. "I love him. That's pretty much the whole story."

André dipped his head at her confession. "And does he know you love him?"

"Nope." She made a popping noise with her lips when she ended the word. She'd told him, yeah. But hearing and knowing were different things. "How about Nikki? Does she know you're still in love with her?"

André's eyebrows lifted into his hairline and his mouth fell open.

"Boom, sucka!" Sabine hollered. "Didn't see that coming, did you?" She pumped her arms in the air and did her version of a victory dance.

"You suck," André said, picking up the bottle of wine. "I'm taking the rest of this." He went back around to the other side of the island, his ears a bright red.

Sabine laughed and the energy shift in her chest helped move some of the pain around. She would be okay. And Dave would be okay. And they would eventually talk about what happened because she was just on the wrong side of crazy to let Dave ghost her.

And honestly, he would probably eventually respect her for wanting to at least clarify some things before leaving him alone.

Maybe.

She hoped.

Because she wasn't going to just let him slam the door on what they had been building. She was at least going to apologize. Even if she had to get past Dallas to do it.

"So are we eating real food or is it just cookies all holiday?" André asked, dipping a snowman body into the frosting.

"Just forgoing the utensils, huh?" she asked, watching him.

He shrugged. "It's just us."

"We're not animals," she admonished. He waggled his eyebrows and she snickered. "I have sandwich stuff in the fridge if you need nutrients outside of sugar."

She eyed the overflowing trashcan and made a face. "How much do I have to pay you to take out my trash?"

He downed the last of the wine and started wrestling the trash into the bag and tying it closed. She left him to it and brought the plate of naked cookies and the bowl of frosting to the couch.

"What are we watching tonight?" She called over her shoulder. "Are we sticking with tradition?" She hoped so, she'd cued up *Scrooged* in anticipation.

"Sabine, can you come here a second?" André called from the doorway.

"Ugh. I should've taken it out myself. Freaking teetotaler can't hold his pink wine." She made it to the door and André was standing there with the trash bag in his hand. He had the strangest look on his face.

"There's someone here for you," he said, and pushed the door all the way open.

Sabine's heart turned over in her chest.

Dave.

Standing at her door. Looking lost and broken.

"Dave…" she whispered, approaching him. She pressed a hand to her heart to keep it from jumping out of her chest and leaving her for good.

He's here.

He's here.

Lost Track

He's here.

"I just needed to see you. Even if…" Dave exhaled heavily.

André patted her shoulder and went back inside the loft.

Her heart strained against her insides. It wanted to climb out and hug Dave with every ounce of love it had beating through it.

She pulled the door closed behind her and they went into the hallway for some privacy. He sat down with his back to the wall and his legs stretched out before him. She took a seat near his hip, facing him.

She swallowed the tears that threatened to take over.

He's here.

If he was here, then it was going to be okay. She wasn't sure how she knew that for sure. It was like his heart was speaking to hers and they had decided between them that it was all going to be just fine.

She reached for him and curved her hand over his cheek. He leaned against her palm.

Those deep blue eyes looked back at her with turmoil and fear, and her broken heart squeezed.

"I'm sorry," she said, not waiting another moment to tell him. She had no idea if he'd gotten any of her messages, but it didn't matter. All that mattered is that he was there, right there. And she could tell him she was sorry.

"I should have never gone into your home without you," she said. She blinked and a tear rolled down one cheek.

He brushed it away with his thumb.

"I wanted to be able to explain," he whispered, his eyes glossing over.

She nodded. It wasn't that she needed an explanation. *He* needed it. To make the ends match. To put it in order in his own head.

All she had to do was let him.

"Do you—" He wiped under his eyes and looked away, shame coloring his cheeks. He took a heavy breath and tried again. "Do you feel differently? About me?" His voice broke and he wouldn't look at her.

Her heart caught in her throat. "No," she replied, and punctuated it with a kiss to his mouth.

He seemed shocked by her reaction, but she was desperate to convince him that nothing would ever make her feel different about him.

"I love you," she whispered against his mouth. She kissed him again.

"I love you." She kissed his cheek.

"I love you." Kissed his other cheek.

"I love you." Kissed the tattoo above his eyebrow.

"I love you." Kissed his nose.

"I love you." Kissed the rose tattoo.

"I love you." Kissed his chin.

"I love you." Kissed his top lip.

"I love you." Kissed his bottom lip.

She climbed into his lap and straddled him. He settled his hands lightly on her hips. She grabbed his face in both hands.

"I love you," she said. "Deeply. For who you are."

He sucked in a deep breath and blinked like he was surprised. "Really?" he asked. "Even the—" He waved a hand to encompass all of his unspoken fears.

"Yeah, really. All of it." She wiped a tear off his cheek with her thumb.

"But I do things that don't make sense."

She leaned forward and brushed her lips against his because it needed to happen again. She looked at him seriously. "I'm not afraid of things I don't understand."

He took in a shuddering breath.

"Dave, you are my hero," she said, gazing at the face that she adored. "You have this incredible, tender heart. It's so big and brave. You make me think I can be brave too. You open up my world to new things every day. The moment you walked into my life you started saving me. And you never stopped."

His hands moved from her hips to her back and he breathed easier.

She kissed his forehead. Then his nose. Then his chin.

"I love you," she said, resting her forehead against his and closing her eyes.

"I'm very sensitive." It was an admission that was part trying to add levity and mostly true.

"I like that you're sensitive."

"I'm crying in the hallway like a little bitch."

She sat back so she could see his face again. "Only bad bitches cry."

His lips twitched and she brushed them with her thumb.

"I overreacted," he said, his eyes getting wet again. He swallowed.

She shrugged. "It's okay to be afraid sometimes. Next time, tell me, and we can be afraid together."

He blinked hard, and she watched him wrestle with that information. "Really?" he finally asked, his voice breaking.

She nodded and he wrapped his arms fully around her and crushed her to him. He buried his face in her neck and held her for several long minutes.

It was warm and safe and whole in his arms.

It was as if he was squeezing her heart back together.

After a minute, it began to beat a whole new rhythm.

One that matched his.

And she just knew, no matter what happened next, they'd be able to get through it. Because they'd get through it together.

He pulled back and looked her in the eye. His expression was fierce as his eyes scanned her features like he needed to remind himself who he was talking to. "I love you. Do you know that?"

She smiled and licked her lips because she was so not even on his level and he had no idea. All she could do was hold on and hope to keep up.

Because he really was a superstar, and she was caught in his radiance forever.

He crushed his mouth to hers and the relief poured into that kiss caught her by surprise. She slid her fingers into his hair. Her entire body rejoiced at being near him again and she could swear that individual cells inside her body were high-fiving each other.

He wrapped his arms around her back and held her close as his tongue slid into her mouth.

She moaned at the sensation, and he tightened his hold.

The apartment door that was *not* hers, opened.

"Uh, do you mind?"

Sabine and Dave both broke away from their kiss to glare at the pale faced neighbor.

She was just about to ask him if he needed help shoving a banjo up his ass, but Dave stood and ushered her into her loft.

"Seriously?" she growled. "The freaking nerve of that guy."

Dave bit his lip and then backed her into the corner of the doorway, and he was kissing her again.

Okay.

Yes.

She could forget about the banjo player if this was the reward.

The kiss went from urgent to tender. He slowed his pace, his hands moved over her back, her arms, her shoulders, her sides.

He lifted his head and gazed down at her adoringly.

She touched the rose near his eye, and he grabbed her hand and placed a kiss to her palm.

They didn't need to talk through this.

Their hearts were rebooting.

She was so glad he'd come home.

Chapter Twenty-Seven
Lifetime

DAVE

Light streamed in through the tall windows and woke him.

He stretched, arms over his head, toes pointed as far as they would go.

He had slept like a damn baby—as usual when he was with Sabine.

It was like peace was just a part of her essence. She bestowed it on anyone and everyone around her.

His arm drifted across the bed only to find it empty.

Hm.

Maybe she was using the bathroom.

Maybe he should jump in there right after her.

And then maybe he could talk her into coming back to bed.

Or not.

Her brother was sleeping in Kara's room. And even though he'd had enough wine last night to make a Real Housewife blush, Dave wasn't comfortable putting the moves on his girl with her brother in the same loft.

No. He wanted to be able to take his time.

And he especially didn't want any distractions.

Not with Sabine.

Never.

She deserved all his focus.

Her brother had been an exceptional cooler last night, which was why they had only kissed a little and no heavy petting.

Which wasn't as bad as you might think.

The bathroom was empty when he got there so he used it, and then went on a quest to find the most beautiful girl in the world.

It was a short quest.

She was standing in the kitchen in a short emerald-green robe and matching fuzzy slippers. She'd taken her hair out of its braids the night before and it hung in kinky, fluffy curls down her back.

He was so distracted by the sight of her that it took him an extra second to realize what she was doing.

She bent her knees and peered at an object on the counter in front of her. Then she went back to the paper instructions in her hand.

He came up behind her and slid his arms around her waist, tucking his chin in the space between her neck and shoulder.

"Is that an espresso machine?" he asked.

"Yes," she grumbled. "I was trying to surprise you. But apparently, I'm not talented enough to figure out how this thing works."

His heart warmed and grew inside his chest.

She had gotten him an espresso machine. Not for her. Not for any other reason than she remembered he had a weird obsession with espresso.

He couldn't remember someone ever getting something for him without him actually paying for it.

It was so simple and gloriously *normal*. Except he knew that nothing about the way Sabine cared for him was normal. It was extraordinary and powerful and he could feel it shifting his fears to the side.

He drew her body as close to his as he could and inhaled the scent of her. Emotion clogged his throat.

How close had he been to losing this?

How close had he come to not having this kind of perfection in his arms? Someone who saw him and loved him.

Just because he was so afraid of being misunderstood.

In that moment he decided that no matter what happened in the future, he would always come back to her. They could talk about it. He was confident that she wouldn't run away and hide, that she would answer his questions. Even if everything went very, very wrong, the truth of her was that she would show up and talk to him.

She would work through it with him.

But for now, he needed to make her an espresso. It was the least he could do.

He pressed his lips to her cheek, and she hummed a happy tune in the back of her throat.

"Well," he said, pushing through the emotion clinging to his voice. "I happen to know how to operate almost every espresso machine in circulation."

"Oh, fancy," she teased, stepping out of his arms and giving him room to work.

He eyed her for a second, wanting to say more but not having a clue where to start. She waited and when he just shook his head and sighed, she smiled and hopped onto the counter.

And he made her an espresso.

* * *

André joined them a few hours later.

"Hangover for Christmas?" Sabine asked. "And I thought I wouldn't know what to get you." She filled a glass with water and handed it to André along with a bottle of aspirin.

He took it and squinted uncomfortably in the sunlight. "It's that damn pink wine. I never know how much is too much."

Sabine rolled her eyes.

And that was when the entire world had a panic attack.

Okay, maybe that was a slight exaggeration.

But Sabine's phone pinged with a text, and then another, and another, then it rang.

"Damn," she said, picking up her phone. "It's Max."

Dave held up a hand, remembering the status of his phone, just as she answered.

"Hello? Yeah, he's here. No. Last night. I don't know. Here, talk to him yourself." She shoved the phone at Dave. "It's your bestie."

"Hey," Dave said, way too casually.

"Really?" Max did not sound amused. "So you're alive. Are you okay? Have you been kidnapped by pirates in the South China Sea?"

Dave chuckled. "I'm fine. Still in Chicago. I'm at the loft."

"Curtis called me," Max said.

"Oh."

"Yeah. But I was in the shower, so ma answered."

"Oh no."

"Oh yes. Where the hell is your phone?"

"I broke it."

Max was quiet. He was probably pinching the bridge of his nose. He did that a lot when Dave had frustrated him.

"You know what? That's fine. It's Christmas. That radio city troll doesn't need access to you on the Lord's birthday. Who does he think he is? Santa? No, ma, that's what I just said. Yeah, the thing about Santa."

Dave stifled a laugh. When Max began to rant, it was best to just let him finish.

"I'll get you a new phone. I'll ship it to the loft. Sound good? I'll have it all set up for you, don't worry. It'll probably be a few days though, okay?"

"Thanks, Max."

Max sighed loudly. "How are you and Sabine? You good?"

Dave glanced up at Sabine and smiled. "Yeah. We're good."

"What happened yesterday was my fault," Max said.

Dave had read enough of Max's text last night that he knew that part. "We can talk about it later. Go spend time with your family."

"You're family too," Max reminded him soberly.

"I know."

They hung up and he slid the phone back across the table.

"Max is going to send me a new phone. He's going to send it here. Is that okay?"

Sabine made a face. "Of course. It's basically your second home."

That was true. It was like his second home. Hm. There was something there that should be thought about, but he'd have to get to it later.

"So, what do the Debois do on Christmas Day?" he asked.

"Hmm." Sabine tapped her chin with a finger. "I mean, tradition says we nurse our hangovers and open presents."

"Presents!" Dave hissed. He slapped his forehead with a palm.

Sabine shook her head with a frown. "Oh, no. I didn't mean you—"

"No, I have something for you," Dave interrupted her. "I left it in my car. And some of it's at my place. But I've had something…for a while."

She narrowed her eyes at him. "Why do you have that smug look on your face?"

He succumbed to the urge and owned his smugness with a grin. "Because I never remember to get things on time. Ever. I need a lot of reminders." But he had gotten her something perfect and he knew it. "I mean, it looks like it was wrapped by wild animals, but it's the thought that counts."

Sabine regarded him thoughtfully, her lips curved into a smile he wasn't sure he'd ever seen on her before. It was soft and tender. And it made his heart race.

"Well then," she cleared her throat. "I better make hangover food for this one, so we can get to the presents."

The rest of the day was so easy it didn't seem real.

They ate, they laughed, they talked, they danced.

Dave went down to his car and brought up her gift.

He'd forgotten about it semi-on purpose because it was that cool. He knew that if he thought about it too much, he'd just blurt it out to her.

It was a really good gift.

He closed the door to the loft behind him and André caught him in the entry.

"Hey, I know my being here last night wasn't…" he made a face and shook his head. "I shouldn't have gotten that drunk."

Dave gripped his shoulder. "No, it's fine. We've all tied one on."

André dipped his chin but he still looked sheepish.

"Still, thanks for not kicking me out."

Dave snorted. "Don't be ridiculous. You're her family. You'd have to be a way bigger douchebag to get me to kick you out."

André smirked.

"What are you two doing over there?" Sabine said when she found them. "C'mon. I want to unwrap presents."

They joined her in the living room, and Sabine passed out the small bundle of gifts that she'd tucked under the tree. One for André and one for Dave.

Dave handed her the shirt box that he'd wrapped in the only paper he could find. Which happened to be "Happy Birthday" paper he'd found tucked in a drawer at the studio.

She shook her head and smirked when she took the package from him.

He loved the sparkle in her eyes that said she thought he was funny.

He was going to amuse the hell out of her for the rest of her life.

André opened his and it was a very nice wool sweater and a bowtie that had dinosaurs on it.

Dave opened his and time stopped.

He couldn't picture certain things about the future. It was a mystery to him and probably always would be. But every once in a while, the universe would stop moving and an image would pass him. Little glimpses of what *might* be in his future.

When he'd lifted the lid and it revealed a basketball jersey, it happened.

He pulled the jersey out and it unfolded so he could see all of it.

It was white with black letters and numbers. The front had a yellow sun emblem on it and the number one. The back also had the number one and the name said "SUPERSTAR."

And in his mind, he saw himself playing basketball with someone much smaller than him. A child. He couldn't see their face, but the jersey matched his and the number was three.

He looked at Sabine and his nose began to burn.

"This is perfect. Thank you."

She smiled bright even though her eyes shone with her own tears. Did she know what he'd seen?

Of course not.

But he wouldn't have been surprised if he found out she had.

She was a remarkable woman, and he was pretty sure he hadn't even come close to discovering all of her talents.

He gestured for her to open her gift.

She pulled the top off and immediately started giggling.

"Oh my god, I love it." The box fell to the floor and she held up the black cardigan.

He grinned when he saw her hold it to her torso and lovingly touch the buttons he'd had custom made for her.

They were tiny, little Dark Helmets.

And again, he caught an image of a would-be future where he was giving her Dark Helmet themed gifts for all their special days.

* * *

SABINE

Dave had asked if she wanted to go look at Christmas lights. She'd never done that before.

They got in his Range Rover and were deep in a discussion about the ethical treatment of droids in the Star Wars universe when she realized they were pulling into the underground garage where Dave lived.

"Wait." She turned sideways in the seat. "What are we doing here?"

He parked the car and turned off the engine before facing her. "I was wondering if you'd like to see where I live."

She pressed a hand to her chest. "We don't have to do that."

"I know. But I want to." His mouth tugged up on one side. "I have to give you your gift anyway."

"What?" she said, confused.

He got out of the car and she did the same. She came around the back of the vehicle as he opened the back and removed a guitar case.

"You already gave me my gift," she reminded him. He was being suspicious.

"I gave you one gift, yes. But I have one more." He shot her a wink.

And her heart gave a little kitten purr.

Yep.

Those winks were going to get her into a lot of trouble one of these days.

He transferred the guitar to the other hand and then reached for her. She took his hand and they walked quietly to the door of his condo.

It felt strange to think about how only two days ago, she'd been in the same place with a completely different mindset. It's probably why she hesitated after he unlocked the door.

Because *this* was what she wanted. She wanted him to lead her into his space and show her all the things about himself he didn't show anyone else.

He stepped inside and turned back to her.

"You comin'?" he asked.

She knew he'd forgiven her. He hadn't said the words exactly, and maybe that's why she still felt unresolved.

"Umm."

He leaned a shoulder against the door jam and waited patiently.

Because of course he did.

It was another reminder of how poorly she'd handled the situation. When Max had suggested she come upstairs she should have said no. Instead, she'd jumped right on the opportunity to peek behind the curtain.

"I need to explain something," she said, feeling brave and seizing the moment.

He tilted his head, concern in his eyes. But he didn't try to stop her.

"I wasn't trying to violate your privacy. When Max asked me to come up to your place, I got excited because…" She shrugged one shoulder and swallowed the uncomfortable lump in her throat. "Because I'm really, *really,* embarrassingly into you. Like…" She rubbed her fingers on her temple. Was she sweating? "Like, I am kind of obsessed. With you."

Oh God. This was super unflattering.

She'd just confessed to being a groupie, hadn't she?

"But not because you're famous or rich or anything."

Why was she still speaking?

"But because you are like no one I've ever met." She held her hand up, palm out. What was she doing with her hand? She squeezed the hand into a fist. "And I can't stop wanting to know everything about you."

She was afraid to look at his face at this point because he was probably two seconds away from signaling security to come and remove her.

"And again, not because you're a celebrity. But because you're really awesome." She finally looked at his face. He had a small smile playing on his lips. "You know I think you're awesome, right?"

"Just get in here," he said around a laugh. He started to turn back into the condo, and she shot an arm out to catch the door. She didn't cross the threshold.

"Do you forgive me?" she asked, holding her breath.

His eyes went soft and he came back to her. He cradled her cheek in a palm and rubbed his thumb back and forth.

"Of course you're forgiven," he said.

She released her breath and pressed her face into his hand. "Thank you."

He dropped his hand and she followed him inside. Lighter than she had been a few moments before.

He set the guitar case down in the living room and then took her coat.

"When it's just me, I throw my coat on the floor." He took both of their coats and made a show of hanging them up.

"Oh! Should I take my shoes off?" she asked.

He shrugged. "Yeah. Let's take our shoes off."

They kicked their shoes to the corner and she lost her balance. But he was there to catch her. He pulled her into his arms and pressed soft kisses to her neck.

"Do you want to see my binders?" he asked, his lips grazing over the sensitive skin just below her ear.

She giggled and tightened her grip on his shirt. "When you say it like that it sounds very dirty."

"Do you want me to do dirty things to you instead?" he asked.

Electricity shot through her and she tugged him closer. "Do you *want* to do dirty things to me?"

"Oh yes," he confirmed, working his lips around her jaw to her mouth. "I have wanted to do dirty things to you for a while now. I have a whole folder in my head marked 'Dirty things to do to Sabine.'"

She giggled even as heat rushed to her belly.

One of his hands curved around her ass while the other ran up her side, around her ribs, swiped a thumb over a breast, on its way to the back of her head.

The sensations were like a trail of fire across her body and she made a noise that was part pant, part whimper.

She felt him grin against her mouth right before he swept his tongue inside.

She greeted him eagerly, grinding her body against his with absolutely no shame.

It was like that morning he'd spent all that time cataloguing what kinds of touches and caresses turned her on had locked inside his mind. He knew exactly how to touch her and where to elicit a response.

Oh, he was clever.

He pulled back and looked into her eyes. It took her a second to focus through the lusty haze. When she did, he was aiming a crooked grin at her like he knew exactly what he did to her mind and body.

He traced the shell of her ear with a finger and it set off tiny fireworks from her hair to her center.

"I love you," he said. "You're it for me. You're all I want."

Her heart did a shimmy and a shuffle before it curled inward and purred like a kitten.

"I love you," she said but before she'd really finished, he was kissing her again. He wrapped his arms low around her back while his tongue tangled with hers. She slid both hands into his hair. He bent slightly and then stood, lifting her feet off the ground.

He walked them backwards into his bedroom and then set her feet back on the floor.

His hands slid under the hem of her sweater and lifted, and it was gone.

His gaze traveled over her breasts, down her torso, back up again, and his eyes darkened. "I have wanted this for a very long time."

"Me too," she said, reaching greedy fingers for his hoodie. She knew she was being too eager but she couldn't help it. She loved him and he loved her and if that made her eager, than so be it.

He took the shirt off, tossed it to the side, and she placed her hands on his inked chest.

Her fingers danced over the lines and art on his skin.

She'd never been with someone with so many tattoos. Had never considered tattoos all that attractive. But these markings were Dave's. He'd chosen them and wore them. Something about that made every design and image personal and important.

He put a finger under her chin and lifted so she was looking at him. In his eyes swirled welcome and desire and joy. She wanted to dive into those deep blue waters and live there.

"I am yours," he said. "Forever."

* * *

DAVE

Her lips curved into a shy smile and his eyes dropped there and held. He inhaled and cupped her shoulders. His thumbs hooked under her black bra straps and pulled them slightly off her shoulders.

He took a step back just to look at her.

He didn't want to miss anything.

His gaze danced over her face, hair, body.

She was exquisite. A work of art. The most beautiful woman in the world.

So much of his life his thoughts were everywhere at once, making it difficult if not impossible to focus even when he wanted to.

But this moment was different.

Everything in the world faded away and all that existed was her and him and what they felt for one another. Call it tunnel vision or hyperfocus, all he knew was her—the softness and heat of her skin, the freedom in her eyes, the seduction in her smile.

He didn't want to get this wrong.

Not with her.

Never with her.

The sound of the icemaker running in the kitchen pulled at his attention and he closed the bedroom door.

The windows in his room were curtained, making it pitch black.

That wouldn't do.

He wanted to see her.

He crossed to the side table and flicked on the small lamp. It was enough light so he could see her fully, but not enough to cause distraction.

Because he hadn't been kidding when he'd said he had numerous ideas about her and him and naked times.

He'd also thought about all the ways his head could screw it up. And he'd prepared for that.

He didn't need weird interferences to interrupt any of his sexy ideas.

So many ideas.

Endless ideas.

Ideas that involved her hair against his chest as she collapsed on top of him. Ideas about the sounds she made when his hands were on her. Ideas about her sighs and cries and eyes.

Lots of ideas.

But he didn't have a plan.

Plans were boring.

He was going to do what he did best—make it up as he went.

He turned back to her and caught the small smile playing on her lips as she watched him make his preparations. He sucked his lower lip into his mouth as his gaze caught on the swell of her breasts and the curve of her waist.

Fuuuuck. He was already half-hard and he wasn't even touching her.

He had to touch her.

"Can I touch you?" she asked.

Thankfully they were on the same page.

"Please do," he replied, coming closer.

His hands curved around her hips and flicked open the button of her jeans. Her hands smoothed over his chest and up his shoulders.

"You know those little skirts you wear for work?" he asked, sliding the denim over her hips and letting them drop to the floor.

"Mm-hm," she replied placing open mouth kisses along his right pec. She got to his nipple and her pink tongue darted out to lick it.

He sucked a breath through his teeth at the sensation.

"I'm gonna fuck you in one of those skirts someday," he promised out loud.

Her hazel eyes darted up to his and her lips quirked in a surprised smile. "Yeah?"

He stepped back so he could see her body entirely. Her red cotton panties made him fully hard and he groaned.

"I'm almost sorry I didn't wear one today," she said, a slight tease in her tone. She had to know what she did to him.

But maybe she didn't.

"Don't be," he replied, his erection straining against the fabric of his jeans. He undid the button and zipper if just to give himself more room.

He wasn't sure when he'd reached for her again but his hands were encircling her waist, running over her hips, finger dipping into the hem of her panties.

She was exploring as well. Her small, nimble hands all over his chest and stomach. When she reached a hand into the front of his boxers and took hold of his erection, he hissed.

Her wide hazel eyes looked up at him with innocence. It was so fucking hot he almost forgot his own name.

She slowly pumped her hand over his length, her lips parted.

While he had said she could touch him, he didn't want it to be over already. And if she kept doing exactly what she was doing, it would be.

He turned her around to face the bed, her hand came out of his underwear. And he missed her grip on him but he knew of a better one if he could just focus.

His thumbs dipped into her back dimples.

"Your skin—" he said, with nowhere to go with his words because it was all sensation.

He ran his hands up her rib cage to the clasps of her bra. He unhooked it and let it fall down her arms and then onto the floor. He pulled her back a step until her skin was touching his.

God, she was so warm.

And soft.

His hands came around her front and gently skimmed over her belly, up her ribs, to hold the weight of her breasts.

His mouth landed on her neck and sucked and licked while his hands kneaded her breasts. He tugged gently at her hard nipples, eliciting soft whimpers from her perfect mouth. Her hips undulated against his, searching for more.

One hand continued to caress and tease her tits as the other slid lower, lower, lower, dipping into the front of her panties.

His fingers found wetness.

"Sabine," he said in her ear, nipping at her earlobe.

"Yeah?" Her voice breathy and distracted.

"Is this for me?" he asked, running a finger over her dampness.

That day in her bed when he'd kissed her all over, he'd wondered about this part. How wet he could get her. How much pleasure he could bring her.

"Baby," she half-moaned, half-whimpered.

He dipped his middle finger in between her folds and back out.

Her tits pressed into his hand and a soft breath caught somewhere in between in inhale and exhale.

He dipped his finger in again, this time deeper, finding her little bundle of nerves.

She gasped and each of her hands grabbed onto his wrists.

He smiled against her ear as he felt her trying to press his hand back into her. He decided to give in, except this time he went to her opening and slid the tip of his finger in.

She was so fucking wet.

That was it.

He needed to be inside her.

He reached into the pocket of his jeans and grabbed the condom that he had stashed earlier.

"Put your hands on the bed," he directed.

She did as she was told and then looked at him over her shoulder.

Her eyes were hazy with lust, her cheeks flushed. She was naked save for the red panties.

He shoved his jeans to the floor and then his boxer briefs. His rock hard erection sprang forward and her eyes dropped to it.

And then she licked her lips.

"God *dammit*," Dave hissed, trying to focus.

He quickly slid on the condom, trying to ignore the way she watched him.

Then he stepped up behind her pert ass that was tipped up for him. He slid her panties off her hips and they dropped to the floor.

The Jamiroquai tattoo should not be as hot as it was. But for some reason it worked for him in a big way.

He gripped her left hip in one hand while he used his other to guide the tip of his cock to her entrance.

He nudged her opening, trying to go slow. He knew he wasn't enormous, but he was on the higher end of average for size. And Sabine was small. What if he hurt her?

"Please," she whimpered, pushing herself backward into him.

He slid inside her hot, tight center and nearly lost it.

Fuck.

Her inner walls squeezed and clenched as she made room for him. A soft, keening wail came from her lips and she arched her back, her arms reaching out in front of her.

"Is that okay?" he asked, holding still, his fingers gripping her hips.

"Yes," she replied. But her voice didn't sound like her voice. It sounded desperate and needy. It sounded like she needed him to make it better.

He pulled out an inch and then slid in deeper. The slickness of her arousal making it easy. He started short, shallow thrusts and increased in tempo and depth as he went.

His heart thundered in his chest and every nerve ending in his body was on fire.

Was this how it felt to have sex with someone you were in love with?

Because this didn't feel like anything he had ever experienced before.

He was so *aware* of her. Of them. Of how their bodies reacted to one another.

He bent over her body and caressed her tits, teasing the nipples. His cock slid back and forth inside of her sweetness. Her sighs and cries gathered strength and volume in conjunction with the grip of her pussy on his cock.

She was close.

He could feel it.

He wanted to fuck her like this forever.

But he also wanted to see her face when she came for him.

He also knew that if he saw her face while she came while simultaneously feeling it, he was going to come too.

And he wasn't ready to come yet.

He straightened and held her hips. It was hard to tell if he was thrusting or she was.

Either way, their rhythm matched perfectly.

He dropped his head back and groaned.

Fucking.

Perfect.

Literally.

He blinked against the haze of lust and arousal and made a decision.

"Put your knees on the bed," he directed. He slid out of her and she made a sad noise. But she did as he asked and crawled forward.

She trusted him so much. He swore he would never make her regret it.

He crawled onto the bed behind her and guided her body upright. Carefully he pointed his cock back to her entrance and slowly lowered her onto him. He shifted his thighs so she was resting most of her weight on him.

Once his cock was seated deep inside her, he wrapped his left arm around her front, holding her tits. Then he used his right hand on her hip to guide her back into a rhythm that would drive them both crazy.

She dropped her head back against his shoulder and he licked and sucked her exposed neck. She tasted like Christmas cookies and sex.

He pinched her nipple while at the same time circling her clit with the middle finger of his other hand.

Her moans changed. They got deeper, more urgent. He could feel her tightening around him and he held her closer to his body.

"Come for me," he said against her neck. "Please. Let me feel you come apart."

Her body bucked and her inner muscles spasmed, squeezing his cock and coating it in her climax. Her cries echoed off the walls and in his heart.

Yes. This was all he wanted for the rest of his life.

Her trust and her love and her pleasure forever.

He grinned against her neck.

Carefully, he slid free of her heat. She collapsed onto the bed. He joined her, placing tender kisses along the back of her arm, the nape of her neck, between her shoulder blades.

She rolled to face him and he met her with kisses to her cheeks, her chin, her mouth.

Her hands ran over his shoulders and smoothed down his chest. He moaned into her mouth as his tongue darted inside for a taste. He cupped one breast, the hard nipple grazing his palm, and he ground his erection against her hip.

"Can you handle more, or do you need a minute?" he asked, brushing the hair out of her face.

She cupped his cheek and ran a thumb over his lower lip.

"I can have more?" she asked.

He turned his face into her palm and kissed it.

He'd give her everything for the rest of their lives.

He lowered himself to her mouth and kissed her deep and slow and languid.

Their tongues slid and played and she sighed into his mouth. His hands were everywhere. Her hair, her breasts, her stomach. Her ass, her hips, her thighs.

Her body writhed beneath him. Responding to his touch in shivers and clinging, clutching grasps and gasps.

His mouth moved to taste one nipple, then the other, then back again. She arched, wanting more of his mouth on her and he loved it. He loved every move, every needy whine, every trembling breath.

But he needed to be inside her again. To see her face when he entered her. To look into her eyes when she came apart.

He grabbed one of the pillows from near the headboard—a firm, decorative pillow that he'd never understood the point of until this very moment— lifted her hips with one hand and slid the pillow beneath her with the other.

He surveyed the position of her body and his gaze tracked up to meet her eyes.

"Is this okay?" he asked.

She nodded. He lifted one of her legs and kissed the inside of her knee while watching her face. He ran his hand down her thigh and back up and again and then threw the leg over his shoulder. Then he did the same to the other leg.

He lined up the head of his cock with her entrance and entered again into that paradise that his cock now thought of as home.

Her inhale turned into a long, indulgent moan.

He watched her response as he slid almost all the way out and then back in again.

And again.

And again.

And again.

Hitting the little button on the inside of her vaginal wall that so many men claimed was a myth.

If the g-spot was a myth, then Dave was a fucking god.

And Sabine was his goddess queen.

And he would worship at her alter for the rest of his life.

Her breaths came quicker as he stoked the fire inside her.

Her cries and whimpers shot straight to his ego which thickened his cock and tightened his balls.

Her face—*holy fuck* her face. Her parted lips, her hazy eyes focused solely on him, her perfect, rosy-tipped tits bouncing in front of him as he increased the tempo.

She was going to come again.

He *needed* her to come again.

He reached down in between them and found her swollen clit. He watched her face as he stroked the nub in time with his thrusts.

"Oh *god*!" she cried out. Her pussy clamped down on him and wave after wave of ecstasy pulsed through her body from her center.

He thrust into her as deep as he could get and his vision exploded in a shower of sparks as lightning rocked through his body with his orgasm. The most beautiful colors and vistas cascaded through his mind as her body convulsed around him, sending him into orbit.

He wasn't there anymore.

He was in space.

He was a shooting star.

His heart and his lungs were stardust now and he'd never be the same. Now, he was only hers.

***

SABINE

Three orgasms (two for her, one for him) and one destroyed pillow later, they were wrapped in his sheets near the center of the king-size bed. They were on their backs. She had her head on his chest and he had an arm wrapped around her shoulder, and he was making lazy circles with his fingertips along her arm.

He sighed the sigh of a very content man and she smiled.

"I'm happy," she said softly. At the same time the confession left her lips, her heart took that final tumble into bliss.

And Dave was waiting there to catch her.

"Me too," he replied.

He stretched his right arm out in front of them. "You see that tattoo on my wrist?"

She grasped his forearm and pulled it closer so she could read the script in the low light.

"The force is with her," she read out loud.

"That's you."

She stared at the words written in fine point and tried to process what he'd said.

"I got it just after the NMAs," he added. He let out a deep breath. "I knew I was in love with you and I wanted to document it."

Her heart pounded, making her hands tremble. She brought his wrist to her lips, closed her eyes, and kissed the words. She held him there, trying to impress upon him how much this small gift meant, how deep it went into her heart.

This man was like no one she had ever known.

So he was confusing to some. So his thoughts moved more laterally than linearly.

But his soul matched hers in ways she never dreamed possible.

He removed his wrist from her lips and wrapped his arm around her, drawing her close.

She hugged his arm with both of hers and hummed softly. "I love you."

He kissed the top of her head.

"Do you want some wine?" he asked.

She chuckled and reveled in the freedom of laughing with him while also being naked with him.

Yep.

She'd reached heaven on earth.

"Maybe some water first," she said. "That was pretty athletic."

She craned her neck up to smile at him and he was looking back at her with a saucy grin. "Tell me when you've recovered and we can go again."

A laugh burst out of her and she rolled to her stomach so she could see him better. "You're joking, right?"

He tugged a strand of her hair. "Not kidding. I've been in love with you for a while so I have a lot of ideas to work through."

She shook her head knowing she was blushing from her breasts to her ears.

He chuckled and knifed up to kiss her again. Then he swung his legs out of the bed and put some sweatpants on.

"I'll get you some water."

She waited approximately two and a half seconds before she got out of the bed, wrapped the sheet around her, and joined him.

His eyes lit up when he saw her. He set the glass of water on the breakfast bar as she carefully slid onto a stool.

"I would like some pink wine, I'll get you some," he said, putting two glasses on the counter.

"You have pink wine?" she asked, lifting her eyebrows.

He smiled and pulled the bottle from the fridge. "I know you like it, so I made sure I got some in case I was ever brave enough to invite you over."

And that settled the last lingering fear she had. He hadn't invited her over because he felt pressured to do it. He had been planning it all along.

She'd just been too impatient.

Stupid Sabine. Rookie mistake.

Nope. No.

She wasn't going to beat herself up about it after he'd forgiven her. They could move on.

And with his energy and creativity they could move on all night long.

"And you taught me that rosé is for when you're feeling just a little bit fancy," he said, pouring the glasses a little fuller than was proper but she wasn't going to complain.

"I am so glad that lesson took."

"You're a very good teacher." He gave her a bright smile as he handed her the glass.

She took a sip. "Speaking of, do you still want to get your GED?"

He narrowed his gaze at the inside of his glass as he swirled the wine. "Hmm. Ask me again later."

"Fair enough."

He took a seat beside her and brought the red binder with him.

He put it down in front of her and nudged it.

"Go for it. I know you want to get a closer look."

She inhaled through her nose as she watched him warily. "I really do."

He snickered at her. "Then go for it."

They paged through the binder together. For the better part of an hour, he answered all of her questions. She laughed at the stories he told about the early days when Max hadn't yet discovered the usefulness of the binders.

"Wait. So how many loaves of bread did he find under your bed?" she asked, her stomach hurt from laughing so hard.

"I don't know. Like five."

"Five!"

"See? You sound just as shocked as he did. I still don't see the issue." Dave drained his wine. "Do you want a refill?"

"Yes, please."

He got up and opened a new bottle.

"Thank you."

She looked up, unsure what he was thanking her for.

"Thank you for not making fun of me. It's nice to be able to talk about this stuff without thinking I'm losing cool points."

She made a very unladylike noise. "You point me at anyone who makes fun of you and I will knock them out. I know I sound very calm right now but inside I'm a complete rage monster. I'm not joking. Stop laughing."

Dave bent over and rested his forehead on the counter, his shoulders shaking.

He eventually stopped laughing and refilled her glass.

"Do you know why my stage name is Sunshine Capone?" he asked.

"Actually, no." She frowned and doubled back. "Wait. I saw some vloggers talking about it—"

"No, no, no. The public doesn't know." He rested his elbows on the bar. "In school I was always in trouble. Not like big, get kicked out kind of trouble. I was just enough of a shit that every teacher knew my name. I got really familiar with the principal's office. But my way of dealing with that was to always be adorable. I always had candy that I shared, and I'd bring flowers to the principal, and I called all the teachers 'sweetheart.' It didn't matter their gender, they were all sweetheart. But one day, I had gone too far. On my way to school I saw these beautiful tulips and I decided that those would be perfect for Principal Summers. So I dug them all up and delivered them right there on the playground." He took a dramatic pause and pumped his eyebrows once. "They were her tulips. From her own yard."

"*Noo*," Sabine gasped.

"Yep." He chuckled at the memory. "She was big mad. She said I was like a little happiness gangster. She was the first one to call me Sunshine Capone. I loved it. I decided that's exactly who I wanted to be."

"Oh my God, that's amazing." Sabine wiped her eyes. "That makes me love you even more."

He smiled and his eyes wandered over her face. "I guess I've always had a thing for teachers."

The blush crept up her neck to her cheeks and she tried a flirty wink. It probably wasn't as effective as his winks were on her. But maybe she'd get there someday.

"C'mere," he said, taking her hand and tugging her off the stool. "It's time for your gift."

She stopped moving to get his attention. When she got it, she pointed down the hall towards his bedroom. "You just gave me three in there."

He threw his head back and laughed. He pulled her into his arms and continued to laugh as he held her. He pressed a kiss to the top of her head.

"You're so great. My favorite human ever."

She hugged him back and smiled. Because she felt the same about him.

And one of these days she was going to show him how amazing he was.

Even if it took the rest of her life, that would be her mission.

She let him lead her to the sofa where she sat down.

He let go of her hands and bent to the guitar case he'd placed on the floor. Unclipping the latches, he revealed a gorgeous acoustic 6-string. Sabine didn't know anything about guitars, but it looked brand new.

He took the guitar out of the case, sat down on the coffee table and set it across his legs.

"You look nervous," he said with a sly smile.

She clasped her hands in her lap. "I don't know anything about guitars, and I'm worried I'm going to say something stupid."

He grinned and his tongue shot out to touch his bottom lip as he began fiddling with the knobs on the instrument. "God, you're cute."

She forced a nervous laugh and waggled her eyebrows. "Yep. Just keep thinking I'm cute. Pretend like my ignorance isn't even here."

He ran his tongue over his teeth, still smiling. "I can teach you whatever you want to learn."

Something about his tone held a lot more promise than when other people said things like that. And she knew he meant it. If she wanted to learn something, he'd show her.

And he'd probably be really nice about it too.

"I wrote you something," he said, doing a test strum.

Sabine thought about all the songs he'd been writing with Zara and what Mandy had said.

Was it one of those?

"Something no one has heard yet," he added.

That answered that question.

He looked up then and caught her with those dark blue dreamy eyes.

"Would you like to hear it?"

She nodded, her heart fluttering around in her chest like a drunk hummingbird.

He strummed a note and stopped. He took a breath and let it out. "I feel like I should warn you, it's not like the stuff I normally do."

"Okay," she said. It could be a Scottish Opera. She was going to love it no matter what. He wrote her a freaking song. No one had ever written her a song. No one had even written her a love note. He could literally do no wrong at this point.

But when he started playing, goosebumps broke out along her arms and legs. And she realized she had greatly underestimated this moment.

And then he sang to her. He was right. It wasn't like his usual stuff. It was soft, and sweet. An actual love ballad.

Lost Track

. . .

"Never did I try,
To think that I,
Could find someone who makes me feel alive.
More than that,
You keep up when I'm too fast,
And you hold me close when I feel like I'm fallin'.

Too many times,
I looked for a way out,
Instead of looking for your love.
But somehow my heart heard you callin'.

So give me a moment,
To get the words right,
I've never been one to make sense the first time.

The thoughts stop,
my mind is calm,
When you look in my eyes,
I am home,
And I,
Don't know how.
But I'll spend my life loving you,
In the now.

People like to plan,
But I just can't,
You ask me questions,
You understand,

When I'm with you,
I see clearly,
A breakthrough,
And your love makes me brand new.

So give me a moment,
To get the words right,
I've never been one to make sense the first time.

The thoughts stop,
my mind is calm,
When you look in my eyes,
I am home,
And I,
Don't know how.
But I'll spend my life loving you,
In the now.

My love won't look the same as someone else's,
But it's yours and no one else's,
Your heart is where my wealth is.

Give me a moment,
To get the words right."

The song faded into the stillness of the condo.

He set the guitar aside and picked his wine up.

She sat in stunned silence, her heart suddenly too big for her body.

He sipped that damned pink wine, a huge smile on his face. Like he knew exactly what he'd done to her.

"You look like you're very proud of yourself," she observed, feigning irritation.

"I am." He pumped his eyebrows. "I'm feeling *very* confident right now."

A surprised giggle escaped her. "Oh really?"

"I mean, I'm pretty sure I started falling in love with you the moment I saw you. And, I know you love me back. So yeah, I'm feeling myself."

He put the empty wine glass aside and came for her. He planted his fists on either side of her hips, caging her in. He brushed his nose along hers and she watched his indigo eyes darken.

"So, you love me?" she asked, sounding way more casual and cool than she felt.

His mouth was inches from hers.

"Hell yeah, I love you," he replied gruffly. "You love me?"

"Hell yeah," she whispered.

He touched her mouth with his and drew back slightly.

"Marry me," he said.

She put her hands on his shoulders and studied his earnest but patient expression.

He didn't say it again. He didn't take it back. He just waited for her to decide.

It was the strangest thing.

She knew without knowing.

She could feel it deep inside.

The details would always be the details. But the big stuff, the stuff that mattered, was already settled in her heart and mind.

This was where they both belonged, and they'd found it together.

"Hell yeah," she replied, voice rough with emotion.

He took a deep breath and wrapped his arms around her, picked her up, and carried her back to his bed.

* * *

DAVE

He brushed his fingers gently through her hair at her temple and watched her sleep.

Never had he felt so still.

Time had always confused him. He knew it existed, and he was tied to its useless rules. But here, with her, time stopped. Because even time had no power over how he felt for her.

He was never going to be able to love her the way she deserved. Not in a normal way. Not the way someone else might.

The way he loved her would be different. It would be the only way he knew how—flat out and constant. Intensity mingled with gratitude.

Most importantly, he would cherish her.

And she would feel cherished.
That was a promise he knew he could keep.

Epilogue

WEDDED BLISS! Sunshine Capone secretly marries Sabine Debois just one month after proposing.

CelebX obtained exclusive photos of Sunshine Capone and Sabine Debois showing PDA outside of a federal courthouse on Friday.

Rumors of a romance between the rapper and the teacher started four months ago when they appeared together at the NMAs. Sunshine's publicist insisted they were just friends—which was reiterated by sources close to both of them.

But over the past few weeks the two were spotted holding hands and hiding from photographers in Los Angeles and again in New York, fueling romance rumors once again.

Sources close to Sunshine Capone have confirmed that the two wed in a secret ceremony in a Chicago courthouse on Friday.

A month ago, sources said he took her ring shopping, but they were trying to keep it low key.

"They're both very down to earth people. It's going really well for the both of them and they're happy," the unnamed source said.

The source that confirmed the nuptials said, "They just didn't have a reason to wait anymore. It might seem sudden to anyone who doesn't know them. But this makes sense for who they are."

The newlyweds are rumored to be honeymooning in the Maldives.

Sunshine's publicist did not comment on the rumors.

THE END

Author's Note

When I sat down to write this story, I knew it wouldn't be easy. I do not pretend to know everything about ADHD and all its intricacies. But as someone who loves someone with ADHD, it's a topic close to my heart. The examples and symptoms displayed in this story were inspired by my personal conversations and involvements with my husband. As such, they in no way cover the vast spectrum of experiences of those who have ADHD, or those who live with someone with ADHD.

All I wanted was to write a story about a character based on someone I love who has expressed feeling underrepresented and misunderstood in books and movies.

I hope I did at least a little of it right.

Love,
Heidi

Playlist/Chapter Titles

1. Sunshine…OneRepublic
2. Rolling Through…311
3. Good Feeling…311
4. Myself…Post Malone
5. Use of Time…311
6. Something Just Like This…The Chainsmokers & Coldplay
7. …Ready For It?...Taylor Swift
8. I'm Gonna Be…Post Malone
9. gold rush…Taylor Swift
10. You (featuring Post Malone)…Neptune
11. Space and Time…311
12. willow…Taylor Swift
13. Get Me (featuring Kehlani)…Justin Bieber
14. Delicate…Taylor Swift
15. Homemade Dynamite (Remix) [featuring Khalid, Post Malone & SZA]…Lorde
16. I Don't Care…Ed Sheeran & Justin Bieber
17. Off My Face…Justin Bieber
18. Intentions (featuring Quavo)…Justin Bieber
19. I Think He Knows…Taylor Swift
20. I Can't Be Myself (featuring Jaden)…Justin Bieber

21. At Least For Now…Justin Bieber
22. Anyone…Justin Bieber
23. Bleeding Love…Leona Lewis
24. hoax…Taylor Swift
25. As I Am (featuring Khalid)…Justin Bieber
26. Lifetime…Justin Bieber
27. Holy (featuring Chance the Rapper)…Justin Bieber

Acknowledgments

As always, this book had a very specific group of supporters without whom I would have never been able to write the darn thing.

Penny Reid. Thank you for creating this amazing Universe with your words, heart, and characters. Thank you for letting me play there. I am forever grateful.

The Smartypants Romance Authors. It's one of the most surreal things of my life to count you all as colleagues and friends. Brilliant, funny, talented writers who blow me away with your grace and kindness.

Scott Colby. You taught me how to be brave. I am forever grateful.

Post Malone. I was a casual fan when I started writing this book. I am no longer a casual fan. If you know what I'm saying.

My readers. I'm so happy you found me. Or I found you. Or however it works. We found each other and my life is all the better for it.

My betas. Thank you for carrying me through this one. Thank you for the encouragement and the love. You never gave up on me even when I had given up on myself. Thank you for believing in these characters and loving them the way I do.

Kati. Thank you for being the best hype girl anyone has ever known. I hope we get to do this a long, long time.

Jo. I hope you know how much I appreciate you. I wouldn't be able to do any of this without you. Thank you for making me look smarter than I am, for your insight, for your grace.

Jamie. It bears repeating: my life would be boring and unfunny without you. I'm so very thankful for the weird, goofy, perfect friendship we have. You make me a better mom and a better human.

AJ. Thank you for the jokes, and the phone calls, and the constant encouragement. You believe in me in ways that are honestly just silly, and you should get that checked. I am so thankful to have a brother like you.

Bria. Thank you for all the wisdom and insight. For the weekly chats and the understanding. You are a beautiful part of my life and I'm so very grateful for you.

Charlie. I love watching you grow. Watching you discover and explore the world around you makes everything worth it. You're an extraordinary human. I am honored that I was chosen to be your mom. You are everything that's right in this world and you give me hope for a better one.

Charles. Captain Awesome. My real life Sunshine Capone. This character has so much of you in him, it's hard to let him go. Your heart, your mind, your soul, are the most beautiful and wild places I have ever known. Falling in love with an explorer has been the greatest adventure of my life. Thank you for taking my hand all those years ago. Thank you for loving me. And thank you for letting me love you.

God. Thank you for all of it. For them. For this. For the next. My cup runneth over.

About the Author

Heidi writes stories that she hopes will inspire her readers to take their hearts on one more adventure.

She still lives in the Black Hills with her alarmingly handsome husband, their fearless child, and a rather large and spoiled dog.

She is fueled by her unwavering and perfectly normal devotion to Dave Grohl and coffee.

And a whole lotta love.

heidih.net
Email: heidih.writer@gmail.com

Find Smartypants Romance online:
Website: www.smartypantsromance.com
Facebook: www.facebook.com/smartypantsromance/
Goodreads: www.goodreads.com/smartypantsromance
Twitter: @smartypantsrom
Instagram: @smartypantsromance

Also by Heidi Hutchinson

Double Blind Study Rock Star Series:

(Interconnected standalones, Adult Contemporary, Romantic Comedy)

Learn to Fly

In Your Honor

Deepest Blues

The Hope That Starts

Brand New Sky

Into the Night We Shine

Matter of Fact (holiday novella)

Things That Shine (crossover with Bria Quinlan)

Soaring Bird Surf Series:

(Interconnected standalones, Adult Contemporary, Sports Romance, DBS spinoff)

Tectonic (#0.5)

Like the Back of My Halo

Sushi and Sun Salutations

Puppy Love and Peanut Butter

Rope a Dope

Caught a Vibe

Smartypants Romance XY Records Series:

(Rock Star Romance)

Key Change

Lost Track

All Mixed Up

Write or Wrong

In Between Series:

In Between the Earth and Sky

In Cold Mud Series:

(Women's fiction)

Stubborn Hearts (prequel to Brand New Sky)

www.heidihutchinsonbooks.com

Also by Smartypants Romance

Green Valley Chronicles

The Love at First Sight Series

Baking Me Crazy by Karla Sorensen (#1)

Batter of Wits by Karla Sorensen (#2)

Steal My Magnolia by Karla Sorensen (#3)

Worth the Wait by Karla Sorensen (#4)

Fighting For Love Series

Stud Muffin by Jiffy Kate (#1)

Beef Cake by Jiffy Kate (#2)

Eye Candy by Jiffy Kate (#3)

Knock Out by Jiffy Kate (#4)

The Donner Bakery Series

No Whisk, No Reward by Ellie Kay (#1)

Dough You Love Me? By Stacy Travis (#2)

Tough Cookie by Talia Hunter (#3)

Muffin But Trouble by Talia Hunter (#4)

Oh Brother! Series

Crime and Periodicals by Nora Everly (#1)

Carpentry and Cocktails by Nora Everly (#2)

Hotshot and Hospitality by Nora Everly (#3)

Architecture and Artistry by Nora Everly (#4)

Small Town Silver Fox Series

Love in Due Time by L.B. Dunbar (#1)

Love in Deed by L.B. Dunbar (#2)

Love in a Pickle by L.B. Dunbar (#3)

<u>**The Green Valley Library Series**</u>

Prose Before Bros by Cathy Yardley (#1)

Shelf Awareness by Katie Ashley (#2)

Dewey Belong Together by Ann Whynot (#3)

Checking You Out by Ann Whynot (#4)

<u>**Scorned Women's Society Series**</u>

My Bare Lady by Piper Sheldon (#1)

The Treble with Men by Piper Sheldon (#2)

The One That I Want by Piper Sheldon (#3)

Hopelessly Devoted by Piper Sheldon (#3.5)

It Takes a Woman by Piper Sheldon (#4)

<u>**Park Ranger Series**</u>

Happy Trail by Daisy Prescott (#1)

Stranger Ranger by Daisy Prescott (#2)

<u>**The Leffersbee Series**</u>

Been There Done That by Hope Ellis (#1)

Before and After You by Hope Ellis (#2)

<u>**The Higher Learning Series**</u>

Upsy Daisy by Chelsie Edwards (#1)

<u>**Green Valley Heroes Series**</u>

Forrest for the Trees by Kilby Blades (#1)

Parks and Provocation by Juliette Cross (#2)

Letter Late Than Never by Lauren Connolly (#3)

Peaches and Dreams by Juliette Cross (#4)

Young Buck by Kilby Blades (#5)

Package Makes Perfect by Lauren Connolly (#6)

All Fired Up by Allie Winters (#7)

Wild Goose Chase by Kilby Blades (#8)

The Teachers' Lounge Series

Passing Notes by Nora Everly (#1)

Band Together by Piper Sheldon (#2)

Ex Marks the Spot by Hazel James (#3)

Past Tents by Stacy Travis (#4)

Story of Us Collection

My Story of Us: Zach by Chris Brinkley (#1)

My Story of Us: Thomas by Chris Brinkley (#2)

My Story of Us: Grayson by Chris Brinkley (#3)

Seduction in the City

Cipher Security Series

Code of Conduct by April White (#1)

Code of Honor by April White (#2)

Code of Matrimony by April White (#2.5)

Code of Ethics by April White (#3)

Cipher Office Series

Weight Expectations by M.E. Carter (#1)

Sticking to the Script by Stella Weaver (#2)

Cutie and the Beast by M.E. Carter (#3)

Weights of Wrath by M.E. Carter (#4)

Common Threads Series

Mad About Ewe by Susannah Nix (#1)

Give Love a Chai by Nanxi Wen (#2)

Not Since Ewe by Susannah Nix (#3)

Ewe Complete Me by Susannah Nix (#4)

Meet Your Matcha by Nanxi Wen (#5)

XY Records Series

Key Change by Heidi Hutchinson (#1)

Lost Track by Heidi Hutchinson (#2)

All Mixed Up by Heidi Hutchinson (#3)

Write or Wrong by Heidi Hutchinson (#4)

Bad Habit Book Club Series

Nun Too Soon by Lissa Sharpe (#1)

Nun the Wiser by Lissa Sharpe (#2)

Second to Nun by Lissa Sharpe (#3)

Educated Romance

Work For It Series

Street Smart by Aly Stiles (#1)

Heart Smart by Emma Lee Jayne (#2)

Book Smart by Amanda Pennington (#3)

Smart Mouth by Emma Lee Jayne (#4)

Play Smart by Aly Stiles (#5)

Look Smart by Aly Stiles (#6)

Smart Move by Amanda Pennington (#7)

Stage Smart by Aly Stiles (#8)

Lessons Learned Series

Under Pressure by Allie Winters (#1)

Not Fooling Anyone by Allie Winters (#2)

Can't Fight It by Allie Winters (#3)

The Vinyl Frontier by Lola West (#4)

Out of this World

London Ladies Embroidery Series

Neanderthal Seeks Duchess by Laney Hatcher (#1)

Well Acquainted by Laney Hatcher (#2)

Love Matched by Laney Hatcher (#3)

<u>**Wolf Brothers Series**</u>

<u>Truth or Wolf by Anne Marsh (#1)</u>

<u>Wolf and Bare It by Anne Marsh (#2)</u>